SECRE

A Just... dispensing his own brand of punishment, overriding the impotent court system by secretly shipping repeat offenders and social undesirables to a desert penal camp—where torture, forced labor and executions are due process. In order to stop the wholesale destruction of the U.S. Constitution, Able Team must recruit a counterstrike force from the very people they help incarcerate and start one hell of a prison riot.

TERROR IN WARSAW by Gar Wilson

As the doors of capitalism open on Poland, so, too, does the ugly side of free trade—narcotics. The nation's drug problem surfaces almost overnight, and America appears to be the chief trafficker in a conspiracy to undermine the country by corrupting Polish youth with drugs. Phoenix Force hits the streets of Warsaw to stop this smear campaign, exposing a bloody plot devised by ousted Communist officials intent on giving democracy a bad name.

Also available in this series:

HEROES: Book I
HEROES: Book II

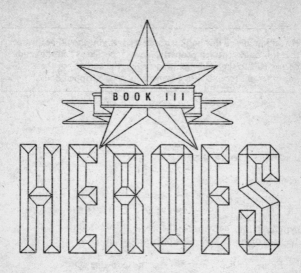

BOOK III

HEROES

SECRET JUSTICE
TERROR IN WARSAW

A GOLD EAGLE BOOK FROM
WORLDWIDE®

TORONTO • NEW YORK • LONDON
AMSTERDAM • PARIS • SYDNEY • HAMBURG
STOCKHOLM • ATHENS • TOKYO • MILAN
MADRID • WARSAW • BUDAPEST • AUCKLAND

First edition September 1992

ISBN 0-373-62406-9

HEROES: Book III

The publisher wishes to acknowledge the following authors
for their contribution to the individual works:

Ken Rose—SECRET JUSTICE
William Fieldhouse—TERROR IN WARSAW

Contents

SECRET JUSTICE

by
Dick Stivers

An Able Team novel

PROLOGUE

It was just after eight in the evening when Angela Perez first noticed the patrol car in the rearview mirror. The streets were still slick from an earlier rain. The tenement stoops were deserted. A wind, smelling faintly of burnt meat and exhaust, had risen from the south. The City of Angels couldn't have seemed less alive.

The cops were vaguely familiar: that was Perez's first thought. Having caught a fleeting glimpse of their faces in the glow of a streetlight, her initial thought was, I know these guys. I interviewed them for the Vivero story. It also passed through her mind that if, in fact, she had spoken to these cops during the course of the Vivero investigation, then they probably didn't like her. Probably even hated her. Because if ever there had been a scathing indictment of police brutality within the Hispanic community, it was her piece on the Vivero shooting.

Given this realization, she was naturally not at all surprised when the flashing red lights finally came to life. In fact, it really couldn't have been more predictable. Two bored Anglo cops on a dead Los Angeles night. In all probability they would not only run her plates against the stolen-vehicle list, but also demand proof of registration.

It was very dark along the stretch of road where she eased her battered Honda to a stop. The overhead lights had been blackened by pellet guns. The warehouses had been gutted for insurance. From somewhere beyond the warren of alleys came a chorus of frantic dogs. But otherwise there were no sounds at all, except for a murmur of metallic voices echoing from the police radio.

The officers waited about six or seven minutes before emerging from the patrol car—six or seven empty minutes probably intended to leave her unsettled. Then, as if on cue, they slowly stepped out onto the oily pavement. The driver was young and blond, with angular features and a thin mustache. The other one was stocky, with vaguely pinched features and graying hair. As they drew closer, moving with their weight on their heels, she noted that their hands were resting on their nightsticks.

They initially asked to see her driver's license, then scrutinized her photograph with the beam of a flashlight. In response she made a mental note of their name tags: Barber, the blond one; McClure, the older one.

"Is this your vehicle?" Barber asked, his voice flat, his gaze fixed on her throat.

She smirked and gazed defiantly into the man's blue eyes. "Yes, Officer, this is my vehicle."

"Would you mind stepping out of it?"

She met Barber's gaze again, held it for a second or two, then asked, "What for?"

"Just step out of the car," McClure snapped.

She was very conscious of their probing eyes when she finally stood before them, very conscious of Barber measuring the swell of her breasts beneath her sweater, while McClure stared at the flare of her thigh beneath her skirt. At twenty-two years old she knew she fitted every Anglo's ideal of a Latin beauty—slender and lithe, with soft waves of dark hair. She was also well aware that the Anglos liked the hint of innocence in her lips and the vaguely girlish tilt to her nose. But rarely were the stares so unrestrained.

Barber moved closer, letting the beam of his flashlight play upon her legs. "Now I want you to step to the front of your vehicle and place your hands on the hood."

She returned his gaze with another quick smirk. "Look, Officer, I have a right to know—"

"Just do what the man tells you," McClure rasped. "Step to the front of your vehicle and place your hands on the hood."

She hesitated, briefly meeting their eyes again in a moment of hard defiance. Then, because she was tired and cold and just wanted to get it over with, she finally obeyed.

There was another whispered exchange, then the crunch of a heel on the pavement. "Suit yourself," Barber said. McClure laughed. Finally, after another three or four seconds of silence, Barber stepped closer and said, "I'm afraid we're going to have to take you in, miss."

Her hands still pressed against the hood of the Honda, she slowly shifted her head to the left in order to meet the police officer's gaze again. "What are you talking about?"

"You heard the man," McClure growled. "We're going to have to take you in."

"On what charge?"

There was another brief exchange of whispers as Barber withdrew a pair of handcuffs. "Parking tickets," he finally said, smiling. "Fifteen outstanding parking tickets."

She rose from the hood, turning with a sudden flash of fury. "That's complete bullshit! I paid those parking tickets. I paid them six months ago, and even if I hadn't paid them, you still don't have the right to—"

"Just assume the position," Barber snapped.

"But this is completely illegal. In fact, this isn't even close to—"

"I said assume the position, miss."

They secured her wrists behind her back, then withdrew to look at her again. Five, ten, fifteen seconds and they just kept looking at her.

"Look, will you please tell me what this is all about?" she asked at last. "Look, I've got a right to know what this is all about!"

Barber escorted her to the patrol car, his left hand on her arm, his right on the small of her back. When he pressed her down into the rear seat, she felt his hand slowly slip to her buttocks. But when she caught sight of the open whiskey bottle, she was suddenly much too frightened to speak.

Then it began to rain again, and another chorus of baying dogs echoed out of the blackness. McClure had unscrewed the cap from the whiskey bottle for a long, slow pull. Barber had lit a cigarette and switched off the radio. Yet, before she could comprehend the meaning of these actions, she found herself pondering an even more horrifying realization. The *Miranda* decision. They hadn't even advised her of her rights.

She took a deep breath and briefly shut her eyes. Her wrists had begun to burn beneath the cuffs, and she was suddenly very cold. But none of it seemed to matter in the face of this slow-breaking horror—why hadn't they Mirandized her? She leaned forward in order to meet Barber's gaze once more. "Excuse me," she said softly "but haven't you forgotten something?"

The blond cop returned her gaze with a dull stare. "What did you say?"

"My rights. If you're going to arrest me, then I want you to read me my rights."

Barber glanced at his partner. "You hear that, Bobby? She wants you to read her rights."

McClure shook his head and leered. "Her rights, huh? Well, I guess I can read the little girl her rights."

Then, faster than she would have ever dreamed possible, he reached out and struck her with an open palm across the face. The blow left her breathless and wide-eyed, her chin against her shoulder and two tracks of tears along her cheeks. There was also a faint taste of blood in her mouth, and the echo of the blow kept ringing in her ears.

But far worse than either the pain or the shock was the icy edge to Barber's voice as he turned from behind the wheel and smiled. "Now, what were you saying about your rights?"

1

Carl "Ironman" Lyons and his fellow Able Team members had spent two days and three nights waiting in a rented Florida bungalow for a search warrant for a scum named Reuben Ramos. All in all, it was a hard wait with pounding rain in the afternoons and sultry winds in the evenings. To make matters worse the team's electronics expert, Hermann "Gadgets" Schwarz, was suffering from nasal congestion, and Rosario "Politician" Blancanales had been forced to sleep on the floor. Then the television had crapped out just as the Miami football game was getting under way. What else could go wrong?

It was about six o'clock in the evening when the district attorney finally showed up: seersucker suit, suede loafers, six-hundred-dollar briefcase, forty-five-thousand-dollar BMW. Lyons placed the man at about twenty-five, and from an obviously wealthy family. Lyons further supposed that the man was on a political track, doing his time in city hall in order to make the right connections.

Lyons was seated on the veranda when the district attorney appeared. Beside the unraveling wicker chair lay four empty cans of beer. Beyond the rusting screen lay a long view of the windblown beach and the palms in black sawtooth against the sunset. In another life, the blond Able Team warrior supposed he might have actually found this view pleasant, what with the running whitecaps and swaying wands of moss. After two dead days of waiting out a judicial tango, however, he was in no mood to appreciate the scenery.

Ironman didn't get to his feet when the D.A. approached. He simply tossed back another beer and asked, "You Singer?"

"Sanger," the young man replied. "The name's Eric Sanger."

Lyons tossed the empty beer can onto the rotting planks. "Well, tell me something, Mr. Sanger, are we going to bust ourselves a drug dealer, or are we going to continue watching the cockroaches?"

Sanger hiked up his trousers and sat on the edge of a rusting lounge. "I'm afraid it's not that easy, Mr. Lyons."

"Why not?"

"Because it's a very tricky case. Because Judge Keefer is nervous, and so am I."

Lyons glanced over his shoulder at Blancanales's vague reflection in the window. Then he looked back at Sanger. "If you think you're nervous now, pal, just wait until those gentlemen in there find out that your office has been jacking them around for the past two days. Then you'll really know what nervous is all about.''

Sanger pressed a thoughtful fist to his forehead. ''All right, I'll tell you what I'll do. I'll authorize an entry tonight if you promise to play it absolutely by the book.''

''Meaning what exactly?''

''Meaning that you'll be accompanied by officers from the local force, that you'll carry only authorized weapons and that you announce your presence before entering. I also don't want any unnecessary bloodshed. If Ramos is willing to go quietly, I don't want you to hurt a hair on his manicured goatee. You understand? Not a goddamn hair.''

Lyons tugged on his earlobe, his hard gaze fixed on the storm-tossed water.

''It's not negotiable, Mr. Lyons,'' Sanger said. ''If you want to move in on Reuben tonight, those are the ground rules. No flash grenades through the windows. No explosives under the floorboards. And a clean, clear announcement at the door.''

Lyons bit his lower lip, then shifted his gaze back to Sanger. ''Tell me something, have you ever faced an AK on full-auto? How about an under-over conversion? Ever faced one of those babies?''

''Look, Mr. Lyons, I don't make the rules. I'm just here to explain them. You go arrest the guy on any other basis and I won't be able to make it stick. Which means that Ramos is going to walk. Which means it's all for nothing or worse. You do it my way, on the other hand, and at least we've got a chance. Now do you want to go for it or not?''

Lyons stared at the shivering palms for another fifteen seconds, then got to his feet. "Yeah, we want to go for it.''

IT WAS JUST after midnight when Lyons and company reached the edge of Ramos's six-bedroom, mock-Tudor home in St. Petersburg. Joining them for this little law-enforcement excursion were two officers from the Tampa police department: a twenty-nine-year-old Texan named Lewis Pauley and a thirty-eight-year-old former Marine named Lester Small. All five men were armed with standard-issue shotguns and .45 automatics. They had also been issued bulletproof vests.

"Looks to me like there's about six of them,'' Blancanales whispered from the low limb of a willow tree. His right eye was pressed to a Starlight scope trained on the lower windows of the target house. His left eye was shut in concentration, and despite the chill, he'd already begun to perspire.

"Where?'' Lyons asked from the shadows below the limb.

Blancanales shifted the scope to an upper window, then to what looked like a sun deck. "Some sort of game room,'' he replied. "Maybe a den.''

"Any idea what they're doing?'' Pauley asked.

Blancanales set the scope aside. "Hanging out. Looks like they're just hanging out.''

From the grassy rise where the willows stood lay a long, shadowy stretch of ground leading to a low stone wall. Beyond the wall was a jungle of orchids, sea grapes and acacias. Then came the winding flagstones beneath the folds of Spanish moss, and finally the actual entrance to the Ramos residence.

Like other homes in the area, the Ramos place had been built on a spur of land that curved into the bay. From the road one saw only a modest view of bleached wood, glass and marble. Somewhat closer, however, it became evident that the house had been decorated in astonishingly poor taste. Hence the pink plaster flamingos on the lawn, alabaster nymphs and the Day-Glo pilasters.

"There's this guy on the force," Pauley said as he moved along with Lyons and the others through the knee-high grass. "Name's Jackson, and he's got this theory that you can always tell a dealer's house by the decor. He even wants to do a book on it, right? Maybe one of those coffee-table things with all those photographs. Call it something like *Houses of the Rich and Nasty* and fill it with pictures of drug dealers' homes. 'Cause I'm telling you, there's some real weird ones out there. There's places like you never even dreamed about."

Beyond the moss-encrusted wall they could see a lily-choked pond and then the shadowy path of flagstones. Riffs from electric guitars issued from a bedroom window; laughter rippled from the swimming pool.

"That's the other thing about these people," Small said. "They're always having a party. You can raid them at six in the morning and they're still having a party."

They paused beneath the thicker folds of Spanish moss. The grass was sodden here, the air heavy with the dampness and stench of leaf mold.

"Man, I hate this," Schwarz whispered as he fixed his gaze on the massive front door. "I mean, talk about asking for trouble."

There were echoes of a fountain closer to the entrance, and faint laughter from an upper window.

"How about I hit 'em from the bedroom window?" Blancanales suggested softly. "How about I just scramble up that trellis and move in from the upstairs?"

Lyons glanced at the darkened window above the eaves, then back at Small. "How about it, Les? You think Sanger's going to object if Pol goes in through the window?"

The beefy ex-Marine peered through the shadows at the massive front door, then up at the ivy trellis to the ledge. He grinned. "What window?"

They waited exactly sixteen minutes before moving out from the shadows of the willows toward the broad marble steps of the entrance. Blancanales by this time had become a dim silhouette on the ledge above. Upon reaching the edge of the reflecting pond, they paused again. Finally dropping the safety on his 12-gauge, Lyons rose for the last, lonely walk to the door.

He hesitated, pressing himself against the marble and listening. The music from within had grown softer, with only the echo of a solitary sax. The laughter had also died. Well, here goes nothing, Lyons thought as he inched closer to the door. Here goes modern law enforcement . . . for better or for worse.

He shifted his weight to the balls of his feet and brought the shotgun up. Then he took a deep breath and shouted, "Federal officers! Open the door!"

Nothing, except the cold notes of the melancholy saxophone and the patter of dripping leaves.

"Federal agents! Open the door!"

Still nothing, except possibly a whispered voice and a footfall on the marble within.

He inched a little closer to the door, heard what might have been the cocking of an automatic and signaled to Schwarz and the two Tampa cops to stay down and back.

But given the play of shadows from the swaying folds of Spanish moss, it was possible that neither Schwarz nor the two officers even saw Lyons's warning.

Of if they had seen it, they simply ignored it.

Small was the first to rise from behind the rim of the reflecting pond. Then, obviously hearing or sensing something he didn't like, he started to drop to his knees again. But not before the first burst of autofire shattered the night.

From where Lyons stood, his back to the cold marble, he was only able to see what transpired in flashes—the white burst from the muzzle through a bay window adjacent to the door, the muslin curtains billowing outward, the shuddering form of Officer Lester Small as the slugs pounded into his body. He heard Blancanales cursing on the ledge above. He heard Schwarz shouting at Pauley. He heard the grunt of pain as Small tumbled back over the marble wall of the reflecting pond. Then he heard nothing except his own silent scream of rage.

Lyons dropped to a low squat to return fire. Although he had no definite target in view, he was fairly certain someone was still moving behind the billowing curtains. So he squeezed off two fast rounds from his 12-gauge.

There were echoes of another maddened cry, and someone, maybe Pauley, shouted, "You bastards!"

Lyons poured in more lead through the window adjacent to the door and saw a bright streak of blood across the curtains. Then, rolling out from behind the marble column, he fired at the doors until the oak began to splinter.

The door, finally bursting open with the impact of the shotgun blasts, offered a quick vision of two figures—two thin, wiry shapes with heavy-caliber automatics in their hands. Lyons squeezed off another slug from his shotgun, but saw only the explosion of porcelain and glass. Three sustained bursts from an Uzi answered his 12-gauge, sending clouds of marble dust into the air. From behind the ledge of the reflecting pond Pauley had also begun firing in earnest. But it wasn't until Schwarz opened up, pumping four rounds from the hip, that the effect became obvious.

The first figure beyond the doorway was a lean, swarthy kid in blue jeans and no shirt. The slugs from Schwarz's weapon lifted him into the air, tossed him back against the mirrored foyer and left him sprawled in a heap of shattered glass. The second figure was a beefy guy in sweats and running shoes. The slugs seemed to kick his legs out from under him, leaving him momentarily suspended before he dropped into a bloody heap. Judging from the tangled screams, there might have been a third and fourth man ducking into the jungle of furniture. But all Lyons saw were shadows.

Ironman waited until Gadgets had reached the staircase before ducking into the doorway. There were still traces of cordite in the air. There were also screams from beyond the foyer where the wiry kid in jeans lay dead or dying in a widening pool of blood.

"See anything?" Schwarz whispered, joining Lyons at the mouth of the marble foyer.

Ironman shook his head and peered down the mirrored corridor to a mess of upturned furniture, splintered chairs and shattered porcelain.

"So how do you want to play it?" Schwarz asked.

Lyons glanced over his shoulder at the outline of Pauley in the doorway behind them. Then he glanced at the slow-shifting shadows ahead. "How about you just keep your eyes peeled while I move on out?"

"What happens if they try to tag you from the balcony?"

Lyons peered out beyond the end of the corridor to the gently curving staircase. "Then shoot them."

Ironman moved out slowly, his weight on the balls of his feet again, eyes still fixed on the darkest parts of the room. As he neared the end of the corridor, he vaguely heard television voices echoing out of the gloom. But apart from the curtains billowing from a bullet-shattered window, there was no actual movement.

I should have brought a flash grenade, he thought. I should have brought something fully automatic. Then, moving a little deeper into the gloom past shattered vases and a wrecked sofa, he thought, I should have told the D.A. to go to hell.

Lyons paused where a mock-Tudor chair had been splintered with shotgun blasts. A Toyota commercial blared from the television. Then he caught another fleeting glimpse of someone moving among the toppled urns in the living room, heard what might have been the rattle of gold chains. But it wasn't until he saw a glint in the lamplight that he actually began to react.

He rolled to his left, scrambling for the cover of a heavy oak table. The figure at the foot of the stairs was short and squat, with shoulder-length hair and a headband. There was definitely some sort of weapon in the man's hand, and Lyons was sure he heard the click of a magazine slipping into place.

Lyons turned on his hip, swinging the shotgun around. But even as his finger began to squeeze the trigger, he knew he was too late. The squat young man at the foot of the stairs had already pegged him with a full-auto AK-47.

A full second passed, one endless second, while Lyons just kept staring at the muzzle of the AK-47. The attacker's features were almost childish in contrast to the hard eyes and gleaming goatee. He saw the guy's lips spread into a strangely boyish grin, while his knees bent slightly into the classic firing position. Yet when the muzzle finally began to flash, the face was suddenly as hard and mature as any killer's.

Six slugs tore into the heavy slab of oak where Lyons had taken cover. Next he heard the windows shattering around him, then the whine of four more slugs ricocheting off the marble floor. He also heard what might have been Schwarz yelling something from the mouth of the corridor, while Pauley screamed from just inside the doorway.

But all these cries were nothing compared to the deafening echo of Blancanales's voice, booming out from the top of the staircase. "Get down!"

Lyons would later recall only one clean image of the Hispanic warrior half-bent over the railing to squeeze off four shots into the shadows below. The figure beneath the staircase seemed to waver before he fell, momentarily growing stiff, then letting loose a long burst of autofire as he stumbled out of the darkness and onto the flawless marble.

Ironman waited another full minute before rising from behind the table and approaching the body. Although the breeze through shattered windows continued to stir the shadows, it was now suddenly very still. It was also very quiet, with only the gentle flicker of the television screen from a darkened room at the end of the hall.

The young man at the foot of the stairs was still faintly twitching, his left hand opening and closing around the stock of the AK-47, his right foot quivering. The eyes, however, were clearly lifeless, and there was no heartbeat.

"Is this him?" Lyons asked, staring at the black goatee and gazing into the filmy eyes.

At the opposite end of the room Schwarz was examining the kid in jeans and the beefy man in sweats. "These two have also had it."

Ignoring Schwarz's comment, Lyons knelt down for a closer look at the lifeless form at his feet. "How about it, anyone? Is this one Ramos or not?"

Pauley approached, his clothing stained with Small's blood, his service revolver dangling in his hand. After a moment's hesitation he nudged the corpse with his boot. "Could be," he finally breathed. "Yeah, that definitely could be Ramos."

However, they could now hear footsteps on the balcony above, and a short, stocky figure emerged from the bedroom. The figure wore a floral bathrobe, leather slippers and a watch that must have set him back at least twenty grand. But in the end all

Lyons saw was the goatee—sleek and perfectly trimmed.

Blancanales responded first, dropping into a half crouch and leveling his automatic. An instant later Lyons and Schwarz also trained their weapons on the stocky young man on the balcony.

In response, however, Ramos merely grinned. "Well, aren't you going to read me my rights?"

2

"What about our rights?" Angela Perez asked softly. "Huh? How can they just completely ignore our rights?"

The lanky black girl shrugged and shut her eyes again. "All I can say, honey, is that something tells me we don't got no rights—not here."

It was midnight, or shortly after. Instead of a formal booking at the downtown station, Perez had been taken directly to a holding tank. From the tank she had been hustled into a windowless van and taken to some sort of warehouse on the eastern edge of the city. There she found herself among thirty other dazed young women—all of them shoeless and terrified.

The black woman's name was Lisa, and she had been arrested at the corner of Hollywood and Vine, where she often picked up clients for eighty-five dollars a trick. Beyond these facts, however, she was unable to tell Perez anything—not what the specific charges were, not the names of the arresting officers, not even why she, too, had never been read her rights.

The warehouse was a vast, poorly lit concrete place. Now and again there were echoes of automobile engines and footsteps from beyond the windowless walls. But, for the most part, it was dead silent, except for the occasional whispers and coughs of the women. It was also very cold, with foul drafts from the ventilation shaft above.

"Maybe it's just some kind of mistake," Perez said after another long silence. "You know what I mean? Maybe the regular holding tanks were filled, so they brought us here as a temporary solution."

Lisa opened her eyes and slowly turned to face Angela again. "Honey, this ain't no mistake."

"But they can't just do this to us. They can't just shove us into some warehouse and lock the door."

Again, however, Lisa merely shrugged. "Yeah, well, they're doing it, aren't they?"

There was the low rumble of another slow-moving vehicle, then the echo of more footsteps. Next came the sound of turning tumblers and the screech of the doors rolling open again. Initially Perez was only able to make out a single dim form. Then, by degrees, she realized there were four men standing in the doorway. They were dressed alike—blue nylon windbreakers and black jeans—and all were armed with shotguns, except the fourth man, who held a cylindrical metal wand. They also wore surgical masks and stocking caps.

"All right, ladies," the chunky one with the metal wand said. "This is how we're going to proceed. On my signal you'll line up single file and board the bus outside. You won't talk, you won't break rank and you won't look directly into the faces of the guards."

There were soft moans as the prisoners stood, and the softer sobs of a teenage prostitute. But the men remained silent and impassive behind their surgical masks.

It was even colder outside, and the streets were still slick from the rain. The bus was waiting at the end of an alley, the yellow glow of its headlights smeared across the pavement, white clouds of exhaust suspended in the air. As the first women in line drew closer to the bus, the masked men closed ranks and cocked their weapons.

Perez was about twenty feet from the door of the vehicle when the disturbance began. Initially all she heard were the choked sobs of a pale girl in a yellow shift. Then she heard one of the men shout, "Let's go! Let's go!" Apparently the girl had slipped to her knees and was unable to rise again.

There were more choked sobs as the guard with the metal wand appeared. A fat black woman attempted to intercede but was thrown to the pavement. The kneeling girl shook her head, whipping her hair back and forth as she screamed, "You can't make me! This is illegal and you can't make me! I've got rights and I demand to speak to my lawyer!"

But by this time the metal wand was shoved against her belly and the electrifying punch of the high-voltage prod left her shuddering and silent.

"Anybody else want to talk to a lawyer?" the heavyset man with the cattle prod asked.

"THE RIGHT OF THE PEOPLE to be secure in their houses," Sanger said, "shall not be violated."

Lyons shifted his gaze away from the moonlit sea and looked at the D.A. "What's that supposed to mean?"

Sanger took a deep breath and exhaled through clenched teeth. "It means Reuben's going to walk."

It was nearly four o'clock in the morning. Lyons and Sanger were seated on Reuben Ramos's spacious tiled patio among the potted palms. There was coffee, but it was cold. There were doughnuts, but they were stale. Although the bodies of Ramos's associates had finally been removed, the grounds of his palatial home were still swarming with police officers and coroners. After an exhaustive search had failed to uncover more than a gram or two of illegal substances, someone had even brought in the sniffing dogs. But the animals, too, were only making a mess of things.

Schwarz and Blancanales appeared, exhausted and edgy. Gadgets slumped into a wicker chair beside Ironman. Pol moved to the low tiled wall and stared out at the glittering bay.

Lyons sighed. "So it was all for nothing. Is that what you're trying to tell us? Lester Small got his head blown off for nothing."

Sanger took another long, hard breath. "Look, I told you to play it by the book. I told you that if you guys went rushing in like the Light Brigade we'd end up losing this case, and that's exactly what happened.''

Blancanales stared hard at the D.A. ''Hey, it wasn't like we had a choice. The moment we announced ourselves, they opened up.''

''Then you should have pulled back,'' Sanger snapped, ''and called for backup. That's the way it's supposed to be done. You get surrounded and you take them out with bullhorns. As it is, we could also be facing an excessive-force suit from the victims' families.''

''Victims?'' Schwarz echoed softly. ''Did I hear you right, man?''

Sanger nodded. ''With three dead kids on white marble, anything's possible.''

''Well, that's insane,'' Schwarz muttered. ''I mean, for Christ's sake, it's not like these guys were just sitting around doing their homework. They were returning fire. Besides, they were drug dealers.''

''Alleged drug dealers,'' Sanger interjected. ''But that's not the point I'm trying to make. What's important here is that we don't have a snowball's chance in hell of putting Reuben away.''

''And what about the weapons?'' Lyons asked dryly. ''How about we go for illegal possession of the full-autos?''

''What possession?'' Sanger countered. ''As far as the law's concerned, Reuben wasn't in physical possession of anything. He was having a little party, and some of his guests happened to bring something they shouldn't have. There's no guilt, not in the eyes of the law."

"And the crack?" Blancanales asked.

Sanger shook his head. "You've got to be kidding. There isn't even enough to make it worth arresting, let alone prosecuting."

"So what's the goddamn consolation prize?" Lyons asked softly, his voice vaguely hoarse from exhaustion.

Sanger looked at him wryly. "The preservation of constitutional freedom. That's the prize. You bend the law, even a little bit, to put a piece of scum like Ramos in the slammer, and from that point forward no innocent citizen is completely safe. To put it bluntly, gentlemen, you fucked up."

IT WAS DAWN when Lyons and his team finally decided there was nothing more to be gained by waiting around the Ramos estate. The air was still heavy with moisture, the sky overcast. As they wearily tramped past the sodden lawns to the circular driveway, they were rewarded with one last look at Ramos, sipping coffee in the back of a patrol car and happily chatting with a pretty anchorwoman. His lawyer, a short roly-poly guy in a twelve-hundred-dollar raincoat and snakeskin boots, was amiably chatting with a couple of arresting officers. A female paralegal in black leather pants was dispensing more doughnuts.

"What's wrong with that picture?" Schwarz asked as he watched from the shadows along the edge of the reflecting pond. There were still traces of Small's blood on the flagstones, along with scattered shotgun casings.

"Yeah," Blancanales echoed, "what the hell's wrong with that picture?"

"Let it go, boys," Lyons cautioned.

"I can't let it go," Blancanales responded as he moved out of the shadows, his gaze fixed on the prisoner's grinning profile.

"Pol," Lyons called softly after him, "back off."

But Blancanales just kept moving forward with slow, stiff steps. As he approached the rank of patrol cars, all eyes turned to him, but only the roly-poly lawyer actually spoke. "Is there something you want to say to my client, Officer?"

Blancanales stopped and glared at the lawyer. "No," he growled. "I don't want to talk to him. I just want to look at him. I just want to make sure I won't forget that ugly mug of his."

The lawyer took a step forward, blocking the warrior's view of Ramos. "Well, I'm afraid this is upsetting my client and that I'm going to have to insist that you leave. Furthermore, I have to warn you that unless you have legal cause to talk to my client in the future, I'll regard any and all communication as intentional harassment aimed at upsetting him."

Blancanales blinked, his eyes now clearly alive with hatred. "Upsetting your client? Is that what you think's going on here, Counselor? Well, let me tell you something, pal. If you think your client's upset now, just wait until I see him again."

The lawyer met Blancanales's gaze, then turned to the uniformed officers around him. "Did you men hear that? This gentleman's threatening my client and I demand that he be restrained immediately."

"It's all right," Lyons interjected, stepping into the circle of cops and reporters. "Everything's all right. My man here's just a little tired, that's all. He's had a hard night, okay?" Then, taking Blancanales by the arm and gently leading him away, he said, "Come on, Pol, this kind of scum isn't worth it."

Lyons and Blancanales continued back along the flagstone path in silence, the wind stirring leaves all around them, the sun beginning to rise among the palms.

"You know what's going to happen now, don't you?" Blancanales asked.

"Forget it, Pol."

"That bastard's going to be out on the streets in three hours. He's going to be having breakfast on the patio of his two-million-dollar house. Now you tell me if that's justice."

3

It was dawn when the bus finally came to a halt and Angela Perez first glimpsed the encampment. A stiff wind was blowing from the east, and it was bitterly cold. There were also heavy clouds of brown dust in the air, which made the place seem like something half glimpsed in a dream, an impression reinforced by the corrugated Quonset huts, a row of gray brick bungalows and coils of barbed wire. Here and there among the bungalows were stooped figures of men and women in gray overalls with yellow stripes.

The women were herded from the bus in single file, most shielding their eyes from the dust, a few staring in disbelief. As they proceeded through the high gates between the coils of barbed wire, someone whispered, "What the hell is this place?" But no one saw fit to answer.

From the gates they were escorted along a half-paved path to a gravel courtyard. There they were assembled in two ranks of three and told to remain absolutely silent. The walls of surrounding bungalows offered some relief from the windblown sand here, but it was still bitterly cold.

Along the walls of the courtyard stood seven guards. All were dressed alike: jeans, sheepskin coats, cowboy boots and blue caps. Some carried shotguns. Others had Winchesters. A few sported fully automatic assault rifles. Now and again they spoke softly among themselves, but no one actually addressed the women until the warden appeared.

He was a tall, angular fellow with graying hair swept back from his forehead. In a leather trench coat and aviator sunglasses he looked like someone from a World War II movie, a German tank commander or a British air marshal. His hands were gloved and his boots had been polished to a high shine.

He looked at them, shifting his gaze from face to face as he slowly walked along the ranks. Finally he withdrew to a makeshift podium at the end of the courtyard and began to speak.

"Welcome to the Experiment. My name is Warden Arthur Merryman and this is your new home. I'm sure you all have many questions, but these will be answered in good time. At the moment I simply want to tell you about the rules. Rule one. Those attempting to cross the wire will be shot. Rule two. Those attempting to incite rebellion will be shot. Rule three. Those attempting to inflict harm on any of the camp officials will be shot.

"To these basic rules I might further add the following. As you might have noticed, this encampment also houses male prisoners. Now and again you'll be working closely with these men. However, any excessive contact, and you all know what I mean by that, will result in severe punishment for both parties. All other infractions, including failure to obey immediately any and all orders given to you by myself or one of the guards, will be met with severe bodily punishment.

"Beyond all that, you need to know this—you're here because you've proven yourself to be detrimental to the society at large. You'll remain here until I deem that you're no longer detrimental. While you're here you'll be given no opportunity to communicate with the outside world, nor will you be permitted to receive any communications. In exchange for your food and clothing you'll be expected to work in any of a variety of projects. Those refusing to work will be punished in a number of ways."

He paused and gazed once more along the ranks of the barefoot, shivering women. Then, just before leaving the podium, he added, "Oh, one last thing. This facility happens to be located a long way from anywhere. Thus, even if you should manage to slip my wire, I seriously doubt you'd live to cross the desert. Have a nice stay."

Immediately following the warden's introductory speech the women were marched along a narrow gravel path to a low complex of cinder-block buildings. En route they passed a dozen male prisoners. Most were young and either black or Hispanic. Although they stared, there was no real trace of desire in their eyes. There was only exhaustion.

Beyond the steel doors of the first cinder-block building stood three female matrons in jeans and workshirts. Two were armed with shotguns. The third carried another cattle prod. The one with the cattle prod introduced herself as Assistant Warden Carol Trask. She instructed the women to remove their clothes and step into a gray-tiled shower. She added that wet skin increased the pain of a cattle-prod jolt. The water was cold, the soap smelled like detergent and there were no towels.

Following the shower, the women were issued their clothing—shapeless gray smocks, cotton underwear and cheap canvas shoes. Then they were herded into what would serve as their dormitory—a low room with bunk beds on either side. The windows had been fitted with wire mesh, and the door was bolted from the outside.

For a long time after climbing onto her assigned bunk Perez simply stared out the window. Twice she saw the rising dust of vehicles on a distant road, and once she saw an airliner high above the far mountains. Somewhere beyond the wire there were sounds of picks and shovels and what might have been a generator. But there were no voices, just the whispers of the women.

"So?"

Perez looked up to meet the tired gaze of the black woman named Lisa on the bunk above. She sighed. "So what?"

"Exactly, honey. So what? They put us here and they don't tell us nothing. So what do we say? We say so what? You understand me, honey? We just say so what, because if we try to figure it all out, we're going to break down and cry. Now the man, he tells you this or he tells you that, and you just think to yourself, So what?"

Perez looked once more at the view of desert and barbed wire. "But there's got to be something we can do. I mean, this is completely against every law there is."

"Tell me about it. So what do you suggest? Find a pay phone? Or maybe we should dig ourselves a tunnel under that wire out there. Forget it, baby. This place is the end of the line. I don't know why we're here, and I don't know what right they have to put us here, but I do know this much—it's the end of the line. So my advice is to make the best of it, honey. This is the only world we got now."

For a long time Perez continued to stare out the window. She watched the long shadows of mountains creep across the empty landscape. She watched the shadow of a solitary hawk circling above. Eventually she realized there were tears in her eyes and that she was growing desperately hungry. At that point she started to cry as she never had before.

CARL LYONS and his team spent five more days attempting to salvage the Ramos case. They dined at a seafood restaurant with Sanger, the D.A., and a personal friend of the judge. They prowled around the marina, hoping to intercept a trawler with contraband in the hold. They spent an evening watching Ramos eating oysters on his patio. They drank a lot of beer with Tampa cops who felt equally frustrated by the law. Then, finally hearing that Ramos was planning to fly to California, they prepared to go home.

It was late Friday afternoon when word arrived that the case was closed. Lyons and Blancanales had spent the day sipping lukewarm beer on the sagging porch of their rented bungalow. Schwarz sat on the steps, fiddling with one of the directional microphones originally procured as part of the surveillance equipment. As with the voice-activated tape recorders and the laser taps, however, Sanger had been unable to secure the necessary warrant. Finally, at around six o'clock, Lewis Pauley appeared, obviously exhausted, clearly angry and slightly drunk.

The Tampa detective fetched himself a beer from the galvanized tub on the porch, then sat on the rough wooden steps beside Schwarz. Another stiff wind was blowing from the west, and the beach was littered with driftwood, hamburger wrappers and beer bottles.

"So what's the point, huh?" Pauley said. "That's what I want to know. We go busting into the bastard's house. Lester takes eight slugs in the face. We find two grams of coke and a mess of full-autos. We know there was more dope, but Ramos probably flushed it. We also know the guy's up to his ears in grass and God knows what else. But now he's officially as free as a bird. He even gets to leave the state. So I ask you, what's the goddamn point?''

Schwarz was the first to respond. He put down the directional microphone and met Pauley's red-rimmed gaze. ''How about we take you out for steak and shrimp, Lew?''

The burly cop shook his head. ''I don't want to eat, man. I don't want nothing, except to get back a little of what they took from my partner.''

Lyons set down his beer and leaned forward. ''It's not worth it, Lew. You go out and pop a guy like Ramos, and what does it get you? A moment of satisfaction that could cost you your whole career. It isn't worth it.''

Pauley smiled slightly. ''Hey, I'm not talking about popping the little bastard. I'm talking about something else. I'm talking about circumventing the whole damn system—the lawyers, the judges, all of 'em.''

Blancanales exchanged a quick glance with Lyons, then turned to Pauley. ''Circumventing the system how?''

Pauley grinned enigmatically. ''Let's just say there are other people who aren't so happy with the way this game's played. Let's just say there are other people who don't like the idea that a good man like Les Small is lying in a morgue while a piece of dirt like Reuben Ramos is on his way to a vacation in California.''

"And what people would those be?" Lyons asked, his voice a little harder.

Pauley didn't reply. Instead, he got to his feet, drained the last of his beer and tossed the bottle over his shoulder. Finally he said, "Look, I'm drunk, okay? I probably don't even know what I'm saying. So what do you say we just forget the whole thing?"

IT RAINED all that night, a hard rain driven by winds that left the beach strewn with palm leaves and more driftwood. Having stayed awake until nearly three or four, Schwarz and Blancanales were still sleeping at ten o'clock the next day. But Lyons was up and gazing out at the wind-tossed sea.

As Ironman sat in the wicker chair on the porch, he glimpsed a white Mercedes moving slowly along the road below. The seventy-thousand-dollar vehicle approached from the east, then finally stopped on the shoulder of the gravel road. From a distance the driver looked vaguely familiar—a prematurely balding, roly-poly guy in white cotton trousers and a blue blazer. As the man drew closer, though, Lyons suddenly remembered who he was—Ramos's smooth-tongued attorney.

The lawyer approached slowly, pausing to navigate around a clump of driftwood and scrape something off his expensive loafers. When he finally drew within speaking distance, he stopped and did his best to smile. "Mr. Lyons, my name is Eliot Brickman. Do you remember me?"

"Yeah, I remember you," Lyons said sourly.

"Then do you think I might have a word with you?"

"About what?"

"About my client Reuben Ramos."

"What about him?"

"He's disappeared."

Lyons fixed a grim look on the lawyer. "Why don't you look in Beverly Hills?"

Brickman coughed. "That's the problem. He never made it to Los Angeles." The lawyer paused as he hoisted his bulk into a chair. "On his way to the airport Reuben was apparently accompanied by a young woman. According to the woman, who prefers to remain nameless, my client was proceeding at high speed along the coastal route when a Tampa patrol car pulled him over. The officers ran a check on Reuben's license. Then, after claiming that he was in violation of several traffic statutes, they insisted that he come down to the station. Accordingly he was handcuffed and placed in the back of the patrol car. That was the last anyone ever saw of him."

Lyons took a deep breath, but his gaze remained fixed on the wind-tormented sea. "What happened to the girl?"

"Nothing. The cops just left her sitting in the car."

"What about the arrest report?"

"There isn't any. In fact, as far as the Tampa PD is concerned, none of this ever happened."

"But you believe the girl?"

Brickman nodded. "Yeah, I believe the girl."

"Which means you think the Tampa police picked him up and dropped him into a swamp?"

Brickman sighed, leaning forward so that his elbows rested on his knees. "Look at it this way. You and I both know there are some pretty hard feelings floating around these days. I mean, after all, you people bust into my client's home in order to catch him in a deal. And what do you get for it? Less than two grams of coke and a roomful of dead bodies. No arrest, no nothing."

"Except that Lester Small is dead," Lyons said.

"Exactly."

"And so you think someone on the Tampa force decided to even the score by taking the law into his own hands. Is that roughly the idea?"

Brickman shrugged. "Well, I do happen to know that Small's partner has been extremely agitated of late. I also happen to know the man can be violent above and beyond the call of duty."

"Well, you can forget about him. Pauley was here when Ramos was due to fly out."

"All right, then maybe it was someone else. A couple of Small's other pals on the force. The point is, we're looking at both motive and opportunity here."

"But no corpse."

"Not yet."

Lyons rose from the wicker chair as Pauley's words flashed through his mind. *I'm talking about circum-*

venting the whole damn system. Yet all Lyons finally asked was, "Why me?"

"Because you're federal. And though you might play rough, I don't think you play dirty."

Lyons turned to face the lawyer, his eyes revealing nothing. "Look, even if I believed you, which I'm not sure I do, there's nothing I can do about it."

"I'm not so sure about that. Like I said, you're federal. You've got connections. You can make things happen. Besides, the cops around here trust you, which means they'll talk to you."

Lyons frowned. "I don't think I'm your man, Brickman. Not over a guy like Ramos."

"But it's not about Ramos. It's about the whole fabric of our legal system. It's about everything this nation's supposed to represent. Can you really turn your back on all that?"

"Why don't you go to the Bureau? That's what they're there for."

"The FBI couldn't find its own feet, and you know it. Besides, I really don't think the FBI's going to have much sympathy for a missing drug dealer, not under the present circumstances."

"Yeah? Well, I don't have much sympathy for a missing drug dealer, either."

Brickman rose and joined Lyons at the railing. "Let me ask you something. Where do you draw the line? If it's okay for the cops to go out and whack a drug dealer, what happens when they start whacking car thieves? Or how about hookers? What do you do when they start offing hookers because they don't like the look of them? Where does it end, or does it?''

Lyons looked at Brickman. "Why don't you save the closing argument, Counselor, and start telling me what's really going on.''

"I don't know what you mean."

"Sure you do.''

Brickman continued to meet Lyons's gaze, then nodded. "All right, the whole truth and nothing but the truth. Reuben Ramos isn't the first to vanish into the legal system around here.''

Lyons cast the lawyer a fierce look. "What are you talking about?''

"I mean that some of my colleagues have also been losing clients lately. Now I realize you probably have a pretty low opinion of lawyers who defend drug dealers, but these people aren't lying when they say something's going on around here . . . something real scary.''

"Is it always the same kind of circumstances? Guy gets pulled over on some minor charge and then he's never heard of again?''

"More or less, yeah. Although there was also a case last month where the suspect was simply dragged from his bed in the middle of the night, Nazi style.''

Lyons clenched his jaw. "All right," he said finally. "I'll see what I can do.''

"But you won't tell the cops I was the one who told you about it, will you?''

Lyons looked at the lawyer again, noting fear in the man's eyes and a faint tremor in his lips. "What difference does it make?"

Brickman gulped. "If I'm right, it makes a lot of difference."

The lawyer's Mercedes was a gleaming reflection on the highway when Blancanales appeared in the doorway behind Lyons. The muscular silver-haired commando was still clutching the blanket he'd slept in. "So what was that all about?"

Lyons shook his head, his voice as distant as his gaze. "I'm not sure. Maybe nothing. Maybe everything."

4

"You're right," Schwarz said. "Something's definitely going on."

It was late Monday afternoon. Having caught a flight from Tampa to Washington and then a chopper to Virginia, Able Team had finally returned home to Stony Man Farm. They were sitting in the complex's War Room, trying to piece together the puzzle they'd stumbled onto in Florida.

"It's still pretty vague," Aaron Kurtzman, Stony Man's computer wizard, murmured after another long spell of silence in front of a monitor. "That's the first thing you've got to realize."

"But there's definitely a pattern, right?" Blancanales prompted.

Kurtzman nodded. "Yeah, there's a pattern. The question is, what does it all mean?"

Schwarz stood and paced. After more than three hours at Kurtzman's side, his eyes were bloodshot and his legs were cramped. He was also hungry and restless. "I can give you a theory," he said softly to Lyons.

The blond ex-cop sighed. "Sure. Give me a theory."

"If you're right, and I'm not necessarily saying you are, but assuming you are, then this is coordinated."

Lyons looked at Gadgets. "Explain."

"He means the pattern is probably federal-based," Kurtzman added. "He means it's some kind of program."

"What kind of program?" Blancanales asked.

"A secret one," Schwarz said. "A very secret one."

Lyons moved over to Kurtzman's side, rested his weight on the back of a wing chair and stared at the computer screen.

"Take a look at this," the computer genius said, his fingers clattering across the keyboard until the screen bore a list of twenty-seven names and addresses. "Missing persons since the first of July. Six from New York. Four from Los Angeles. Two from Houston. Two from Dallas. Three from Chicago...and so on. Now what do they all have in common?" His fingers danced across the keyboard again, and a second set of figures appeared on the screen. "In and out of trouble with the law, right? Every one of them had a record. And what else do we know?" His fingers performed another quick dance. "According to relatives and friends, each one had supposedly been arrested just prior to their disappearance."

"So what are you trying to tell me?" Lyons asked. "That these people are vanishing into some sort of Bermuda Triangle in the legal system?"

Gadgets smiled slightly. "I wouldn't exactly call it a Bermuda Triangle. I'd call it a black hole, and I'd say it was almost definitely manufactured."

"Manufactured by whom?" Lyons asked.

Schwarz nodded at Kurtzman, and the computer wizard's fingers began their keyboard dance once again. This time, however, the screen replied with only the vaguest notations—a short series of single-digit numerals and a seemingly unrelated list of letters.

"What do you make of that, Gadgets?" Kurtzman asked.

Schwarz studied the screen for a moment and shrugged. "A Justice code?"

"Or judicial," Kurtzman suggested.

"Meaning what?" Lyons asked.

"Meaning," Schwarz said softly, "that we'd better be careful who we talk to about this."

"Real careful," Kurtzman added.

CARL LYONS and Hal Brognola, Stony Man's chief of operations, moved quietly through the woods outside the building housing the War Room.

"Let's just say that at the moment it's a hunch," Ironman began, his hands in his jeans pockets, his eyes on the trail before them.

"But you want to turn it into a full-blown case, right?" Brognola asked.

"Well, I don't think we can just ignore it."

They came to a circular clearing where patches of frost hugged the ground. "Any idea how many people in this country vanish every year?" Brognola asked.

Lyons shrugged. "Not like this."

"Besides, what's your proof? The word of some drug dealer's attorney?"

"What about the stuff Kurtzman found?"

"Come on, Carl, I can play that game, too. Give me a couple of hours in the data banks and I'll make you a list out of anything."

"Yeah? Well, I don't think we can write it off that easily. In fact, I don't think we can write it off at all. Something's definitely going on—something weird."

"So what do you want to do about it? Take another Florida vacation?"

"Not necessarily, no."

"Then what?"

Lyons picked up a stick and poked at a clump of leaves. "I want to run it back to the source."

"And by the source, I take it you mean...?"

Lyons stared at the big Fed. "I mean Washington."

They sat down on an old stone bench. Although it was cold, neither man seemed to notice.

"How about you just give me the bottom line?" Brognola suggested.

Lyons sighed. "Are you sure you want to hear it?"

Brognola nodded. "Why shouldn't I?"

"Because I think this thing might go all the way to our front door."

"Meaning?"

"Meaning it might involve some of the same people who pay us."

"Which is another way of saying the bad buys are in the inside this time. Is that it?"

Lyons took another deep breath. "Look at it this way. You're working for law and order. Maybe as a cop on the beat, maybe as a federal prosecutor. You've spent half your adult life trying to clean up the streets, trying to put society's scum away. But everywhere you turn you find yourself hamstrung with this or that law. You find your cases broken faster than you can count, shredded by smooth-talking lawyers in two-thousand-dollar suits. So what are you going to do about it? You're going to start bending the rules. You're going to try to set up your own legal system and start dispensing your own brand of justice."

"And how far up do you think it all goes?" Brognola whispered.

Lyons shook his head. "I'm not sure. But seeing as how we could be talking about the preservation of this nation's Constitution, I think we'd better find out... and fast."

THERE WERE two primary industries at the encampment—a license plate factory and a glassworks. Added to these were a few service industries, including laundry and food preparation, but most of the inmates made either license plates or bottles. No one was certain who consumed the finished products or even if they were consumed at all. All they knew was that crude license plates were forged in one shack while even cruder glass bottles were blown in another. It was said that the license shop was preferable to the glass furnace because it was slightly cooler. But after eight unbroken hours pounding and trimming sheets of steel, Angela Perez couldn't imagine that any place was worse than the machine shop...except maybe hell.

The typical day began at dawn, with a few spoonfuls of oatmeal and a glass of milky water. The inmates were then herded single file into their respective factories and work commenced. At noon the prisoners were generally served two slices of luncheon meat on white bread or canned beans. Work would then continue until supper, when the inmates were served reconstituted beef or a slice of canned chicken, more white bread and occasionally canned corn. Those judged to be flagging at any point during the day were usually transferred to one of the punishment assignments, which meant either digging ditches or laying bricks in the desert sun. There were, however, far worse punishments.

The first formal punishment came on the evening of the seventh day. Perez and the others had just finished a supper of sausage and cold beans when a general assembly announcement blared over the public address system. Fifteen minutes later a hundred women and two hundred men were herded into the central yard and lined up in front of the whipping posts.

After another ten or fifteen minutes a Puerto Rican woman and an Oriental boy were marched to the posts. Although only the woman was actually crying, the boy looked pretty frightened. The prisoners' wrists were fastened to the posts with leather straps. Then a brawny male guard, known among the inmates as Toma, approached and peeled off the boy's shirt and the woman's gray smock.

The charges were read by one of the female guards, a tall, big-shouldered woman named Lily. Although Perez was no longer really listening, it seemed that the offenders had been caught attempting to steal tins of fruit cocktail from the camp stores. After what was termed a "formal investigation," it had been decided that each offender was to be given ten lashes.

The whip was broad, designed to hurt but not cut. The big-shouldered woman positioned herself to the right and three paces behind the Puerto Rican. Toma positioned himself similarly behind the Oriental. The first crack left the woman shuddering and whimpering with pain. The boy was able to remain silent for a little longer, but eventually he, too, couldn't help screaming. At one point, after about eight or nine strokes, Perez let her eyes stray beyond the yard to the warden's tower. Merryman was at the window, watching intently through a pair of binoculars.

Presumably the public whippings were designed to instill obedience in the inmates. It was felt that if they regularly witnessed others screaming under the whip or howling, thanks to the cattle prod, they'd be less likely to rebel. On the whole the theory proved successful. With images of pain constantly in everyone's mind there was very little talk of defiance or insubordination. Yet every now and then, despite pain and suffering, there was always someone who refused to lie down and roll over.

It was a Friday morning when Perez first laid eyes on the rebel. She had risen with the desert chill, obediently eaten her insipid breakfast and taken her station in the license plate factory. What with the continual echo of pounding hammers and clattering metal, she'd been entirely unaware of exactly when the rebel first appeared. At one point, however, he was standing beside her—a squat, slightly rotund young man with gleaming eyes and a devil's face. Under any other circumstances she supposed she would have despised him. After all, he was basically just another sleazy punk, and thus the epitome of everything that was wrong with today's Hispanic youth. But given the grim humiliation of the camp, she found something comforting in his defiant eyes.

"So what do you say, honey?" he whispered as he pretended to pound out imperfections in another sheet of steel. "Is this the pits or is this the pits?"

"You're not supposed to talk," she told him.

"What do you mean I'm not supposed to talk? What's the point of being in this hellhole if I can't talk to a pretty chick like yourself?"

A guard passed, a wiry weasel of a man named Smythe. In addition to his walkie-talkie he carried a stun gun.

"Some kind of creep, huh?" the rebel whispered as Smythe ambled past.

"Look, he'll hear you and then we'll both be in trouble," she whispered back.

"Hey, what's life without a little trouble? Besides, what are they going to do to me? What could be worse than this?"

She gave him a sideways glance. "You'd be surprised."

A slightly dazed black woman named Julie appeared with another barrelful of uncut plates. Perez heaped a stack on her workbench and began methodically pounding out the flaws. Although there might have been something admirable about the rebel's attitude, it was definitely not the way to survive. To remain alive you kept your head down, your eyes fixed on your feet and your mouth shut. Otherwise they'd notice you. And if they noticed you, you were dead.

"Hey, let me ask you something," the rebel whispered. "What did a good-looking woman like you do to get in here?"

Perez intensified her blows on the metal.

"Come on, baby," he persisted. "You can at least tell me what you did to get in here."

"Nothing," she finally whispered. "I didn't do anything."

Out of the corner of her eye she saw him smile. "Now ain't that a coincidence. 'Cause I didn't do nothing either...or at least nothing they caught me for. They just grabbed me one night, threw me into this big old bus and here I am, which wouldn't be so cool except for you. So how about it?"

"How about what?"

"How about you and me being friends? What do you say?"

She chanced a look at the guard, then ceased her hammering. "Look, I don't know where you think you are, but if you keep talking, you're going to get us both into a lot of trouble. So would you please just be quiet."

He gave her another slightly demonic grin, then a fairly casual nod. "Okay, baby, I'll be quiet. But first I want to show you what a guy like me can do around this place. So keep your eyes open and you'll see something fine."

Although Perez tried to keep her gaze fixed on her work, she couldn't help but notice the rebel's foot gently nudging a can of lubricant out from under the bench. Next, having somehow managed to overturn the can, he casually spread a thin film of oil across the concrete. As the guard drew closer, the rhythm of the rebel's hammer blows grew faster and louder. Then everything seemed to stop as Smythe's legs flew out from under him and he hit the floor with a sickening thump. The guard got to his feet slowly and glared at the bowed heads around him. "Who the hell did that?"

All eyes returned to the benches, all hands in clear sight.

"I asked you people a question! Who the hell put that oil on the floor?"

"I think it just happened," said a female voice at the end of the factory.

The guard met the speaker's eyes for two or three hard seconds. "What did you say?"

"I think it just spilled," said another voice from the shadows of the factory.

The guard turned and looked in the direction of the second voice. "It just spilled, huh? Well, if it happens to spill again, there's going to be some real trouble around here. Do I make myself clear?"

Nothing was quite the same after that. Although no one had the nerve to discuss the incident in public, the image of Smythe sprawled on the floor was clearly on everyone's mind. It was in their eyes when they broke for lunch and in their faint smiles when they returned to the benches. It was probably the first real act of defiance any of them had seen since arriving at the camp, and it wouldn't be forgotten.

As for the rebel, Perez spoke with him only once during the days that followed—a brief encounter outside the factory door.

"Hey, baby, what did you think of my little move on that guard the other day? It was pretty cool, right?"

"It was pretty stupid," she said.

"Oh, come on, baby. You don't really believe that, do you?"

"Look, just leave me alone."

"Hey, I'll leave you alone. But first, how about telling me your name?"

"Angela."

"Angela? Hey, that's a pretty name."

She nodded, started to move away, then suddenly stopped. "What's your name?"

He flashed a devilish grin at her and stroked his gleaming goatee. "Ramos. Reuben Ramos."

5

In the fantasy Agent Jay Sole was a dark knight. He moved through the streets of industrial cities like a furious wind, sweeping away every piece of human trash in his path. He regularly matched wits with the world's most devious criminal minds, and when his .38 spoke, no one talked back. He also, of course, always got the girl and never ate his lunch from a brown paper sack on a pigeon-stained bench in the park.

It was a crisp, clear Thursday, with vaguely pink clouds above the nation's capital. Having spent the morning bent over a filing cabinet in a windowless room at FBI headquarters, Sole was pleased to get a breath of air finally. He was also pleased that the weekend was near and that he had finally managed to get hold of the complete set of "The Untouchables" on videotape. Indeed, if only there hadn't been two very disturbing men approaching from the shadows of an oak tree, he might have been reasonably happy.

He had first spotted the men while unwrapping the ham-and-swiss sandwich his mother had packed that morning. Next, while sipping root beer, he'd seen them again on the grassy knoll. Then, when he glanced up from his pickle, he caught another glimpse of them moving out from under the oak...and definitely coming straight toward him.

"What you got there?" Lyons asked, smiling as he sat on the bench. "Ham and cheese?"

Sole swallowed hard, then turned to his left where Blancanales now sat. "Do I know you gentlemen?"

Lyons smiled again and shook his head. "Not really. But we know you, and that's all that's important at the moment."

Sole stuffed what was left of his lunch back into the sack and glanced around nervously. Although there were one or two others from the Bureau seated on benches in the distance, he doubted whether anyone could really help now. "Look, do you mind telling me what you guys want?"

Lyons leaned a little closer to the pale agent, his lips only inches from Sole's ear. "Well, it's kind of like this, Jay. It seems we're conducting a little survey and we'd like to ask you a couple of questions."

"What kind of questions?"

"Questions regarding certain papers you've been processing, certain records pertaining to the apprehension of certain individuals by local law-enforcement agencies."

Sole cautiously eyed Blancanales's hands, then shifted his gaze back to Lyons. "Look, I don't know who you guys think I am, but I happen to work for—"

"We know who you work for, Jay," Lyons cut in.

"Then you obviously know I've got nothing to do with local law-enforcement agencies."

"We know you *should* have nothing do with local law-enforcement agencies," Blancanales interjected. "But sometimes what should be and what is aren't always the same thing."

"Case in point," Lyons said, "the arrest of one Reuben Ramos."

Sole ran a hand across his forehead, knocking his glasses slightly askew. "Hey, you guys got to understand something here. I'm just a clerk. I just process the papers."

"Exactly," Lyons rasped. "You just issue the warrants. Only problem is, how come the FBI's issuing warrants for the arrest of a suspect who isn't even in their jurisdiction?"

Sole swallowed hard again as perspiration broke out on his forehead. "Look, it's not exactly that we're issuing warrants for the arrest of these people. It's more like...well, a recommendation. We're just advising some of the local PDs that we think maybe they should pick these suspects up on a kind of informal basis."

"And then what happens to them?" Blancanales asked.

Sole shrugged. "How should I know?"

Lyons and Blancanales stood, lifting Sole by his arms. From a distance they might have looked like three slightly intoxicated buddies leaning on one another for support. A closer inspection, however, would have revealed that the arms around Sole's shoulders were fully ready to snap his neck.

"It's like this," Lyons said as he and Blancanales led the skinny clerk into the darker recesses of the park. "We were doing a little checking in some of the national data banks, and it seems your name popped up quite a lot."

"Hey, I just channel the information, that's all."

"What kind of information?" Blancanales demanded.

"Little things. Like if some cop in Chicago wants to know if he can lean on some local dealer, then I process the request up through the ranks. I make sure it doesn't cross anyone's lines, that it's all coordinated."

"Meaning the local cops have to ask the Bureau if they can do their job?"

"Of course not. It's just that—"

"It's just what?" Lyons interrupted impatiently.

Sole's knees buckled, and Lyons eased him down onto another pigeon-spotted bench. "Let's just say there's some kind of project."

"What kind of project?" Blancanales asked, sitting beside Sole.

"A special federally coordinated project utilizing volunteers from various PDs around the country. The cops go out and pick up some local creep and then we coordinate the handling."

"And by 'handling' you mean what?" Lyons asked.

"I don't know exactly. I just know the cops haul these guys in and some of our boys take over from there."

"And what happens to the arrest reports?"

Sole smiled faintly. "The arrest reports?"

"You said these suspects were hauled in by local police, so how come there's never any local record of it? No arrest reports. No fingerprints. No mug shots. Nothing."

Sole rubbed his pointy jaw. "Well, I guess there's no record of it because no one's ever actually arrested. They're just . . . well, you know, pulled in."

Lyons and Blancanales exchanged a quick glance, then rose from the bench to face the clerk again.

"Let me ask you something," Lyons said. "Did you ever stop to think that maybe what's going on here isn't completely legal?"

Sole bit his lip. "What do you mean?"

"I mean, the Bureau's telling local cops to drag people off the streets without any regard for the law."

Sole shook his head. "Hey, we're talking about the real scum of the earth here. We're talking about drug dealers and gang bangers."

"Yeah? Well, we're also talking about the Bill of Rights, Jay. Which means you could be in a whole lot of trouble."

"But I don't have anything to do with it!" Sole protested. "I just channel the information."

"Channel it to whom?" Lyons pressed.

"To the project coordinator."

"And who's the project coordinator?"

"Hey, I can't just—"

Lyons leaned closer. "What's his name, Jay?"

Sole hesitated, shifting his eyes from Lyons to Blancanales.

"Come on, Jay. Spit it out."

"Grabowski. Special Agent Lenny Grabowski."

Lyons straightened. "Thanks, Jay. You've been a big help."

Ironman and Pol had already begun moving back into the shadows of the oaks when Sole finally got to his feet. "Hey, you never told me who you guys are."

Blancanales turned, his face as grim as death. "That's right, Jay. Let's keep it that way. You'll stay healthier."

BLANCANALES LIFTED his eyes to the stony gaze of Abraham Lincoln and sighed. "How do you think he would have felt about all this?"

Lyons shook his head. "Not good."

Although the skies had cleared, leaving the lawns bathed in sunlight, the surrounding park was still deserted. There were a few schoolchildren near the reflecting pond and some elderly women with infants seated on benches beneath the cherry trees. And, as usual, a few listless tourists wandered in the shadows of the Washington Monument and the Jefferson Memorial.

"So what do we know about Lenny Grabowski?" Lyons asked as he slowly ascended the steps with Schwarz and Blancanales.

Schwarz withdrew a notebook from the pocket of his windbreaker and flipped it open. "Old guard. Been with the FBI more than twenty-five years. Made quite a name for himself in the sixties harassing campus radicals, Vietnam War protestors and black activists. Headed up one of the Patty Hearst teams, then moved to an administrative post on the inside. Officially he's listed as the team leader for something called the National Urban Task Force."

"Which way do you think he'll jump under pressure?" Blancanales asked.

Schwarz shrugged. "Hard to say. Politically he's known to be slightly to the right of Attila the Hun. But at the same time he's also known to have a drinking problem, and they say his marriage is a mess."

"So how do you suggest we make the approach?" Lyons asked.

Schwarz paused and gazed at the dark silhouette of the Washington Monument and the flocks of wheeling gulls. "How about we get him alone and in the dark?"

AGENT LEONARD GRABOWSKI lived in a whitewashed colonial estate just off the Shirley Memorial Highway. It was a large, rambling place, originally built with the help of his ex-wife's father. There were still touches here and there of the woman's original vision—the green shutters, the gently sloping portico, the brass fittings. But on the whole it was no longer really a home; it was just an old house that was slowly going to seed.

The long, winding path between the circular drive and the portico was lined with twisted oaks that tended to deepen the evening shadows. There was also no light on the porch or light from the street. Thus, when Lyons and Blancanales initially made their approach, Grabowski couldn't even see their faces.

"Hey, Lenny, how the hell are you?" Lyons growled as he stepped out from the blackness and took hold of Grabowski's right arm.

The FBI man spun, attempting to twist free of the stranger's grip. But by this time Blancanales had also appeared, taking hold of Grabowski's other arm.

"Uh-uh," the smooth-talking Hispanic chided as he casually removed a .38 revolver from Grabowski's jacket.

"We just want to have a little chat," Lyons said. "Nothing too heavy, just a little talk about life in the big city."

"Who the hell are you?" Grabowski demanded, still struggling against the blond stranger's iron grip.

"The research committee," Blancanales replied. "We're the research committee, come to ask a few questions."

Grabowski grew still, his face perspiring heavily. "Look, I don't know who you people think you are, but I happen to be a federal agent. You understand? You'll be—"

"We'll what?" Lyons snapped, his voice suddenly cold and menacing. "Disappear off the face of the earth, maybe?"

Grabowski was escorted into the house and deposited on a sofa in the den. In the yellow lamplight he looked old and tired. His face was slightly puffy and still studded with sweat. His wandering eyes were laced with red and ringed with dark circles.

"We spoke with Sole," Lyons said. "We also pulled your files from the data banks."

"What the hell is this all about?" Grabowski demanded.

Blancanales moved past the dusty desk to examine a framed certificate from the American Legion. Also on the far wall were two photographs of Grabowski shaking hands with J. Edgar Hoover.

"It's about a lot of things," Blancanales said. "But mainly it's about the National Urban Task Force."

"That's a classified project, for Christ's sake. You people have no right to—"

"Ah, but we do," Lyons interjected. "We've got every right."

From the far wall Blancanales moved to a dusty curio cabinet filed with miniature cameras and weapons taken from Soviet spies. There was also a pair of mink-lined handcuffs and a photograph of Grabowski beside Richard Nixon.

"I guess you might say it's a question of priorities as much as anything else," Lyons continued after another long pause. "Sure, there's a hell of a crime problem in this country. But, on the other hand, there's also the Constitution to protect. And that's where we come in."

Grabowski seemed to digest the tall, muscular man's words for a moment, then suddenly rose from the sofa. "Look, I don't know who you people are or what you hope to gain, but if you think you can come in here and ask me about official FBI business, then you're sadly mistaken. Now, if you don't leave my house immediately, I'll be forced to call the police."

Lyons looked at the aging FBI agent and smiled thinly. "And exactly what police would you call, Lenny? The regular local cops... or those secret federal ones?"

Blancanales slipped back around the desk and pressed Grabowski down onto the sofa again. "See, we already know the general outline, pal. We know you've got a special arrangement with certain cops around the country to pick up suspects without an arrest warrant. We also know these suspects have a way of simply disappearing before anyone even knows they're missing. What we don't know, however, are the specifics."

"Like who gives you your orders," Lyons added. "And who gives that person his orders."

Although suddenly very pale, Grabowski's voice was still firm. "I've got nothing to say to you guys."

"Really?" Lyons smiled. "Well, that's too bad. Because, you see, this *is* official, which means that if you don't talk to us, you may end up talking to a grand jury."

Grabowski grew very still again, his eyes shifting to the photograph of Hoover. "All right, all right. But this is off-the-record, okay? Way off-the-record."

There was some bourbon in the cabinet, and Blancanales poured Grabowski a large one. The FBI agent lit a cigarette, blew some smoke into the air, then looked at Lyons. "It's not a Bureau project. The task force, I mean. It's not really under the FBI umbrella. We're just the liaison to the local police departments."

"A liaison to whom?" Lyons pressed.

"The Center."

"What Center?"

"For the Study of Urban Violence."

"And what's the Center for the Study of Urban Violence?"

"I'm not sure exactly. I think it's some kind of private foundation. Kind of like one of those think tanks that contract with the White House."

"And they're the guys who call the shots?" Blancanales asked from behind the sofa.

Grabowski nodded. "Yeah, that's about the size of it."

"You got a name for anyone up there?" Lyons asked.

"Not really."

"What's that supposed to mean?"

"It means I deal with a guy named Jerry White, but I don't think he's a player."

"Then who's the player?"

"I'm not sure. All I know is that these guys are connected. They got people all over Washington, people way up at the top of the heap."

"And by top of the heap, you mean what?"

Grabowski shifted his gaze to the portrait of Nixon on the south lawn of the White House. "I think you know what I mean."

6

It was after midnight when Able Team returned to Stony Man Farm and nearly three in the morning when the preliminary facts were assembled. After dozing for an hour on a leather couch, Lyons joined Brognola in the War Room. Also present were an exhausted Gadgets Schwarz and a restless Pol Blancanales.

"Why don't you give me the finer points first?" Brognola suggested.

"Such as?" Lyons rasped.

"Like who else knows you boys are onto this?"

"Basically no one."

"And what about those two clowns from the Bureau?"

Blancanales responded first. "We didn't exactly introduce ourselves, but I'd still put Grabowski on ice for a while. At least until we make our move."

"And what about Ramos's lawyer in Florida?" Brognola asked.

Lyons shook his head. "Supposedly he's on our side."

"How about fingerprints in the data banks?"

"Didn't leave any," Gadgets said wearily.

"Which means that apart from Grabowski, you boys are still operationally clean," Brognola said. "Is that about the size of it?"

Lyons nodded. "I think so, yeah."

"Then I guess we'd better start thinking about moving on in, because this could be bigger than any of us imagine." Brognola tossed a buff folder bearing four classified stamps onto the massive table. Then came the photographs—two shots of a columned mansion on the dark bend of a wide river, and a studio portrait of a square-jawed man. "Jack Lang and his Hudson River Center for the Study of Urban Violence."

Lyons picked up the portrait and studied the square-jawed face. "Now, when you say Jack Lang, you're talking about *the* Jack Lang, right?"

Brognola nodded. "All fifty million dollars' worth."

"And you're sure he's the one behind the Hudson River Center?"

"I wouldn't have kept you boys up so late if I wasn't sure. He operates it out of his own Jack Lang Foundation, the mansion you see there in the photo."

"So where do we stand now?" Blancanales asked.

Brognola shrugged. "Well, I can give you a theory."

"Sure," Lyons said, "give us a theory."

Brognola slid his stocky body back into his chair and pressed his fingertips together. "What do you know about Lang?"

Lyons shook his head. "Only that he's rich, that he owns about half the state of Arizona and that he's pretty good friends with some damn important people."

"Including the President," Schwarz muttered.

"That's right," Brognola said. "He's a good friend of the President. He's also chairman of the Committee for a Strong America."

"Which all adds up to what?" Lyons asked.

Brognola sighed. "A guess?"

"Sure," Lyons said. "Give us your best guess."

"All right. I think we might be looking at some sort of clandestine urban control experiment."

Brognola rose from his chair and withdrew a loosely bound sheaf of papers. "Recommendations for a crime-free America. Two hundred and twelve pages. Dry as hell and apparently innocuous. But when you read between the lines you find some pretty interesting stuff."

"And by 'interesting' I take it you mean...?" Blancanales asked.

Brognola let the papers drop back onto the table. "Scary." He slid back into the chair and sighed. "Story goes like this. About four, five years ago Jack Lang got himself appointed to the President's Commission on Urban Violence. It's one of those titular posts that people like Lang get awarded for having figured out a way to donate fifteen times the legal limit to the President's campaign fund. So it doesn't mean anything. It's just, you know, one of those useless commissions designed to make people think something's being done about the crime problem in our godforsaken cities.''

"And then Lang gets an idea,'' Schwarz said.

"Something like that,'' Brognola replied. "Yeah, Lang gets an idea—why not really make something out of that so-called President's Commission on Urban Violence? Why not really give the thing some teeth? So he starts making a few telephone calls, spending a little money, networking with some like-minded law-enforcement people in the Bureau. A new administration comes in, Lang briefs them on what he's got going and lands himself a sort of unofficial position as adviser on the urban crime problem. And by this time he's got his Hudson River think tank in high gear and he's got some real support for his ideas.''

"And what exactly are those ideas?'' Lyons asked, leveling his eyes at the Stony Man chief.

Brognola returned the gaze with a strangely sad smile. "Ever read *Mein Kampf?*''

They all fell silent for a moment.

"Like I said,'' Brognola continued softly, "it's just a theory at this point. But I think it's entirely possible that Lang has set up some sort of experimental prison system.''

"You think the President knows?'' Blancanales asked.

Brognola shook his head. "Not really, no. I think it's buried somewhere in Justice, the local police departments and the Bureau. But the real force behind the whole scheme is private and entirely under Lang's control."

"So how do we proceed?" Schwarz asked.

Brognola glanced at Lyons. "Carefully. Very, very carefully. After all, as far the world's concerned, Lang is still a very respectable man. He's got friends in all sorts of high places, and he's got the money to make more friends."

"So what's the bottom line here?" Blancanales asked. "What are we ultimately looking at?"

Brognola exchanged another glance with Lyons, then took a deep breath. "Worst case?"

"Yeah," Blancanales replied. "What the worst case?"

"That Lang, with the help of a few like-minded bureaucrats, has built himself his own justice system within the justice system. It's got no judges, no juries and no lawyers. It's just cops and executioners. It drags suspects off the street or out of their beds and hauls them away, maybe to a grave, maybe to some kind of concentration camp. Either way it's not how we do business."

"Still," Blancanales said softly, "it's kind of strange when you think about it."

"How do you mean, Pol?" Lyons asked.

"Well, here we've spent the past ten years or so busting our chops to keep the bad guys off the streets.

Now all of a sudden you're telling us the bad guys are on the inside and we're supposed to go out and protect a bunch of drug-pushing creeps. It just seems kind of strange, that's all.''

Brognola shrugged, then shook his head. "Well, all I can tell you, Pol, is that it's going to seem a lot stranger if someone like Jack Lang succeeds in turning this nation into a police state."

IT WASN'T UNTIL the twentieth day of her stay in the camp that Perez began to realize inmates were dying all around her. When she first began to notice that names kept dropping from the roll call, she had innocently assumed the missing prisoners had either been transferred to another camp or had become ill. Likewise, when she heard the shots in the night, she had innocently assumed the guards were either testing their weapons or killing coyotes. Then there were the rumors about the graves beyond the wire, and finally the talk about executions.

"I mean, who's going to stop them, you know?" Ramos had told her, fear evident in his voice. "They want to take someone out into the desert and blow him away, like who's really going to stop them?"

"But that's murder!" Perez had whispered back.

"Yeah," Ramos had replied gravely. "It's murder."

There were at least four more executions during the weeks that followed. Yet the question that ultimately kept Perez awake every night, the question that burned in her brain every minute of every day was: how was it determined who was to live and who was to die?

It was late Sunday evening when Perez's name was finally called. The barrack lights had been extinguished. Exhausted inmates whispered softly among themselves. From somewhere beyond the women's compound came the mournful notes of a blues harmonica. Then came the crunch of boot heels on the gravel, and finally the guards shone a light in her eyes.

"Perez! Front and center, now!"

She rose from her cot as if in a trance, mostly conscious of the blood draining from her face and the electric silence around her. The first guard, Toma, locked her arms behind her back. The second guard, a muscular woman named Rita, secured her wrists with a pair of plastic cuffs. Then they shoved her into the cold and marched her along the gravel path to the bungalows beyond the wire. As she approached the last stucco building on the left, she was vaguely aware that this was where Warden Merryman lived. But none of it really registered until she saw the man standing in the doorway.

The warden's quarters were simple but scrupulously clean. The pine furniture suggested a Southwest lawman's office, and there were framed sixshooters on the wall. She also saw Indian rugs, stuffed coyote heads and a collection of bullwhips.

He told her to stand in the center of the room while he eased himself into a chair behind an old desk. Then he withdrew a manila folder and began to leaf through the pages casually. Although it wasn't cold, she couldn't stop shivering. She also desperately wished they had let her slip on her shoes.

"Let me ask you something," he said at last. "Do you know why you're here?"

She raised her eyes from the floor, no longer certain whether to laugh or scream. "Excuse me?"

"I said, do you know why you're here?"

She shook her head. "Not really, no."

"Well, then I'll tell you. You're here because you were a very bad girl."

He rose from behind the desk and began to circle her slowly. "Every three minutes someone in this nation is victim to a major crime. Rape, murder, theft, assault, extortion. Every three minutes some decent American citizen suffers because of the scum out there. It's an intolerable situation, absolutely intolerable."

He hesitated, remaining just beyond the periphery of her vision, his lips only inches from her ear. "Now I realize you've never committed any of those crimes yourself, Angela. But, in a sense, you've committed a far worse transgression. You've attempted to ruin the reputation of those men and women charged with protecting honest citizens against the rising tide of scum. You have, as a so-called crusading journalist, attempted to smear the good name of your city's law-enforcement establishment. And that, my dear Angela, is why you're here tonight."

He moved to her other side, his breath now on her neck. "Oh, I know what you're thinking. You're thinking that what we're doing here is illegal. Maybe you're even thinking it's ultimately fascist. Well, in a sense, you might be right. But the fact remains that radical problems need radical solutions. Our cities have become cesspools. Our citizens spend their lives in fear while their children are exposed to every imaginable kind of filth. It's a problem that the normal legal system can't even being to deal with, and thus this camp was established as the final solution."

He stepped around to face her again, then lifted her head with a finger beneath her chin. "Look, I know you're not like the others out there. I know you probably shouldn't even be here. But the fact is, you're here and there isn't anything either of us can do about it . . . except maybe try to make the best of it."

She looked at him, meeting his blue eyes for a moment. "What are you talking about?"

He slid his hand to her shoulder, and began to trace the collar of her drab gray smock. "I can make things easier on you, honey. I can make it so that you have yourself a nice hot bath every day and real food. I can make it so you have something nice to wear and someplace warm to sleep." He hesitated, running his finger along her throat, then lower to the swell of her left breast. "I can even give you a nice warm bed. Now what do you say about that?"

She met his gaze again, feeling the scream of outrage rising from the pit of her stomach and exploding into her brain. But in the end her response was hardly more than a whisper. "Go to hell."

A brief smile played on his lips. Then, stepping back with his left foot, he brought his right hand across her face. The blow knocked her to her knees, blurring her vision with tears.

"Now how about we try it again?" he snarled, wrenching her head back with a handful of hair. "You want to work with me, or do you want to work against me?"

She shook her head and rasped, "You can't do this."

"Is that so? And why is that?"

She shut her eyes, arching as he yanked on her hair again. "It's not legal," she moaned.

He smiled again, his lips only inches from her ear, his breath warm on her face. Then he took hold of her smock and ripped away a single strip of gray cotton from her shoulders to her waist. "It's not legal, huh?" He grunted. "Well, I'll tell you what's legal and what's not."

He grabbed her cuffed wrists, dragged her to the adjoining room and threw her facedown onto the mattress. The rough wool bedspread smelled of cheap cologne. The pillows were cold and smelled of fabric softener. "Not legal, huh?" he muttered. He yanked her panties down and wedged his left knee between her legs. "Nothing's illegal here. You understand?"

He slapped her two or three times before she finally rolled over onto her back and surrendered. Then she simply shut her eyes and fixed her mind on the odors: deodorant, male sweat, kerosene, and the whiskey fumes on Merryman's breath.

It surprised her how little of anything she felt when it was over—not hatred, not fear, not even disgust. She simply lay very still with her knees drawn up to her breasts and her dull gaze fixed on the gently swaying curtains. Although he had finally removed the hand-cuffs and tossed her an old terry-cloth robe, she made no attempt to cover herself. She just watched the slight movement of the curtains and the shifting shadows on the wall.

"Now, that wasn't so bad, was it?" he asked, reaching for a pack of cigarettes on the nightstand.

She shifted her gaze to the wash of lamplight on the ceiling, but still didn't respond.

Merryman extended a hand to caress her left breast, then brushed the hair away from her face. "Well, how about it? Was it really all that bad?"

She managed to shrug, then shut her eyes again to hide the first tears. "No."

"Then maybe we should make it a regular thing, hmm? How about it?"

She propped herself on an elbow and looked at him. "Do I have a choice?"

Merryman reached out and grabbed a handful of her hair. "What do you think?"

7

The Jack Lang Foundation stood on a rise eight miles from where Benedict Arnold had attempted to betray the American Revolutionary Army. It was an imposing place, dark and shuttered and surrounded by massive oaks. There were willow groves closer to the Hudson River banks and a short stretch of marsh and tangled woodland.

Originally the house had supposedly belonged to the widowed bride of a Civil War general, then to the half-mad son of a New York industrialist. Some said it was haunted by the ghost of a murdered child, while phantom horsemen were sometimes heard on midsummer nights. After falling into the hands of Jack Lang, however, the rambling old house had soon taken on other associations.

Like other privately funded advisory groups, the Jack Lang Foundation essentially represented a shadow government. Among its directors were more than a dozen men and women with standing invitations to the Oval Office, while at least six of the last thirty cabinet members had been drawn from the foundation's roster. It was all part of an American system of government that few citizens understood, and still fewer trusted.

It was close to midnight when Lyons, Schwarz and Blancanales reached the edge of the foundation grounds. They came by a circuitous route, first by van along Old Mill Road, then by foot across the stretch of marshy woodland. "I guess you might say it's a question of priorities," Brognola had told them. "Do we want to play it by the book and get nowhere, or do we want to bend a few rules and get right to the heart of the matter?"

And by "bend a few rules" he was referring to unauthorized entry and the theft of classified documents.

It was cold beyond the woodland, with a stiff breeze off the river and an early-winter chill. It was also quite dark, with only a quarter moon in the trees and the occasional sweep of headlights along the highway. Yet, as the team drew closer, moving in a half crouch through waist-high grass, there were definitely no lights in the windows of the old Lang house.

"Anything?" Lyons asked.

Schwarz lowered his eye from the Starlight scope and shook his head. "I'm not sure."

From the edge of the wood the ground sloped steeply to the marsh, then rose again to the copse of oaks. From the opposite bank came the echo of a midnight train. There were also cries of night birds and what sounded like an owl.

"It's your call," Lyons whispered to Schwarz. "You take us up there and you get us in."

The mustached electronics wizard picked up the Starlight scope again and began to scan the eaves and shutters. "We're probably going to figure on at least two sets of motion sensors. One on the outside, one on the inside."

"What about trip wires, alarms and all the rest of it?" Blancanales asked from over his shoulder.

Schwarz shook his head. "Probably don't need them with a state-of-the-art motion-sensing system."

"So how do we handle it?" Lyons asked.

Schwarz shrugged. "Depends how it's rigged. If it's internal, we can probably work around it. If it's integrated with an outside security system, then we probably have to cut the power."

"And what do we do if the guards show up?" Blancanales asked.

Schwarz looked at him. "Good question."

From the copse of oaks they moved to the edge of the sloping lawn. Although there were mounted floodlights above the portico, the canopy of hanging leaves still offered shelter. Yet closer to the broad steps and the columned front there were only low hedges.

After Gadgets neutralized the exterior alarm, they slipped on surgical gloves and entered a sort of pantry. There were tins of imported soup on the shelves, crackers and caviar, along with bottles of vintage wine and champagne.

"Think of it as a mousetrap," Schwarz whispered as he rummaged through his little black bag of electronics gear. "We want the cheese, but we can't afford to release the spring until we're well out of the way."

"But we're in, aren't we?" Blancanales whispered back. "I mean, here we are, so what's the big deal?"

Schwarz pointed at a slender line of wires leading from the doorjamb to the flashing red light on a visual-display camera above the staircase. "That's the big deal. Keep out of its line of vision."

A modest kitchen that no one obviously ever used lay beyond the pantry. Then came a long corridor lined with eighteenth-century landscape etchings, and finally what might have once served as a dining room. There were apparently two sets of security installations beyond the dining room—cameras, possibly monitored from an outside security room, and a second array of motion detectors.

"They screwed up," Schwarz whispered as he slowly approached the first motion detector. "See that?" he said, pointing at the power unit. "It's all on the same circuit. Cut the juice and it all goes down."

It took Schwarz just a few minutes to locate the main power source and reroute the alarm systems, then a few more minutes to make his way back to Lyons and Blancanales in the dining room. From the foyer they moved on to an oval living room filled with dark furniture and moody seascapes of the New England coast. There was also a portrait of Jack Lang here, his eyes apparently burning with conviction, his left hand clutching some sort of scroll.

"Looks like an interesting guy," Blancanales cracked as they moved past the imposing portrait.

Lyons grinned. "Yeah, fascinating."

From the sitting room they moved into what probably served as the main conference room. The motif was somewhat more contemporary here, with a rattan sofa and stainless-steel sculptures. Then came another long corridor lined with early twentieth-century etchings, and finally the staircase to the second-floor offices.

It was darker along the second floor, with only dim shafts of moonlight seeping through the oval windows. What had once been bedrooms were now offices and conference rooms. The overall motif was still quite ornate, however, with more dark landscapes and portraits of long-dead faces.

"Any idea what we're looking for?" Blancanales asked, peering into a corner room with a view of the dark river.

"We'll know it when we find it," Lyons replied.

"How about I try to gain access to this baby?" Schwarz suggested, pausing to examine a video-display terminal in a smaller office adjacent to the staircase.

Lyons shook his head. "I don't think these guys are stupid enough to leave the real goodies on an unprotected system."

Beyond the staircase were two more doors. The first led to what might have been some sort of waiting room, with early twentieth-century etchings of trains and barns on the walls. The second, a substantially larger room, featured another imposing portrait of Lang seated against a background of heavy damask.

"The director's office?" Blancanales whispered, hovering in the half-open door.

"Yeah," Lyons replied. "The director's office."

Schwarz entered first, running his fingertips along the doorjamb, then along the edge of the rug. Even though he found no sign of wires, he still continued cautiously. In addition to Lang's portrait there were also pictures of Ronald Reagan and Barry Goldwater. Deeper within the curtained gloom there was even a portrait of a young Richard Nixon.

Two mahogany filing cabinets were adjacent to the desk, and it took Schwarz only a few minutes to spring the locks. Then, although there were several apparently fascinating documents, Lyons primarily focused on one—"An Interim Proposal for an Emergency Justice Act."

"What do you make of this?" Ironman asked as he withdrew a hand-held photocopier from Schwarz's little black bag.

Pol quickly leafed through the pages, glancing at such phrases as "an effective countermeasure to the rising tide of urban terror" and "the complete, self-contained penal system above and beyond current limitations." Then, continuing his perusal, he came across: "Inasmuch as the need and resources exist, it would seem that the project, at least experimentally, could begin anytime.'' The last fifteen pages of the document were devoted to a list of names, some obviously members of local police departments, other apparently agents within the FBI. There were also what might have been lists of accomplices within city detention centers and federal correctional institutions.

In all it took Lyons another five minutes to assemble and copy all the interesting documents. While he worked Schwarz carefully examined a wall safe behind the bookshelves. "I could probably bust this baby,'' he told Lyons.

"How long?"

Schwarz shrugged. "Ten minutes or so."

Lyons stepped to the window and eased back the curtains. Even though the grounds below were still silent, something told him that time was running out, that their luck wouldn't hold much longer. "I think we'd better just get the hell out of here."

They were halfway down the staircase when they first heard the sound of tires on gravel. Lyons responded first, switching off his flashlight and moving into the deeper shadows. A moment later Blancanales drew his .45 auto, but kept the safety on.

There was a harsh crackle of voices from a radio and the rattle of a doorknob. Blancanales mouthed the words, "Security guard," and Lyons nodded an acknowledgment.

Then came the soft tread of footsteps along the floor below and a whispered name. "Charlie? Hey, Charlie, you see anything?"

Schwarz had also drawn his weapon by now, although Lyons had given them both a sign of caution.

"Charlie?" the voice from below called out again. "Charlie, what the hell's going on in there?"

Seconds passed, and Lyons led his men to the landing.

"Charlie, you all right?"

The footsteps drew closer, and Blancanales began to eye the window above, the doorway and the steps.

"Charlie? *Charlie!*"

Then, from directly below the staircase, they heard, "It's nothing, Bill. Probably just a short in the system. Let's report it and move on."

Lyons waited until the security vehicle pulled away before he motioned Schwarz and Blancanales forward again. Then, silently descending the staircase to the first floor, they quickly moved back out into the night and away from the foundation.

"LET ME ASK you something," Brognola said as he continued to scan the documents Able Team had retrieved forty-eight hours earlier. Once again they were all sitting in the Stony Man War Room. "How far are you guy's willing to go in order to stop this thing?"

Lyons stared hard at the big Fed. Schwarz and Blancanales also shifted their gaze to the chief. "Why do you ask?" Ironman asked.

Brognola tossed the last of the pages down and spread his hands on the table. "Because I think from here on it could get pretty hairy." He rose from his chair and began to pace the length of the room. "It's like this. I still don't know exactly what's going on, but I'm pretty sure about this much—somewhere in this country Jack Lang has built himself a full-blown concentration camp, and I don't know how to shut it down without hurting some very important and probably innocent people."

"Which means you don't want to move in from the outside," Blancanales said. "That about the size of it?"

Brognola nodded. "I start making phone calls to the White House and there's no telling which way the tree will fall. I mean, does this go all the way up to the cabinet? Can the President be implicated even if only by association?"

"So why not go directly to the Man himself?" Schwarz suggested. "Call him on the special phone and tell him you've got to talk privately."

"And tell him what? That one of his heaviest supporters has been a naughty boy? That the Third Reich is upon us, and unless we act fast we'll all be goose-stepping to Jack Lang's tune? Anyway, the President is in no position to move openly against something like this. A scandal like this would make the Iran-Contra affair look like a delinquent tea party."

"Then go to the attorney general," Blancanales said. "Tell him he's got a serious civil rights problem on his hands and he needs an investigation."

"That will just scatter them," Brognola countered. "Lang will close up shop and run. Or worse, he'll implicate the President and the rest of the Administration."

"Then what?" Lyons finally asked.

Brognola looked at him. "An inside move."

Blancanales rubbed his jaw. "How inside?"

"Very inside." There was a brass ashtray, a fountain pen and four pencils on the table. "Let's say this is the installation," the big Fed said, picking up the ashtray. "Now, as far as I can tell, it's supplied by several outside sources." He put down a pencil, a pen and then another pencil. "You've got your local cops giving them prisoners. You've got the FBI plugging in tactical Intelligence. You've obviously got a pool of men drawn from federal pens, and naturally you've got Lang pumping in cash."

Brognola picked up a crystal paperweight from a bureau behind him and placed it in the circle of pens and pencils. "And this is us. Now, we can either try to hit Lang through regular channels, or we can do something real smart. We can move in on him from directly within the camp itself."

The Stony Man chief stepped away from the table and contemplated the wall. Although his hands were casually thrust into his pockets, his face was hard with tension. "I'm not saying it's going to be easy. I don't even know if it's possible. But assuming we can work it, would you guys be willing to go undercover inside the camp?''

Schwarz and Blancanales exchanged a quick glance, while Lyons shifted his gaze to Brognola. "How do you propose to work it?" he asked.

The beefy Fed shook his head. "I'm not sure yet. But assuming we can find an entrance, I think it might be possible to slip you guys in as guards."

"As guards?" Blancanales echoed. "Don't you think we'd be more convincing as inmates?"

Brognola smiled. "Hey, you want to play an inmate, Pol? Be my guest."

"What kind of backup could we expect?" Lyons asked.

"Providing you can get me enough to seal the case, I should be able to get authorization for at least the National Guard."

"And assuming we don't get enough to seal the case?" Blancanales asked.

"Then you'll have nothing to worry about, will you?"

"And exactly how far will we have to take it?" Schwarz asked.

Brognola shrugged. "Just far enough to get me some hard proof. Far enough to let me know what the hell's going on out there."

"Assuming, of course, there really is a camp," Lyons reminded him.

Brognola took a deep breath, his eyes now fixed on a relief map of the continent. "Oh, it's out there all right. Somewhere. You can bet on it."

"So where do we start?" Lyons asked.

"We begin by running those names you picked up last night, tracking the positions back to some sort of point of entrance into the Lang project."

"Such as?"

"Off the top of my head I'd say try someone in the Justice Department, maybe the Bureau of Prisons."

"From what I've seen so far it could be a pretty tough one to crack."

Brognola shrugged. "Maybe, but then there's always a weak link somewhere. All we have to do is find it."

8

"Here goes nothing," Lyons said as he and Blanca-nales rose from the shadows of the Justice Department parking garage stairwell. Then, drawing their .45s, they moved out at a quick walk. Edward Duffy, a top honcho in the Federal Bureau of Prisons, was their mark. The overweight bureaucrat didn't seem particularly alarmed when he saw the two Able Team commandos headed his way, though he did quicken his pace.

Lyons took Duffy from behind, applying a fore-arm to his throat and jamming the .45's muzzle into the man's meaty ribs. "Wallet," he barked.

Duffy responded with a terrified nod. "Just don't hurt me, okay?"

Lyons took the man's wallet and handed it to Blan-canales. Pol flipped it open, examined the credit cards and driver's license, then said, "Edward Duffy in the flesh."

"Then let's roll," Lyons said.

A moment later, amid a screech of radial tires, Schwarz appeared behind the wheel of a windowless van. Then, although Duffy attempted to break free, Lyons had little trouble heaving the man into the rear seat.

Blancanales secured Duffy's wrists with plastic cuffs, then shoved him onto the floor of the van. Lyons drew the .45 and pressed it into the bureaucrat's groin. As the van screeched out of the garage and into the evening, Duffy rasped, "Look, if it's money you want, I can get you all you want."

Lyons increased the pressure of the weapon against the man's groin and told him to shut up. It was fully dark when they reached a wooded area.

"Look, can't you just tell me what's going on?" Duffy squeaked.

Lyons glanced at Blancanales, then shrugged. "What do you want to know, Eddy?"

"Just tell me what this is all about, okay?"

Lyons inched up the muzzle of the .45 until it rested on Duffy's throat. "It's exactly what you think it is, Eddy."

The cottage was hardly more than a shadow among the pines. There were no lights, no moon and the hills seemed to be an extension of the night sky. As Schwarz stopped the van, Duffy began whimpering, demanding again to know what was going on. The Able Team warriors ignored him, though.

"Little cold out there, Eddy," Lyons said as he pulled a green blanket from beneath the seat. "Wouldn't want you to catch your death now, would we?'' He placed the blanket over Duffy's head and led him from the van.

"Look, I happen to be a federal agent," Duffy said from beneath the blanket. "You can't just kidnap me."

There were patches of frost along the path and pine needles suspended in ice. The door was frozen shut, and Blancanales had to shoulder it open. The prisoner was deposited on a wooden stool and the blanket was removed. At first, like a child refusing to acknowledge reality, Duffy wouldn't open his eyes. Then, finally looking around him, he whispered a desperate little oath.

"Here's the deal," Lyons began, slowly pacing in front of the prisoner. "There's a group of people in Washington, and one day they got it into their heads that something had to be done about crime in this country. I mean, we all know it's way out of hand, right? So these guys decided they had to do something about it."

"Regardless of constitutional guarantees," Blancanales added.

"That's right," Lyons said. "Regardless of the Constitution, these guys decided to clean up the streets. So what did they do? Well, I'll tell you what they did. They got a few stooges like you to bend the rules a little. You know, lend them a hand to establish their own penal system. Then they got a few cops to grab suspects off the street, people who ended up in a secret penal camp, and that's supposedly the end of crime in America. Pretty neat, huh?''

''Very neat,'' Schwarz said from the kitchen where he was attempting to coax a flame from a Sterno can.

''The only catch,'' Lyons continued, ''is that the cure turns out to be worse than the illness. I mean, after all, Hitler's Germany didn't have a crime problem, either.''

Blancanales rose from his rickety wooden chair in the corner and slowly approached the prisoner until he was only inches from the man's face. ''This is the deal, Eddy. We know the broad outline, but we don't know all the details.''

Duffy swallowed hard, then shook his head. ''Look, I was just following orders, okay? I don't make the policy. I just follow orders.''

''That sounds like a familiar song,'' Lyons said. ''Now tell us something we don't know.''

Duffy shook his head. ''I don't know anything. All I know is that they've got this program.''

''What kind of program?'' Lyons shot back.

''To clean up the streets, to get rid of drug dealers, gang bangers and prostitutes.''

''And who thought up this program?''

''I don't know. Some big names.''

''Such as?''

''Like that Arizona millionaire.''

''Jack Lang?''

''Yeah, Jack Lang.''

''Who else is involved?''

Duffy shook his head and wiped perspiration from his face with his jacket sleeve. "Look, I'm just a cog in the machine. I'm nothing."

"That's right, Eddy," Blancanales growled from just beyond the edge of Duffy's vision. "You're nothing. Which means no one's going to miss you if you vanish off the face of the earth."

"So how about it?" Lyons pressed, poking his .45 into Duffy's ample stomach. "Why don't you tell us what it's all about before it's too late?"

For two or three awful seconds it seemed as if Duffy couldn't move his head at all. Finally, sucking in a mouthful of air, he whispered, "All right. I'll tell you what I know."

Blancanales removed the handcuffs, and Schwarz brought the man a cup of black coffee. Lyons, however, jammed his .45 into the waistband of his jeans and stared at their prisoner. "Okay, Eddy," he said at last, "let's take it from the top. Who do you take your orders from?"

Duffy gulped some coffee. "I only deal with Lang's people. I know it goes higher than that, but I only deal with the foundation."

"And what exactly do you do for the foundation?"

"I'm the camp recruiter."

"Explain."

"I'm the one who staffs the camp, brings in the guards, that sort of thing."

"And you run it all through the Bureau of Prisons?"

Duffy shook his head. "No, nothing about the program is official. It's basically all private—privately funded and privately managed."

"But still utilizing government personnel, right?"

Duffy nodded. "Not officially. But let's face it. There are a lot of law-enforcement people who are fed up with this nation's failure to clean up the streets, fed up with collaring suspects on Monday and seeing them out on the streets again by Tuesday. So naturally with that kind of frustration the scene was ripe for a radical solution. It was just a question of getting funding and pooling the right sort of resources."

"Which is basically your job, right?" Lyons asked.

Duffy nodded again. "Like I said, I help staff the camp. I find guys in Federal Corrections who are willing to start making a difference."

"How high up does it go?" Blancanales asked.

Duffy mopped his forehead with his sleeve. "I'm not sure exactly. I know the White House originally gave the Lang Foundation a contract to come up with some proposed solutions to the urban crime problem, but I don't think anyone from the Oval Office ever imagined Lang would actually put one of his proposals into action."

"And how does this so-called proposal work?" Lyons asked.

Duffy took a deep breath, then shut his eyes and exhaled with a soft curse. "There are lists of various local police departments drawn up each month. The lists are composed of the names of all the outstanding creeps in the area—dealers, pimps, political radicals and so on. The lists are then submitted to some guys in the FBI. If everything checks out, then the pickup order is issued."

"Pickup order?" Lyons prodded.

"An unofficial authorization for the cops to go ahead and pick up the suspects."

"So there's never any actual warrants drawn up, never any sort of judicial review?"

Duffy smirked. "What do you think?"

"And once the suspects are picked up," Blancanales asked, "then what happens?"

Duffy shrugged indifferently. "There are holding centers in all the major cities. Mostly they use warehouses or old buildings. The suspects are taken to one of these centers and then loaded onto the buses."

"And the buses take them where?"

Duffy shifted his gaze to the far wall and held it there for some time.

"Where, Eddy?" Lyons demanded menacingly. "Where do the buses go?"

Duffy pressed a worried fist to his mouth, then glanced up at the ceiling. "Look, it's not like we haven't got a problem in this nation. I mean, just walk out the door and look around. We've definitely got a crime problem and something has to be done about it."

"Skip the speeches," Lyons snapped. "Where do the buses go?"

Shutting his eyes again, Duffy finally whispered, "Diablo."

Lyons and Blancanales withdrew to the filthy alcove that served as the kitchen while Schwarz kept an eye on Duffy. When Ironman and Pol finally returned to face their prisoner again, Duffy looked at them and said, "You guys are going to kill me, aren't you?"

Lyons smiled. "Not if you cooperate."

Duffy ran his tongue over his lips. "How do you mean?"

Lyons dropped to one knee and stared into the bureaucrat's frightened eyes with burning intensity. "It's like this, Eddy. We want you to get us all the way in."

Duffy twitched. "You guys are out of your mind."

Blancanales grinned. "Is that so?"

"Besides, it won't work," the Federal official insisted.

"Why not?" Lyons asked. "After all, you're responsible for supplying guards to the camp, aren't you? They need a new guard to keep the prisoners in line, you're the man they call. Well, we just want you to supply them with a couple of new guards, that's all."

"But they check these things out. They review the service files. They check the records. And if the records don't check out, you're dead meat."

"Then you'll just have to make sure our records do check out, won't you? Give us a history, give us a cover. The point is, Eddy, you're going to place us in that camp one way or another. Understand?"

"What do I get out of this?"

Lyons grinned. "Well, let me put it like this. You play ball with us and we might just save your skin when this whole thing blows up."

Duffy's shoulders sagged. "Okay, I'll get you into the camp. But don't blame me if you all get early funerals."

If ever there was a godforsaken place on earth, Hal Brognola said, it had to be the Diablo badlands in Arizona. In support of this remark he showed them four aerial photographs of the landscape. There were two shots of brown canyons extending into the rocky wastes, one shot of bone-dry arroyos, and finally a photograph of the installation itself—dung-colored bungalows, coiled lines of barbed wire, a regular concentration camp.

"Naturally we couldn't risk a direct overflight," Brognola said as if to explain the quality of the photographs. "But at least these will give you some idea of what you're up against."

"Yeah," Lyons muttered as he continued to examine the photograph of the camp.

It was nearly dawn. Having shuttled Edward Duffy to a Stony Man safehouse, Lyons and his team had caught a chopper to Delaware. There, in a sealed briefing room at the southeast end of Dover Air Force Base, Brognola had been waiting with the photographs. Also in his possession were three packets of identity papers, including credit cards and employment records.

"The way I figure it," Brognola said, "these covers only have to last you about a week. After that we should have enough on them to call in the cavalry and shut it down."

"Who else knows we're going in?" Blancanales asked.

"Just the President."

"And he says?" Schwarz asked.

"Bring us some hard evidence and he'll move in like the hand of God."

Blancanales smiled. "So then we don't really have anything to worry about."

"Not a thing in the world," Lyons remarked, once more eyeing the photograph of the Arizona desert wastes.

Brognola's closing brief was delivered on the airstrip itself. The waiting plane, half-submerged in ground mist, couldn't have looked more ominous. The voices of attendants, shouting in the distance, couldn't have sounded more haunting.

"Basically it's going to work like this," the big Fed said. "Carl and Gadgets, you guys are going in as guards. You'll have about eighteen hours to memorize your roles, get to know the ropes and so forth. No one's going to expect you to be anything more than prison guards, however, so you shouldn't have to worry about too much in the way of specialized skills."

"What about the paperwork?" Lyons asked.

"That's all being taken care of," Brognola replied.

"And Duffy's playing ball and all that?"

Brognola nodded. "So far so good."

"So then what about me?" Blancanales asked, his eyes on the third sealed envelope in Brognola's hand. "If those two are going in as guards, what do I go in as?"

Brognola smiled. "Well, let me put it like this, Pol. According to your profile, you're about the meanest dude who ever walked the streets. In fact, you're so bad—"

"Never mind," Blancanales interrupted. "I think I get the picture."

Schwarz and Blancanales climbed into the plane while Lyons remained outside for a moment.

"I guess I don't have to tell you what's riding on this one," Brognola said.

Lyons shrugged. "You mean apart from the basic fabric of the Constitution?"

Brognola nodded. "Yeah, something like that. This one's a tough one, Ironman. Watch your back."

Lyons grinned. "Is there ever any other way?"

PEREZ IGNORED the warden's touch and watched the green van slowly enter the compound. It was a warm night with another hot wind from the flatlands and a cloudless sky above. As the van drew closer, she caught a glimpse of a tall blond man behind the wheel.

"Who's that?" she asked.

Merryman slid his hand away from her naked spine and glanced out the window. "Two new boys. Two new tough bastards come to make life a little harder on everyone concerned. They've got a new prisoner with them."

"Anyone special?"

"Just another piece of scum, baby."

She rose to her knees on the sweat-drenched mattress and gazed out the window to the three slow-moving figures in the compound. Earlier, in her dream, she had been seated on a terrace above the Santa Monica beach. She had been drinking an espresso with a croissant, and a breeze was playing in her hair. There had been frolicking dogs on the sand, but now she realized they were only the distant coyotes.

She turned to look at Merryman again, no longer even concerned about her nakedness. "May I take a shower?"

He smiled. "Hey, baby, you can even use the soap."

She climbed off the bed and went into the bathroom. Turning on the tap, she adjusted the temperature and stepped into the stall. As the water beat against her face, she sobbed quietly to herself in the only privacy she got in this hell of hells.

"I won't be able to see you the day after tomorrow," Merryman said when she emerged from the shower. "I've got to break in those new guards. Anyway, I think maybe I need a vacation from you. I haven't been getting much sleep these days, you know."

Perez nodded dully.

She slipped on the rough cotton dress and canvas shoes, then ran a finger through her hair. In the beginning she had always dried her hair before leaving his bungalow so that the other inmates wouldn't suspect she'd taken a shower. But now there was really no point in pretending. Everyone knew she was Merryman's whore.

"Hey, aren't you going to kiss me good-night?" he said as she moved to the doorway.

She stopped, hesitated, then finally moved back to the bed. When she was finally facing him again, he took hold of her wrists and drew her closer. Then, slipping his hand right up her dress, he forced her lips to his. As always, the revulsion only lasted a moment, then she felt virtually nothing.

"Oh, by the way," he said suddenly, "there's a little something I want you to do for me."

She dropped her eyes, knowing it was going to be bad, possibly very bad.

"It's about that new prisoner. Supposedly he's one real mean bastard. His name's Blanco or something like that. Anyway, I was thinking maybe you could keep an eye on him for me."

She shrugged, still not looking at him.

"Hey, I know what you're thinking. But listen, I'm not asking you to spy or anything like that. I'm just saying that if you hear something, you might pass it along." He took hold of her hair and drew her down for another hard kiss. "I really could make it worth your while. You should know that by now."

The sky was alive with stars and the moon hadn't yet dropped below the mountains when a rat-faced guard escorted her back to the barracks. He tried to engage her in conversation, commenting on the weather, the moon and the stars. As always, however, she ignored him.

Most of her fellow inmates were still sleeping when she slipped back into her cot, not that they would have talked to her even if they'd been awake. Ever since she'd begun to spend nights with Warden Merryman, virtually no one would speak to her. It wasn't that they resented her for having slept with the man. Indeed, they all knew only too well that Merryman took whatever he wanted. Even so, though, Perez wasn't one of them anymore.

The only exception was Lisa, the black prostitute Angela had met at the warehouse. In the six weeks that had passed since she'd arrived at the camp, Lisa had turned into an old woman. Physically she might not have changed a great deal. On the inside, however, she'd grown bitter and old. She'd also developed a wasting cough that continually tore at her lungs.

"So?" Lisa whispered from the bunk above.

Perez glanced up at her friend's haggard face. "So nothing," she said and sighed.

"Well, at least you got your shower."

Perez flushed. "What's that supposed to mean?"

"Don't mean nothing 'cept—"

"Except what?"

"Let me put it like this, honey. When I used to turn a trick, I always got me more than a hot shower and a piece of chicken."

Perez propped herself on an elbow. "Look, you think I like what he does to me?"

"No, honey. I don't think you want it. I just think maybe you never stopped to examine your choices."

"What choices? He wants me, so he takes me. That's all there is to it."

"No, baby, you always got your choices. They might not always be too pleasant, but you definitely got your choices."

"What are you talking about?"

Lisa smiled, then slowly sank back down on her cot. "Oh, I think you know what I'm talking about."

And it was true. Perez did know. Her friend was talking about killing the man. She was talking about taking off her clothes for him, making passionate love to him and then waiting until he fell asleep. It wasn't a new thought. In fact, it passed through her mind almost every time she looked at Merryman, every time she felt his touch or saw the scissors gleaming in the moonlight on his desk. *Kill him!*

10

At approximately the same time Angela Perez had begun to think about murdering the warden, Reuben Ramos was devising ways of killing at least a dozen more members of the camp staff. It wasn't necessarily a task that excited him. But having spent the previous nine days pondering the question of escape, he'd finally come to the conclusion that nothing short of a bloody uprising would save him now.

"Got to think of it as a war," he'd told a South Bronx street fighter who called himself Christoph. "They got the guns, but we got the numbers."

Christoph, however, hadn't been so certain. "Hey, man, numbers don't mean nothing against full-autos."

But Ramos hadn't risen to the top of the central Florida marijuana trade for lack of determination. And so he continued to plan. He made a point of counting the guards, noting the angle of fire from the towers, memorizing the types of weapons carried, assessing their proficiency. It wasn't going to be easy, he told himself. But given a fast, spontaneous uprising, it was just possible that the inmates could grab enough weapons to fight their way out.

Assuming, of course, they fought as one. Which meant, in turn, that they needed a strong, charismatic leader, a man they would follow without question, without hesitation—a real general, so to speak.

And that was where the plan fell apart.

As much as it pained him to admit it, Ramos knew he wasn't the kind of man the inmates would follow to the death. People might have been afraid of him back in Florida, but here he was just another punk. And the prisoners wouldn't follow a punk through the wire.

In all Ramos had spent about four days pondering the problem of leadership before his eye finally fell on the stranger. It was another hot, waterless morning. The day before, two new guards had arrived escorting someone who was rumored to have been a particularly vicious prisoner—an Hispanic with more killings to his name than Ted Bundy. As usual, Ramos hauled sheets of steel into the factory and half-heartedly pounded out the imperfections. Then, at some point just before lunch, he finally laid eyes on the new prisoner.

There were three things that immediately intrigued him about the stranger. First, the man was older than most of the other inmates. He wasn't over the hill, but he had definitely been around the block. Second, the man was a killer. That was obvious from even a quick glance. Finally, and perhaps most intriguing of all, Ramos was almost certain he'd seen the stranger before. He couldn't put a time or place on the memory, but he was somehow certain it was connected with heavy violence... very heavy violence.

It was just about finishing time when Ramos finally worked up enough courage to address the stranger. The guards were growing restless and hungry. The inmates were exhausted and starved.

"You're new here, aren't you?" Ramos asked, edging up to the silver-haired stranger.

The man turned slowly. "What's it to you?"

"Hey, man, I'm just asking, that's all. See, I only just got here a few weeks ago myself. So I thought, you know, maybe we could, uh—"

"What? Grab a beer?"

Ramos laughed nervously, and glanced at the man's hands. Killer's hands. "So, uh, what are you in for?"

The stranger grinned sardonically. "Jaywalking."

"Jaywalking, huh? Hey, that's pretty funny. Well, listen, Mr. Jaywalker, maybe we should have a talk sometime."

"About what?"

"Well, there's some things about this place I could tell you about."

"What kind of things?"

"I can't really go into them right now. But let's just say I've been keeping my eyes open and I've been working on some plans. Get my drift?"

"Yeah, I get your drift."

As Ramos continued to observe the stranger, it became increasingly obvious to him that this was just the sort of man needed to lead the uprising. Not only were the other prisoners respectful of him, but even the guards seemed a little wary.

Later that evening, for example, the stranger was sent out to help stack a load of bricks for the construction of another isolation box. On duty were Warden Merryman's two new goons: a tall, blond guy and a shorter man with brown hair and a mustache. As far as Ramos had been able to ascertain, these two new guards were definitely people to be avoided.

But the stranger didn't care one bit about them. In fact, he even appeared to welcome a confrontation, actually went out of his way to knock over a pile of neatly stacked bricks right in front of the guards' eyes.

"Hey, you!" the blond one shouted. "How about picking up those bricks?"

The stranger turned, smiled and started walking away.

"Hey, I'm talking to you, greaseball! Stack those bricks right now!"

But the stranger kept moving.

Finally the blond guard sent the mustached guy to fetch the stranger. But the moment the guard laid a hand on the stranger's arm the silver-haired inmate turned and looked right into his eyes. Then, although it was hard to see what passed between then, it was pretty obvious that even the guard was rattled.

Naturally that wasn't the end of the incident. Later that night the two new guards came into the barracks and dragged the stranger away. But given the stranger's defiant smile, Ramos was pretty certain the man would survive just about anything the guards could dish out. What made the drug pusher happy, though, was the realization that he had found his leader. Still, something bothered him about the man. Try as he might he couldn't shake the feeling that he'd seen the guy somewhere. But where?

THERE WERE FOUR uncompleted barracks just beyond the wire. Eventually these crude brick-and-timber structures would hold another eighty inmates, one on top of another. Also under construction was a punishment cell and another sweatbox. Yet for the moment this was still a relatively quiet part of the camp.

"Together at last," Blancanales said, smiling.

"Yeah," Schwarz said. "Just like old times."

"So how's it going, Pol?" Lyons asked.

Blancanales glanced back at the barracks where Ramos and the other prisoners were locked in stuffy darkness. "Reuben might remember me, but I don't think he can place me back at his bust in Florida. In fact, I think he's looking for any excuse in the world to trust me. As for the others, I think they're pretty convinced I'm just another hard-assed inmate looking to survive in this place. Now what about you guys? How's life as a ball-busting guard?"

Lyons shrugged, adjusting the .45 on his belt and gazing out at the moonlit stretch of desert. "Well, we haven't had much chance to get a real close look at this place, but I'm starting to get a basic idea of what's been going down.''

"Have you had a chance to talk with Merryman?" Blancanales asked.

Schwarz shook his head. "Apparently the official welcome comes tomorrow morning over the warden's weekly power breakfast."

"The main thing," Lyons said, "is that we've got to find out what's really going on here. Who's doing what to whom, if you know what I mean."

"Well, I can tell you one thing straight off," Blancanales said. "Merryman has got himself one hell of a nice little setup. Did you know, for example, that he regularly takes the women back to his bungalow? His current girlfriend is apparently some Los Angeles girl named Perez."

"You got a line to her?" Schwarz asked.

Blancanales shook his head. "Not yet, but I think I can probably get myself transferred into the same factory where she works."

"That might not be such a bad idea," Lyons said. "Because if Merryman's sleeping with her, he's also probably talking to her."

"And while I'm checking out the Perez girl, you might want to check out that guard named Toma," Blancanales said.

"Toma?" Lyons repeated.

"Big guy, looks like he eats steroids for lunch."

"Yeah," Schwarz said. "I've seen him around."

"Well, you might want to check him out," Blancanales repeated. "Word has it that he's the one who arranges the executions."

Lyons grew silent for a moment, scanning the empty prison yard and the coils of barbed wire beyond. "Right," he sighed. "Then let's just do it."

"Oh, and one last thing," Blancanales said.

Lyons frowned. "Yeah? What's that?"

"Well, I think in the interest of maintaining my reputation, one of you guys better hit me."

Schwarz looked at Pol. "Huh?"

"Well, since you guys just dragged me out in the dead of night, I think I ought to return with a bruise or two. Know what I mean?"

Lyons smiled, then shrugged. "Sure, Pol, I know what you mean." Lyons jabbed Blancanales twice, first on the bridge of the nose, then on the jaw.

When Blancanales managed to rise again, he spit out a mouthful of blood and grinned. "Thanks. I needed that."

Lyons smiled. "Don't mention it."

Pol fingered his jaw. "Maybe I can do the same for you someday."

11

"I want to apologize for not having had a chance to welcome you boys sooner," Merryman said, extending his hand.

Lyons shook the warden's hand. "Thank you, sir. It's a real pleasure."

Merryman turned to Schwarz. "And you, too, soldier. Welcome aboard."

Schwarz grinned. "Thank you, sir. It's a real honor to be here."

Merryman smiled. "Exactly. It's an honor."

Breakfast was served in what Merryman called his staff room. In all there were fifteen guards seated at the long steel table, the burly Toma among them. Although the sun still hadn't risen above the distant mountains, the flatland beyond had already begun to glow with a strange orange light.

"So how about telling us a little about yourselves?" Merryman suggested as he helped himself to a mound of fried potatoes and a half-dozen slices of bacon.

According to the cover Brognola had established, Lyons was supposed to have originally been a cell-block guard disciplined for excessive brutality. He was also supposed to have been ex-Air Cavalry with a drawerful of decorations. All Lyons said now, however, was that he was fed up with the crime problem in the country, fed up with seeing obviously unreformed criminals walk out of America's prisons and back onto the streets.

"Well, the fact is, gentlemen," Merryman said, addressing the new arrivals, "we're doing something very special here. Now I'm not going to tell you that it's always easy. I mean, you boys are going to be guarding the worst kind of scum on earth, but I'll tell you one thing. No one here is going to give you a hard time for any so-called excessive brutality."

There were questions about Schwarz's past next, particularly his supposed role in putting down riots at Attica. Then a big-shouldered black guard asked about the prisoner Schwarz and Lyons had brought with them. "That Hispanic guy, what's his story?"

Schwarz stuffed some bacon into his mouth and grunted. "Not a whole lot to tell except that the guy's a stone-cold killer. They had him out at Terminal Island, but they couldn't make the charges stick. So, seeing as how we were flying out here, anyway, they figured why not save the bus fare."

"What were they trying to hold him on?" another guard asked.

"Apparently he does contract work," Lyons replied. "Some for the mob, some for the dopers. Either way he's bad."

"Then maybe you boys should keep a special eye on this Blanco fellow," Merryman suggested between mouthfuls of fried egg.

"Pretty much what we intend to do, sir," Schwarz said. "Keep an eye on him."

THE FORMAL ORIENTATION began after breakfast with a tour of the women's compound. "Strictly speaking, this is what you might call a coed camp," Merryman said, grinning. "Now that may pose special problems, but it also poses special pleasures ... if you boys get my drift," he added with a wink.

From the women's compound Merryman escorted Schwarz and Lyons to the punishment cells. "I guess, in a way, you might say this is the heart of the facility. This is what it all comes down to in the end—enforcing what I call the word of the law."

Of particular note were the automobile batteries and the electrodes, presumably intended for fingers, toes, nipples or whatever.

"Pretty neat," Schwarz rasped.

Merryman shrugged. "Well, it's like this. A guy starts giving us trouble, all we got to do is hook him up to one of these devices. Then we put a little juice through him, and bingo, he's not giving us trouble anymore."

"And what about the women?" Schwarz asked.

"Same thing. They give you trouble, you just take 'em down here. That usually puts them straight in pretty short order."

From the punishment cells Merryman led his new guards across the sandy courtyard to the administration office where the duty rosters were drafted. En route, however, Lyons couldn't help noticing the bullet holes along one of the outer walls. "Trouble?" he asked.

Merryman hesitated, as if carefully choosing his words. "I wouldn't exactly say there was trouble. Let's just say every now and again we have to employ a little harsher methods on these people. Put a head on the pike to let them know who's boss."

Also visible from this vantage point were the mounds of freshly turned earth beyond the wire—more than two dozen graves in the distance.

"SO WHAT DO YOU THINK?" Schwarz asked when he and Lyons finally returned to their bungalow.

It was a stark room with two tiny windows cut into the brick and a bare linoleum floor. The lamps had no shades, and the furniture was covered with desert dust.

"I think it's still too early to tell," Lyons replied as he inched the curtains aside and gazed out at the expense of sand.

"But you don't have any doubt it's dirty, right?"

"None at all."

"So then maybe we should start thinking about moving up our schedule a little. Like how about shutting this place down first thing tomorrow? It would save us all a lot of grief in the long run."

But Lyons shook his head. "I don't think so, Gadgets. I think we better wait until we've got this case completely sealed . . . right, left and center."

"And you don't think we've got a case against them now?"

Lyons let the curtains fall, then turned with a hard sigh. "You got to remember something. Unlike the prisoners here, Merryman and his goons are going to stand trial. They're going to have smart lawyers and a jury of their peers. Now I'm not saying they don't deserve that. I just want to make sure they don't walk on some technicality. I want to make sure American justice is done."

"SO HOW DO YOU LIKE IT?" Ramos whispered as Blancanales bent to retrieve another sheet of steel. "Pretty nice place they got here, huh?"

Pol gave the drug peddler a sidelong glance. "What do you want from me?"

Ramos grinned. "Hey, I don't want nothing from you, man. I'm just trying to be friendly, that's all."

Blancanales hefted a sheet of steel onto the wooden bench and began pounding. "Yeah, well, you keep talking and you're going to get us both into trouble."

Ramos smiled. "Hey, I saw you last night with those two guards and you didn't strike me as the kind of guy who's afraid of a little trouble. In fact, you look like the kind of guy who *wants* a little trouble."

Without ceasing his work Blancanales glanced into Ramos's eyes for a moment. "I'm listening."

Ramos took a quick glance over his shoulder at the guard, then said, "This ain't your first time in prison, right?"

Blancanales shrugged. "What's that got to do with anything?"

"Well, haven't you noticed that something's weird about this arrangement? Like they never let you see no lawyer and you never went to no courtroom?"

"So?"

"So this ain't no prison camp. This is a concentration camp. You know what I mean? This is like what the Germans had going for them in World War II. And I'll tell you something else about this place. Nobody gets out of here alive. Nobody."

Blancanales tossed the sheet of steel aside and picked up another. "And so what's your point?"

Ramos shrugged. "No point except that you don't look like the kind of guy who takes crap sitting down. You look like the kind of guy who's willing to take a chance if the odds aren't too steep."

Blancanales glanced up at the guard in the doorway. The man's face was a grim mask behind his mirrored sunglasses, the 12-gauge resting in the crook of his arm. "Odds don't look too good from this vantage point," he grunted.

"That's because you're thinking about doing it alone. Well, I'm not talking about doing it alone. I'm talking about doing it with a group."

Blancanales looked around him, his eyes shifting from one bent and broken inmate to another. These were once the worst children of America's inner cities, the worst of society's victimizers. Yet now they were nothing more than victims themselves—frightened, hungry and lost. "Doesn't look too promising to me."

"That's because up until now they never had a leader," Ramos countered. "But you, man, I think you're that guy. I think you're the guy who's going to make a real difference around here."

"Yeah? And what gives you that idea?"

Ramos smiled and tapped his forefinger against his temple. "Intuition, man. I've always had this real good intuition about people. In fact, sometimes I can just look at somebody and know where they're at. Besides, I think I've seen you before. I can't remember exactly where. But I'm pretty sure it was somehow connected with heavy business, and that's exactly what we're up against here—heavy business."

Blancanales hefted another sheet of steel onto the workbench and wondered how long it would take Ramos to remember where they'd met, how long before the man got a good look at Schwarz or Lyons and recalled their faces busting through the door of his palatial Florida home.

It was noon when Pol witnessed his first beating. One of the inmates, a half-dead ex-junkie, had dropped a bucket of rivets on the floor. A moment later a guard was on him like a bulldog, repeatedly beating the prisoner with a rubber hose. Even after the prisoner had slipped into unconsciousness the guard continued to beat him. Like the others, Blancanales simply watched. Despite the outrage and fury, the indignation and the horror, he simply stood by and watched.

When it was over, two more guards appeared, a bull of a man named Dickerson and some woman. They dragged the lifeless prisoner away, leaving a trail of blood across the filthy concrete. Then came the order to return to work.

"It doesn't get any easier," a soft voice said behind Blancanales.

He turned to meet the gaze of a pretty woman he'd noticed before. She was currently Merryman's number-one squeeze.

"You can see it a hundred times, but it doesn't get any easier."

Blancanales tossed a smooth sheet of steel onto the pile to his left and hefted another onto the workbench, but this time a little closer to the Puerto Rican woman. "You're Perez, aren't you?"

She nodded. "And you're the new one, the one they dragged out of the barracks last night."

Blancanales shrugged. "Wasn't too bad. They just wanted to work me over a little. Sort of like Merryman works you over, or so I'm told."

She lowered her gaze and flushed. "That's not my doing."

"I know that."

"The warden wants, so the warden takes, and there's nothing anyone can do about it."

He shrugged. "Maybe, maybe not."

She glanced at him suspiciously. "What do you mean?"

"I mean that maybe if you were to keep your eyes open you just might see something that could make a difference."

She shook her head wearily. "Nothing will make a difference around here. Nothing at all."

12

"She's what they call an eco-raider," the guard named Toma told Lyons as they slowly crossed the dark yard past the punishment block. "Political radical dedicated to the violent destruction of anyone they feel is messing with the environment. Normally the warden leaves her alone. But apparently someone at the top wants the names of her friends. So the warden figures a night on the electrodes should do it."

The electrodes, attached to a standard automobile battery, had been fastened to the woman's breasts by means of electrical tape. The skin had then been moistened with water from a garden hose in order to better distribute the charge. To keep the victim from thrashing around, her wrists and ankles had been secured to a heavy table by means of leather straps. Plenty of buckets of ice water were on hand to keep her conscious.

"How long does this go on?" Lyons asked, trying to sound casual, trying to hide his revulsion.

Toma shrugged. "Thirty minutes or an hour usually does it. But something tells me the warden might want to stretch it out with this one."

"And the people who ordered it, who are they?"

Toma shrugged again. "I don't know. I guess it was probably the foundation. The point is, we're into saving this nation. Sure, some of the things that go down around here might be unpleasant, but that's the price you got to pay for freedom. Know what I mean?"

"Sure," Lyons breathed. "For freedom."

Another flurry of screams echoed out of the bungalow, and Lyons had a clear vision of the girl arched and shuddering as the electricity shot through her body. But apart from his left hand clenched into a fist, he remained entirely casual. Because now wasn't the time to move, he told himself. Move now and they'd only cut him down.

He left Toma in the yard and slowly made his way back to the bungalow he shared with Schwarz. The electronics wizard was seated on the bed, rigid and staring out the window. In his left hand he held a .45 auto. Across his knees was a shotgun. "You know what they're doing to her?" he asked when Lyons entered the bungalow.

Lyons nodded. "Yeah, I know."

"So are we just going to stand by and let it happen?"

Lyons removed his side arm, laid it on the chair and slumped onto the cot. "What the hell do you want us to do, Gadgets? Go in there with guns blazing?"

Schwarz shut his eyes as another hollow scream tore through the night. Then, very calmly he said, "I don't know what to do. I just know I can't sit here and listen to that anymore."

Lyons stood and started to slam his fist against the wall, but then pulled back. "All right, listen to me. We need more information about the guys pulling the strings in this hellish operation. We need more proof of Lang's involvement."

"So what do you suggest?"

"I suggest we wait until we can get hold of the camp records. Then we find a way to get to the radio and call in reinforcements."

Schwarz took a deep breath. "Okay, we play it your way. But within forty-eight hours this place better be history or I take this shotgun and start opening up. Got it?"

Lyons nodded. "Yeah. Forty-eight hours."

THE WARDEN SLOWLY RAN his finger down the length of Perez's spine and watched her shiver in the moonlight. Although he hadn't planned on spending the entire night with her, he hadn't been able to help himself, not after torturing the other girl. Watching the environmental activist thrash under the leather restraints, pleading with every fiber of her being, screaming until her throat was raw, that kind of excitement demanded gratification. Yet now it was dawn. His need was reasonably satiated and his mind was beginning to turn to other matters.

"So why don't you tell me about him?" he asked as his finger continued its lazy course along her back.

Perez lifted her head from the sweat-drenched sheets. "About who?"

"That new man. That Blanco character."

She sighed. "There's nothing really to tell. He's just another inmate."

Merryman marginally increased the pressure of his finger on her spine. It was one of a thousand ways he had of telling her that despite his apparent affection he could crush her at a moment's notice. "Come on, baby. I think you can do better than that."

She shivered beneath his touch. "All I know is that the other inmates are kind of afraid of him, but they also respect him."

"Why?"

"Because he stood up to those two new guards. And because he has a certain way about him, a certain defiance."

Merryman rolled onto his back with an almost wistful smile. "Ah, yes, defiance."

He rose from the bed, slipped on his shorts and moved to the window. All night there had been sounds of more coyotes in the desert. He kept giving orders for the tower guards to shoot the creatures on sight, but still they kept calling, taunting. Defiance. "Ever read about the concentration camp system in Nazi Germany?" he asked suddenly.

She shrugged, then secretly shut her eyes in disgust.

"Not that I necessarily approve of everything that went on there. I mean, the gas chambers and all that were pretty excessive. But on a clinical level it was fascinating. In fact, it was very fascinating."

He let the curtains fall and moved back to the bed. Although the dawn breeze had left her shivering again, she didn't dare attempt to cover herself. She knew he liked to pontificate while she lay naked in front of him. He liked to watch her shivering as he spoke.

"The point is," he continued slowly, "in Hitler's Germany they understood control. They understood how to crush the will of a defiant prison population." He paused, running his hand along her thigh, casually kneading the flesh. "But there's this catch, see? It seems that no matter how effective your control methods are, there are always one or two spirits that can't be broken. There are always one or two little flames that can't be extinguished."

He slid his hand up to her neck and grabbed a handful of her hair. Then, slowly drawing back her head until she couldn't help but look at him again, he asked, "Is there a flame out there that refuses to be extinguished, baby?"

He let her head fall back onto the mattress and stepped back to the window. The dawn had grown red, leaving every twisted branch and rock in black relief against the sky.

"I have a feel for these things," he said at last. "I can't exactly explain it, but I always get this feeling when things are brewing out here, when the whispers start growing a little too intense, when the embers start glowing a little too brightly.''

He turned to face her again, his eyes suddenly dark and furious, his voice hoarse. ''The question is, where does it start and how far does it go? Is it just that Blanco character? Or does it involve others? That's the burning question, baby.''

She left him just as the sun was starting to rise above the mountains. He was still standing by the window, gazing out at the torrid wastes and working his jaw in quiet fury.

Something was definitely not right, he told himself. Someone was definitely making plans of murder and rebellion. And yet what could he do about it? Of course, the simple solution would be to drag Blanco into the yard, put him against the wall and shoot him. But what if there were others? What if it went deeper and farther than Blanco? What if, and he actually felt himself shudder at the thought, it went into his own staff?

He stepped to the closet, threw an old bathrobe over his shoulders and moved to the filing cabinet. There he hesitated, drumming his fingers on the cold steel and staring at the swirling dust in the shaft of sunlight through the window. Then, without really knowing why, he withdrew the files on his two newest guards.

I'll give it forty-eight hours, he told himself. I'll give it another forty-eight hours and then I'll start busting heads.

13

Blancanales was seven paces from the factory door when the guards yanked him out of line and dragged him behind the piles of brick and scrap lumber. He was struck twice, first in the stomach to double him over, then across the back of the neck. That neither blow actually caused him any real discomfort, however, wouldn't have been obvious to anyone watching.

"I figure we got eight minutes," Lyons said to the groaning Blancanales at his feet.

Pol nodded, then struggled back to his knees with a convincing groan. "Ramos still can't figure where he saw me before, but he wants to go ahead with his plan."

"Which is?" Schwarz asked, glancing over his shoulder to make sure no one was watching.

"Mass move on the guards. Grab some weapons and start shooting."

"And how does he figure you fit in?" Lyons asked.

Blancanales gave another grunt of pain as if he'd just taken a boot in the stomach. "For some reason he's got it in his head that I'm the guy to lead it all."

Schwarz took another quick glance over his shoulder, then withdrew a rubber hose and brought it down an inch away from Blancanales's left shoulder. Pol responded with a moan, then collapsed back into the dust. "I also spoke to the girl," he whispered. "The one Merryman's taken as his mistress."

"And?" Lyons asked, cocking his leg as if to lay in another boot.

"She obviously hates the bastard, but I don't think she's ready to start working for us."

"I don't blame her," Schwarz said, recalling the screams the night before.

Blancanales moaned with pain as Lyons faked a kick to his groin. "Yeah, well, Merryman's got everyone pretty scared around here. Especially after last night."

Lyons stepped back as if to survey the damaged man at his feet. "Apparently it's even worse. Apparently Merryman's got a regular cemetery out there."

Blancanales struggled to his knees again, then sagged as if the pain were simply too great. "How far away are we from proving it all?"

Schwarz swung the rubber hose again, missing Blancanales by less than an inch. "Carl and I are going to try to get into the files tonight. See if he's got a list of who's been terminated."

"How do you plan to get in there?" Blancanales asked after yet another convincing groan.

"That's kind of up to you," Lyons replied as he bent to deliver another mock blow.

Blancanales yelped, then fell back as if only barely conscious now. "I knew I was going to love this."

Schwarz took a handful of Blancanales's hair and yanked the man to his knees again. "It should be a piece of cake, Pol," he said between clenched teeth. "All you got to do is convince that Perez girl to get Merryman out of the office for a few minutes."

Blancanales tried to struggle free, but Schwarz's grip remained firm. "I've hardly established a basis of trust," he grunted.

Schwarz faked two quick jabs to the prisoner's face, then let him fall back to the ground. "Just tell her to ask him to take her for a walk or something. That's all she's got to do."

Pol rose to his knees again, hesitated for a moment, then rasped, "All right. I'll talk to her."

"Oh, and one last thing," Lyons said as he yanked Blancanales back to his feet.

"What's that?"

"Nobody goes through a beating like you just had without a little blood."

Blancanales opened his eyes and looked at his friend. "Huh?"

"For that little touch of realism," Lyons said, ramming a fist directly into Blancanales's mouth.

For a good five minutes after he was tossed onto the factory floor Blancanales remained motionless. The pig-faced guard had more or less ignored him while the other inmates merely looked at him. Then, by degrees, as if pulling himself together through waves of nausea and blinding pain, he dragged himself over to the bench beside Perez and picked up a rawhide hammer.

His first few blows were unsteady and apparently sent more stabbing pain through his ribs. After yet another six or seven minutes, however, he finally settled into a bearable rhythm, waiting to make his next move.

"You all right?" he heard Perez ask.

He gave her a pained look, but couldn't entirely suppress a smile. "Never better."

"Why did they do that to you?"

He shrugged. "They love me."

"Is there anything I can do?"

He hesitated, glanced up to see if the guard was watching, then nodded. "Yeah, there's something you can do."

ALTHOUGH MALE AND FEMALE prisoners weren't technically permitted to speak to each other except on job-related matters, the rule couldn't always be enforced. During the evening break, for example, when the weary inmates were herded into the yard for another foul meal of cold beans, Blancanales had no trouble slipping away to meet Perez. He met her in the shadow of corrugated factory walls, amid heaps of scrap metal shavings. It was the one relatively free hour of the day, a time when most of the guards retired to the towers for a beer.

"So?" she asked.

He looked at her, peering into her tired eyes. "So how about sitting down?"

She brushed a stray lock of hair from her eyes and sat on an old tire. "We could both get in a lot of trouble, you know."

He smiled. "I thought we already were in a lot of trouble."

That got a faint smile, but it quickly faded. "You know what I'm talking about."

"Sure. But I don't think you know what I'm talking about."

She gave him a quick glance and brushed another strand of hair from her eyes. "Who are you?"

He cocked his head to one side and grinned. "Not who you think I am."

"What's that supposed to mean?"

"It means there are still people around who believe in the Constitution."

He drew her a little deeper into the shadows, his hand clutching her left arm. "Listen to me, Angela. This is America, not Nazi Germany, and this place is operating way outside the law. But unless we do something about it no one's going to know. You understand?"

She shook her head, her eyes suddenly filled with tears. "What are you talking about?"

"I'm talking about getting enough evidence to shut this place down. I'm talking about cutting out this cancer once and for all."

She gave him a look that lay somewhere between hope and horror. "But how can I possibly...?"

"Merryman's going to bring you to his quarters tonight, right?"

"I don't know. Probably."

"Well, I want you to get him outside for a while. Tell him you want to see the open desert or something. Tell him anything, but just get him away from his quarters for fifteen or twenty minutes. Can you do that?"

A shrill whistle sounded from the tower, calling the inmates back to the factory.

"What do you say?" Blancanales whispered. "Will you do it?"

A second blast of the whistle sounded as the guards began barking, "Let's move it! Right now! Move it!"

"Come on, Angela," Blancanales whispered. "Will you do it?"

The outline of a guard appeared. "Hey, you two by the shed. Let's move it!"

"Angela?"

She nodded. "Okay."

"NICE NIGHT, isn't it?" Merryman asked. He was standing at the window of his office, his hands resting on the sill, his eyes fixed on the starry sky. "The kind of night that makes you glad to be alive."

She had showered, dried her hair and now stood wrapped in a towel. He still hadn't actually looked at her.

"I got something for you," he said. "Over there on the desk."

She moved to the desk and picked up a package. It was addressed to A. J. Merryman, Federal Bureau of Prisons.

"Go on, open it," he said.

Her hands were shaking so badly that she could hardly manage to pull the perforated tab. She also had difficulty tearing the tape. But when she finally saw it, she felt a wave of nausea.

"Came all the way from Reno," he told her.

It was a black string bikini with a matching transparent camisole, exactly the sort of thing a whore would wear.

"Well, what do you think?"

"It's..." Her eyes began to fill with tears again and her blood turned to ice water.

"Well, put it on. Go on, let me see what it looks like."

She slipped it on in the bathroom, then paused for a last moment alone in front of the mirror, revulsion plain in her face. When she finally emerged from the bathroom, he was seated in the leather armchair with a glass of bourbon in his hand and a dull grin on his face. "Well, aren't you something. Aren't you the prettiest something in the whole damn desert."

He spun a finger in the air, motioning her to turn around. "Outstanding. Absolutely outstanding." His gaze was like fire on the back of her thighs, and she could actually hear his breathing. "Yes, sir, you're a real treat tonight, baby."

He gently forced her down to her knees, then idly began to toy with her hair. "Now didn't I tell you Daddy would take care of you?"

But before she could mumble a reply he pressed her face to his groin.

IT WAS ABOUT midnight when he finally stopped pawing her. Perez lay on the unmade bed, her left leg extended, her right leg slightly bent to accentuate the curve of her thigh. Her eyes were fixed on the curtains. Her heart was pounding. "May I ask you something?"

He stirred in the leather armchair and took another sip of bourbon. "Shoot."

"I was wondering if I could ask you a special favor."

He looked at her, his eyes following the curve of her thigh to the slope of her breasts. As always, his hands had left faint bruises on her skin, reminders of his passion that bordered on cruelty. "What kind of favor?"

She propped herself on one elbow, slightly arching her back in a pose she knew he liked. Her voice, too, couldn't have been more seductive. "Well, you see, I was kind of wondering. I mean, it's been so long since I've been outside. I mean, really outside. Well, I was just wondering if maybe we could go for a little walk together."

He looked at her, the desire starting to burn again in his eyes. "A walk?"

She nodded. "I know it's against the regulations and everything, but I thought that maybe for just a few minutes we could, you know, be like real lovers."

His eyes narrowed, but his lips slowly spread into a thin smile. "A walk? That's all you want from me?"

"Just for a few minutes."

He rose from the chair, moved to the bed and took her face in his hands. "You want to go for a goddamn walk in the desert?"

"Like real lovers, away from the fences and the wire. Just you and me under the stars."

His smile grew broader and he shook his head. "You're something else, baby. I thought you were going to ask me to get you out of here. But all you want is a little walk under the frigging stars."

She parted her lips and gazed innocently into his eyes. "Does that mean you'll do it?"

He smiled again, drawing her in for a fierce kiss. "Hey, you want a little walk in the desert, hell, I'll take you for a little walk in the desert. But first, how about you let me make a call to the watchtowers? Otherwise, you see, my boys might just put a few holes in us by mistake."

14

Schwarz put down the Starlight scope and turned to Lyons. "I think she really did it."

It was just after midnight. Although the lights in their bungalow had been extinguished for some time, neither Schwarz nor Lyons had slept. Instead, they were stationed at the window, gazing out across the compound to the warden's cottage. They had been watching when Perez first arrived, and were still watching when Merryman closed the curtains.

"Where are they now?" Lyons asked.

Schwarz returned his eye to the hand-held scope, carefully adjusting the aperture until the view of Merryman's cottage was distinct and shadowless. "Just outside the door and moving toward the main gate."

Lyons picked up a penlight and slipped it into the breast pocket of his shirt. Also in his pocket was an assortment of lock picks and a length of industrial wire.

"They're at the gate now," Schwarz said.

"Where's the guard?"

"Tower."

"Anyone else?"

"Not that I can see."

Lyons picked up the hand-held photocopier and his automatic. "All right, then, let's go do it."

They moved out in a half crouch, keeping to the shadows of the bungalows and skirting the edge of the gravel beds. Although there were lights in three or four other bungalows and soft strains of country music from the open windows, there were no actual signs of guards. Even the towers seemed empty.

"Is that them?" Lyons whispered, peering at the shadows of two figures moving through the scrub.

Schwarz picked up the scope. "Arm in arm like a couple of real lovers."

"Which way are they headed?"

"Out across the desert."

There was a relatively open stretch of ground between the last guard's bungalow and the warden's quarters. Lyons and Schwarz hesitated, crouching beneath the shadows of a juniper tree. Schwarz scanned the compound once again with the scope, this time fixing on the death strip between the fences where patrolling guards sometimes paused for a cigarette. Then, shaking his head, he and Lyons continued moving.

The door to the warden's bungalow was shut but not locked. Inside, they could smell whiskey and cheap cologne. Although the bedroom lamp had been left on, the outer room was dark and Lyons had to move slowly in order to avoid the furniture. The floor was littered with articles of clothing—Merryman's boots, Perez's dress, torn panties. Dangling from the arm of a chair was a pair of handcuffs.

"Why don't you keep watch at the window?" Lyons suggested as he moved past the desk to the filing cabinet.

Schwarz nodded and trained the scope on the desert again. "Don't see them anymore," he whispered. "Don't see much of anything."

Lyons withdrew his collection of picks and trained a narrow beam of light on the filing cabinet lock, which was new but not fancy. The problem was how to get it open without leaving scratches. He began by inserting the wire to test the action. Next, withdrawing a dental pick, he began to toy with the tumbler. Then, finally extracting a thin strip of steel, he managed to release the catch.

"You in?" Schwarz asked softly.

"Like a rat in the pantry," Lyons replied as he gently slid the first drawer open.

Because he was essentially a bureaucrat at heart, Merryman had constructed his files with an almost frightening logic. Individual prisoners were arranged alphabetically and according to sex. There were subcategories for those with drug problems and yet another category for those suspected of violent crimes. Finally there was a file on those with unsavory political connections and what Merryman referred to as anti-American sentiments.

Yet what ultimately left Lyons chilled to the bone were the files of those who had been summarily executed in the dead of night. "Hal was right," he whispered. "It's like Nazi Germany here."

Schwarz turned from the window. "You found something?"

"Yeah," Lyons sighed. "I definitely found something." He spread the files out on the floor and picked up the hand-held copier. "Listen to this," he whispered as he slowly rolled the copier over the pages. "Arnold T. Gibbs, twenty-four years old. Exterminated July 18 after executive review. Alice Hopper, twenty-six years old. Exterminated August 7 after executive review. Nolen Andrew Tyler, nineteen years old. Exterminated September 7 after executive review."

Schwarz put down the scope and glanced over his shoulder. "What does executive review mean?"

"It means Merryman must have made a telephone call to Jack Lang, and the two of them decided to kill these people."

Lyons took out another file and placed it on the floor. In addition to the prisoner's name, age and date of execution there was also a photograph. It showed a dark shape sprawled in the shadows of a wall. Apparently the prisoner had been shot twice, once in the belly and then again in the back of the neck.

"You want to hurry it up a little?" Schwarz whispered as he scanned the desert. "I think they're heading back."

"I'm hurrying," Lyons replied as he quickly gathered up the files and stuffed them back into the cabinet.

PEREZ CLUNG to Merryman's thigh and tried to pull him back down onto the sand. "Just a few minutes more," she whispered. "Just five more minutes."

But Merryman stared at his bungalow. "I'm telling you I saw something in the window."

She pressed her face to his hip and ran her hand along his crotch. "It was probably just a shadow. Now come back here and make love to me. Come on. Let's do it right here under all these beautiful stars."

He pushed her hand away and took another step toward the compound gates. Although there were only thin trails of moonlight across the grounds, there were definitely shadows that shouldn't have been there. "Over there. Look over there!"

"I don't see anything," she said, sliding her palm along the inside of his leg. "Except this," she giggled. "Now come on and make love to me."

But he caught another glimpse of something hovering in his doorway, so he continued tramping forward. Perez rose to her feet, drew the raincoat he'd given her around her shoulders and hurried to his side. "Well, if there's someone there, maybe it's not such a good idea to barge in on them."

Merryman ignored her and drew a Colt Python. Closer to the main gate he thought he saw another shadow slip through the doorway of his bungalow. But rather than signal the guards in the tower, he simply continued onward.

"Don't you think we should at least check this out first?" Perez asked. "I mean, it's probably only—"

"Shut your mouth," he snarled, clutching her arm very tightly now, virtually dragging her behind him. He hesitated just outside the door of his bungalow, cocked the Python and dropped to a half crouch. "Stay behind me and don't say a frigging word," he whispered to Perez.

He opened the door by inches, scanning the shadows for a moment. When his eyes fell on the footprints, he swore softly under his breath, then continued slowly into the room.

"Maybe those are your prints," she whispered. "Maybe you just never noticed—"

He whirled around to face her and savagely gripped her arm again. "Do I own a pair of goddamn running shoes like that?"

She shook her head, feeling the tears starting to burn in her eyes again, feeling her heart pound in her chest.

He shoved her into a corner, then moved through the living area, noting that the Navaho rug was out of place. There were also faint boot prints near the window along the linoleum in the study. But it wasn't until he found the Starlight scope that he knew for certain.

He withdrew a handkerchief and gently picked it up by the lens cap and returned to where the woman was crouched. "Know what this is?" She started to extend her hand to the object, but he pulled it away. "Don't touch it," he snapped. "You'll smudge the fingerprints. Just tell me what you think it is."

She shook her head, fighting back a fresh storm of tears. "I don't know."

"Well, then let me explain. It's a Starlight scope. It's an extremely expensive piece of equipment and generally used only by professional spies. Now do you get the picture?"

She took a slow, deep breath, consciously willing herself to stop shivering. "But why would someone want to spy on us?"

He looked at her for a moment, then smirked. "Not us, baby. They were spying on me."

He set the scope aside, then took hold of her arm again and walked briskly to the study. "Look at that. Look at those goddamn scratches. You think those just happened? Hell, no. Someone just got through picking the goddamn lock and reading my frigging files. Only problem was, I caught a glimpse of them through the window. See? The son of a bitch was standing right here when I saw him. The other one was probably crouched here, keeping an eye on us with the scope. When we started marching back, they panicked and left the scope behind. End of story."

He eased back the cabinet drawer and began to leaf through the files. "Yeah," he said to himself. "Well, that makes sense."

She lifted her gaze to him. "What makes sense?"

"They were looking at the extreme cases, the ones we had to bury."

She sank down into a chair with a hopeless sigh. "But I don't understand. I mean, how can you be sure—"

He turned again to face her. "Oh, come on, baby, who are you trying to kid?"

She looked at him, as if still not quite sure what he was implying. "What do you mean?"

"You know exactly what I mean, baby. Do you think I was born yesterday? You were just trying to get me out of here, weren't you? You were in on it from the start."

"Arthur, that's not true!"

"Come on, sweetheart, let's not play games anymore. These guys put you up to it, didn't they? They told you to get me out of my quarters for a while so they could search the files. Not that I blame you, baby. I mean, after all, despite our fun and games, we're still enemies, aren't we?"

She shut her eyes. "Arthur, it's not what you think."

"Why don't we stop playing games?" he insisted again.

"Arthur, I don't know what you're talking about."

"Sure you do. In fact, the only thing I'm not one hundred percent certain about is who your friends are. Although, frankly, I'm pretty sure about that one, too. It's those new guards, isn't it? Maybe also Blanco. All of them in it together. Well, believe me, I know how to handle that kind of crap."

She caught another glimpse of his furious eyes and whispered, "Please, Arthur, just listen to me for a moment."

Ignoring her, he moved to the desk and picked up the telephone—a direct line to the tower. "Charlie, this is the warden. Tell Earl to get four or five guys and come down to my quarters immediately. Oh, and, Charlie, tell them to bring some weapons."

"Arthur, please, I can explain everything."

He slammed the receiver down, then turned to look at her. "Why don't you stick around, baby? The fun's just beginning."

15

When Schwarz and Lyons realized the Starlight scope was still in Merryman's room, they simply turned and looked at each other. They were back in their bungalow.

"All right," Lyons said calmly. "Let's not panic."

Schwarz reached for his automatic, then for his jacket. "Facts are, Merryman has our fingerprints on record, which means it's going to take him about fifteen minutes to identify us. Facts are, Blancanales is still in the compound, which means his ass is grass unless we do something right now."

Lyons moved to the window and caught a glimpse of at least five guards sprinting through the night. "Tell me something. If you were Merryman, what would you expect us to do at this point?"

"I guess I'd expect us to make for the desert. Maybe try to steal one of the jeeps and head for the mountains."

"Exactly," Lyons said. "Which is why we're going to play it differently."

"What are you talking about?"

Lyons moved to a footlocker at the base of his bunk and began removing his weapons—an AR-15, a Remington shotgun and his spare .45 auto. He also began withdrawing the ammunition, nearly fifty rounds. "What I've got here isn't nearly enough, but it's a start."

"A start for what?" Schwarz asked as he knelt to help pack the spare ammunition into his coat.

"To start ourselves a prison riot."

Four minutes later Lyons and Schwarz moved out across the dark compound. They moved at a half crouch, keeping to the shadows of the bungalows. When they reached the last row of bungalows, they paused in the shadow of a water tank to scan the far ground. Although there was now definitely activity all around them, it wasn't synchronized yet.

"Figure it this way," Lyons whispered. "Merryman finds the scope, realizes someone was in his quarters and then gets on the horn to the tower. If he's smart, and we can't assume he's not, the first thing he'll do is organize a team to check our bungalow. Then, assuming we've made a break for it, he'll send a dozen or so men out to the desert."

"Which should give us what—ten, twenty minutes?"

Lyons nodded. "Something like that."

"So then what are you proposing?"

Lyons glanced to his left and out at the inner gates of the compound. "I'm proposing we get our hands on as many weapons as possible, then get ourselves inside that compound and start building ourselves a strike force.''

''You mean with the inmates?''

Lyons shrugged. ''Well, you got a better idea?''

Schwarz cocked his head with a worried sigh, then said, ''And how do you suggest we get the weapons?''

Ironman shifted his gaze back to the bungalows. ''We borrow them.''

Although technically the guards were supposed to keep their weapons in the main armory, the rule had never been strictly enforced. So when Lyons and Schwarz kicked in the door of the last bungalow on the left, they initially found two more Remington shotguns, two rifles and another hundred rounds of ammunition. They also found a sleeping guard named Wiley, but he was inconsequential.

When Lyons and Schwarz kicked in the door, Wiley had hardly stirred. Then, rising to an elbow, he grinned and asked, ''Hey, guys, what's going on?''

Lyons drew his .45 and placed it against the kid's head. ''Lie still, keep your mouth shut and you probably won't get hurt.''

The young guard stared in disbelief as Schwarz began methodically stuffing the weapons and ammunition into a canvas duffel bag. ''Hey, don't you think—''

''Shut up!'' Lyons growled.

''What about the handguns?'' Schwarz asked.

Lyons increased the pressure of the .45 against Wiley's skull. "Handguns?"

The guard pointed to a closet where Schwarz recovered three more weapons—a Colt Python and two Beretta 93-Rs. When these were also loaded into the duffel bag, Schwarz lugged the cache to the door and peered out across the compound. He could see lights sweeping across the bungalows and could hear echoes of voices in the distance, but the immediate vicinity was peaceful. "Looks pretty clear to me. But I can't tell what the hell they're doing beyond the wire."

Lyons slid the muzzle of his weapon beneath Wiley's chin and spoke softly into the boy's left ear. "How about it, pal? What's the procedure around here when there's a security problem?"

Wiley slowly sat up on his cot and gulped. "We're supposed to seal off the compound, then send out search parties if there's a break."

"And what are the procedures if the inmates happen to get hold of some weapons?"

Wiley shifted his frightened gaze to the duffel bag. "Weapons? You can't give those animals weapons. That's insane."

"You hear that?" Lyons said. "Wiley thinks we're insane if we give these weapons to the inmates."

Schwarz smiled. "Yeah, we're completely insane."

Eight minutes later, after securing Wiley to the steel frame of his cot and gagging his mouth with a pair of shorts, Schwarz and Lyons moved on out again. They kept mainly to the shadows of the storage bungalows, then moved along the drainage ditch that ran between the coils of barbed wire. By the time they reached the gates of the inner compound, the night was alive with wailing sirens and sweeping searchlights. The fat was in the fire.

BLANCANALES WAS FACING the window when the barracks door burst open. Ramos was seated on the cot, while the other inmates were whispering to one another.

"Everybody stay cool!" Lyons shouted.

Blancanales slid past Ramos, moved to the doorway and accepted one of the shotguns from Schwarz's sack of goodies.

"What the hell's going on?" a burglar named Leiser demanded.

"Yeah," a junkie echoed. "What the hell's going on here?"

Lyons stepped forward, a Remington pump in the crook of his arm, his .45 on his hip. "It's like this. You people are about to be given a choice. You can either stay out of our way or you can help us."

"Help you do what?" a heavyset black man named Collier asked.

"Shut this place down once and for all," Blancanales said.

Lyons dragged the duffel bag into the center of the room and withdrew another shotgun. "Now, we don't have enough weapons for all of you, but we've got enough to get started. So who wants to take the plunge? Which one of you is ready to give them back a little of what they've been dishing out?''

A full thirty seconds of silence passed before anyone stepped forward. From beyond the compound there were finally sounds of approaching jeeps and incoherent voices over the bullhorns. But in the end nothing seemed louder than the footsteps of the first volunteer.

He was a thin junkie named Lee Harper. His back still bore traces of a whipping he'd received for attempting to steal an orange from the guard's mess.

"You know how to use this?" Lyons asked as he extended the shotgun to the boy.

Harper accepted the weapon and slowly turned it over in his hands. "Yeah, I do."

Lyons turned to face the nervous eyes of the others. "All right, who's next?"

Five more inmates rose and slowly stepped forward. But before they could accept their weapons a sixth prisoner got to his feet—Ramos.

"Wait a minute," he said. "I finally recognized you guys. You were in on my bust. How do we know this isn't some trick? How do we know this isn't some sort of experiment to find out which of us is willing to fight?"

Lyons waited until the ensuing whispers died down, then stepped forward. "Ramos is right, up to a point. We are special agents, but we're not working for Merryman. We're here to close him down. Now are you guys going to join, or not?"

But the five volunteers still didn't pick up their weapons.

Blancanales stepped forward, addressing the inmates with a soft, steady voice. "I guess you might say it's kind of like this," he told them. "You men may be guilty of all sorts of crimes, but nothing you did warrants your stay in this place. Nothing anyone has ever done warrants a stay here. So what's it going to be, gentlemen? You want to sit down and keep on letting them mess with you, or do you want to pick up these weapons and help us fight?"

At that moment Ramos reached down and picked up a rifle. "Let's kick ass."

The others joined in with a cheer.

16

Searchlights swept the prison grounds while another dozen guards watched from beyond the wire. A bullhorn blared metallic warnings, and another siren sounded from the walls. Then, responding to a shadow on the gravel, twenty or thirty rounds of autofire burst from the towers above.

"We've got to get out of here," Blancanales whispered. "We've got to draw the fire away from these people."

Lyons nodded from beside the radiator, then turned to face the inmates behind him. "Those of you with weapons, listen up. On my word we move out. You other people stay here until we can get more arms."

There were more bursts of autofire as Lyons led his team through the barracks doors and out to the compound. When Ironman and his team attempted to cross the open ground to the factory, however, the fire suddenly grew deadly.

"Maybe we'd better do something about that tower," Schwarz whispered after scampering back into the shadows of the barracks.

Lyons and Blancanales glanced up at the looming tower. Although nothing was visible, there was obviously something heavy up there, some sort of Squad Automatic Weapon with a laser sight.

Lyons glanced over his shoulder at the huddled forms of the inmates. "Which one of you guys has a Remington?" he whispered.

"Right here," a Hispanic kid named Coco replied.

"You know how to use that thing?" Lyons asked.

The boy nodded. "Sure do."

"Then get yourself over to the corner of the building and start feeding them fire when I give the word. As for the rest of you, stay down."

When Coco scrambled off along the barracks wall, Lyons slid over to Blancanales. "What do you think?"

Pol peered up at the vague forms of the guards above. "I think we'd better knock out that big gun before we're cut to shreds."

"Then go for it," Lyons whispered.

Blancanales nodded, got on his haunches and moved out, breaking into a run when the first rounds began sparking off the gravel.

"Now!" Lyons shouted. "Open up now!"

Although clearly not an experienced killer, Coco began pumping 12-gauge rounds up at the tower with savage accuracy. A moment later Schwarz and another inmate rose and let loose a barrage of their own. A spray of automatic fire answered from the perimeter, but by now Blancanales had become just another shadow below the tower.

Politician hesitated, pressing himself against the concrete supports of the tower and peering up at the steel beams. Then he swung himself onto the ladder and began his ascent. Although the guards were distracted by the fire from behind the barracks, Blancanales couldn't have felt more exposed.

He paused just below the rim of the platform. Apparently there were two guards in the shelter, squeezing off bursts at anything that moved. Blancanales finally eased himself over the edge of the tower's platform, rolled onto his side and leveled his shotgun at the guards. The first guy never knew what hit him as a blast from the Remington tore his chest apart.

The second guard spun the Squad Automatic Weapon in Pol's direction, but the Able Team warrior cut his intention short. The guard screamed as his stomach disintegrated and a cloud of blood sprayed out of his mouth.

"Hold your fire," Lyons whispered. "Pol's taken the tower, so hold your fire."

Although the searchlights continued to sweep the gravel yard, there were now only random shots from the perimeter—a heavy round from a hunting rifle, two or three quick rounds from a 9 mm pistol.

"What do you think?" Schwarz asked, sliding along the barracks wall until he reached the shadows where Lyons was crouched.

"I think they're worried," Lyons replied.

"Which means what? That they'll probably start moving up in force?"

Lyons nodded. "Wouldn't you?"

Stoker, a former L.A. drug dealer, appeared, scrambling up from the far end of the barracks walls. Crouching in the shadows behind Stoker's shoulder was Ramos. "Looks like they got something going on out there," Stoker said. "Out there beyond the gates."

Lyons inched his way to the corner of the barracks and peered out across the forty yards of gravel to the double chain-link gates of the inner compound. Among the darting shadows there were probably at least another dozen guards watching from behind uncompleted bungalows and storage tanks. Then, finally but steadily, he heard the rumble of an approaching truck.

"What do you think?" Schwarz asked. "Does that sound like the makings of a frontal assault?"

Lyons nodded. "It's logical. We take the inner compound and they come right through the gates with a couple of four-wheelers and some .50 calibers."

"So what do we do?"

Lyons glanced around him, his eyes moving over the faces of the inmates. Then he looked at Ramos. "Tell me something, Reuben. Do you think you can get me more men?"

Ramos offered a smile that lay somewhere between a smirk and a grin. "You kidding, man? You get me the guns and I'll get you the meanest bunch of hoods you've ever seen."

Lyons nodded with a hard frown, then turned to Schwarz again. "What do you think? Are we completely out of our minds even to consider giving these guys weapons?''

Schwarz glanced over his shoulder at the far gates where yet more shadows were gathering. ''Probably. But, on the other hand, I don't think we have much choice.''

17

Merryman scowled at the map on the wall as he repeatedly worked his hand into a fist. Behind him stood his senior administrative assistant, a pale, hawk-faced man named Leo Kern. Beside Kern, also slightly at attention, stood Hank Toma. Although not visible from Merryman's study, Angela Perez was also present—handcuffed to the steel bedpost in the adjoining room. Occasionally there were shots from the compound and the metallic shouts of voices through bullhorns. But here, in the lamplit gloom of the warden's quarters, it was still very quiet.

"So basically you're telling me they've taken over the prisoners' yard," Merryman said softly. "Is that it?"

Kern stiffened slightly. "Well, I wouldn't say *complete* control, sir."

Merryman looked at him, the scowl still on his face. "Yeah? Well, what would you call it?"

Kern stepped forward and ran his hand along the portion of the map representing the rim of the men's compound. "Well, for one thing, we still control all this area, including the north and east towers."

"And what about this one?" Merryman frowned, indicating the southern tower above the barracks.

Kern wet his lips. "Well, sir, that one might—"

"It's been taken," Toma said. "Guy went through the wire, climbed the ladder and wasted both guards with a shotgun. Also got hold of the weapons, including a SAW."

"But like I said," Kern added, "we still have the north and east towers."

"Which does us about as much good as a raincoat in a shit-storm, because there's no direct line of fire."

"Well, we still have some alternatives," Kern countered.

"Yeah? Like what?"

Toma stepped forward and pointed at the section of the map that represented the main gates. "I got forty-two men forming here and here. I also got one of the gravel trucks moving up like a tank to ram the gates."

Merryman frowned. "Well, I still don't like it one bit. This thing is just too organized. These guys know exactly what they're doing."

"Does that mean you want me to call in help?" Kern asked.

"Like what?" Merryman shouted, turning to face the administrator. "The National Guard? The Army? Christ, man, what the hell do you think this experiment is all about? It's about secrecy. It's about keeping our damn mouths shut. No, we're not calling in anybody. We have to handle this ourselves and then bury the scum in the desert—real deep in the desert. Now, if you'll excuse me, I've got other business to attend to.''

"YOU HEAR THAT?" Blancanales whispered.

Lyons nodded, his hand growing slightly tighter around the butt of his weapon. "Yeah, I hear it."

"So what are we going to do about it?"

Lyons shook his head as another faint scream echoed high above the compound.

"It's Perez, and you know it," Pol rasped. "We can't just let him tear her apart like—"

"I know," Lyons interrupted. "But there's nothing we can do about it now."

It wasn't quite three o'clock in the morning. Having returned from the tower with four more Remington shotguns, two .357 Magnums, the SAW and at least a hundred rounds of ammunition, Blancanales had joined Lyons and Schwarz in a half-constructed bungalow. From there they had a fairly unobstructed view of the shadows massing at the main gate. Upon Blancanales's return, Ramos was dispatched to barracks four to enlist another six volunteers. Although the other three barracks were silent, they knew every inmate in the compound was awake and listening.

Another faint scream cracked the silence, and Blancanales winced. "Got to do something," he mumbled.

But there were also sounds of another gravel truck moving up from between the bungalows, and a flurry of boot steps spreading out from the main gate.

"Looks like they're going to try to hit us from the flanks," Schwarz said, his fingers nervously toying with his shotgun.

When Ramos returned with more inmates, they moved out in a low sprint to the factory. To their left, one of the prisoners led four of his colleagues into the shadows of a water tower. Schwarz and the others remained behind with the SAW. Although there was still a fair amount of lateral movement along the main gates and adjoining fences, the guards hadn't attempted to enter the compound yet.

"Any ideas?" Blancanales whispered as the three Able Team warriors slipped between the heaps of scrap metal that lay beside the factory.

Lyons peered out across the compound. "Looks like they're planning to come right through the center."

"Could be a trick," Ramos suggested.

Lyons looked at the goateed man, then turned back to Blancanales. "He could be right, Pol."

Blancanales shrugged, then glanced up at the roof of the factory. "Well, in that case, maybe I should cover it from both ends."

He moved out slowly, a patch of blackness within the deeper blackness. From the heaps of stacked sheet metal he slipped between piles of smashed crates, then finally took cover behind a Dumpster. Every thirty seconds or so one of the northern tower searchlights swept the compound in a lazy arc. But it was very dark where Blancanales chose to make his move.

He moved silently, easing himself onto the rim of the Dumpster and then sliding the shotgun onto the corrugated roof of the factory. Muscling himself onto the roof, he picked up his weapon and saw that he had a clear view of the compound gates. He still didn't have the range, but he definitely had the angle.

The roof sloped slightly from where Blancanales lay. Then, too, the corrugated steel was probably thick enough to deflect anything the guards could throw at him. In fact, the only thing that ultimately concerned him was the .50-caliber machine gun mounted on the back of the gravel truck.

Blancanales heard the truck before he actually saw it. Then, sliding up to the edge of the factory roof and peering over the eaves trough, he caught the first glimpse of the hulking gray machine slowly inching over the gravel.

The first bursts of autofire were panicky shots from the guards behind the truck. Yet when two of the inmates attempted to return fire from beneath the water tower, the .50 opened up with murderous accuracy.

From where Blancanales lay on the factory roof the view of the kill couldn't have been more vivid. The impact of the heavy slugs lifted one of the prisoners into the air, held him for a shuddering moment, then tossed him back onto the gravel. The second burst severed his left arm, while the third burst virtually cut him in two.

"Get back!" Lyons shouted. "Get the hell back!" There were shouts from the inmate named Collier, directing the others to take cover behind a pile of old tires. But when the second prisoner attempted to scramble out from under the water tower, another .50-caliber burst cut him to shreds. He seemed to dance before he fell, a crazy little jig on the gravel. Then, as plumes of blood sprayed from his chest and back, he crumpled to the ground and lay still.

There were more .50-caliber bursts as the truck gathered speed, plowed through the gates and entered the compound. Blancanales caught a quick glimpse of Lyons rolling under a heap of sheet metal as a spray of lead kicked up gravel in his wake. Then he caught another glimpse of the guards, at least twenty of them, fanning out from behind the truck and moving into the shadows of the number-two barracks. But it wasn't until he caught another quick vision of the flashing .50 that he finally opened up.

The truck, continuing slowly into the heart of the compound, had drawn roughly parallel with the factory. Although two or three inmates had managed to squeeze off a few 12-gauge rounds, nothing had slowed the truck down. But from where Blancanales lay, prone on the sloping roof, the angle of fire was ideal.

He squeezed off the first shot as the truck passed into the shadow of the water tower. He aimed for the gunner and nailed him in the head. Blancanales squeezed off his second shot as the belt feeder started to scream. It was a clean shot, and it threw the guard to the bed of the truck in a shower of crimson. But it wasn't until Blancanales squeezed off his third, fourth and fifth 12-gauge rounds into the top of the cab that the truck finally began to slow.

There were screams from behind the truck and a tortured cry as the driver tried to spin the wheel with his shot-mangled hands. Flying glass from the windshield sparkled in the air while the engine seemed to roar in anguish.

From where Lyons lay, deep in the blackness beneath the corrugated sheets of steel, the effect of Blancanales's barrage was even more dramatic. Although he hadn't been able to see the machine gunner's death, he had definitely seen the driver die, saw the man's eyes grow wide with pain and horror as the 12-gauge spray of lead ripped through the top of the cab and pulverized his skull.

Ramos appeared, hunkering down between the heaps of steel. "Did you see that, man?"

Lyons propped himself on one elbow. "Listen to me. We've got them on the run. Now get your people up here and tell them to open up."

A random spray of fire from an AR-15 peppered the stacks of steel where Lyons and Ramos lay, and there were muzzle-flashes of at least ten more automatic weapons from behind the stationary truck.

"Now, Ramos," Lyons hissed. "Get your people up here now!"

WHEN THE LAST GUARD melted back through the gates and into the darkness, Lyons drew his men to a halt. Among the bodies sprawled along the compound fence were at least two guards who had been particularly hated by the inmates. When Collier, Ramos and the other prisoners finally approached the bodies, however, they said nothing. They simply squatted on the gravel and stared.

"It's not over," Lyons said. "That's the first thing you people have to realize. This thing isn't even close to being over. We bloodied them a little, but that's all. Nobody's walking away from this one yet."

Ramos appeared, followed by a dozen new volunteers who had slipped out of the barracks. There were also inmates now watching from the doorways and huddled behind the truck.

"I think these guys also want a little piece of the action," Ramos said. He swept his arm in a wide arc to indicate the other inmates beginning to emerge from the barracks. "In fact, I think they all want a little piece of the action."

Lyons rose from the shadows of the main gate and gazed out at the faces around him—some frightened, some determined, some unreadable. "What do you think?" he asked Schwarz.

Schwarz shrugged. "I think we're probably going to need all the help we can get."

Lyons nodded, then turned back to Ramos. "All right, but make sure they understand the ground rules."

Blancanales appeared, moving out from behind the factory and then skirting the chain-link fence until he reached the spot where Lyons crouched. "Looks like they retreated into the women's compound," he said. "I also got a glimpse of more lights along the outer gates."

"Headlights?" Lyons asked.

Blancanales shook his head. "Tactical lights, probably those 650 high beams."

"So what's your point?"

Blancanales squatted and cocked his head to one side. "I think they might start shooting the women pretty soon."

"So what do you want to do?"

Blancanales shifted his gaze back to the compound where the inmates were collecting weapons from the fallen guards and searching pockets for ammunition. "How about you lead these guys into a main thrust while I go after Merryman?"

Lyons ran a hand across his mouth as he watched the inmates scurry across the yard with their new-found weapons. Although most of the men seemed reasonably familiar with their weapons, they clearly had no real concept of organized combat. Yet before Lyons could voice an objection to Blancanales's plan, Perez's tortured screams started again—frantic and pleading.

18

Beyond the gates of the men's compound lay four more half-constructed barracks intended to hold another hundred inmates. Beyond these structures lay another stretch of chain link, another tower and a row of storage sheds. Then came the women's compound, the punishment huts and finally the radio shacks. Although there were no definite signs of guards in the darkness, Lyons was fairly certain they had been deployed.

"We're going to have to kill all of them," he said softly, almost to himself.

Blancanales looked at Lyons. "So what's your point?" he asked at last.

Lyons peered out from above the lip of the drainage ditch that paralleled the outer fence of the men's compound. Although shadows could be misleading, he was fairly certain he was still looking at perhaps twenty-five guards. All he finally said, however, was, "We're just going to have to get real mean."

Schwarz appeared, slipping along the drainage ditch with Ramos in tow. Now thoroughly involved in the battle, Ramos had stripped off his shirt and draped himself with ammunition belts. He also wore a headband. "My guys are definitely ready," he told Lyons. "You just give the word, man, and we'll move on out."

Ignoring the drug dealer's comment, Lyons shot a questioning glance at Schwarz.

Schwarz shrugged. "Well, they're not exactly the 101st Airborne, but they're ready."

"All right," Lyons breathed. "Then start moving them out in two groups." He pointed at the outer fence of the women's compound. "The first group out there," he added. "The second group over by those storage units."

Schwarz nodded. "And meanwhile you'll be going in for a closer look, that the idea?"

"Yeah," Lyons rasped. "I'll be going in for a closer look."

"And so what about Merryman?" Ramos asked.

Blancanales, who up until now had been silent and motionless beside Lyons, suddenly came to life, jamming a fresh magazine into his shotgun. "Merryman's mine."

WITH THE NEW RECRUITS there were fourteen inmates in the first team to move out. Lyons drew his men to a halt in the shadows of the first storage shed and signaled to Blancanales. From where he was crouched beneath a water tank, Blancanales returned the signal. Once again the ground ahead was silent and dark. The blackness was particularly thick within the women's compound.

"Hey, you mind if I ask you something?" Ramos whispered, sliding up on the gravel beside Lyons.

Lyons turned and looked at him. "No," he finally breathed, "I don't mind if you ask me something."

"How come you guys are doing this? I mean, first you blow away my people in Florida and try to throw my ass into jail. Then you come out here and try to save our necks. So what's your story, huh? I mean, what do you guys really want out of this?"

Lyons peered past the drug dealer at the outline of the women's compound and what looked like six guards sliding up to the firing line behind the cinder-block wall of another unfinished structure. "We want justice—real justice."

The first shots broke just as Schwarz's team slipped through the gates of the women's compound—eight fast rounds from an M-16 on the tower above, another ten or twelve rounds from an AR-15. But it wasn't until the searchlights bore down with terrible efficiency, that Schwarz's team returned fire.

The lights exploded into thousands of fragments, and there were screams of pain from the tower above.

At the same time there were also bursts of autofire from behind the cinder-block wall, and the first inmate crumpled to the ground with a sucking wound in his chest.

Schwarz scrambled for cover beneath one of the rusting water tanks and motioned his team to follow. Ahead, beyond the open stretch of ground that formed the edge of the women's compound, another ten or fifteen guards had slithered into the drainage ditch. Eighty feet to his left were sporadic shots from the first team of inmates—12-gauge blasts, cracks from the .45 Lyons had given to Ramos and two or three fast bursts from an AK-47 that an inmate named Sonny had picked off the body of a guard beneath the truck. But the bulk of fire still came from a wall where at least fifteen guards had now opened up with M-16s.

Another inmate, a black kid from Chicago, took a bullet in the forehead, pitched forward and died. Schwarz dropped to his belly, heard six more heavy rounds slamming into the water tank, then slithered forward into the coils of barbed wire. What I need, he told himself, is a grenade or two. But by the time he slithered forward to the far end of that cinder-block wall, rose and hoisted the SAW, he actually needed nothing but timing.

Gadgets lifted his left hand as a signal to Lyons, then saw the blond leader return the gesture. He lifted his right hand as a signal to an ex-gang member from the Bronx and watched as the signal was returned. Then, waiting another four seconds, he inched out of the coiled wire and into the shadow of the wall.

From the coils of wire where Schwarz now lay the wall ran fifty feet across the gravel to the edge of the first barracks. But here and there the cinder blocks hadn't been firmly cemented in place, and there were also gaps where the doors were to hang. So that when Schwarz finally made his move, swinging through the nearest gap, he had a clean line of fire to the guards.

He fired from his hip, sweeping the muzzle of the SAW in a forty-five-degree angle. The first guards to fall were two Texans from the state facility at Yuma, and they fell with muffled screams as slugs tore into their backs. The next man to fall was a sullen Californian whose body was ripped to shreds in seconds.

Confused shouts broke from the far end of the wall, and someone screamed an order to fall back. But Schwarz squeezed off another two-second burst, and four more guards stumbled to the ground as the spray of lead cut through their ranks. A thin, pockmarked face briefly loomed in Schwarz's vision, then faded back with an explosion of blood and bone.

Schwarz squeezed off another burst as his team of inmates poured through the wall behind him and Lyons drew his men up to the opposite end of the wall. He saw two more guards reeling to the gravel, then still another crumpling with a shotgun blast in the back.

Schwarz heard Lyons shout, "Go! Go! Go!" Then he heard one of the inmates scream, "Get some! Get some!"

By now there were lights again, fierce beams from the southern tower that left two inmates cleanly etched against the compound yard. And when bursts of automatic fire began tearing chunks of cinder from the wall, the inmates' advance was quickly halted.

At Schwarz's signal his team withdrew to one of the excavated foundations just inside the wall. Thirty feet to Schwarz's left the first team under Lyons's command had slipped behind the lower portion of the wall. Then, finally dragging themselves along the drainage ditch, Schwarz and Lyons came together again.

"That was nice work," Lyons said as he drew alongside Gadgets.

Schwarz glanced at one of the guards sprawled in a heap of cement. Although the man's face was unmarked, his torso had been virtually cut in two by a long burst from the SAW. "I don't think it's going to be so easy next time."

Lyons peered out over the edge of the drainage ditch. There was more than eight feet of empty ground before the first rows of bungalows. Although the guards had once more vanished into the blackness, there were still faint signs of them out there—flitting shadows here and there, a glint of metal in the moonlight. Then, like an image from a bad dream, there was also something else, something like a snared animal struggling in a trap between the first and second bungalows.

It wasn't however, until they heard a woman's frantic scream unnaturally silenced by a pistol shot that any of it made sense.

Then all Lyons said was, "I think you'd better tell your people to collect whatever weapons they can find around here and start moving out. We've got to move fast."

19

"Now," Lyons whispered. "Give them the signal to move out now."

He lay in the dry ditch that ran along the edge of the compound. Fifty feet to his left, crouched among the tumbled cinder blocks, were sixteen inmates under Schwarz's command. Forty-five feet to his right, squatting behind another rusting water tank, were eight more inmates under the command of Blancanales. Somewhere along the wall behind lay two sharpshooters recently liberated from the special-treatment barracks. Yet when Lyons turned his head and whispered his command, he was speaking to Ramos.

The former Florida dealer squatted directly over Lyons's shoulder. In addition to his shotgun and .45 automatic he had picked up a long-handled flashlight. It was the sort of flashlight that the guards had used to beat prisoners into submission time and time again. Now, however, it was put to another use.

Cupping the head of the flashlight with his left hand and aiming it at Schwarz's team, Ramos rapidly switched it on and off twice. In response there were two soft whistles from the darkness, then the equally soft sound of footsteps on the gravel. Repeating the signal to the team on his right, Ramos watched another band of shadows rise from the darkness and move forward. Then, replacing the flashlight in the waistband of his trousers and picking up his rifle, he also rose to his feet. As he started forward, he turned to Lyons and asked, "Hey, man, you scared?" And when Lyons simply smiled, he added, "I sure am."

The two teams moved in short bursts of speed, first to the last row of water tanks, then to the storage sheds. Beyond the sheds, however, there was only open ground.

"They're in there pretty tight," Ramos whispered to Lyons as they hunkered down behind the corrugated shed. "We start letting loose with the shotguns, we're going to take a few of the women with us."

Lyons inched himself forward, his boot heels whispering on the gravel. His plan had been to let the first team draw the fire while Blancanales led the second team through the gates of the women's compound and into the barracks. From this vantage point, however, it looked bad. Very bad. "Give them the signal to hold up," he told Ramos.

Ramos withdrew the flashlight again, aimed it to his left and switched it on. He then repeated the signal to his right and switched the flashlight off. "Now what?" he asked, sinking down beside Lyons again.

"Now we have a little change of plans," Lyons replied.

Ramos eyed the blond warrior cautiously while fingering his shotgun. "What kind of change?"

Lyons pointed at the low fence of the women's compound. "Instead of sending in your pals, you and I are going in alone."

There were two long stretches of open ground between the storage sheds and the entrance to the women's compound. Although the shadows of the blown tower offered a degree of cover, it was basically as hard a crawl as any Lyons had ever made. For the first twenty feet he and Ramos kept to the shadows of the tower, then into the shadows of an electrical generator above the medical center. Beyond the generator, however, there was nothing except the open ground and the low drainage ditch to the wire.

They paused at the start of the ditch, watching, listening. Although they weren't directly in the main line of fire, there were at least a dozen guards who could have nailed them to the gravel in an instant.

"Figure it this way," Lyons whispered. "They're expecting a big push over the wire and into their flanks. They're not going to think we're crazy enough to send in only two guys.''

Ramos shook his head and thoughtfully stroked his goatee. "Yeah," he breathed to himself. "No one would think we're crazy enough to send only two guys."

They started moving again when the breeze picked up and the chain link began rattling softly in the wind. Sixty feet from the fence they were able to make out the heads of guards above the drainage ditch. Fifty feet from the fence they were able to make out the faces of guards peering down from the barracks roof. But it wasn't until they actually entered the shadows of the gate that anyone started shooting again.

"Don't move," Lyons ordered. "They haven't spotted us. They're just getting nervous."

Ramos slowly lifted his face from the gravel, softly spitting out dust. "Yeah, they're just getting nervous."

There was a low depression in the ground just opposite the entrance to the gate. Although it didn't offer anything close to real cover, it definitely diminished the target.

Lyons slid into the shallow trench and motioned Ramos to follow. Then, turning to the drug dealer, he said, "Once I'm through I want you to signal the guys and then open up with everything you've got. Understand?''

Ramos returned the blond warrior's gaze, then nodded. "Sure, I understand."

Lyons moved out on his belly again for the first fifteen feet. Once past the gates of the women's compound he rose to a low crouch and scurried into the shadows of a storage shed. From there he was able to get a pretty good idea of how the guards had arranged themselves—ten or twelve along the drainage ditch, another ten or fifteen between the first and second barracks, still more behind the barracks, and finally a few on the roof.

And although the three nearest guards might have caught a glimpse of him, might have even pointed at the unreal shape slithering through the darkness, it wasn't until he reached the relative cover below the tower that the shooting actually began.

He fell back to the gravel as the first rain of bullets tore through the aluminum siding of the shed, then drew himself into a ball behind the steel girder. But even as the fury of lead screamed through the air around him, he was conscious of the covering fire—round after round of 12-gauge shells pouring in from Blancanales's team, long, rapid bursts of full-auto from the men under Schwarz's command. And when he heard the cracks from Ramos's shotgun, he finally rose again.

There were three guards huddled against the corrugated siding of the last barracks. Although they were well out of the firing line from the gate, there was no way Lyons could miss them once he opened up.

He fired on the run, moving out from the tower and squeezing off four fast rounds from the Remington. The first two guards fell instantly, thrown back against the barracks walls by the impact. The third, catching only the edge of the spread, managed to return a quick burst with his M-16. Then Lyons squeezed off a fourth shell that virtually took off the man's head.

Lyons paused among the bodies, pressing himself against the barracks wall and avoiding the glazed eyes of the guard at his feet. Just beyond the corrugated siding were the terrified whispers of women obviously huddled beneath their bunks.

Lyons hesitated before moving to the trash bins. Then, gently heaving himself up, he peered over the rainspout along the sloping roofline. There were two prone guards returning fire from the opposite end of the corrugated roof. But given the clatter of autofire from below, they obviously had no idea Lyons was behind them, inching up his shotgun and resting on the rainspout. Then all they could have known was that something like a sledgehammer had slammed into their torsos, throwing them off the roof and into the blackness below.

Lyons waited a few more seconds before lifting himself onto the barracks roof. The dark courtyard seemed ablaze with flashes of autofire and the deeper crack of shotgun blasts from inmates beyond the gates. There were also occasional screams of women in the barracks and the howls of men rocking in the blackness with bullet wounds. But it wasn't until Lyons had crawled to the opposite end of the roof, peering over the edge of the rusting steel rainspout, that he began to understand what was going on.

Fifteen guards fired from the shadows below, eight or nine more lay in the drainage ditch, returning fire from the inmates beyond the gate. There were also three guards on the adjoining roof, and still more in the shadows of the water tanks.

Lyons went for the guards on the opposite roof first because they posed the greatest threat. He worked efficiently and quickly, shooting for the silhouette of the closest guard first. Then, almost before the target could even respond to the impact, Lyons squeezed off the second round and dropped another guard off the roof. He squeezed off the third round as the last guard turned, this time aiming for the chest. He saw the guard stiffen before he fell, and the quick flash of an M-16 tumbling into the darkness.

There were shouts from below and another fast spray of autofire from the drainage ditch. But by then Lyons had inched himself up to the edge of the roof and lowered himself into a firing position—eighteen feet above the main stretch of the guard's defensive line. It was like shooting fish in a barrel.

20

Lyons and Blancanales slipped into the shadows adjacent to the barracks door and examined the blood on the concrete step. There was also blood on the surrounding gravel and more blood on the path.

"What do you think?" Blancanales asked softly, the fingers of his left hand continually opening and closing around the stock of the shotgun.

Lyons pressed his palm against the barracks door. "I think they're inside."

There were heavy footsteps closing in from the corner of the building, and Blancanales instinctively dropped into firing position. A moment later, however, Ramos appeared with six or seven inmates in tow. "We got the bastards running, man," the drug dealer said.

Lyons exchanged a quick glance with Blancanales. Yet all Blancanales actually said was "I think we better do something about Hank Toma. We know he's in there. Kern, too."

Lyons extended a hand in the air to silence the whispers around him. Then he pointed at Blancanales and nodded. Pol returned the nod and moved off along the side of the barracks. Finally, turning his gaze to Ramos, Lyons gestured to the door. "Once I kick in the door," he said softly, "all hell will break loose. So you keep your people down and out of the firing line."

Ramos shook his head. "Uh-uh." He smiled. "Not this time. This time you're going to cover me."

Lyons took a deep breath. "You don't have to do this," he finally said.

"Yes, I do. Besides, those women in there, they're my people. You know what I mean?" Then, without waiting for Lyons to reply, Ramos picked up his weapon and moved to the door.

"Now?" he whispered.

"Now," Lyons replied.

Ramos rose to his feet and attacked the door. He moved in with a skipping kick, focusing his weight and momentum in the heel of his boot. He also shouted as he came on through, a deep grunt of rage and determination.

The door exploded open, sending slivers of wood spraying into the air. There were screams from beneath the cots where the women had huddled, and a black girl named Sheila shouted out some sort of warning.

But Toma didn't need a warning. All he needed was the target.

Toma's first burst caught Ramos in the legs, shredding the flesh along his left thigh and shattering the shinbone. But even as Ramos fell, screaming in shock and pain, he brought up the shotgun and squeezed the trigger when Toma's female hostage shifted slightly. Just then Kern, Merryman's assistant, moved in front of Toma, and Ramos's 12-gauge load demolished his skull.

Toma responded next, sliding his Beretta past his hostage's ribs and squeezing off six fast rounds. The first three rounds struck Ramos in the back, then another burst tore open his throat. But even as the blood filled his eyes the drug dealer still kept grinning. He rolled onto his side for his last shot. Then, screaming out a mouthful of blood, he squeezed off a final round and annihilated another guard.

There were shots from the door now, high shots splintering the beams above Toma's head and wrenching more screams of fear from the cowering women.

"I'm going to start shooting the ladies!" Toma shouted. "You pricks hear me? Keep it up and I'll start wasting these bitches in here!" And just to prove his point he swung the Beretta to his left and blew off the face of the nearest female.

A full six seconds passed while Toma pressed his new hostage a little closer to his body and Lyons flattened himself against the wall outside the door. Also motionless now were Blancanales and Schwarz.

"You hear me out there?" Toma roared. "Next bastard moves a muscle, I drop another one of these bitches."

"Yeah," Lyons growled, "I hear you."

And in the split second of ensuing silence one of the female inmates made her move. She sprang for Toma's left arm, reaching for the wrist that held the Beretta. Then, throwing her shoulder into the man's chest, she slammed her fist into Toma's face. But compared to the slug Blancanales unleashed from the window, the fist was nothing.

Pol actually squeezed off two shots, one to break the glass, the second to kill. The bullet struck Toma square in the forehead, slammed his head against the wall and left him briefly staring in horror.

Lyons entered the barracks slowly, first glancing at the women beneath the cots, then at Toma's mutilated head, then at the lifeless body of Kern. But when he finally reached Ramos, he knelt.

"You going to arrest me now?" Ramos whispered, his eyes clouding with pain, the blood still pouring from his mouth.

Lyons shook his head. "Nah, I think you've already paid your debt to society."

Ramos seemed to consider these words quite seriously for a moment, then said, "Well, in that case, how about you do me a little favor in return?"

"Sure," Lyons breathed. "Anything you want."

"Get the pricks responsible for setting up this place, Merryman and Lang. Get those pricks and blow them away for me, okay?"

"No problem," Lyons breathed. "No problem at all."

But by this time, of course, Ramos was dead.

MERRYMAN TOOK HOLD of Angela Perez's arm and shoved her out the door. Then, scanning the yard ahead, he drew her back into the shadows. In addition to the Python he wore on his hip he had picked up a sawed-off shotgun—a murderous-looking thing with his name crudely carved into the stock. At the sound of footsteps pounding on the gravel he pressed the double barrels into her throat. Still weak from torture, Perez didn't resist.

"I hope you don't think I wouldn't use this," he whispered as the footsteps drew closer.

"No, Arthur," she breathed. "I don't think that at all."

When the footsteps faded, he took hold of her arm again and led her out along the stretch of coiled barbed wire marking the outer perimeter. The gravel hurt her feet, and twice she stumbled with soft cries of pain. But Merryman just ignored her.

They had nearly reached the entrance of the motor court when the figure finally appeared. He seemed to appear out of nowhere, stepping from the shadows beside a row of jeeps and one of the old school buses used to transport prisoners. At first glance Perez took him for a guard. But then she saw the slow-burning hatred in the eyes and she realized this was no guard.

Blancanales casually leveled his weapon at Merryman's chest and smiled. "Going somewhere, Warden?"

Merryman encircled Perez's waist with his left arm, eased the double barrels into her throat and rasped, "Just be cool, baby. Just be real cool." Then, to Blancanales, he said, "I'll blow her damn head off, pal, if you try to stop me."

There were echoes of more shotgun blasts from the yard, then the hoarse shout of a guard yelling, "Okay! Okay! We're putting down our rifles. Look, we're putting 'em down!" There were also echoes of more approaching footsteps—obviously inmates.

But Merryman and Blancanales just continued looking at each other while Perez shivered against the barrels of the sawed-off shotgun.

"I'm serious," Merryman said at last. "You want to see this pretty little thing in one piece, then you're just going to have to let me walk over to that vehicle and watch me drive off."

For a moment it seemed as if Blancanales was considering a lot of things—the distance, the trajectory, the odds of squeezing off a decisive bullet before Merryman could squeeze his own trigger. But in the end he simply said, "I don't think so, Warden."

Merryman nodded. "All right, if that's the way you want to play it. But just to show you I'm serious, how about I blow off her head first?" And to underscore the point he slowly inched his left hand down from her waist to grab hold of her slender wrist.

But even as Merryman made his move, Perez was also making a move—inching her right hand along the warden's waist until her fingers reached the butt of his holstered revolver. Then, suddenly yanking the weapon free, she spun away from the shotgun and faced him.

At that moment Blancanales dropped to one knee, Merryman whirled in horror and tried to bring the shotgun around and Perez shouted, "You bastard!"

And before she even really knew it the revolver was kicking in her hands.

She shot for the belly, a gut shot, but actually ended up hitting him in the groin. She saw his eyes widen with disbelief, saw his lips form around her name. Then she must have shot him at least four more times before he finally collapsed in a mess of blood.

EPILOGUE

Jack Lang stepped to the window of his executive suite and stared out across the Phoenix skyline. Behind him a portly attorney named Stuart Sly was methodically feeding sheets of stationery into a portable shredder. It was late, at least two o'clock in the morning. The offices below were empty, the streets mostly deserted.

Sly fed in the last sheet of stationery, switched off the shredder and said, "Well, that should do it."

Lang nodded, gazing at his reflection in the dark glass—the finely chiseled features, the slightly arched eyebrows, the bloodless lips. "Then you might as well go home, Stuart."

Sly rose to his feet, then hesitated. "As your attorney, Jack, I should probably warn you that you're not in the clear. If somebody decides to launch a full investigation and the inmates are questioned, well, I don't have to spell it out, do I?"

Lang, however, merely smiled. "Oh, I don't think I have much to worry about. After all, the President has almost as much to lose over this one as I do. Big trial, lots of publicity..." Lang broke off with a shake of his head. "No, I really don't think the present Administration is going to allow anything like that to happen, not in our lifetime."

"Still, there were laws broken, Jack. You illegally imprisoned people, you—"

Lang turned, the trace of his smile still on his lips. "But, Stuart, I happen to be above the law—way above the law. Now go home."

Alone in the half-lit suite Lang stepped to the portable bar and poured himself a large whiskey. Then, returning to the window, he continued to stare out at the skyline. When Lyons and Blancanales finally stepped through the doorway, Lang was still at the window, still staring out at the city he'd helped build and the nation he'd tried to save.

"May I help you, gentlemen?" he asked without turning.

"Federal agents," Lyons said.

Lang still didn't turn around. "Ah, yes, federal agents."

"I'm afraid you'll have to come with us," Blancanales said.

Lang smiled. "Come with you? In what capacity? Am I under arrest? Is that what you gentlemen are trying to tell me?"

Lyons nodded. "In a manner of speaking, yeah, you're under arrest."

Lang shrugged. "Well, in that case I suggest you read me my rights."

But by this time Blancanales had stepped closer, drawn his .45 and jammed it into the base of Lang's spine. "What rights?" he whispered.

TERROR IN WARSAW

by
Gar Wilson

A Phoenix Force novel

PROLOGUE

November 10, 1989

The celebration was still in progress. The crowds sang and danced in the streets as people chipped off pieces of the wall with chisels and hammers. The enthusiastic crowd waved banners and cheered as chunks of the wall fell to the ground. Soldiers stood by and watched civilians embrace and share food and drink.

Colonel Yuri Isakovich Durnov smoldered with anger as he witnessed something that had seemed impossible for twenty-eight years. They were having a party along the Berlin Wall. People were tearing it apart and no one was stopping them. The East German government had literally thrown open Brandenburg Gate and granted its citizens freedom to cross to West Germany. The unthinkable had become a reality.

News journalists and television cameras covered this incredible event. For most this was an impossible dream that had somehow come true. To Durnov and his companions it was a nightmare. The Soviet colo-

nel watched Germans from the East and West join
hands as they stood along the stone platform of
Brandenburg Gate. Durnov considered this display an
obscenity.

"My people are a disgrace," Klaus Schoffer muttered, and looked away.

Schoffer was a control officer in the State Security
Service of East Germany. A small, slender man with
features that seemed pinched together to fit his lean
face, Schoffer looked more like a soured civil servant
than an espionage agent. His expression didn't improve as he watched his fellow countrymen literally
dance on the Berlin Wall with West Germans.

"In my country things are even worse," Zbigniew
Zablocki stated with disgust. "I've already been removed from office and I'll be lucky if they don't
charge me with 'violations of human rights,' thanks to
the support those idiots have given Lech Walesa and
his ilk."

Zablocki wore a dark brown false beard, the same
color and texture as his real hair and Stalin-style cow-
horn mustache. Although Zablocki wasn't well known
outside Poland, he was still a public figure and a former member of the Sejm or parliament. The beard,
hat and dark glasses were a precaution in case someone in the crowd was familiar with Zablocki's face and
career.

"You should have had that union dissident shot
years ago," Schoffer commented gruffly. "Letting
Walesa live was a mistake."

"That would have accomplished nothing," Zablocki told the SSD agent. "Walesa didn't start Solidarity, and if we executed him, someone else would have taken his place. The same thing happened in Poland as we've seen here in the German Democratic Republic. The ignorant masses turned against us and betrayed communism. The government was spineless and gave in to their demands."

"And it's happening everywhere," Durnov said grimly as he peered out the car window at the raucous celebration at the Berlin Wall. "Even in the Soviet Union. That bastard Gorbachev has sabotaged international communism with his talk about reform and granting 'self-government' to the nations of Eastern Europe. What that really means is he wants the USSR to abandon you and leave you to fend for yourselves."

"And he dares to call this 'freedom,'" Schoffer scoffed. "Freedom to allow these capitalist swine to corrupt our people. Gorbachev has forgotten that communism is the workers' revolution to be free of the imperialism and oppression of the bourgeois. The ultimate goal is the total equality of all people throughout the world. Now he's betrayed that struggle in favor of the materialism and lies of the West."

Floodlights and flashbulbs illuminated the figures along the Brandenburg Gate. Some stood between the pillars of the great stone arch. Flags waved with the German national colors of black, red and gold. Durnov didn't see any banners bearing the East German coat of arms, which distinguished the flag from that of West Germany. Even more disturbing to the Russian colonel was the sight of several American flags among the crowd.

"I think we've seen enough," Durnov announced. He turned from the window and addressed the big man in the front seat of the car. *"Vam na'da pryah'ma."*

The driver started the engine and drove straight ahead. He knew Durnov intended the instructions for him because none of the men in the back seat had spoken a single word of Russian until that moment. Of course, the driver understood German fluently, but he had been told to act as if he didn't know the language. This was in case Schoffer or Zablocki said anything in Durnov's absence that the colonel might want to know about. They would be more apt to speak freely in the presence of someone they thought didn't understand German.

The big black Russian car headed along Unter den Linden toward the heart of East Berlin. The vehicle was forced to crawl through the streets due to the masses of civilians still headed for the border. Thousands of East Germans were making the migration to the West. They were cheerful and eager as they strolled toward the wall. Schoffer cursed softly as he peered through the tinted windows to see a girl hand some flowers to an East German soldier. The man smiled and stuck one flower in the lapel of his tunic.

"If I had the authority," Schoffer muttered, "I'd have that traitorous soldier in front of a firing squad."

"I understand your emotions," Durnov assured him. "I even sympathize with them. However, we're faced with a situation that can't be solved with executions and brute force. Look at those people. More than a million of your countrymen have already crossed into the West. Millions more will do so, and neither the government nor the military will stop them. That doesn't include the millions of people in Poland, Czechoslovakia, Hungary, Bulgaria and the Soviet Union who favor these so-called 'reforms.' We're faced with a crisis we can't solve with the barrel of a gun."

"The colonel's right," Zablocki admitted. "Poland now considers itself to be a democracy, and the same will probably happen in Czechoslovakia within a year. It may well happen in East Germany, as well. We'd have to slaughter the majority of our own people to make changes by force. That would certainly be amusing to the Americans and Western Europe!"

"We have to use different tactics," Durnov stated. "That's why I've contacted you and arranged this meeting. The only hope we have of restoring the strength of international communism and the people's revolution is Mácka."

"Mácka?" Schoffer said with a frown. He wasn't fluent in Russian, but guessed what the word meant. "Mask? What does that mean?"

"A mask conceals one's face," Durnov replied. "We must conceal the true nature of our plans and pretend to accept and embrace the policies of *glasnost, perestroika* and this disgusting nonsense about 'democratic reforms.'"

The car pulled off Unter den Linden and headed onto a less-traveled side street. Durnov had told the driver to avoid the Marx Engels Platz to the north of the city. It would be too depressing to see cheering crowds among the war memorials in a place named in honor of the founders of modern communism.

Durnov and his companions were true believers in the doctrines of Marx, Engels and Lenin. Their version of history regarded World War II as a struggle between communism and fascism. They were unaware that Hitler and Stalin had actually been allies in the late thirties before the Nazi invasion of Poland. They had to admit grudgingly that the United States and Western Europe were allies of the Soviets during the war, but dismissed any moral significance. Didn't the capitalist democracies fight the fascists simply in hopes of gaining more territory for their own selfish reasons?

Since Durnov saw little difference between the fascists and the capitalists, he considered it an insult to the memory of the dead heroes of socialism that supporters of democracy dared celebrate at the war memorials. He glanced at the brown and gray shapes among the shadows. The buildings were monoto-

nous. In daylight East Berlin was less than pictur-
esque. At night it was drab and grim.

"Tell us more about Mácka, Comrade Colonel,"
Zablocki urged as the car headed south.

"As you both know," Durnov began, "I've spent
more than two and a half decades with the Eleventh
Department of the First Chief Directorate of the KGB.
I've established contacts with hundreds of dedicated
Communists in high positions of government
throughout Eastern Europe. Many of the most important officials in these nations have known me as an
adviser and representative of the Kremlin. There are
others who feel as we do. If we work together, we can
build Mácka into a powerful covert network to combat the threat of democratic reforms and restore the
fires of international communism and the socialist
revolution throughout the world."

"How can we do this?" Schoffer demanded. "The
people have been duped by the promise of materialism and the illusion of freedom sold to them by the
capitalists and that traitor Gorbachev."

"Our people see that those of the West have more
material goods and they envy this apparent wealth,"
Zablocki remarked. "They don't realize capitalism is
nothing more than a philosophy of greed."

"That's exactly what we have to teach them," Durnov declared. "Mácka will accomplish this. Eventually the people of our nations will realize the mistake
they're making, but by then it could be too late. We
have to bring the realities of the oppression and cor-

ruption of these false democracies to the masses now
before the changes are complete.''

Zablocki nodded. The Polish official knew Durnov's motives weren't as unselfish as his speech suggested. Zablocki had known Colonel Durnov for more
than ten years. The stocky, middle-aged Russian had
always been a good talker. Durnov was a master ma-
nipulator and had the rare talent of convincing others
that his machinations were actually their own.

Yet Zablocki was aware Durnov was more worried
about losing his own position of authority and power
than ''protecting'' anyone from democratic reforms.
Indeed, all three men had enjoyed wealth and privi-
leges far greater than most of their countrymen could
imagine. Despite the Marxist theories that everyone
would work equally and share equally under a true
Communist regime, the reality was that a small elite
group ruled over the masses.

Zablocki didn't intend to give up his power and live
like a peasant. He knew the same was true for Durnov and Schoffer and whoever else the colonel intended to enlist into his Mácka conspiracy. Not only
did these men intend to cling to their power, they also
had concerns for their very survival. They had all
participated in actions that had cost the lives of hundreds, if not thousands, of their countrymen. If this
information became public knowledge, they would be
lucky to be simply deported or sentenced to long
prison terms. These men who had sent so many oth-

ers to the firing squads might well find themselves facing the same fate.

"So we have to appear to agree with these damn reforms," Schoffer began. "It shouldn't be too difficult to give lip service to that nonsense, but how can we convince these reformers our conversions are genuine?"

"There are ways," Durnov said grimly. "It saddens me to say this, but we'll have to give up some of our fellow comrades in order to save ourselves. We all know some secrets about others that can prove they committed what are now being called 'crimes against humanity.' For example, I know a certain doctor in Kiev who's been certifying dissidents as insane so that they can be committed to asylums and drugged to keep them silent. When I expose him, I'll appear to be very 'progressive' to these *glasnost*-loving idiots."

"So we have to sacrifice some of the men who have served the Party as devoutly as ourselves," Schoffer said with a frown. "That's going to be difficult to live with."

"*Da,*" Durnov agreed. He knew Schoffer would be willing to cut his own mother's throat to save himself and had no doubts the SSD agent would serve up as many scapegoats as necessary. "Yes. It will be very difficult, but it will have to be done for the sake of our cause."

The driver brought the car to a sudden halt. Several figures blocked the road as they crossed the street. They waved at the car and cheerfully strolled north toward the border. They carried suitcases and knapsacks. One month ago they wouldn't have dared to display luggage openly as they headed for the Wall.

"Mein Gott," Schoffer muttered, shaking his head. "These terrible changes are everywhere. This is anarchy!"

"We realize that," Durnov replied. "But we have to make people such as these understand that, as well. They must see the dark side of the politics of the West."

"This won't be easy," Zablocki remarked. "We need something that will spark our people into carrying out the equivalent of the storming of the Winter Palace."

"And they'll have to be willing to accept the bloodbath that will follow," Durnov added. "The bloodbath that will take the lives of our enemies and wash away these alleged democratic changes."

1

David McCarter looked in the mirror as he adjusted the flight cap. The uniform fitted fairly well, although it was a bit large for the Briton's lean frame. A grin appeared on his foxlike features as he tapped a finger on the gold wings above the left breast pocket. Although he had never been a pilot for a commercial airline, McCarter had certainly logged more than enough hours of flying time to qualify.

He was uncomfortable because the familiar Browning Hi-Power wasn't holstered under his arm. McCarter didn't like being unarmed, and the lack of the pet 9 mm pistol felt as if part of his anatomy had been removed. The British ace didn't relish the idea of going into the figurative lion's den without a weapon, but he had volunteered to do so.

"You really can be a crazy bastard at times, McCarter," he told the face in the mirror.

He leaned over the sink and washed. He placed a palm, damp with cold water, against the nape of his neck and breathed deeply. McCarter was nervous.

Most people who knew him thought he was immune to fear. He wasn't.

The door to the men's room opened. Calvin James entered. The tall, lanky black warrior looked at McCarter and grinned slightly. He was dressed in a dark suit, a white shirt and a thin houndstooth tie. James took a pair of black frame glasses from his pocket and slipped them onto the bridge of his nose.

"Do I look respectable enough?" he inquired.

"You might fool somebody who doesn't know you," McCarter replied with a shrug.

"Cute," James said dryly as he moved to the mirror and placed a shaving kit on the sink. "You look sort of goofy in that pilot's outfit, too. Maybe that's just because I know what a nutcase you are."

"Probably," McCarter answered. "Anything happening out there?"

"The situation hasn't changed much," James told the Briton. He opened the kit and removed a small brush and a metal disk with gray makeup. "The terrorists haven't changed their demands and efforts at negotiation haven't made any progress. Looks like we'll have to go in, David."

"Well, we wouldn't be here if things weren't already desperate," the Briton remarked.

McCarter and James were accustomed to desperate situations. They were members of Phoenix Force. The five-man commando team, which besides McCarter and James included Yakov, Katzenelenbogen, Gary Manning and Rafael Encizo, consisted of the best trained and most highly skilled experts in unconventional combat and special covert operations in the Western world. Phoenix Force specialized in dealing with missions others would consider impossible. Despite their superb training, exceptional in-the-field experience and uncanny abilities, the commandos weren't superhuman. Every assignment was dangerous and a single mistake could be fatal.

James considered this as he raised the brush to his temples and applied a slight tint of gray to his hair above the ears. He needed to appear a few years older, but it was important the illusion be convincing. James used the brush sparingly so that the gray wouldn't appear pasted on or more excessive than his youthful features suggested. Even a small mistake could make a paranoid opponent suspicious and quite possibly violent.

"I'll let you powder your nose in private," McCarter told him. "See you out front."

The Briton emerged from the rest room. He walked past a pair of airport security guards in the hall and headed for the terminal gate. The sound of shoe leather echoed in the hall. The airport was all but deserted. It seemed unnatural for a major international airport to be so quiet. McCarter felt a chill.

The Istanbul police and Turkish Parachute Brigade soldiers at the terminal seemed tense and frustrated. A heavyset man paced like a caged beast. His shaved head and black handlebar mustache resembled those of an old-style circus strongman. The man was as tough as he looked. General Yildiz had taken part in three military coups in Turkey. The coups had been undertaken to overthrow corrupt governments, prevent anarchy and fight terrorism. On each occasion the military had stepped down from power after a civilian government was reestablished. The reason Turkey wasn't a military dictatorship was because of officers like General Yildiz.

A true patriot, Yildiz was willing to do whatever was necessary to protect the Republic of Turkey. This sense of dedication had earned him the position of head of the internal affairs section of the Turkish National Security Service. The current threat didn't concern the safety of Turkey, but jeopardized the country's reputation and relations with the United States. That was enough to involve the NSS and General Yildiz.

Crises like the one at the Istanbul International Airport had been played out many times before throughout the world. A Turkish Airlines commercial 747 had been seized on the runway by a band of armed terrorists. The fanatics had broken into a passenger loading bridge and avoided airport security, charging into the plane after most of the passengers were already on board. The copilot had tried to close the door to keep the terrorists out. They had shot him and bullied their way into the craft.

The terrorists had forced the pilot to taxi away from the apron to a runway farther from the terminals. Then they had contacted air traffic control by radio and announced they were holding the crew and passengers hostage. Any attempt to rescue the prisoners would get them all killed, the hijackers had warned.

Painfully long hours had crept by since then. Yildiz and others had established radio contact with the terrorists and tried to negotiate for the lives they held captive. The hijackers claimed they were members of an outfit called the Islamic Rescue Forces. They demanded that Shiite "warriors of the Jihad" be released from "political prisons" in Israel, the United States and Western Europe. The terrorists also wanted Israeli forces to withdraw from Lebanon, the United States to pull all Navy vessels from the Persian Gulf, and Turkey to sever relations with all nations holding Islamic political prisoners.

Yildiz had convinced the hijackers to release the women and children. The IRF terrorists had reluctantly agreed to allow even female passengers with American passports or Jewish names to leave the aircraft. They had found two American servicemen among the passengers, hauled them to the door, shot them and dumped their corpses onto the runway. The pilot had attempted to stop them and was also shot and shoved out of the plane.

Reluctantly the terrorists had agreed to let the police retrieve the bodies. Both Americans were dead. The assassins had pumped a bullet into the back of each man's skull. The courageous pilot was alive but in critical condition. He had been shot point-blank in the stomach and several bones were broken from the fall. The IRF hijackers had told negotiators they regretted what had happened to the pilot, but that he shouldn't have interfered.

Yildiz had told the Islamic Rescue Force they could only serve to debilitate the image of Islam by such appalling behavior. He had also told the IRF terrorists that the pilot they had nearly killed was himself a Muslim. They weren't disturbed by this and had said that any Muslim who would try to protect "infidels" deserved to die. If their demands weren't met, the terrorists claimed they would start killing more hostages.

The accents of the hijackers suggested they were Arabs, not Turks. The Saudi embassy had sent its ambassador to try to talk the terrorists into surrendering. Since most of the hostages were Americans or Europeans, ambassadors had also arrived from the U.S., British and West German embassies. Discovering that at least two of the terrorists spoke English, they had also tried to reason with the abductors. These efforts had had limited success. The IRF members had grudgingly admitted that the demands for Israel and the United States to withdraw military forces from Lebanon and the Persian Gulf were unrealistic. Expecting Turkey to break off relations with allies was even more absurd.

Although the terrorists had agreed to drop these demands, they had stubbornly insisted that their comrades be released from prisons throughout the world. They had refused to allow any of the hostages to leave the plane, but they had realized they couldn't stay on the runway with the improvised 747 prison in-definitely, so they had announced they wanted a pilot and enough fuel to fly to Iran.

Phoenix Force had arrived in Istanbul as these ne-gotiations were in progress. The prime minister had personally contacted General Yildiz at the airport and told him these five specialists from America had White House authority. The President of the United States had given them jurisdiction over all American intelli-gence personnel in Turkey, including the case officers of the CIA and NSA in Istanbul. Yildiz was to coop-erate fully with this mysterious team.

Now, as McCarter gazed out the window at the captive airplane, he asked, "We ready to move on these bastards?"

"Well," Gary Manning began as he turned away from a detailed diagram of the interior of a 747 air-liner, "Rafael and I are going to attach ourselves to the underside of the fuel tanker when they drive the truck out to the plane to deliver the additional fuel."

Manning explained this as calmly as one might dis-cuss the weather. The big Canadian's stoic nature and steel nerves were as useful as his uncanny ability as a demolitions expert and exceptional skill with a rifle. His rugged face seemed tranquil, but he knew the risks involved in his profession. Manning knew his life and many others were at stake.

"These IRF lunatics don't seem to be the brightest chaps we've ever come up against," McCarter com-mented as he examined the chart of the plane's construction. "But I reckon they're smart enough to expect us to try something like this. Since the plane is pretty much out in the open and far from the terminals, no one's been able to get close enough to carry out a raid."

"When the police retrieved the bodies of the dead Americans and the wounded pilot, they got closer than anyone else has," Yildiz explained in heavily accented English. "Major Ayvalik's paratroopers have established a ring of trained snipers and shock commandos ready to hit the plane if an opportunity occurs. So far the terrorists haven't made any mistakes."

"They made one," McCarter said with a wolfish grin. "They hung around here long enough for us to get here."

"I hope you know how to do more than boast, Englishman," an Istanbul police officer remarked bitterly. "You volunteered to play pilot, but those terrorists will kill you if they suspect this is a trick."

"I am a pilot," McCarter assured him. "And I actually do just about everything better than I can boast."

"He's still working on modesty," Rafael Encizo commented as he screwed a nine-inch silencer to the threaded barrel of a Walther P-88 pistol.

A handsome, muscular man in his early forties, Encizo was a tough Cuban who had survived the Bay of Pigs, Castro's prison and a hundred covert campaigns with the FBI and DEA before he had become a member of Phoenix Force. Now he slipped the pistol inside his white coveralls and pulled up the zipper.

"If the truck parks close to the plane when it fuels up the tanks," Encizo began, "we should be able to slip out from under it unnoticed and hide under the belly of the 747. But we won't be able to do anything else until the terrorists are preoccupied."

"I still question the wisdom of this attack on a plane loaded with civilians," the U.S. ambassador said, shaking his head with dismay. "Many of the passengers are American citizens. Most of the others are Europeans. It will be an enormous tragedy if this plan goes wrong and all these people are killed."

"Sometimes it's best to negotiate for a while," Encizo admitted, "but this isn't one of those times. The terrorists are ready to leave for Iran. They may or may not be allowed to land there. That would be up to the Iranians. If they allow the IRF gang to bring in the hostages, it'll be even more difficult to rescue them. Past experience shows us what can happen when Iran has hostages. We've got a better chance of dealing with this situation here and now."

"Better for you perhaps," the ambassador said grimly. "What about the hostages?"

"Their odds will be better, too," Manning assured him. The Canadian also attached a silencer to his Walther pistol and shoved it inside his coveralls.

"It'll be very crowded in the plane," an Istanbul cop commented. "A lot of innocent people are on board. A stray bullet could easily hit one of them, or a round could go through an opponent and strike an innocent bystander.''

''That risk is genuine, but we've reduced it as much as possible,'' Manning stated. ''That's why we're taking only semiauto handguns. They're not as indiscriminate as full-auto weapons. We're using subsonic 9 mm ammunition that will reduce the penetration of the round. Less chance of a bullet passing through one person to strike another. The silencers will also reduce velocity. Of course, this also cuts down on the effective force of the projectile when it hits a target. That's why we're using a variation of the Glaser Safety slug with the subsonic loads. The slug fragments on impact and close to a hundred percent of the energy is absorbed by the target. It produces nearly twice the stopping power effect of standard hollowpoint ammo.''

Calvin James walked from the hall to the terminal gate. With glasses and the gray dye at his temples, James appeared to be roughly ten years older than his true age. The tall black dude from Chicago joined the others and moved to a table. He opened a black medical bag and examined the contents. ''I can't have anything that looks suspicious,'' he remarked. ''They'll search this thing and frisk me for anything that might be a weapon or a listening device.''

''The radio transmitters you and your British friend wear can't be detected without special equipment,'' Yildiz assured him. ''Disguised as buttons on your jackets, they seem innocent enough. You know the frequency for these devices is very short-range."

"The range only needs to be adequate for us to hear them when we're under the plane," Manning told the general.

"What part of the plane did you decide to cut through to enter?" James asked the Canadian and Cuban warriors.

"The lavatories," Encizo answered as he pointed at the diagram. "A pair are located at the front, between the nose and wings. Two more are at the tail. We're going to try to get in at both front and back to cover the interior of the plane from both ends."

"I just hope nobody is in the rest room when one of us starts burning a hole through the floor," Manning added. "A screaming, panic-stricken passenger could wreck our operation and get a lot of people killed."

"So you admit something could go wrong with this plan?" the American ambassador demanded, his eyes wide with accusation.

"Any one of a hundred things could go wrong," James answered. "If somebody else has a better plan, please let us hear it. If somebody knows a way we can do this with less risk to the hostages or our lives, I'd sure like to know what it is."

"We might be able to stall them," a policeman suggested. "Hold off delivering the fuel and try to talk them into releasing hostages before giving them any assistance."

"They've already killed two captives and nearly killed the pilot," Manning reminded him. "The longer this takes, the greater the likelihood more will die."

"That's true," Yakov Katzenelenbogen, Phoenix's leader, announced as he appeared from the hall.

Katz was dressed in a robe and keffiyeh headdress. The Arab clothing was virtually identical to that worn by the Saudi ambassador who accompanied Katz. The Israeli also wore a pair of dark glasses and a black glove on his right "hand." The five-fingered steel prosthesis was less practical or functional than the three-hook device Katz favored, but the prosthesis better suited his role in the rescue plan.

"The sooner we hit them, the better for all involved," the Phoenix commander declared. "Except the terrorists, of course."

"You're going to try to impersonate a Saudi official?" General Yildiz asked with astonishment. "You'll be exposed the moment they speak to you in Arabic."

"No, he won't," the Saudi ambassador declared, and glanced at Katz. "This gentleman speaks fluent Arabic with a proper Cairo accent."

"Really?" the Turkish intel officer inquired as he raised an eyebrow. "Arabic as well as English and German?"

Katz nodded. He spoke six languages fluently and had a limited expertise in several others, but he wasn't apt to boast and even less inclined to give details about himself unless someone had a need to know.

"My Cairo accent may be a problem," Katz stated. "If the terrorists notice I don't sound like a Saudi, I'll have to tell them I'm originally from Egypt and became a Saudi citizen after family members were killed in the Six Day War and I was injured."

The Israeli raised the prosthesis attached to the stump of his right arm. "I'll tell them that's how I got this," he added. He didn't mention that he really had lost the arm in the Six Day War when he was an officer in the Israeli army. "Hopefully they'll believe me and accept the story if I say my only living relatives were in Saudi Arabia and I've been living there since the mid-sixties."

"That's another risk," Yildiz said with a frown.

"One that puts me in jeopardy, but not the hostages," the Phoenix commander explained. "That makes it more acceptable than others. There's no way we can exclude imperilment for the hostages, but they're already in a precarious situation."

"Well, they demanded a pilot and agreed to let a doctor come aboard to check on the hostages," McCarter said. "They didn't say anything about letting a Saudi representative onto the plane."

"Hopefully they won't object," Katz said. "None of the three of us will be armed. We can all play our roles convincingly and we shouldn't seem threatening. Of course, these terrorists are suspicious and paranoid. It won't take much to set them off."

"We received a telephone call from the hospital," General Yildiz declared. "Captain Elekdag, the pilot, has recovered consciousness. He's a tough character. The doctors say he'll pull through.''

"That's good news,'' Manning remarked with a nod. "The captain's a brave man.''

"He also told my agent at the hospital some details about the terrorists,'' the general added. "There are seven of them. All male and young. Mid-twenties to early thirties. At least two of them have submachine guns. The others are armed with pistols. Elekdag thinks all seven are carrying at least one hand grenade each.''

"My God,'' the U.S. ambassador rasped.

"You might pray to Him while we're headed for the plane,'' Encizo suggested. He turned to Manning and said, "Let's do it.''

2

The tanker truck parked alongside the airliner. While genuine airport workers pumped gallons of fuel into the 747, faces peered from windows to watch them. The terrorists' features were concealed by cloth masks across noses and mouths. They wore caps and only their eyes were visible. The night was broken by the bright glare of floodlights surrounding the runway. The hijackers clearly saw the men outside the airplane but not the two figures that crawled from under the truck.

Rafael Encizo and Gary Manning had attached themselves to the frame of the truck by leather loops fixed to the bars for wrists and ankles. The commandos slipped loose and crawled from the truck to the plane. They moved under the fuselage of the 747 as the airport employees continued to feed fuel into the airliner.

The Phoenix pair carried compact blowtorches on their belts and radio receivers with earphones. They remained beneath the plane and waited tensely as the truck began to pull away. The commandos stayed out of view from the windows of the 747 and hoped the terrorists wouldn't send one of their comrades outside to check under the aircraft.

As the vehicle departed, three figures walked from the terminal to the runway. McCarter, James and Katz marched to the captive 747. The floodlights cast distorted shadows across the pavement. The glare seemed to oscillate around the outlines of the three men to create an unearthly appearance, as if a trio of space aliens were headed toward the plane.

The door at the nose of the plane opened. A masked figure dressed in a checkered shirt and denim jeans leaned through the opening and pointed a Soviet-made PPS-41 submachine gun at the approaching figures. He shouted something in Turkish, and Katz replied in rapid Arabic.

"Your friend claims you speak English," the terrorist declared. He was obviously addressing McCarter and James. "What are you?"

"What are we?" McCarter replied. "Take a look at this British Airways uniform. You figure that means I'm a hotel doorman?"

James jabbed the Briton in the ribs with an elbow. McCarter tended to wag his sarcastic tongue too freely. He needed a reminder that he was playing the role of a civilian pilot and ought to tone down his usual flippant remarks. The British ace grunted. He knew what James was trying to express, but McCarter figured it wouldn't be out of character for a pilot, even a civilian, to present haughty behavior if he was the sort to volunteer to fly a plane held by terrorists.

"I'm Dr. John Kilroy," Calvin James announced quickly, trying to cut off McCarter before the Briton's smart-aleck act convinced the hijacker to open fire. "I'm an American employed by the United States embassy."

The hijacker turned his attention to Katz once more and addressed him in Arabic. "Why are you here?"

"I was sent to speak with your group about the demands you've made concerning political prisoners held in the Middle East," Katz replied in the same language. "I can also serve as a translator if necessary."

"Wait here and stay exactly where you are," the terrorist instructed. "Don't move forward or try to go back. We'll shoot you all if anyone moves."

He vanished within the plane. Katz glanced under the craft. Encizo and Manning crouched in their hiding place and nodded at the Israeli. Katz lowered his head and spoke softly into the receiver button on the shirt beneath his robe. "Nod twice if you can hear me," he whispered.

Manning and Encizo responded as requested.

Another masked figure appeared at the door of the plane. He wore a tan leather jacket, and the butt of a pistol jutted from his belt. A black cap covered the top of his head and a green scarf concealed his lower features. The eyes above the mask seemed as cold as black diamonds. He pushed a rope ladder from the threshold and it dangled to the ground.

"Climb up," the terrorist ordered in English.

Katz scaled the rungs of the ladder. The terrorist waited for him at the door and offered a hand to haul him inside. Katz extended the gloved prosthesis. The hijacker grasped the artificial hand and immediately released it and pulled away. Katz climbed up to the threshold without the man's assistance.

"What's that thing?" the terrorist asked, eyes fixed on the prosthesis.

"A war souvenir," Katz answered. "Are you in charge here?"

"Yes," the man with the green mask confirmed, "you may call me Ali. Move to the wall and place your hands on it, over your head."

Katz followed instructions and faced the wall, arms raised and feet shoulder-width apart. Another hijacker frisked him. The man pulled off the keffiyeh and pulled down the sleeves of his robe. The terrorist examined the prosthesis with interest and unbuckled the straps to the leather sleeve of the plastic-and-steel limb. He gasped when the prosthesis came loose.

"Satisfied?" Katz inquired in Arabic as he waved the stump of his abbreviated arm.

The man seemed embarrassed and returned the prosthesis. Katz slipped it onto the end of his right arm. The terrorist offered to help him with the straps and buckles, but Katz shook his head. He attached the device to the stump with ease. Katz had been an amputee for more than two and a half decades, so he was accustomed to putting on the prosthesis by himself.

McCarter and James also climbed the ladder to enter the plane. The terrorists were less considerate with the younger men. They shoved them into a wall and held guns to their skulls as they frisked the pair. The search was expert. The terrorists were familiar with carrying concealed weapons and checked for ankle holsters, sleeve guns, neck pouch weapons, the small of the back and crotch as they patted down the commandos.

"I thought you wanted me to fly the bloody plane," McCarter commented. "You blokes are acting more like you expect me to entertain you in the shower room."

"What's that supposed to mean?" a confused terrorist demanded.

"He's just babbling," James told the man. He was glad the hijacker didn't understand the implications of McCarter's comments and didn't intend to explain them.

The IRF goon dressed in a checkered shirt opened James's medical bag. He found a stethoscope, blood pressure gauge, bandages and other items that didn't worry the terrorist. However, he grunted when he discovered some hypodermic syringes and scalpels.

"These could be used as weapons," the man announced.

"Oh, yeah?" James scoffed. "I'm gonna try to cut and stab you guys when you're packing all those guns?

Gimme a break, man. Hold on to the damn bag if you're worried about that. If I need anything to treat injured passengers, I'll ask for it and you can hand me what I need. Fair enough?''

"All right," Ali said, and nodded at the man in the checkered shirt. He turned to a wiry terrorist clad in a green windbreaker. "Take the Englishman to the cockpit. If he isn't a real pilot and can't fly the plane, bring him out so we can get him off the plane."

Ali didn't say whether McCarter would be alive or dead when ejected from the craft. He didn't have to.

"May I see the passengers now?" James asked the terrorist leader.

"They've been humanely treated," Ali declared. "We only struck those who tried to resist us and we didn't use more force than necessary."

"Uh-huh," James said with a nod. He remembered how "humanely" the hijackers had shot the two American servicemen earlier. "Well, if all we have are some minor cuts and bruises, I can examine the passengers and go back and report to the embassy."

"And you'll tell them we're not savages, but soldiers in a war for the liberation of our people?" Ali asked, an eyebrow cocked above a challenging dark eye.

"I'll tell them the condition of the hostages...I mean, the folks on the plane," James answered. "If you want me to deliver any other messages, I guess I can do that, too. Write 'em down if you got a lot of them so I don't forget anything."

"We'll see," the IRF ringleader told him. He gestured for two terrorists to accompany James and turned back to Katz. "Since you're from Saudi Arabia, I assume you're a Sunni Muslim. We're Shiites."

"I didn't come here to discuss religious conflicts within Islam," Katz explained. "The ambassador wants to understand your demands well enough to relay the information to his superiors. Perhaps some of these are negotiable and my country may agree to support them if they don't seem beyond reason."

"What is unreasonable about wanting our people released from prisons?" Ali demanded.

"I didn't say it was unreasonable," Katz assured him. "My opinion in this matter isn't important. I don't make decisions about Saudi politics. I'm a very low-level diplomat and my greatest worth consists of knowing my limitations. It isn't my place to agree or disagree with you. My only duty is to return with a clear grasp of what your organization wants."

"Very well," Ali announced. "Let's talk. Please follow me."

Ali mounted a stairwell to the upper lounge in the first-class section at the front of the plane. This part of the plane was a luxury for wealthy travelers only. Ali marched among the leather-backed sofas to the small galley bar. Katz guessed beneath his mask that Ali was smiling. He seemed pleased with his conquest.

Another IRF gunman followed behind Katz as the Israeli moved to a sofa and took a seat. Ali's bodyguard was a large man dressed in a military field jacket and armed with a French MAT-49 submachine gun. Two Soviet-made F-1 hand grenades were visible on the terrorist's belt.

"Listen well, my Saudi friend," Ali began as he poured some coffee into a plastic cup. "I don't want to repeat myself."

McCARTER STEPPED into the cockpit, accompanied by the IRF guard. The Briton removed his cap and tossed it into the first officer's seat as he examined the array of gauges, altimeters, indicators and other instruments. He leaned forward and pressed a switch in the center of the control panel.

"What are you doing?" the terrorist demanded in broken English. He pointed a blue-black pistol at McCarter's head.

"Checking the computer display unit," the British ace answered as he glanced over his shoulder and saw the muzzle of the gun inches from his ear. "Get that thing out of my face. It makes me nervous."

"You have reason to be nervous, English," the goon sneered.

"I don't need to be reminded of that, mate," McCarter muttered, and studied the rows of altimeters at the pilot's seat. "You know, there are two seats here because that's usually how many blokes fly one of these big metal birds. It's going to be hard enough for me to handle this entirely solo. I don't need you waving that damn gun around."

McCarter turned a knob near the top of the instrument panel at the pilot's seat. The terrorist again asked what he was doing. The commando rolled his eyes and uttered a weary sigh.

"Checking the navigational radio," he answered. "There's a lot involved with handling a 747. I can't keep taking time from my work to explain everything I have to do."

"We don't fly until the Saudi and the black one leave the plane," the terrorist stated.

"We don't fly at all if the vertical speed indicator doesn't work. Or if there are any problems with the radar altimeter, manual stabilizer, weather radar, horizontal direction indicator and about two dozen other instruments I'm checking out."

"Even if some of those things don't work, we'll fly," the guard insisted.

"Bloody wonderful," McCarter snorted. "We could clear this runway and get a couple of hundred feet in the sky and smash into a DC-10 in a cloud bank if the radar and radios aren't working. This is an international airport, not a little airstrip out in the plains. Planes are coming in and going out constantly. One mistake and we'll all be bloodied scraps mixed in with burning wreckage from a collision with another aircraft."

The terrorist considered the Briton's remarks as he watched McCarter climb into the pilot's seat. The Phoenix pro worked the control yoke and grunted as if less than satisfied. The guard leaned forward, concerned that something bothered the Englishman. The man seemed to know what he was doing, and the terrorist didn't want any flaws in the baffling controls of the 747 to cause an accident that could cost all their lives.

"Maybe it's okay," the Briton remarked. "Maybe it isn't."

"What's wrong?" the terrorist asked urgently.

McCarter glanced over his shoulder. There was no one at the entrance to the cockpit. He also glimpsed the pistol still in the IRF flunky's fist. It was an American Colt Government Model—a single-action, semiauto pistol. The hammer was set at full-cock and the safety was in the off position.

"We might have a couple of problems here," McCarter said grimly, and glanced up at the overhead switch panel. "Turn on the speed mode selector, will you?"

The terrorist looked up at the instruments and started to raise a hand, although he wasn't certain which switch to touch. McCarter turned and took advantage of the distraction. His hands shot out. The Briton grabbed the Colt and jammed his thumb between the hammer and firing pin. With his other hand he swung high to deliver a backfist to the gunman's face.

McCarter's attack caught the terrorist off guard. He grunted from the blow and squeezed the trigger of his Colt. The hammer pinched McCarter's thumb, but didn't hit the firing pin. The IRF thug didn't understand why the pistol failed to fire. McCarter chopped his fist across the man's wrist to jar the Colt from numb fingers. The Briton immediately followed the stroke with an elbow smash to his opponent's breast-bone.

The terrorist tried to wrap his left arm around McCarter's neck, but the Phoenix fighter slammed another elbow stroke to the man's jaw. The hijacker started to sag as McCarter rose from the pilot's seat. He shoved his dazed opponent into the first officer's seat, then hammered his fist into the goon's sternum and slammed another punch to the guy's jaw. The terrorist slumped across the copilot's seat.

McCarter raised his hand and prepared to deliver another blow. The man was already unconscious, but the Phoenix commando couldn't risk the chance the opponent might regain his senses before the raid was completed. McCarter could kill the hijacker with a final well-placed stroke to a vital spot. However, he chose to chop the guy across the side of the neck with moderate force to make certain the fellow wouldn't regain consciousness for a while.

If the situation had been reversed, the terrorist wouldn't have spared McCarter's life. The men of Phoenix Force weren't murderers. It wasn't necessary to kill the man. McCarter removed his dark blue necktie and used it to bind the senseless opponent's wrists to the post of the yoke controls by the copilot's seat. He used the terrorist's own scarf mask to gag the flunky.

"Hope you can hear me," McCarter said into his button microphone as he finished securing the unconscious man. "One bastard down. I'll leave the cockpit in thirty seconds. Everybody better be ready."

The Briton wished he had a receiver unit so Encizo and Manning could tell him their status or at least let him know they had gotten the message. McCarter trusted his fellow Phoenix warriors with his life, but he didn't have unfettered faith in technological gizmos.

McCarter checked the terrorist's pistol. The hammer was at half-cock from the Briton's jamming action during the struggle. He thumbed it back to full-cock and pressed on the safety. The Briton removed the magazine from the buttwell. It was loaded with six rounds of copper-jacketed ammo. Probably 230-grain, McCarter guessed. The .45 Colt was a big gun with plenty of knockdown.

He returned the magazine to the butt and jacked a shell into the chamber. McCarter put the safety on and slid the Colt into his belt at the small of his back. The pilot's jacket concealed the weapon. He frisked the unconscious terrorist and found two hand grenades and three spare magazines for the .45 pistol. McCarter pocketed the weapons and glanced at his watch. It was time to go.

THE HOSTAGES had been corralled into the business-class section in the center of the plane. Restricting the hostages there was convenient for the terrorists. Guards were posted at the front and rear of the aisle.

The terrorist assigned to watch Calvin James stood in the center of the aisle while the black commando examined a hostage who had been pistol-whipped. The captive passengers huddled silently in their seats. Several had been beaten by the terrorists. Few seemed to have much defiance left. They were tourists and businessmen, not soldiers. Many of the hostages were dressed in expensive suits and had probably been seated in first class before the IRF hijackers had rearranged seating aboard the plane.

As James attended to the bruised and battered passengers, some asked questions about what was going on outside the plane. The gunman guarding James told them only to speak to the doctor about physical ailments. James didn't volunteer any information. His guard was already suspicious, and the Chicago badass couldn't risk doing anything that might convince the guy to haul him back to Ali for interrogation or possibly shoot him outright.

James applied some disinfectant to the cuts on the brutalized passenger's face and suggested the man put some ice on the bruises to reduce the swelling. He glanced up and saw McCarter approach from the nose of the plane. An IRF gunman stepped into the Briton's path and pointed a submachine gun at his chest.

"I wish you people would stop poking about with those bloody firearms," McCarter complained. "Do you speak English?"

"I do," the terrorist assigned to accompany James replied. "What are you doing here? You're supposed to be preparing to fly the plane."

"That's why I'm here," McCarter answered. "I studied the flight log and maintenance records on this bird. There's a problem with the explosive bolts to one of the emergency exit doors."

"Explosive bolts?" the confused terrorist asked. "I don't understand."

"The explosive bolts are supposed to blast the exit doors open in certain types of emergencies," the Briton explained. He hoped the gunman didn't know enough about commercial aircraft to realize McCarter was deceiving him. "If the plane goes down at sea or there's a fire on board, the bolts can be activated. You understand?"

"I think so," the IRF follower said. "What sort of problem is connected with these explosive bolts?"

"The damn things malfunctioned in Ankara four days ago and haven't been replaced," McCarter lied smoothly. "I don't know what's wrong with these Turks. You'd think they'd realize something like this is a serious hazard. Bloody bolts could go at any time. Everybody could be sucked right out the door if the damn thing bursts at twenty thousand feet."

"Sort of like in the movie *Goldfinger?*" James inquired.

McCarter grunted and rolled his eyes toward the ceiling. The four terrorists in the aisle conversed briefly in rapid Arabic. McCarter had learned some

Arabic when he was stationed in Oman with the SAS, but he could understand little of the discussion. The hijackers who didn't understand English wanted to know what was going on and the fellow McCarter had told about the bogus equipment hazard answered them.

The explosion startled terrorists and hostages alike. The blast sounded like an oversize firecracker. An emergency exit door suddenly popped loose and fell away from the body of the plane. Hostages cried out in alarm. Some ducked low and others started to rise from their seats in panic.

James immediately jumped the distracted terrorist assigned to guard him. The black commando's arm flashed and the side of his hand chopped the IRF stooge across the wrist. The blow struck the subgun from the terrorist's hand. The Phoenix pro slashed his arm in a sideways arch and swung another chop at the man's throat.

The hijacker still held the medical bag in his other hand and raised it to block James's attack. The Phoenix fighter's hand chopped the leather case, and the terrorist rammed a shoulder into the black commando's chest. The blow staggered James and knocked him backward into the lap of a startled hostage.

"Excuse me," he growled without looking at the passenger. He gripped the backrest of the seat in front and pulled.

James sprang from the man's lap and jumped back to the aisle. The terrorist had dropped the bag and pulled a grenade from his belt. James swiftly snap-kicked him in the groin. The toe of his shoe connected with the man's genitals, and the terrorist groaned and began to double up but still tried to reach for the pin to the grenade.

James hammered both fists into his opponent's forearms to prevent him from yanking the pin from the grenade. Then he rammed an uppercut into the hijacker's solar plexus and grabbed the wrist above the grenade. The black tough guy swung his elbow high to clip the front of the elbow under his opponent's jaw. The terrorist's head recoiled from the blow, and James quickly grabbed the fist that still held the grenade.

The black Phoenix commando jammed his thumbs into the ulna nerve at the back of the man's hand as he twisted the hijacker's arm. Fingers opened and the grenade fell to the floor. The dazed terrorist's free hand reached for the second grenade in his belt. James swung a high kick and slammed the heel of his shoe into his opponent's mouth. The man fell into the armrest of a seat and toppled across the lap of a passenger. The hostage gasped and stared down at the terrorist's bloodied, unconscious face.

McCarter also made his move against the terrorist who had accompanied him to the business section. He swept his left forearm under the barrel and frame of his opponent's submachine gun to shove the muzzle to the ceiling. The hijacker triggered his weapon and blasted a short burst into the metal skin of the plane. The shots roared within the confines of the plane and hostages screamed in terror. McCarter ignored everything except his opponent as his right hand emerged from the small of his back with the Colt .45 pistol in his fist.

There were too many innocent lives at stake to take any chances. McCarter thrust the barrel of the Colt into the thug's chest and opened fire. He shot the man through the heart and quickly jammed the muzzle of the big Colt under the guy's chin and fired once more to make certain the terrorist was dead. Since the hijacker still held the submachine gun, McCarter had to shut down the man's brain to prevent a muscle reflex from triggering the chopper before he could take it from the dead man's grasp.

"Oh, my God!" a hostage cried out as he saw blood and brain tissue splatter the ceiling of the plane.

"Sorry about the mess," McCarter muttered as he grabbed the slain terrorist's weapon and allowed the corpse to sink to the floor.

GARY MANNING HAD SET a small charge at the exit door outside the plane. The CV-38 plastic explosive was equipped with a radio detonator. The Canadian demolitions expert didn't trigger the remote control to set off the explosives until he and Encizo had cut holes in the belly of the plane with their blowtorches. After both men climbed through the holes to enter the lavatories at the front and rear of the 747, Manning pressed the button.

The explosion was the signal for Phoenix Force to act. Manning trusted his three teammates within the plane to do their part. He opened the door to the rest room and stepped into the aisle, Walther P-88 in his fist. The Canadian warrior moved behind the terrorist guard posted at the front of the aisle as James and McCarter were taking out their opponents. The guard started to point his weapon at the combatants but hesitated, afraid of hitting his own comrades.

Manning did what he had to under the circumstances. He pointed the silencer-equipped pistol at the back of the terrorist's skull and squeezed the trigger. The Walther rasped harshly, and a 9 mm slug crashed through bone and burrowed into the brain of the enemy. The guard fell to the floor.

Manning stepped over the corpse and saw that James and McCarter had already dispatched their opponents. At the end of the aisle Rafael Encizo stood over the body of the guard who had been posted there. The Cuban had entered from the lavatory at the rear of the plane and dealt with his target in the necessary manner. Encizo held his Walther in one fist as smoke curled from the muzzle of the silencer.

"Stay in your seats and keep down!" Manning shouted at the passengers. He repeated the order in French and German to make certain they all understood.

In the upper lounge above the first-class section Ali and his terrorist bodyguard heard the explosion and gunshots and turned from Katz. The Phoenix Force commander rose from his seat and quickly thrust his prosthetic toward the heavily armed guard.

Flame jetted from the tip of the gloved index finger. An explosion with a loud crack filled the lounge as a .22 Magnum round blasted through the bridge of the terrorist's nose, pierced the man's brain and punched out the back of his skull. The fellow's head bobbed forward as his subgun dropped. The terrorist slumped against the post at the head of the stairwell. His body tumbled over the edge and rolled awkwardly down the metal risers.

Ali was stunned by the unexpected attack. He cursed himself for not suspecting a weapon might be built into the "Saudi's" artificial limb. Furious, the terrorist leader reached for the pistol in his belt as Katz charged, but the Israeli's prosthesis smashed into his chest and knocked him against the backrest of a sofa, winding him. Then, when Ali grabbed for a grenade in his belt, Katz stepped closer and swung the prosthesis, chopping the steel extremity between the terrorist's neck and shoulder and snapping the collarbone.

Crying out in pain, Ali still managed to draw his pistol with his right hand.

Katz grabbed the hijacker's wrist and pushed down as the fanatic squeezed the trigger. A shot roared and Ali shrieked as hot agony jolted through his left thigh to fill his groin and spine with fire. The terrorist had shot himself in the leg. Katz slapped the steel palm of his prosthesis against the side of Ali's head. The man sighed as if relieved to surrender consciousness.

Calvin James mounted the stairwell to the lounge, a confiscated pistol in his fist. The black warrior found Katz disarming the senseless terrorist ringleader. James stuck his weapon into his belt as he approached.

"You okay?" he inquired.

"Fine," Katz assured him. The Israeli tossed Ali's pistol and grenades onto a sofa. "How did it go downstairs?"

"Our guys didn't get a scratch and none of the hostages were hurt," James answered. "We had to kill most of the terrorists, but we managed to take a couple of 'em alive."

"Good," Katz said with a nod. He glanced at the bloodied, broken figure of Ali on the couch. "This man could use some medical care. We don't want him to bleed to death before the Turkish authorities take him off our hands."

"Yeah," James agreed as he opened the medical bag. "We can afford to show a little mercy now. More than he would have shown us."

"That's one of the ways we're different from men like this," Katz said, casting a brief glimpse at Ali. "Thank God."

3

"I'd tell you guys you did a great job handling that skyjacking in Istanbul," Hal Brognola began as he placed a stack of folders on the table, "but I don't want to give you all swollen heads."

Phoenix Force sat at the conference table in the Stony Man Farm war room. The five-commando unit was part of the enforcement arm of Stony Man. The ultrasecret organization consisted of a small dedicated group of professionals who handled the most difficult missions against international terrorism, criminal syndicates, destructive conspiracies and other threats to freedom in general and the United States in particular.

Brognola was the chief of operations for Stony Man. His only superior was the President himself. The highest-ranking federal officer in America, Brognola had access to information from virtually all U.S. intelligence organizations, although his own status in the government was as well guarded as Stony Man itself.

"We can't take full credit for the raid," Katz said with typical modesty. "General Yildiz, the Turkish military, the Saudi ambassador and others cooperated with us. It would have been far more difficult, if not impossible, to accomplish the mission without their assistance."

"The President figures you guys saved the day and asked me to pass on his personal congratulations and thanks," Brognola told them. "I met with the man in the Oval Office about an hour ago."

"Oh, boy," Calvin James said with a sigh. "That means he called you to the White House and it wasn't for a social visit. He gave you another mission for us. Right?"

"I know you guys could use some R and R," the head Fed said, giving Phoenix Force a sympathetic smile. "Your last major assignment was only two months ago, and handling hijackers in Istanbul isn't exactly a vacation even if you did wrap it up in less than twenty-four hours."

"But the President has a problem and we're the only people who can do the job," Gary Manning said dryly. "Sometimes I wonder if we don't do our job a little too well."

"In our line of work you're either very good or very dead," Rafael Encizo remarked. "So what does the President want us to do?"

"The whole world knows there have been some remarkable changes in Poland and all of Eastern Europe since 1989," Brognola began. "Communist regimes have folded and Poland is one of the most dramatic examples. Five years ago, who would have believed Poland would have free elections after forty years of communism?"

"Or that the once-outlawed Solidarity movement would be in control of Poland," Katz added. "An East European Communist country becoming a democracy would have seemed impossible five years ago. However, I assume we're not discussing Poland because everything is going so well there."

"For almost a month there's been an alarming increase in drug-related crime in Poland," Brognola began as he opened the top folder. "A number of robberies and assaults appear to be linked to addicts after money to support their habit. Three days ago six students from the University of Warsaw were found in an apartment rented by two of the kids. They were all dead. Autopsy reports claim the cause of death was arsenic poisoning. Somehow it got mixed in with the cocaine they were snorting. The Warsaw cops found a bag of coke laced with arsenic in the room."

"Drugs are a problem all over the world," James remarked.

"Communist countries haven't had any major problems with narcotics," the Fed explained. "That's one form of free enterprise Poland doesn't want. The situation gets worse, guys. An American businessman named Peter Henderson was in Warsaw to meet with Polish industrialists concerning a trade agreement with his corporation. Henderson's outfit figured they might be able to import cement cheaper than producing it in the U.S. That's not important. What matters is a maid at the Intercontinental Hotel went into Henderson's room to change the sheets and found him sprawled on the floor, dead. A little mirror with a razor blade and white powder was on the night table by his bed.''

"I reckon it was cocaine and not talcum powder," McCarter said dryly as he got out a pack of Player's cigarettes.

"Arsenic-flavored coke at that," the Fed confirmed. "That's not all. The cops also found nearly ten kilos of cocaine in Henderson's luggage and twenty-five thousand zloty stuffed in a cardboard box. Zloty is the main currency in Poland. Maybe you guys knew that, but I sure as hell didn't."

"So this low-level businessman was supposed to be a dope dealer who was a victim of his own tainted drugs," Encizo commented thoughtfully. "Did Henderson have a criminal record?"

"Not unless you include parking tickets," Brognola answered. "The Justice Department and the FBI checked Henderson's background and couldn't find anything more sinister than a divorce when the guy was in his twenties. No drugs, alcoholism, wife abuse or anything to suggest Henderson was anything less than a pretty decent guy. His second wife—now his widow—was astonished to hear her husband had supposedly died from taking drugs. She's outraged by the claim he may have been a dope pusher."

"Family members don't like to think their loved ones might be less than good and noble," Manning said with a frown. "Still, this does sound pretty odd. Henderson's background doesn't fit the pattern for an international drug dealer."

"Criminals don't always fit patterns," James reminded him. The black former police officer had a special hatred toward drugs and pushers. "But I agree it sounds pretty screwy. I'm not up on Polish money. How much is a slutty worth?"

"Zloty," Brognola corrected. "And it's about eighty zlotys to one American dollar."

"Eighty?" James asked, raising his eyebrows. "So they found twenty-five thousand zlotys in Henderson's room, and that's supposed to suggest he was making a fortune selling cocaine to college kids? This dude was allegedly smuggling dope into Poland and selling the shit so he could make less than four hundred bucks?"

"Three hundred and twelve dollars and fifty cents to be exact," the Fed replied. "Maybe that's a lot of money in Poland. I don't know what the average income is for Polish citizens."

"Approximately four thousand dollars a year," Katz stated. Brognola stared at him with surprise. The Israeli shrugged and added, "I read it in a magazine article a while back."

"Okay," Brognola said with a nod. "The point is, three hundred and twelve bucks isn't much money by American standards. Cal's right. It seems damn unlikely Henderson or anybody else would be smuggling dope and selling it for that kind of chicken-feed profit."

"So the poor guy was probably set up and murdered," Encizo remarked. "Unless he had a couple of million zloty stashed away somewhere the cops haven't found so far."

"Nasty business," McCarter admitted, blowing smoke through his nostrils. "But not the sort of thing Phoenix Force handles. Sounds like it's strictly a police matter. Warsaw police, maybe Interpol, ought to deal with it."

"The President sees this differently," Brognola declared, consulting another file report. "Certain members of the Polish parliament—I'm not even gonna try to pronounce it—are already demanding their country ban Americans from their soil. They seem to think these incidents are proof of some sort of conspiracy by the United States to undermine their nation by corrupting Polish youth with drugs."

"And why would the U.S. want to do that?" Manning asked, amused by the absurdity of this idea. "Poland's a democracy now. The United States and other Western nations couldn't be happier about that."

"Poland is still a very new democracy," the Fed answered. "Solidarity candidates won the vast majority of seats in the elections of June 1989, but there are still Communist party members in a few seats in the parliament. Those Commies don't like Americans, and a lot of Poles probably still distrust Uncle

Sam. A lot of Europeans are suspicious of the United States, especially now that the Soviet Union seems to have been knocked out of the superpower ring. What worries the President about Poland is it's currently sort of a blend of democracy and socialism. It's already discovered that democratic reforms aren't going to solve economic woes overnight. There's still strong support for Marxism among many Poles, and communism could be revitalized if people start associating increased crime with capitalism."

"Whatever else one can say about Communists," Encizo said, a truculent trace of bitterness in his tone, "they do believe in law and order...unless you count the crimes committed by the government itself."

The Cuban's experience in his homeland had been a harsh lesson about the realities of communism. Most of his family had been slaughtered by Castro's troops, and Encizo himself had been beaten and tortured while a political prisoner in El Principe.

"After forty years of oppression under communism," Katz remarked, "I doubt Poland would volunteer to have that form of government again. Nonetheless, I see the President's point from a different angle. America's relations with Europe are of vital interest to this country and the nations of that continent. Most Poles will realize the idea that the U.S. government would deliberately try to infest Poland with drugs is absurd, but many may question whether it's safe to allow U.S. citizens into their country for fear they might be syndicate drug smugglers or free-lance narcotics traders.''

"Henderson was probably murdered, and whoever did it may have selected him simply because he was an American businessman,'' Manning added. "If they set up one American to be the dead fall guy for drug-related deaths, they can do it to others.''

"I still say the police and Interpol should deal with this sort of thing,'' McCarter said with a sigh. "Criminal investigation isn't our bleedin' field, Hal. You know that.''

"The President wants the best people possible for this mission,'' Brognola insisted. "That's you guys. The reports on this case are still incomplete. You can go to Warsaw, check it out firsthand and, if you decide there's nothing you can do the authorities already involved can't do just as well, then, hell, you let me know and take a holiday in Europe for a week or so.''

"That sounds okay to me,'' James announced. "Phoenix Force has carried out missions in about a dozen European countries and we've never really had a chance to enjoy any of those trips.''

"I always did,'' McCarter said with a shrug.

"Yeah,'' Manning muttered. "But the rest of us don't like being shot at. When do we leave for Poland?''

4

Stanislaw Rzewuski turned to avoid looking at Pierre Gautier and Philippe Vaché. He considered the Corsicans unprincipled, loathsome gangsters. Rzewuski didn't like being forced to work with such trash, but Zablocki had told him it was necessary to do business with the Corsicans, and Rzewuski trusted the former Sejm official.

Thirty-two years old and athletically trim, Rzewuski remained as efficient a fighting machine as he had been when he served in the Sixth Pomorska Airborne Division. A sleek, cunning man with a deceptively bland face and polite manners, Rzewuski had been recruited into the Polish Security Service when he was twenty-five. His intelligence, aptitude for languages and deciphering codes, skill with weapons and total dedication to the Communist party had made him an ideal choice for espionage work.

Indeed, Rzewuski's loyalty had always been to the party rather than his country. He was a product of a family of dedicated Communists and an education that had drilled in the belief that the struggle for socialist unity for all people was the most noble cause on earth. Young Rzewuski had studied the works of Marx, Engels and Lenin with the intense devotion of a religious zealot.

When General Jaruzelski imposed martial law to repress Solidarity, Rzewuski had infiltrated the trade union to gather intelligence about the leaders of the movement. He was proud of the fact that he had personally presented information about union activities that had helped the government justify the arrest of Lech Walesa and many other prominent Solidarity members. Rzewuski was praised for his "patriotism" and promoted to case officer.

Then things had started to change. The Communist party had actually disciplined forty-five thousand members of its own party for their efforts to restrain the Solidarity movement. Martial law was lifted, and Walesa and others were released from prison. To Rzewuski this was nothing short of treason. Horrified, he had watched the party buckle and surrender to more and more demands. Communism, his creed since childhood, was slowly coming apart at the seams.

Now the once outlawed Solidarity union had taken control of Poland and the former renegade Walesa was regarded as a national hero. Rzewuski was stunned that the men he considered traitors now ruled his country. It seemed everything Rzewuski believed in had been dashed to the ground and shattered.

He felt as if the situation was hopeless. Eastern Europe and even the Soviet Union had surrendered to the enemy. They had lost faith in the goals of communism as taught by Karl Marx. These nations had been seduced by what Rzewuski regarded as the short-term advantages of capitalism.

However, Colonel Durnov and Zbignew Zablocki had contacted Rzewuski and recruited him for Mácka. The Polish intelligence agent had met Durnov in the early 1980s, although the Soviet officer was known by a different name at the time. As an agent in the KGB's Eleventh Department, Durnov had been an "adviser" to the Polish Security Service. Such Russian operatives were known as "uncles" by East European intel personnel. Sometimes they were referred to as "perfumed uncles" due to the habit many dedicated Soviet Communists had of using liberal doses of perfume. This was supposed to suggest they labored so hard for the party they didn't have time to bathe.

Rzewuski was eager to join Mácka, although Durnov's plan to regain power for communism was ruthless and would require harming and killing many innocent people. Yet Rzewuski doubted anyone was truly innocent. Those of the West were part of the capitalist system and those of the East had become coconspirators with the enemy. Since Rzewuski had no living family, his only sense of duty was to the party, and now to Mácka.

Nonetheless, Rzewuski hadn't anticipated working with Corsican gangsters. Gautier and Vaché were ironic partners in Mácka's battle against the blight of democracy in Eastern Europe. The Polish agent sat at the old, scarred desk in the drab office of the warehouse. He still wore his topcoat due to the cold draft. The Corsicans remained close to the wood-burning stove and Rzewuski didn't want to get closer to the pair even if that meant he couldn't enjoy the warmth of the stove.

Pierre Gautier felt the Communist agent's contempt. That didn't disturb the stocky Corsican hoodlum. A smile tugged at Gautier's wide lips, and his small, dark eyes glittered with amusement. Rzewuski, Zablocki and the other Polish Marxists were such hypocrites. They considered the Corsican Union to be immoral trash, yet they had hired Gautier's mob to help them kill their fellow countrymen and wreck the lives of hundreds of other Poles by introducing them to narcotics.

At least the Corsicans were honest about their motives. They were interested only in money and the luxuries that accompanied wealth. The Communists claimed their reasons for their actions were noble goals that required hideous methods to accomplish. Gautier doubted any of them would be upset with the democratic reforms in Poland if they could have maintained their previous positions of power and privilege.

Philippe Vaché sat on a crate near the stove and picked his fingernails with the steel point of an ice pick. A tall, slender, bald man, Vaché was Gautier's lieutenant. He had earned a fearsome reputation as a mob assassin. Vaché generally kept his thoughts to himself and seldom spoke unless required to do so. He didn't care what the Poles thought of the Corsican syndicate or what torment their activities might bring to Poland.

Vaché wasn't even particularly interested in the profits the mob would make through its alliance with the Communist league. He worked for Gautier because he enjoyed it. Vaché was a sadist and found great pleasure in inflicting pain and death. The ice pick was his favorite tool for torture and murder. Vaché was a freak who could never fit into civilized society. If he hadn't belonged to the Corsican Union, he would have surely become a deranged serial killer and murdered random victims for recreation.

However, like many sociopaths, Vaché was very intelligent and possessed a high degree of cunning and survival instincts. Vaché was a valuable adviser and security chief because he had a talent for assessing dangerous situations. He knew how killers thought because he was a killer himself. Vaché could look at a street, a lonely country road or a hotel room and judge how an assassin would most likely attempt to use the setting for an ambush or murder attempt. It was a unique talent and one that had saved Vaché's and Gautier's lives on several occasions.

"This damn weather," Gautier complained as he held his palms close to the stove for warmth. "This Baltic climate is too cold for my Mediterranean blood.

Those Scandinavian countries are even worse this time of year. I've spent too much time in the north. After this business is finished, I'll say *au revoir* to this climate and return home."

"*Bon,*" Rzewuski told him. The Corsicans didn't understand Polish so they communicated in French. "When this is finished, I think we'll all be glad to be rid of one another."

"*Oui,*" Gautier readily admitted. "But we're not going anywhere until we've been paid in full. So far the profit has barely covered Captain Vatten's services and our people in Sweden."

"This is Poland," Rzewuski replied, "not the capitalist empire of the United States or an oil-rich Arab country run by a heartless despot monarch. We have limited finances. Our organization is devoted to political ambitions, not mere profit."

"How admirable," Gautier said dryly, "but *our* interest in this matter is purely financial and your people knew that from the beginning. So far you've failed to meet your obligations to us, obligations that involve cash payments."

"It's a very dangerous thing to cheat a Corsican," Vaché added with a thin smile as he waved the ice pick in a circular pattern in the air. "I'm sure you've heard stories about the misfortune that happens to those who betray us." Vaché rose from the crate and raised the ice pick in front of his own face. "Sometimes they get their eyes poked out or eardrums punctured. I recall one bastard who had his testicles pinned to a stool." To emphasize his point Vaché suddenly drove the steel tip of the ice pick into the top of the wooden crate. Then he looked at Rzewuski, folded his arms on his chest and chuckled softly.

Rzewuski turned away and shifted slightly in the swivel chair behind the desk. Vaché was pleased by this reaction because he thought he had unnerved the Pole by his dramatics. Suddenly Rzewuski spun around in his chair and thrust an arm above the desktop. A Makarov pistol was clenched in his fist. Gautier gasped when he saw the gun, and the smile vanished from Vaché's face as the Polish officer pointed the pistol and fired.

The pistol roared in the confines of the room. A 9 mm bullet smashed into the ice pick and split the wooden handle. Splinters flew from the instrument, leaving the naked blade wobbling in the top of the crate. Vaché jumped back and cursed under his breath as he reached inside his coat. Rzewuski calmly placed his pistol on the desk, confident Gautier wouldn't permit his stooge to draw another weapon.

The door to the office burst open. Henryk Wankowicz, one of Rzewuski's most trusted agents, appeared with a gun in hand. Mikolaj Kochanowski, another Polish agent, stood behind him for backup.

"Relax, Comrades," Rzewuski assured them. His ears were ringing from the gunshot, but he knew their hearing wouldn't be affected to the same degree. "Just a small accident. No one was hurt. If anyone heard the shot on the docks, tell them a gasket from a boiler exploded."

"Are you certain you don't need help?" Wankowicz asked, casting a suspicious glance at the Corsicans.

"*Tak, dziekuje,*" Rzewuski answered. "Yes, thank you. Everything's under control now."

The agents left and closed the door. Gautier thrust an accusing finger at Rzewuski and demanded an explanation. Vaché simply stared at the intel officer and nodded as if he approved of what had happened.

"I used extreme methods to be certain you Corsican savages would understand me," Rzewuski declared. "You two think you can threaten me? This isn't a back street in Paris. It's my homeland and I still have considerable influence here. I've also been a soldier and a security service officer since I was eighteen. I've killed a few men myself and had others disposed of when necessary. Your gangster tactics don't impress me. Not here in Poland. Not against me."

"*Très bien,*" Gautier replied. "Very well. We understand each other, but you still owe us money, *monsieur.*"

The office door opened once again. A large, powerful figure filled the doorway. Kochanowski clutched the big man's arm and tried to keep him from entering. The burly brute easily slammed the Polish agent into the doorframe and shoved the dazed man aside.

"Merde alors!" the big man bellowed. "What the hell are you people doing? I thought this was supposed to be a covert operation and you're in here firing at one another!"

His French was fluent, although the accent revealed it wasn't his native tongue. His cobalt blue eyes glared beneath bushy blond brows and a beard rimmed his lantern jaw. A navy blue greatcoat hung on his muscular six-foot-six frame and his boots stomped the floor as if he were trying to break the boards beneath his feet.

"Everything's all right, Captain Vatten," Rzewuski assured him. "As you can see, no one was shooting, and there's no corpse here."

"I'm about to take my ship to sea," the captain announced. "I don't care to be stopped because the authorities are suspicious about what goes on here. I damn sure don't intend to return with another shipment of that South American poison if you Poles and Corsicans are at one another's throats. Drag yourselves down if you like, but don't take me with you."

"You've been paid, Captain," Gautier told Vatten. "This has already been a profitable enterprise for you. My people aren't as fortunate, but they've had to be patient while you receive full payment for doing the least hazardous part of this assignment."

"If you think you can get cocaine into Poland by another route," the Swedish captain began, "go ahead and try. I don't particularly like this business, anyway."

"None of us do," Rzewuski stated. "We just had an argument that got out of hand, Captain. Messieurs Gautier and Vaché are unhappy about some delays in finances, but they have the same interests as myself, although their reasons are different. Don't worry. We'll work this out in a civilized manner without any threat to the security of our operation."

Vatten saw that Kochanowski had gotten to his feet and drawn a pistol. Rzewuski told him to put the gun away. Kochanowski reluctantly obeyed and glared at Vatten. The Swedish hulk merely shrugged and turned back to the men in the office.

"Contact me after I reach Oland," he announced. "If this financial impasse is solved and both sides have dealt with their grievances, then I'll deliver the next shipment."

"There won't be any problem concerning payment," a familiar voice declared from the doorway.

The others turned as Zbignew Zablocki entered. The Polish politician's expression revealed he was unhappy with their behavior as he jammed his hands into the pockets of a camel-hair coat. Zablocki was less than fluent in French, but he was aware both Rzewuski and Gautier understood English. The Sejm veteran switched to this language to better express himself.

"My associates have provided us with an additional ten million Swiss francs," Zablocki explained. "That should relieve some of the apprehension about working for us, Monsieur Gautier."

"How did you come upon this fortune?" the Corsican gangster inquired suspiciously.

"That's not your concern," Zablocki answered. "We have the money and we can afford to pay you quite well for your goods and services. That's all that matters, isn't it?"

"It is," Gautier admitted. "Now if you can convince your henchman to keep his gun holstered..."

"You just keep your psychopathic friend under control," Rzewuski told him. "If he threatens me again, I'll kill him. Vaché is hardly necessary for this operation. He's too unstable to trust beyond the limits of this warehouse. The man's just a killer, and we can't even use him for that because he's too fond of his ice picks."

"Philippe has other skills," Gautier stated with a shrug. "Don't worry about him. If we're receiving our payments, we're not a threat to anyone."

"Fine," Zablocki said wearily. "Make certain Captain Vatten understands the situation. We have enough problems without quarreling among ourselves. I can't afford to return here to check on you people. Comrade Rzewuski will return with me to Warsaw. That should put an end to the personality clash between him and your group."

"I certainly welcome returning to Warsaw," Rzewuski declared. "My control officer may be trying to contact me by now. Officially I'm on vacation, but they're probably calling in every active duty intelligence operative to investigate the death of the American.''

"They're about to learn that what's happened so far is just the beginning,'' Zablocki added with a grim smile.

5

Ignacy Jowialski pointed at the thirty-seven-story architectural oddity at the corner of Marszalkowska and Swietokrzyska. It was constructed in layers, like a giant wedding cake of concrete and glass. The foundation featured Greco-Roman–style pillars and nondescript block-shaped walls. The second layer resembled a Gothic church, flanked by four abbreviated keeps similar to those found in Norman castles. The top portion seemed to be an odd combination of a modern skyscraper and a Gothic design, capped by a cupola and steeple.

"That's the Palace of Culture and Science," Jowialski announced as he turned to address Phoenix Force. "The best view of Warsaw can be enjoyed from the top of that building because it's the only place in the city one doesn't have to look at the Palace of Culture and Science."

Jowialski chuckled at his own joke. Captain Potocki also smiled at the remark. Anton Staszic, a CIA case officer, realized Phoenix Force failed to understand the joke. He explained that the Palace of Culture and Science had been a gift from Stalin to Warsaw during the reconstruction after World War II.

"You'll hear that joke about the palace fairly often in Warsaw," Staszic added. "It was popular long before now. The Poles have never been fond of being a satellite country under Soviet rule and they always objected to Stalin's 'gift.'"

"Objected?" Jowialski scoffed. "I'm surprised someone hasn't blown that building apart. Down the street is the Museum of Struggle and Martyrdom, another monument to Communist propaganda."

"Yeah," Staszic admitted. "But at least most of the history covered in the museum concerns Poland's resistance against the Nazis. This country was right in the middle of World War II. About six million Poles were killed during the war. No place was hit harder than Warsaw. Two-thirds of the population was wiped out."

"That's what I heard," Katz commented. He recalled stories from Polish Jews in Israel. Roughly three million of the Polish victims of the war had been Jewish.

The reconstruction of Warsaw had been very successful. The capital of Poland was a beautiful city that combined modern buildings with restored historical sites. Phoenix Force had admired the view as the limousine bus had traveled from Okecie Airport to the heart of Warsaw.

The five commandos had arrived on a special Polish airline flight. Staszic, Jowialski and Potocki had met them at the airport and waived customs for Phoenix. The team had loaded their luggage and themselves into the limo bus. Introductions had been exchanged even as Potocki had driven the vehicle away from the airport.

Phoenix Force had recognized Anton Staszic from a photo in a CIA file faxed to Stony Man headquarters. The forty-year-old Company case officer was the son of Polish immigrants and had been raised in a bilingual family. His language skills and obvious familiarity with Polish culture made him an ideal operative for American intelligence in Poland. Staszic had been stationed in Eastern Europe for more than a decade.

Ignacy Jowialski had formerly been "the other side." A member of the Polish Security Service, Jowialski didn't seem a likely candidate for a "secret police" outfit. Indeed, the good-natured, intellectual Jowialski had been a failure when Poland was a Communist country because he had only given lip service to the party line. However, his devotion to the changes in the government and support of the democratic reforms had made him a good choice for the new Security Service.

Captain Potocki was a member of the Warsaw police militia. A tough, hard-nosed cop, he wasn't unlike policemen found anywhere in the world, aside from his exceptional linguistic ability. Potocki spoke four languages fluently and had a working vocabulary in three others. He didn't speak much as he drove the bus along Marszalkowska.

"You guys have never been to Poland before?" Staszic inquired as he took a pack of cigarettes from his jacket pocket.

"No," Katz confirmed. "I can guess your next question. You wonder why anyone would think we could learn anything about the drug-related deaths here in Warsaw that you gentlemen haven't already done."

"This is our country," Jowialski stated with a shrug. "We clearly know more about it than you, and Captain Potocki has considerable experience dealing with crime in Warsaw. What we seem to be faced with is a criminal case, not espionage or terrorism."

"I know you guys have White House authority," Staszic added. "The Polish government has agreed to cooperate with you, but I just don't see what can be done. Sad as it may be, Peter Henderson was a damn dope pusher who croaked from his own poisoned cocaine. The pity is he got some kids killed before he died."

"What about the autopsy?" Calvin James inquired. "Was there any evidence Henderson was a regular user? According to the information we got on the dude, he didn't even smoke and drank only an occasional glass of wine. No history of drug use and no criminal record. That sure doesn't sound like the background of a drug smuggler and coke addict."

"Perhaps he was never caught in the past," Jowialski suggested. "More likely he was new to the drug trafficking trade and had only started using the cocaine himself. Isn't that what your department suspects, Captain?''

"Something like that," Potocki answered, keeping his attention on the road. "The biggest concern is how many other smugglers have brought cocaine into Poland."

"Somebody brought the coke into your country," McCarter said with a shrug. "No doubt about that. The questions we have to answer are *who* did it and *why*."

"The reason behind drug peddling is always money," Staszic remarked. "That seems obvious."

"If our information's correct, Henderson didn't have enough money in his room to justify smuggling cocaine into Poland," Encizo replied. "Besides, there have been political reasons behind drug trafficking rings in the past. There were the Opium Wars of the nineteenth century because England found the opium market useful in maintaining its hold on Chinese ports. The KGB was involved in the heroin trade and established at least one refinery for processing heroin in Bulgaria. There's also evidence the CIA has been mixed up in at least one dope-dealing scheme. A lot of Third World countries have sold narcotics to help support their governments. In Nicaragua, for example, it's very likely both the right-wing contras and the leftist Sandinistas were involved in cocaine trafficking. The former to finance their rebel efforts and the latter to undermine the United States while making a profit in the bargain."

"You seem well versed on this subject," Jowialski commented. "Yet I think you may be grasping for straws. That is the expression for a desperate effort to claim an explanation based more on wishful thinking than solid proof, no?"

"We're just considering all possibilities until we know enough facts to extrapolate about these incidents," Katz assured him. "Frankly our expertise isn't primarily investigations. We're a direct-action unit. If Henderson was a drug dealer, Interpol and other law-enforcement organizations can deal with this case and we'll happily let them do so. However, if someone's trying to undermine Poland's democratic reforms and your country's relations with the United States, then we need to stop them."

"Well, there are already some small demonstrations outside the U.S. embassy at al Ujazdowskie," Staszic commented. "People are protesting American 'criminal influence' and a few even think the drugs were brought into Poland by the U.S. government."

"That was quick," McCarter said with a grunt. "Somebody stirring these folks up?"

"Communist party leaders have been rather critical of the democratic reforms," Jowialski answered. "They also seem most eager to blame the cocaine-related deaths on the United States. Most are saying it's a criminal syndicate like the Mafia. A few claim the loathsome business is a CIA plot."

"Any of them have any idea what the hell the CIA would gain by bringing drugs into Poland?" Gary Manning asked.

"Not that I know of," the Polish intel agent admitted. "Nonetheless, all the evidence currently points at the United States, one way or the other."

"Not all of it," Katz reminded him. "We need more information. Has Interpol been called in?"

Potocki reacted with surprise. "Polish law enforcement isn't part of Interpol yet. Why Interpol?"

"Narcotics are associated with this mission," Katz answered. "Interpol knows more about cocaine traffic in Europe than we do. If Henderson didn't smuggle the cocaine from the United States to Poland, it must have reached your country by another route. If Henderson was a pusher, we need to find out how he smuggled more than ten kilos of coke past customs or brought in the drugs through another source."

"It's a place to start," Staszic agreed with a sigh. "I just hope this incident doesn't undo all the progress made by Poland in the past two years. Is something wrong, Mr. Wallburg?" he inquired when he noticed Katz gazing out the window.

"There's always something wrong," the Israeli replied with a faint smile. "Wallburg" was his current alias, but he was accustomed to changing identities with each new mission.

"We've reached the safehouse," Potocki announced as he steered the bus up Prezedmiescie Street to the offices of Orbis Travel.

"You gotta be kidding," James commented when they pulled into the parking lot. "The travel bureau is the safehouse?"

"No," Jowialski replied with a smile. "The bus is Orbis property. The safehouse is up the street. Do you want to bring your luggage or have it delivered to your hotel?"

"We'll carry it," Encizo answered. "We don't like to be separated from our gear."

"I was told you brought your own equipment," Jowialski began as he opened a briefcase and removed five leather folders. "These special permits authorize you to carry firearms, even fully automatic weapons."

"That might save us some headaches," Gary Manning said as he took the folders. "I imagine local police would get pretty bent out of shape by foreigners with firearms."

"Actually, one can legally bring guns and ammunition into Poland with the proper permits," Staszic explained. "That was possible even before the democratic reforms."

"Really?" McCarter said with surprise. "Communist countries have always been opposed to allowing anyone except party members and the military to own firearms. Bloody remarkable they allowed tourists to bring guns into the country here."

"Tourists were more apt to be allowed to have guns than native-born Poles," the CIA man explained. "When the Communists found out tourism was good for the economy, they took advantage of the good hunting territory found in the mountain and lake regions. Elk, deer, chamois, bison and boars are among the game animals. If you want to hunt bear, this is the best place in Europe."

"Perhaps you'd care to do some hunting if we can find the time," Potocki suggested as he turned off the engine.

"I love to hunt," Manning admitted. "But I won't kill an animal unless the meat will be used. I won't do it just for blood sport or to have a rack of antlers for my wall."

"It's against my beliefs to shoot at anything that can't shoot back," McCarter stated with a shrug.

"Odds are there won't be any time for recreation," Katz said. "There never is."

They emerged from the bus and followed Jowialski and Potocki. Passersby smiled and nodded at Phoenix Force. Some greeted the five foreigners with *Dzien dobry* or "Good afternoon" in English. They seemed delighted to see visitors. Polish people had a well-deserved reputation for being warm and friendly. Even under communism Poles were noted as xenophiles with an enormous interest in Western culture, fashions and music.

Phoenix Force carried their luggage as their companions led them to a pharmacy a block from the travel bureau. They entered the shop. A middle-aged man behind the counter nodded at Jowialski and turned to an elderly couple who paid for some merchandise. Staszic pretended to be the translator for the five "tourists" and explained what different labels on bottles and jars meant in English. They played their roles accordingly and concentrated on the shelves of medicines and ointments until Jowialski asked them to follow him.

When the customers left, the pharmacist locked the door. Jowialski led the others into a storage room. A stocky figure met them at the entrance to a basement. Jowialski briefly spoke with him in rapid Polish.

"This is Hugo," he explained to Phoenix Force. "He's our communications expert. Hugo has quite a computer downstairs. Perhaps he can help us contact Interpol."

"It would probably be better if I did that," Staszic announced. "I can do it through the U.S. embassy."

"I want to see the autopsy reports on Henderson and the kids who died from the arsenic-laced cocaine," James said. "If any of the bodies are still in cold storage, I'd like to examine them personally."

"We also need a list of Henderson's business associates and anyone else he may have been in contact with here," Encizo added.

"My department has already interviewed them," Potocki said. "They weren't much help, but you may talk to them if you wish."

"Excuse, please," Hugo said haltingly in English. "I received a message on a fax machine just before you arrived. Three more young people were found in a car by the river. Two are dead and the third is in a coma. Cocaine was found with the bodies.''

"Jesus," Staszic rasped. "It's happening again."

"Did you think it was over?" Katz inquired with a sigh. "We'd better get to work, gentlemen. Circumstances have gone from bad to very bad."

"Yeah," James agreed. "Business as usual."

6

Dan Pulaski entered the lobby of the Orbis-Vera. His company had made reservations at the hotel because it was not far from Okecie Airport. Pulaski had no complaints about the Orbis-Vera, but he was annoyed that no one in his company had told him he would have to commute from Warsaw to Cracow.

The desk clerk greeted him cheerfully in English. Pulaski wearily replied with as much enthusiasm as he could manage after spending all day traveling hundreds of miles by train and being given a tour of the Wieliczka salt mines. Maybe some people found the underground passages of the thirteenth-century salt mines fascinating, but Pulaski found them boring.

Pulaski was a representative from an American tour agency that specialized in European vacation arrangements. Since Eastern Europe had gone through phenomenal changes, the agency had decided to include extended tours of Poland, Czechoslovakia, Hungary and Romania. Because he was of Polish descent, Pulaski had been chosen for his current assignment.

Unfortunately Pulaski didn't speak Polish and knew virtually nothing about the country. He had to rely on a translator and guide, but he had discovered Warsaw to be an intriguing city with friendly people. It was also a modern city, similar to metropolitan areas in the United States and Western Europe. Cracow was more traditional and filled with ancient architecture. The only major city to be spared the devastation of World War II, Cracow boasted many historical sites.

That was fine with Pulaski, although his interest in such matters was limited and he was more attracted to contemporary settings. The salt mines had been a total bore in Pulaski's opinion, and he didn't intend to advise his company to include it in its tour package.

Crossing the lobby to the elevator, he removed his overcoat and draped it across a forearm. When an elevator arrived, he stepped inside and pressed the up button. As the lift ascended the shaft, Pulaski loosened his tie and thought about relaxing in a hot tub after a long day. He wanted to call home and talk to his wife and kids in Ithaca, New York, but it was too late. He would call in the morning.

The doors opened on the fourth floor. Pulaski walked through the hall to his room and fished the key from a pocket. He unlocked the door, opened it and started to reach for the wall switch, but the lights were already on. Pulaski was surprised, yet not alarmed by this. The maid had probably left them on.

"Oh, shit!" Pulaski exclaimed upon discovering a man by the foot of the bed.

"Don't be alarmed, Mr. Pulaski," the stranger urged as he extended an ID folder and badge. "My name is Stanislaw Rzewuski. I'm a police detective."

The American looked at the guy. Rzewuski was neatly dressed in a gray suit. His expression seemed nonthreatening and his manner was polite. Pulaski hadn't associated much with cops, but the man seemed like a plainsclothes detective. The credentials looked real, and Pulaski had no reason to suspect the stranger wasn't what he claimed to be.

"You scared the hell out of me, Detective," he admitted as he reached for the door. "What's this about?"

"Better close and lock the door," Rzewuski urged. "Believe me, you don't want anyone in the corridor to get curious about what's going on in here."

"I'm pretty curious about it myself," Pulaski answered as he bolted the door. "How did you get in here?"

"The night manager lent me his passkey," Rzewuski replied. "He didn't ask any questions. That's good because I wanted to talk to you first. I'm sure you don't want a scandal any more than we do."

"Scandal?" The American glared at him. "What kind of scandal? I spent all day at the salt mines—literally. How could I be involved with any sort of scandal?"

"Please, Mr. Pulaski," Rzewuski began with a sigh. "I'm aware you've been out of Warsaw most of the day. You have an alibi. That's the word in English, isn't it?''

"What do I need an alibi for?"

"We received a phone call from an anonymous caller who claimed we'd find a dead girl in this room," Rzewuski explained as he moved to the bathroom.

"Wait a minute!" Pulaski said, frightened. "I don't know anything about this!"

"I'm not saying you do," Rzewuski assured him. "Nevertheless, someone made that phone call. Someone must have been in this room while you were gone." He canted his head toward the bathroom. "Someone left that girl in there."

"Oh, my God," Pulaski whispered, and crossed himself.

"I'm afraid I have to ask you to look at the body," the bogus detective declared. "You may be able to identify her."

"I don't know any girls," Pulaski insisted. He looked away from the bathroom. "I'm married, for Christ's sake. I don't screw around on my wife."

"No one's accusing you of anything, sir," Rzewuski said sympathetically. "I'm sorry, but this really is necessary. Please, Mr. Pulaski, let's get this over with."

"Okay," the American reluctantly agreed. His legs shook as he approached the bathroom. "How bad is it? I mean, is there a lot of blood?"

"No," Rzewuski replied. "She apparently drowned in the bathtub. There's no blood, but it isn't a pretty sight."

Pulaski took a deep breath and stepped to the threshold of the bathroom. He had never considered himself to be squeamish, yet he trembled as he moved through the doorway. Rzewuski stood clear and allowed Pulaski to enter. The American timidly approached the bathtub. Water filled it to the brim.

He inched closer and leaned forward, eyes squinting, ready to close the instant he saw the girl's body. Pulaski peered down at the water, his stomach already knotted. He blinked with surprise when he discovered there was no body, alive or dead, in the tub.

"What the hell is this?" Pulaski demanded as he turned to face Rzewuski. "Some sort of sick joke?"

However, Rzewuski had moved behind the American and seized him. He slipped his arms under Pulaski's armpits and clasped his hands together at the nape of the neck. Pulaski cried out, but Rzewuski held him in the full nelson hold and shoved the American into the bathtub. Pulaski hit the water face first.

"I really am sorry," Rzewuski rasped as water splashed from the tub.

He held one hand at the back of Pulaski's neck in a half nelson and twisted the other in a hammerlock. Rzewuski pressed his opponent into the tub and planted a knee in the small of Pulaski's spine. The American thrashed wildly and more water spilled from the tub. However, Rzewuski held him fast and kept Pulaski's face under the surface.

The American struggled vainly for almost a minute. Then Rzewuski felt the man's body go limp. The Polish assassin kept his victim pressed against the bottom of the tub until he was certain Pulaski had drowned.

He looked down at the man's corpse and shook his head. Rzewuski found this job disgusting. He had murdered people before, but Pulaski had seemed a decent man. This assassination had been particularly distasteful to Rzewuski, although he told himself it was necessary and all Americans were enemies of communism.

Rzewuski removed his wet jacket and trousers. He leaned over the tub and grabbed Pulaski's corpse. The dead man was heavy, his clothes soaked and weighted by water. Rzewuski struggled with Pulaski's suit jacket and managed to strip it from the corpse. Then he unbuttoned the dead man's shirt and peeled it back over Pulaski's left shoulder.

The assassin moved to the medicine cabinet and removed a syringe from the shelf. He knelt by the tub and injected the needle into Pulaski's armpit. Rzewuski pressed the plunger and watched the milky liquid drain from the hypo. He withdrew the needle and continued to strip the dead man's body. Rzewuski searched the clothing and removed all items from the pockets. He placed the wallet and passport in the sink.

He dried his feet with a towel. In the next room Rzewuski took a large plastic bag from a closet. He removed a pair of boots, gray coveralls and a cap from the bag and replaced them with his own and Pulaski's soaked clothing.

Returning to the closet, he removed a bottle of vodka and a small package of white powder. He opened both and placed the bottle in the tub beside the corpse. He put the open plastic bag of cocaine on the tile floor nearby. Rzewuski examined the items from Pulaski's pockets. The wallet, passport and some papers were already soaked. He placed these on the floor and dried the keys, coins, watch and other belongings before putting them in a dresser drawer.

He tossed Pulaski's bathrobe onto the bathroom floor and nodded with grim satisfaction. Then he turned the faucet handles. Water flowed from the spout into the tub as Rzewuski left the bathroom. He donned the coveralls, cap and boots, slung the large plastic bag over his shoulder and left the hotel room.

Rzewuski checked the corridor to be certain it was empty, then headed down the hall to the stairs. He descended the fire exit to the bottom floor and pushed open a door to the alley. The agent left the building and walked to a car parked by the curb. Henryk Wankowicz emerged from the vehicle when he saw Rzewuski approach. The henchman unlocked the trunk and raised the lid. Rzewuski tossed the bag into the trunk and slammed it shut.

"Did everything go well?" Wankowicz inquired.

"It's done," Rzewuski replied. "Let's get out of here."

They climbed into the car and drove away as snow fell from the cold dark sky.

7

The slushing of the wet carpet sounded as if the investigators were walking in mud rather than a hotel room. Captain Potocki spoke with the Warsaw police who had first arrived at the scene. Calvin James headed for the bathroom to examine the body of Dan Pulaski while Rafael Encizo watched a police lab technician test some samples of white powder in a test tube. The chemical reaction confirmed the identity of the substance.

"Cocaine," the technician stated with a sigh.

"Large amounts were hidden under the shirts and underwear in the bottom drawer," Potocki informed Encizo, sharing information he received from the other cops. "At least five kilos. That's not including the drugs found in the bathroom with the body."

"Anything to suggest Pulaski knew Henderson?" Encizo asked as he noticed a cop reading an address book.

"Not so far," Potocki answered. "They were both American businessmen, but they worked in different fields and came from different cities."

James stepped from the bathroom and moved aside as two men passed with the corpse of Dan Pulaski on a stretcher. A sheet covered the naked body. The tall black American turned to Encizo and Potocki. "Looks like he drowned in the tub," he announced. "No wounds or bruises. The vodka bottle and dope suggest he got high and passed out."

"The water was still flowing when the local police arrived," Potocki said. "Another guest noticed water coming from under the door. The bathtub must have been running for hours."

"You think Pulaski's death was an accident?" Encizo asked his fellow Phoenix pro.

"It could be," James replied. "In the United States close to five thousand people die from drowning each year. That's more than the number of deaths from airplane, train and firearm accidents put together. If Pulaski was screwed up with cocaine and booze, he could have drowned. It could be a setup, too. I'll have a better idea after an autopsy. It is kind of weird that his wallet and passport happened to be on the bathroom floor."

"Perhaps he was carrying them when he was drowned in the tub and the killers had to leave the wallet and passport to explain why they were soaking wet," Encizo commented. "It would have been too suspicious if those items were missing."

"He may have had them in his bathrobe pockets," Potocki stated with a shrug. "I don't know why he would carry them into the bathroom, but that isn't proof he was murdered."

"Just another odd coincidence," James remarked dryly. "Two American businessmen just happen to die in drug-related incidents within less than a week. Both just happen to have evidence that suggests they were dope dealers. How much you want to bet Pulaski didn't have a criminal record?"

"No bets," Encizo told him. "But I suspect the Polish people aren't going to be happy with the theory that somebody's been setting up Americans to take the blame for the drug traffic that's costing the lives of many young Poles in Warsaw. People are going to be apt to see the drug trade as an American phenomenon and America as a threat."

"Forensics will dust for fingerprints and examine the room for any evidence of foul play," Potocki declared. "Do you want to stay here and help?"

"I think I can do more good with the medical examiner and the autopsy of Pulaski," James announced. "I might be able to find some answers in the dead man's body tissues. I've handled lots of autopsies and blood tests. If nothing else, we can find out for sure what killed Pulaski and whether or not he has any drugs in his system."

"You go ahead," Encizo said thoughtfully. "I think I'll ask the desk clerk some questions. Is the man downstairs the same one who was at the desk when Pulaski came in?"

"Yes," Captain Potocki confirmed. "He speaks some English, but you'll need a translator. I'll go with you. The clerk has already been questioned. We have his statements."

"I still want to talk to him," Encizo said. "If nothing else, we can compare his answers with those he gave to your men earlier and see how reliable his powers of observation and memory might be. If everything's consistent, it'll suggest he's an accurate witness."

"Well, I'll see you guys later," James commented as he checked his watch. "It's almost 4:00 a.m. Maybe we'll all have breakfast in a couple of hours. I always like to start off the morning with an autopsy and a hearty meal."

"Some guys get all the luck," Encizo said dryly.

NONE OF THE MEMBERS of Phoenix Force got much sleep during their first twenty-four hours in Poland. Anton Staszic used his contacts with the CIA and the U.S. embassy to get assistance from Interpol. Konrad Schmidt was sent by the Interpol central office in Vienna. The Austrian special investigator met with Katz, McCarter and Staszic at the embassy while James and Encizo were at the scene of Pulaski's death.

The CIA man escorted them to a small conference room in the embassy. Staszic assured the others that the room was soundproof and secure. Inspector Schmidt placed a briefcase on the table and slipped off his overcoat. Schmidt was a tall blond man with a fair complexion and pleasant features. His suit was expensive but conservative and practical. The Austrian's appearance was neat and fastidious. He cast a woeful glance at McCarter's wrinkled jacket and Katz's old-fashioned tweed suit. Schmidt wondered what organization these two belonged to. He thought they ought to show a bit more care for their public image.

"*Sprechen Sie Englisch, Herr Schmidt?*" Katz inquired.

"Yes, I speak English," the Austrian replied with a nod. He was surprised that the one-armed stranger spoke German with a proper Bavarian accent. "That's one reason I was chosen for the job when the American embassy contacted Interpol in Vienna. Another reason is I've been involved with narcotics investigations for more than a decade. How may I help you?"

"There have been a number of crimes, including some deaths, associated with drugs here in Warsaw," Staszic began. "Since drug trafficking is a new problem in Poland, it's causing some major concern—"

"Let's just cut to the important questions," McCarter said impatiently. "Who's involved with most of the drug trade in Europe these days?"

"Most of the heroin and opium trafficking is conducted by the Triad," Schmidt replied, taking out a cigarette case and lighter. "That's a Chinese criminal organization. Modern version of the old Tong societies. They've come a long way from the days of little opium dens and hatchet-wielding killers. The Triad is probably the largest criminal syndicate in the world."

"Chinese gangsters?" Staszic remarked with surprise. "They're bigger than the Mafia?"

"More widespread and certainly more members," the Interpol man answered. "Triad operations extend from Southeast Asia to the United States and Canada. One of the reasons the Triad has been so successful is that so many police departments underestimate them and assume Chinese crime consists of simple street gangs. Actually the Triad is sophisticated and very clever, Mr. Staszic."

"Just call me Toni," the CIA agent urged. "Mr. Staszic was my father. I'm still getting used to hearing my real name after using a cover in Poland for so long."

"You're using your real name now?" Schmidt inquired as he fired up a cigarette. "I take it you're not involved in covert operations?"

"Not anymore," Staszic answered. "I'm part of an intelligence liaison section formed by the Company to improve relations between our embassy and the Polish intel since Solidarity replaced communism here—"

"Save it for your bloody biography," McCarter growled.

"Relax, Mr. Masters," Katz said, using McCarter's cover name. "We're not preparing to attack an enemy stronghold. No need to get nasty. We were discussing narcotics in Europe?"

"Ja," Schmidt replied, blowing a smoke ring. He watched the semitransparent gray ring dissolve as he spoke. "The Triad has been particularly active in Holland and Great Britain. However, it has also been involved in heroin trafficking in Germany, Sweden, France and elsewhere."

"What about cocaine?" Katz inquired. "Is the Triad in control of that trade, as well?"

"Cocaine is a different story," the Interpol agent said. "Since the coca shrubs are grown in South America and the cocaine is processed there, the drug comes from a different part of the world than those derivatives of the poppy. The syndicates in Colombia and Bolivia don't have much contact with the Asian networks, but they do have connections with at least one Mafia family in the United States. They, in turn, have roots in Italy and Sicily. That's how cocaine is getting into Europe."

"It isn't being smuggled in by free-lance operators?" Staszic asked eagerly.

"A great deal of it may be getting in that way," Schmidt answered. "Cocaine is a relatively new problem in Europe. Heroin has declined in the United States, but cocaine use has escalated there. Heroin addiction is still a major concern here, although cocaine use is growing at an alarming rate. However, I haven't heard of a major drug problem in Poland. My guess is the Combine must be involved, either directly or indirectly."

"The Combine?" McCarter said with a frown. "That's sort of a cooperative effort by the Mafia and the Union de Corse?"

"Better known as the Corsican Union in English-speaking countries," Schmidt said with a nod. "It's sometimes incorrectly called the French Mafia. Corsicans don't consider themselves to be French, although most of the hoodlums who belong to the Corsican Union are Frenchmen. Usually apaches from Paris. The Mafia and the Corsican Union discovered it was best to cooperate in Europe. They've divided up territories and tend to operate independently most of the time. The Combine is a very loose partnership. There was an organization called MERGE that tried to create a powerful united crime network in the mid-1980s."

"I've heard about that," Katz told him. The Israeli didn't mention that Phoenix Force had clashed with MERGE more than once in the past.

"This is all fascinating stuff," McCarter said with a shrug, "but MERGE obviously isn't involved in cocaine traffic here. Based on your experience, Mr. Schmidt, who would be most likely to peddle coke in Poland?"

"The Corsican Union," Schmidt answered without hesitation. "What little drug traffic existed in the Baltic countries under the Communists was usually linked to the Corsicans. They're also more active in Germany and the Scandinavian countries than the Mafia segments of the Combine."

"That's an interesting hypothesis," Staszic remarked with a sigh. "Unfortunately all the actual physical evidence still points to the American businessmen as the smugglers and dealers."

"It's possible American businessmen may be smuggling cocaine into Poland for the Corsicans or someone else to peddle to the locals," Schmidt stated. "I doubt that outsiders would be able to operate effectively as dealers in Poland. Nonetheless, someone would have to supply the drugs to the Polish trash that sold it to their countrymen. You may not want to hear this, but there have been U.S. businesses involved in the cocaine trade."

"What?" Staszic glared at the Austrian. "Where did you get that anti-American propaganda?"

"I'm sorry, Toni," Schmidt told him. "I know your President talks a great deal about a war on drugs and there's lots of talk about keeping drugs from getting into the United States. However, at least one major oil company delivers tons of a chemical compound known as MEK to Colombia every year. MEK is used for many things. It's a necessary ingredient of rubber cement, for example. It's also used to transform coca leaves into cocaine. Since Colombia isn't noted for its vast exports of rubber cement, I think it's obvious what the MEK is being used for."

"Jesus," the CIA man rasped. "And the Administration is letting this oil company get away with this?"

"MEK isn't illegal," Schmidt replied. "They're not breaking the law by doing this, although I'd say their ethics leave a lot to be desired."

"One crisis at a time," Katz urged. "We certainly appreciate your input, Herr Schmidt. Unfortunately we can't share all the details of this matter right now. We may need your help again in the next few days."

"I've been assigned to Warsaw and attached to U.S. embassy intelligence until further notice," Schmidt answered. "Of course, I'll be in touch with my country's embassy. I'd like to get diplomatic immunity while I'm here just in case something goes wrong. It's much easier to avoid trouble with local authorities if one has diplomatic immunity. Less problem if I need to carry a gun."

He had noticed the bulges of the weapons that Katz and McCarter carried beneath their jackets. The pair obviously packed some serious hardware, Schmidt realized. Large handguns with big frames and long barrels, the Interpol agent guessed. The weapons were for combat situations, not conventional self-defense. Schmidt was accustomed to dealing with undercover cops and occasionally intelligence operatives. They were inclined to carry small concealable weapons with short barrels.

Schmidt wasn't sure what sort of men the Phoenix pros were, but knew they were a different breed than Staszic or most of the others the inspector encountered in his business. One thing seemed clear: if they were carrying such firepower, Schmidt ought to have a gun, too.

"That sounds fine," Katz assured the Austrian. "We'll stay in contact with you however things work out."

"I must admit I'm curious," Schmidt confessed.

"So are we," McCarter declared. "Trouble is we've got a hell of a lot more questions than answers so far."

8

"The background checks on the young people who died from the poisoned cocaine revealed they had a history of delinquency," Gary Manning explained as he carried a cup of coffee to the table. "They had been arrested for disorderly conduct, public drunkenness, and a couple had been busted for possession of hashish."

"All the charges were less than a year old," Hugo, the Polish communications and computer expert, added. "Apparently they felt democracy meant they could do whatever they pleased."

"Sound like standard delinquents," David McCarter commented as he popped the lid from a chilled bottle of Coca-Cola. The Briton was sincerely grateful the American soft drink was available in Warsaw. "My old neighborhood in the East End was filled with kids like that. Most of them straighten out if they live long enough."

"Speaking from personal experience?" Manning inquired.

"I can't say I had a halo when I was a teenager," the Briton admitted, "but I had some sense of direction concerning what I wanted to do with my life. If a kid has some goals to go after—even a poor kid in a rough neighborhood—he'll turn out all right. Just as long as he's got a bit of hope, he can succeed without getting mixed up in crime, drugs and that sort of thing."

"Not everyone accomplishes their goals," Staszic stated. A trace of sorrow in his tone suggested he spoke from a personal point of view.

"These sociological observations won't help us with this mission," Ignacy Jowialski said wearily. "So far it's cost us all a night's sleep and we don't know any more than we did before."

"We've learned a couple of things," Katz corrected. "The drugs may be coming into Poland from other sources than American smugglers. It's certainly suspicious that two alleged U.S. businessmen have died in their hotel rooms and conveniently left plenty of evidence that they were involved in drug trafficking."

"One died from arsenic poisoning and the other drowned in his bathroom," Jowialski stated. "That's not a definite pattern."

"If they were murdered," McCarter began, "the killer or killers would be pretty stupid to knock them off in the same manner if they wanted the deaths to look like accidents."

"That's hardly proof," Jowialski insisted as he spread some butter on a slice of *czarny chleb*.

Sitting at a table in the basement of the safe house, the men ate an unusual breakfast while they discussed the mission. In addition to the *czarny chleb,* a type of rye bread, the meal included sausage, potatoes, cabbage and beetroot soup. Since the sausage was made of pork, Katz had politely passed on this offering. Hugo realized the man known as "Wallburg" had religious objections to pork and gave Katz some whitefish to replace the sausage.

Hearing someone on the stairs, McCarter rose, hand poised by the holstered Browning under his left arm. Hugo approached the foot of the stairs and looked up to see Rafael Encizo. The Cuban descended the steps and smiled as he smelled food.

"I hope there's enough to go around," he announced, heading for the table. "The others are on their way. They're probably hungry, too. It was a very long night."

"Any luck?" McCarter inquired as he returned to his chair.

"A couple items of interest," Encizo replied. He nodded his thanks to Hugo as the Polish agent handed him a plate. "I spoke with the desk clerk at the hotel. He remembered seeing Pulaski enter the lobby at approximately 8:00 p.m. He said the American looked tired, but he didn't appear to have been drinking or using other types of chemical substances. I asked if he noticed what Pulaski was wearing. The clerk replied that Pulaski took off his overcoat before he got into the elevator and had a brown business suit on underneath.''

The Cuban scooped some food onto his plate and opened a bottle of beer. "However, we didn't find a brown suit in Pulaski's room."

"The clerk could have been mistaken," Jowialski stated.

"Pulaski had three suits in his closet," Encizo explained. "One was a black-and-white pinstripe, another was dark blue and the third was gray and still wrapped in a clear plastic bag from the dry cleaners. It hadn't been worn. Even if the clerk was color-blind, he wouldn't have mistaken either of the other suits as being brown."

"But you found the overcoat?" Katz inquired.

"It was laid across the bed," Encizo confirmed. "Potocki and I then went to the U.S. embassy. The ambassador mentioned Toni was there with Wallburg, Masters and an Interpol investigator from Austria, but I missed you guys. I think the ambassador wished we hadn't shown up, because we had him telephone Pulaski's home in Ithaca, New York, and tell his wife what happened."

"Couldn't you wait to do that?" Staszic said with distaste. "At least until we cleared up this business about the cocaine?"

"None of us wanted to do it," Encizo said with a sigh. "It was depressing, but it had to be done in order to ask Mrs. Pulaski some questions. She had helped her husband pack for the trip. She confirmed that he had four suits, including a brown one. He also packed two pairs of black dress shoes. We only found one pair in the hotel room.''

''Why do you think someone would have taken the clothes?'' Hugo inquired, confused.

''If Pulaski was drowned in the bathtub while still dressed,'' the Cuban answered, ''the killer would have been forced to get rid of the clothes. It wouldn't have looked like an accident if the guy was found fully dressed in the tub. The wallet and passport, along with some report sheets, were found on the bathroom floor. Pulaski may have been carrying them in his suit when he was drowned. The killer could have left them on the floor and let the tub water overflow to explain why they were wet. It would have been too suspicious if those items were missing.''

''But there were reportedly no signs of a struggle,'' Jowialski remarked. ''How did anyone manage to drown this fellow? Wouldn't he have put up a fight?''

''Potocki and I discussed that,'' Encizo said with a nod. ''There are a couple ways it could have been done. The killer probably had the tub filled with water before Pulaski entered. He could have hidden in the closet and waited for Pulaski to step into the bathroom, then grabbed him from behind, pushed him down into the tub and held him in some sort of judo or wrestling hold under the water. More likely the killer managed to get Pulaski to trust him, lured the unsuspecting victim into the bathroom and jumped him.''

"How could a stranger get the man's trust?" Jowialski asked, still doubting the theory.

"Maybe he wasn't a stranger," Staszic answered. "Maybe it wasn't a man. Pulaski may have been more trusting of a woman in his room. Maybe the killer is a strong but not unattractive female."

"Anything's possible," Encizo allowed. "Potocki and I think the most likely ruse would be if the killer pretended to be a police officer or hotel security. People tend to trust cops, especially if the killer seemed to be a patient, understanding type who was trying to get Pulaski's cooperation rather than playing storm trooper."

"It's still all theory and not facts," Jowialski said wearily.

They heard more footsteps on the stairs and saw Calvin James and Captain Potocki descend into the basement. The tall black commando headed for the coffeemaker as he spoke to the others. "I just came back from doing some autopsies," he explained. "Not what I consider to be a lot of fun, but it certainly was enlightening. Got a news flash for you guys—Pulaski *was* murdered."

"Are you sure?" Staszic asked eagerly. "He didn't drown?"

"Oh, he drowned all right," James answered as he carried a cup of coffee to the table. He glanced at the food, but it was too soon after carving open human beings for his appetite to be interested. "We also found traces of alcohol and cocaine in his system. That is, we found it in his blood, but not in his liver or stomach. Pulaski was already dead before the booze and coke entered his body. So it settled in the blood and didn't get processed through the stomach, liver and such."

"How did the killer manage this stunt?" McCarter asked.

"It was a cute trick," James said with a nod. "If we hadn't checked everything, it might have gotten past us. One thing we noticed was the lack of cocaine traces or membrane damage to Pulaski's nostrils. That meant he wasn't a regular user who snorted coke. No needle tracks on his arms or legs, so he wasn't shooting up. No trace of alcohol in his mouth or throat, either. Yet there was still alcohol and coke in his blood."

"How did it get there?" Manning inquired.

"We couldn't find the way at first," James continued. "No obvious needle marks on the skin. Then we found the mark in Pulaski's armpit. Small puncture from a hypo, concealed by the hair in the armpit, the sort of thing that could easily be overlooked. Real cute."

"Good work." Katz looked from James to Encizo. "You both did well and so did Captain Potocki. We now have some solid evidence to support what we suspected from the start. Someone is trying to make the public and the Polish government believe the cocaine traffic in this country is coming from the United States."

"The motive for setting up American businessmen is probably political," McCarter stated. "It seems pretty obvious the blokes who'd most want to discredit the United States and Poland's relations with the West would be the hard-core Communist party members. They sure as hell don't like what's happened here since 1989."

"Most have adjusted to it better than you might think, Mr. Masters," Jowialski declared.

"Still, the Communists are definitely the big losers in Poland," Katz stated. "They've also got the most to gain if the reforms fail."

"And the rest of Eastern Europe is looking at Poland as the model for how Western-style reforms will work," Staszic added. "If they fail here, you can bet they'll start running into trouble in other countries, too."

"There's a lot at stake," Encizo agreed. "But I doubt the people of Eastern Europe are going to throw away democracy because a few bastards are bringing drugs into their society. Still, it could set back a lot of progress, and a lot of people will die if we don't stop this."

"Well, the old guard is certainly pumping the cocaine scandal for all it's worth," Staszic remarked.

"Janicjusz, Zablocki, some of the other former Sejm members and representatives of the Communist trade unions all claim this is an example of the ultimate corruption of the capitalist concept of goods and services. The drug dealers are creating a demand in order to profit by providing a supply."

"Zablocki is the worst of the lot," Captain Potocki said bitterly. "That bastard's lucky he wasn't in Romania or they would have executed him when they got rid of Ceauşescu."

"That's a rather harsh evaluation," Jowialski told the Warsaw cop. "Zablocki might be an overzealous Marxist-Leninist, but there's no proof he had anyone killed when he was in the Sejm. He was very pro-Soviet and opposed to Solidarity, but that used to be the position of the government."

"What's Zablocki doing now?" Katz inquired as he took a pack of Camels from his pocket. He fitted a cigarette between the steel hooks of his prosthesis and got out his lighter.

"He's still a party official," Jowialski answered. "I'm not sure what his status is or how he makes a living these days, but Zablocki certainly retains some influence among the Communists."

"He doesn't sound like the sort to acquiesce to the changes in the government," Katz commented. "That doesn't mean he would go to extreme methods to reverse the reforms. Still, we should look into what he's been doing lately.''

"Agreed," Jowialski said with a nod. "Why don't you and your men get some sleep, Mr. Wallburg? My people can handle this. You haven't even had a chance to see your hotel rooms since you arrived.''

"We probably should try to get some rest," Katz agreed. "I suspect we won't get too many chances until this mission is over.''

9

The Victoria Intercontinental was located on Królewska Street, only two blocks from the safehouse. One of the most modern hotels in Warsaw, it featured restaurants, an indoor pool, sauna and its own nightclub. The accommodations were far more luxurious than Phoenix Force was accustomed to during a mission.

David McCarter felt awkward as he crossed the plush lobby to the stairs, suitcase in one hand and hotel key in the other. The opulent setting made the British warrior uncomfortable. His cockney upbringing and life-style didn't suit the ostentatious hotel. He almost envied the other Phoenix Force commandos, who were still investigating potential leads before heading for the hotel.

At the safehouse Jowialski had received word that another dead teenager had been fished out of the Vistula River, which bisected Warsaw. James had assisted Captain Potocki during the autopsy of this unfortunate youth. Formerly an insurance investigator specializing in maritime claims, Encizo had also joined James and the Warsaw cop to search for possible evidence in the victim's clothes and hair.

Inspector Schmidt had contacted the U.S. embassy and spoken with Staszic. The CIA man had relayed the news to Phoenix Force. Katz had gone with Staszic to the Austrian embassy. McCarter had volunteered to accompany them, but Katz had told him to go to the hotel instead. The Phoenix commander had said it would be better if Manning joined him and Schmidt because the Canadian spoke fluent German. The British ace had suspected the real reason was due to his displays of bad temper when they previously met with the Interpol agent.

So McCarter had reluctantly gone to the Victoria Intercontinental alone. Although the hotel was lovely, McCarter wasn't in a good mood. He didn't like being pushed out of the activities of his team and felt as if he was being punished for being a nasty lad. The Briton's sharp tongue and short temper had caused him problems in the past, but he had never been able to properly control either.

The British commando mounted the stairs. His phobia of elevators was due to Gary Manning. The Canadian demolitions expert claimed elevators were too easily sabotaged. A person was virtually helpless in a sealed box suspended by cables, traveling within a long shaft. Explosives could be used to blast the cables or attack the elevator car itself. Little could be done to defend oneself against such an attack.

Paranoia was a necessary trait for individuals in a dangerous profession. McCarter headed for the stairs without considering the reason until he was halfway to the second story. He continued to the fourth floor and strolled the hallway in search of his room. Finding the door with numerals that matched those on the key, he unlocked it and entered the spacious, handsomely furnished suite. The Briton closed the door, locked it and scanned the room.

A sofa with matching armchairs, a breakfast table with two chairs and a massive bed offered appealing comforts. McCarter placed his suitcase on the bed and removed his overcoat and cap. The Briton unbuttoned his jacket and drew his Browning pistol. Gun in hand, he checked the bathroom, closet, under the bed and other places where an opponent might hide. The commando's search turned up no intruders.

A buzzer sounded. Surprised and suspicious, McCarter approached the door. He moved to the side of the doorframe and stood clear of the wooden panels, pistol clenched in both hands, barrel pointed at the ceiling.

"Kto tam?" he called out, using one of the few expressions in Polish he had learned for the mission. McCarter repeated it in English. "Who is it?"

"Toni Staszic sent me from the embassy," an unfamiliar voice replied with a nondescript American Midwest accent.

"What embassy?" McCarter inquired.

"Don't be cute," the voice growled. "This is important."

"All right," the Briton said as he returned the Browning to shoulder leather inside his jacket.

He unlocked the door, and it suddenly burst open. The edge of the door struck McCarter above the right eye. The unexpected hard blow staggered the Briton as pain lanced his eyebrow and brilliant dots of scarlet popped across his vision.

McCarter instinctively reached for the holstered pistol as two figures rushed him. A powerful man with broad shoulders and a square-shaped head pointed a small black pistol at McCarter's face. The gun looked like a toy in the guy's big fist, but McCarter immediately raised his hands to shoulder level.

"Don't do anything stupid, Masters—or whatever your real name is," the other intruder warned as he shut the door and hastily locked it.

"I think I already did," McCarter muttered.

The second man was smaller than his companion. An oversize trench coat hung from his wiry physique like a tent. Wire-frame glasses were perched on his nose and he carried a brown briefcase.

The big square-headed intruder stepped closer, his eyes fixed on McCarter's face, pistol still pointed at the Briton's forehead. The other man fumbled with his valise while his companion slowly reached inside McCarter's jacket. A slight smile tugged at the brute's lips as he dragged the Browning from the shoulder holster.

The skinny guy was busy getting something from his briefcase instead of backing up his partner with a weapon in hand. Whoever the pair were, they obviously wanted him alive or he would already be dead, McCarter figured.

The big guy stood directly in front of him as he liberated the Briton's pistol. McCarter hoped the man would be slightly distracted as he pulled the Browning from leather. The Phoenix commando figured he couldn't hope for a better chance to take action. Discarding the risk, he made his move.

McCarter's left hand snapped downward and snared the big man's wrist above the little black gun. He pushed it toward the floor as his right fist descended like a hammer to club the Browning from the brute's other hand. The Hi-Power pistol fell to the carpet as McCarter snapped his head forward and slammed his skull into the nose and mouth of his burly opponent.

The larger man groaned and McCarter pumped a knee into the guy's groin. He hit a solid thigh muscle instead. McCarter didn't let this deter him as he punched the big man's jaw. The opponent's head bounced from the stroke, and McCarter's right arm smoothly rose and swooped over the enemy's right shoulder.

McCarter still held the man's wrist with his left hand. He snaked his other arm through the crook of the guy's elbow and grabbed his own left wrist. The Briton turned slightly and pulled hard. The man cursed in a Slavic language as his elbow folded and pain stabbed at his shoulder due to McCarter's double-wrist lock.

The Briton applied more pressure to the guy's elbow and shoulder as he moved behind his opponent. He pressed a thumb into the ulna nerve at the back of the guy's fist. The tiny black pistol dropped.

"Hold it!" the skinny opponent demanded as he took a blue-black pistol from the pocket of his trench coat. "That's enough, Masters!"

He stepped forward. The pistol in his fist resembled a Walther PPX, but he seemed reluctant to use it. McCarter twisted his captive's arm harder and turned to put the big guy between himself and the gunman. The fellow with the pistol tried to step around them to get a clear aim at McCarter's head.

The Phoenix commando rammed a knee into his captive's tailbone and shoved, using him as a human battering ram, which slammed into the uncertain gunman. All three men catapulted across the room and crashed into the wall. The skinny man moaned from the weight of the other two on top of him. McCarter quickly released the big man and chopped a hand across the other guy's wrist to strike the gun from his grasp.

The big guy swung a malletlike fist at McCarter's head. The Briton tried to duck, but the heavy knuckles connected and sent him staggering back. The big man charged and swung a kick at McCarter's groin. The Briton caught his opponent's ankle with both hands, pulled sharply and kicked the man's other leg, smashing the kneecap. The large man cried out as his leg buckled. McCarter twisted the captive ankle and sent his opponent hurtling to the floor.

The smaller intruder reached for his fallen pistol. As the guy's fingers touched the steel frame, McCarter's foot stomped on the man's hand, crunching bone. Then the Briton whipped a backfist at the thin man's face. The wire-frame glasses flew from the guy's nose as he fell.

With a bestial bellow the larger man rose and charged like a half-blind bull, slamming into McCarter's abdomen. The breath was driven from the Briton's lungs when his back hit the wall. His attacker rammed a fist into his stomach and the commando doubled up with a groan.

As the big man prepared to deliver another blow, McCarter snapped his body upright and whipped the top of his skull under the guy's jaw. The thug's head recoiled from the unexpected buttstroke and McCarter nailed him with a hard left hook. The guy retaliated, but McCarter dodged his big fist, which struck the wall with knuckle-punishing force.

McCarter hooked another punch to the guy's kidney, then sidestepped a return punch. He delivered a left jab to the brute's chin, which caused him to sway and stumble backward. He hopped awkwardly on his good leg and tried to retain his balance. McCarter lunged and shoved his opponent into the breakfast table. The big man fell into a chair and took it with him when he hit the floor.

The skinny guy once again reached for his pistol. McCarter kicked the gun away from the man's groping fingers. The fellow withdrew his hand, afraid it would be stomped again. The British warrior hurried to his fallen Browning and scooped up the pistol.

"If you bastards are room service, you're not getting a tip," McCarter announced as he pointed the Hi-Power at the smaller man. "Get on your belly with your arms stretched out in front of you. Explain it to your mate in case he doesn't understand English. Keep your hands where I can see them. I'm a bit jumpy now. It won't take much to startle me into pulling the trigger."

Both men obeyed. The big fellow moaned softly from the pain in his mangled knee. He lay on his stomach with his arms extended, palms flat on the floor. His partner adopted the same stance and looked up at McCarter, squinting as he tried to watch the Briton without his glasses.

"I don't suppose you two want to explain what the hell this is about," McCarter commented as he located the handguns of the intruders. "Save us all some time and trouble if you did."

He examined the pistols. McCarter recognized the Cyrillic letters stamped in the metal frames. He was also familiar with the Soviet-made Makarov, similar to a Walther PPK in design. The other gun was a 6.35

mm Tula Korovin, sometimes referred to as a "baby Tokarev."

"Well, freeze my arse and call me a Siberian," McCarter said with a chuckle. "You blokes are KGB. They must be scraping the bottom of the barrel at the Kremlin these days."

"I don't know what you're talking about," the small man replied, his voice an unconvincing monotone.

"Maybe I jumped to the wrong conclusion," the Briton admitted with a shrug. He stuck the Makarov in his belt and pocketed the little TK auto. "You fellas probably just picked up these Soviet weapons at an auction."

He watched the pair as he walked backward to the discarded briefcase by the door. McCarter knelt beside it. The valise was open and he glanced inside. He moved some papers and a large brown envelope. A leather kit was hidden behind the curtain at the lid. McCarter unzipped the packet to discover three syringes wrapped in plastic and a trio of small vials of liquid.

"Hello," the Phoenix pro remarked with interest. "What have we here? I suppose you're gonna tell me you're a diabetic?"

"I'm not telling you anything," the intruder replied in English.

"You will, chum," McCarter assured him.

There were no labels on the vials, but the caps were different colors. McCarter glanced over the papers.

Some were printed in Russian and others in a Slavic language with a Roman alphabet; McCarter guessed it was Polish. The Briton opened the envelope and dumped the contents onto the floor.

Several photographs fell from the envelope. Mc-Carter was surprised to see his own face and the faces of his fellow Phoenix commandos, Staszic, Jowialski and Potocki. The grainy pictures suggested they were blown-up copies of smaller photographs, probably taken by a surveillance camera with a long-range lens.

"This is getting bloody intriguing now," McCarter said. "You chaps forming a fan club? Want me to autograph this picture?"

The English-speaking captive told McCarter to perform an impossible act of self-copulation.

"I take it that means no," McCarter commented as he shuffled to the bed, Browning still pointed at the opponents on the floor. "You two try to get comfortable, because you're going to be there for a while."

He reached for the telephone and heard a woman's voice talking in Polish. McCarter asked if she spoke English. When there was no response, he attempted to repeat the question in Polish.

"*Czy pan...*" the Briton began, but he recalled that *pan* was used when addressing a male. He tried again. "*Czy pani... uh... mówi po angielski?*"

"*Angielsku?*" the woman's voice inquired.

"Yeah, that's what I meant," McCarter replied. "*Angielsku.* English. You don't speak it, do you?"

"*Chwileczke,*" she told him.

"What the hell does that mean?" the frustrated Briton asked, but there was no response from the woman. He hoped she had told him to wait a moment.

"Hello, sir," a man's voice sounded over the receiver. "I am Tomasz and I speak English. How may I help you?"

"Can you put me through to the American embassy, please?" McCarter requested. "My wife's brother works there. She wants me to look him up while I'm in Warsaw, but I've got some work to do here and I won't be leaving my room for a while. Fellow's name is Staszic. Anton Staszic."

"I'll see what I can do, sir," the voice on the phone assured him. "Please wait on the line."

"Believe me," McCarter replied as he looked at the two captives on the floor, "I'm not going anywhere."

10

Fifty miles west of Cracow was a place called Oswie-
cim. It was better known by another name—Ausch-
witz.

Katz stared at the infamous Nazi death camp.
Fences with layers of barbed wire surrounded the grim
brick buildings and drab wooden barracks. The insid-
ious gas showers and crematoriums still stood, monuments to one of the most hideous atrocities in history.

"This is a depressing place, isn't it?" Jowialski remarked.

"Yes, it is," Katz quietly agreed.

He turned up the collar of his overcoat as the cold
wind howled through the barbed wire. Half-frozen
snow crunched underfoot as Katz and Jowialski
walked toward a brick building outside the camp. A
large black Russian car was parked near the structure. Two men stood beside the big vehicle, waiting for
Katz and Jowialski.

"Dobri d'yen," a tall man dressed in a long dark
coat and fur cap greeted.

"Good afternoon," Katz replied, also speaking Russian. He knitted his brows as he saw the tall man's face. The strong Slavic features with a trace of Tatar blood seemed vaguely familiar. "You chose an unusual place to meet, Major. You are Major Aleksandr Reutov?"

"Da," the Russian officer said with a nod. "You may not remember me, but I have good reason to remember you. We met once before in Mexico City more than a year ago."

"Mexico City?" Katz said with a frown as he tried to recall the incident Reutov was referring to. "I remember encountering Colonel Kalinin when I was there...."

"I was one of his aides," Reutov said. His eyes hardened as he spoke. "I still have a scar under my right rib cage from where you gouged me with those steel hooks of yours."

"Really?" Katz said. "I remember now. You tried to attack me to protect Colonel Kalinin. Didn't I kick you in the face, as well?"

"Broke two teeth," Reutov grated in reply.

"I apologize for any pain or discomfort caused by that," the Phoenix commander assured him. "It wasn't a personal matter. I understand why you attacked me and surely you understand why I had to defend myself. I could have killed you, but neither I nor any of my men wanted to harm you, Kalinin or any of the other KGB personnel. We just needed information."

"Kalinin supplied you with it," Reutov replied in a flat voice. "You were pretending to be some sort of French mercenaries when we met in Mexico. I was surprised to discover you're really CIA."

"Mr. Masters was surprised when two of your men attacked him in his hotel room this morning," Katz told the Russian.

"They were just supposed to keep you and your friends under surveillance," the Russian replied glumly. "They stepped out of line and thought they'd interrogate him with scopolamine. You found truth serum in Sarkisov's valise, didn't you?"

"And a vial filled with enough morphine to kill a bull elephant," Katz added. "What did your men intend to do after they questioned Masters? Give him a nice, peaceful drug-related death?"

Reutov frowned. "The drug deaths that have plagued Warsaw have involved cocaine, not morphine. It seems to be connected with Americans, one way or the other."

"One of your men referred to Staszic by his nickname Toni when they rapped on Masters's door," Katz began. "If the KGB knows those sort of details, you must have been picking up a lot of information about CIA activities from the U.S. embassy. You've also had us under surveillance since we arrived. Obviously the KGB's been keeping tabs on Jowialski's outfit, as well. Isn't it clear we're not involved in the cocaine traffic here?"

"You must know enough about espionage to realize nothing is obvious or clear in this profession," Reutov replied.

"That's not true, Major," Katz said with a thin smile. "It's obvious CIA operations in Poland have degenerated to a level that's left so many holes in security that the term hardly applies anymore. Staszic is using his real name and is more concerned with good relations between the U.S. embassy and the Polish government than any sort of covert operations. Staszic and Jowialski are on first-name terms and act like old college chums."

"It sounds as if you're criticizing us," Jowialski remarked. He was having some difficulty following the conversation because it had again switched to Russian. "The security service has tried to cooperate with your people as much as possible."

"Your organization is agreeable to work with," Katz told him, "but it's less than professional. That's not your fault. Poland is still going through a lot of transitions. I'm sure you don't like to think of this, but the Polish Security Service functioned as a secret police organization closely linked to the Communist party and the Soviet KGB until recently. Your organization spied on citizens, denied freedom and arrested people committing 'crimes' that are now part of Polish internal policies. The Security Service was basically the enforcement arm of the Communist regime that's now out of power. Fortunately it no longer operates that way, but unfortunately it isn't quite sure how it should function under a free government."

"Freedom?" Reutov snorted with contempt. "The freedom to have drugs and crime tearing apart society, just as it is in the United States? This freedom means there's no law and order and people aren't safe. The cities will become jungles with gangs of drug-crazed hoodlums roaming the streets."

"That's a bit of an exaggeration," Katz said. "I won't deny there may be a higher crime rate in a free country versus a dictatorship. But that's no reason to treat a population as prisoners within their own homeland. Be that as it may, I think your people and mine have a common goal here in Poland. You're trying to find out who's responsible for the drugs and murders, correct?"

"And I suspect you Americans," Reutov insisted. "This could all be some sort of elaborate camouflage to make it appear you're trying to investigate the conspiracy as a way of concealing the truth."

"That's such an absurd notion I'm sure you don't really believe it, Major," Katz replied. "I'll admit we suspected the KGB might be responsible, but the fact that your men intended to question Masters with scopolamine and you agreed to meet with us suggests we're looking for someone else."

"How considerate," Reutov said sarcastically. "That doesn't convince me your group is innocent."

The Phoenix commander shrugged. "Maybe we can cooperate. The KGB clearly has a better intelligence network here than the CIA at present. It may well be better informed than the Polish Security Service simply because you've got more experience and you still conduct a lot of surveillance here."

"The Soviet Union is still interested in Poland," the Russian agent admitted. "So is the United States. But our reasons are different. My government has decided Poland and the other Eastern European countries can have self-rule and choose their own form of government, yet there are conditions. Similar to Finland we expect Poland to maintain certain cooperative relations with the USSR."

"I understand that," Katz assured him. "What does that have to do with the drug trafficking and murders in Poland?"

"It may not be the KGB's concern if you Americans aren't responsible," Reutov answered in a flat voice.

"You're not interested?" the Israeli inquired. "The smugglers and dealers could be right-wing members of Solidarity. Wouldn't you like to know about that? A nice propaganda coup if that's the case. If extremist members of the Communist party are responsible, it would certainly be better if the KGB was involved in stopping them rather than being accused of being their allies."

Reutov considered Katz's remarks and heaved his chest and shoulders in an exaggerated sigh. His austere manner softened slightly as he glanced from Katz to Jowialski. "What do you have in mind?" he asked.

"Has the KGB been conducting surveillance on any Western Europeans who might be involved in criminal activities?" Katz inquired. "Especially any from France or, more precisely, from Corsica?"

11

Captain Potocki slid a magazine into the butt of his Polish Wz-63 submachine gun, which resembled a cross between an Israeli Uzi and a Czech M-61 Skorpion. The gun was compact, weighed less than twenty pounds and fired a 9 mm cartridge.

The police captain hadn't fired such a weapon since he was a soldier in the Polish naval infantry. Potocki used it only on the firing range. He had never fired a weapon at a human being. He hadn't expected to be called upon to participate in a military raid, and his lack of experience and limited skills troubled him.

By contrast the five mysterious commandos from the United States seemed almost nonchalant as they prepared for battle. Phoenix Force had returned to the safehouse where the bulk of their gear was stored. Potocki watched with fascination as the veteran warriors unpacked their equipment. The Phoenix pros had changed into black camouflage fatigue uniforms, paratrooper boots and black berets. Each man carried a Walther P-88 autoloader in a shoulder holster except McCarter, who stubbornly refused to part with his pet Browning Hi-Power.

The British ace also carried a snub-nosed .38 Special Smith & Wesson revolver in a holster at the small of his back and checked an Uzi machine pistol before loading a long magazine into the buttwell. The weapon, a compact version of the world-famous Uzi submachine gun, was an efficient little chopper with a stubby barrel and a selector switch for full or semi-auto firing.

Rafael Encizo slipped the strap of an Uzi machine pistol over his shoulder and allowed the weapon to hang at hip level. In addition to the Uzi and Walther pistol the Cuban carried a Walther PPK at the small of his back, a big Cold Steel Tanto fighting knife in a cross-draw position on his belt and a double-edged Gerber Mark I dagger in a boot sheath.

Calvin James was armed in a similar manner. A Walther P-88 was holstered under one arm, a Blackmoor Dirk with a six-inch blade sheathed under the other. The black commando carried a medical kit at the small of his back instead of a backup piece. Reluctantly he didn't prepare his favorite weapon, an M-16 assault rifle, for the planned action that night.

Gary Manning was even less happy about leaving his FAL assault rifle unpacked. The big Canadian was a superb rifle marksman and preferred long-range weapons to subguns or pistols. However, circumstances dictated the use of close-quarter weapons and a wise man never carried more than necessary onto a battlefield. Nonetheless, what Phoenix Force considered necessary was an impressive arsenal. All five men carried grenades, ammo pouches loaded with spare magazines and other equipment. In addition to his weaponry Manning had strapped on a backpack containing a variety of special explosives.

Ignacy Jowialski stood beside Hugo's computer terminal as the communications expert tapped into a computer linkup with the Austrian embassy. Anton Staszic looked at the men of Phoenix Force and shook his head in dismay. The CIA case officer turned toward Katz as the Israeli studied a map of Warsaw tacked to a wall.

"I have to question the wisdom of a police raid based on claims from a KGB agent who's hostile toward you because of a past incident," Staszic told the Phoenix commander.

"Reutov certainly has no reason to like me or my unit," Katz replied as he tapped the hooks of his prosthesis on the Lazienkowski Park section of the map. "His political ideology is very different from ours, as well, but I think the information he gave us about Jean Jacques Perse is reliable."

"I'm just not very comfortable with the idea of cooperating with the Russians, or having them cooperate with us," Staszic admitted. "*Glasnost* and all the changes that have happened are all well and good, but the KGB is still on the other side."

"Believe me, we've had enough clashes with the KGB to be suspicious under the best of circumstances," Katz assured him. "However, this agreement between Reutov and ourselves is based on mutual self-interest. We've still got Reutov's two overeager agents in custody. They may not be very good agents, and they certainly were no match for Masters, but Reutov wants them back nonetheless. He certainly doesn't want us to pump them with scopolamine and learn any secrets about the KGB those two may have managed to retain within their walnut-size brains."

"So that's additional leverage to get Reutov's cooperation," Encizo added. "Plus the fact that this drug scandal could either be a major embarrassment for the Communists or a propaganda bonanza. Either way the Russians have a stake in finding out what's really going on."

"Reutov is no doubt disappointed we're not responsible for this mess," Katz said with a shrug. "But he'll get over it."

"Wallburg," Jowialski began as he approached the Israeli, "we just got the additional information from Schmidt at the Austrian embassy. He used his connections with Interpol to run a check on Perse through the Sûreté in Paris."

"According to Reutov, the KGB surveillance of Perse confirmed he's been dealing hashish in Warsaw since March 1991," Staszic remarked. "Does the Sûreté have evidence that Perse was dealing dope in France?"

"If you'll allow me a moment," Jowialski said, annoyed by the CIA man's interruption, "I'll explain. Perse does have a criminal record in France. He received ten years for assault and possession of illegal drugs and firearms in 1979. He was released after six years because he was supposedly rehabilitated. However, in 1989 he was arrested again for possession of cocaine and suspected narcotics dealing for the Union de Corse. Perse had a very good lawyer and charges were dropped after several witnesses claimed a notorious gangster who had been killed that week in a traffic accident had actually planted the drugs on Perse."

"Sounds like the Corsican Union protecting its own," Encizo remarked. "A dead man makes an excellent scapegoat."

"It worked for Perse," Jowialski confirmed, "but he decided it wasn't wise to remain in France afterward. He moved to Sweden for a few months, then came to Poland. He's been living in Warsaw for roughly a year. He owns a bakeshop that specializes in French pastries. Just the sort of novelty to appeal to Poles. We have a national weakness for pastries, but we didn't get many of the French varieties until recently."

"This all fits Reutov's information on Perse," Katz said with a nod. "Except, of course, the claim that he's been involved in hashish trafficking in Warsaw."

"If this is true," Staszic inquired, "why didn't the KGB give this information to the Polish authorities, or use it to blackmail Perse?"

"The KGB doesn't seem particularly interested in helping any country that rejects communism," Encizo answered. "That obviously goes double for Major Reutov, who's apparently still a hard-line Communist. Reutov seems to see capitalism as evil and democracy as a form of anarchy controlled by a greedy ruling class."

"They probably began surveillance of Perse in hopes he'd prove to be an undercover agent for the Sûreté or even a cutout working for the CIA or MI6," Katz added. "When the KGB discovered he was just a hoodlum, they probably continued watching him in case they needed to use him in the future."

"We had problems with hashish in Poland even before 1989," Jowialski stated. "Some hashish was getting into my country, mostly from West Germany. Hashish is a popular drug there. Hash and marijuana have also been coming from the Netherlands."

"So the fact that Perse was involved in hashish might not seem like much to the KGB," Staszic commented. "Still, we can't be sure the bastard's into coke now."

"We know he's with the Corsican Union or at least he was in France," Katz replied. "We know he was involved with cocaine then and he's still dealing drugs. That's enough reason to talk with the man."

Staszic pointed at the Uzi that hung from Katz's shoulder. "You aren't taking that just to talk with Perse."

"Reutov says Perse usually has six or seven hoods at his shop and in his home over the bakery," Katz explained. "The KGB isn't sure if these men are armed, but we'd better assume they are."

"The shop is located near Lazienkowski Park," Jowialski said, glancing over the map. "It's a well-populated area. Two historic palaces are located there. If any shooting occurs, innocent bystanders could be harmed."

"We'll reduce the risk to civilians as much as possible," Katz assured him. "That's one of the reasons we're taking so much firepower and Captain Potocki's bringing extra men. People are less apt to fight when they're outnumbered and outgunned. It's rare for us to have those kinds of advantages in a battle. It might be a pleasant change."

Hugo rose from his seat at the computer terminal and approached the others. He carried a printout and his expression displayed consternation. "I ran a background check on Perse's bank account," the computer jockey declared. "It seems he's paying the rent on a young woman's apartment and giving her financial support. This woman must be his mistress. It's possible she may be at his home. She may even have a child...."

"That seems unlikely," Jowialski said with a sigh. "We can't foresee every possibility."

"But if I can have another hour or two to try to track down more information on this woman—" Hugo insisted.

"We need to get on with our raid," Katz said in a hard, flat voice. "If Perse is paying for the woman's apartment, he probably visits her when he's amorous. I doubt he'd have her at his place unless she's part of his illegal trade."

"In which case," Encizo added grimly, "she'd better not grab a gun. An armed female is as dangerous as a male."

"Jesus," Staszic muttered. "I've never shot anyone and I sure don't want to start by being forced to kill a woman."

"You don't have to worry," Katz assured him. "You're not going with us. Neither is Jowialski. You two don't have the experience or training for this sort of job. That doesn't mean anyone doubts you have the courage, but that doesn't compensate for necessary skills. Frankly Potocki and his police officers aren't really suited for the task, either. We'd rather have commandos or paratroopers instead of cops, but at least Potocki's presence will provide us with some official authority that will be recognized by Polish citizens."

"Ordinarily that's not a major concern for us," Gary Manning commented as he joined the conversation. "But this time we have to operate within city limits and a well-populated area."

"Well, are we going to do this tonight or just bloody talk about it?" David McCarter complained. The British ace was restless and eager to move.

"We're leaving now," Katz assured him. "Everybody bear in mind we don't know what we'll find at Perse's place. Don't jump to conclusions and overreact, but don't underestimate the situation, either."

LAZIENKOWSKI PARK, in the southern part of Warsaw, featured lawns that were green and well tended, as well as the Lazienki Palace and the Belvedere Palace, stunning monuments of Poland's past and the success of the restoration following Warsaw's destruction during World War II.

Phoenix Force and the police officers who assisted them were glad the park wasn't crowded. Warsaw was a cultural center with many theaters, opera houses and museums, but none were located near Lazienkowski Park. The bitter cold and snow also discouraged people from strolling that night. To reduce the risk to civilians and tourists, Potocki's men had set up roadblocks at both ends of Agrykola Street. Most of the shops and restaurants were already closed, but two policemen entered the popular Trou Madame Café to tell customers and employees to remain inside until they received confirmation that it would be safe to leave.

A truck rolled past the two-story French bakeshop and pulled into a nearby alley. The five men of Phoenix Force, accompanied by Captain Potocki, emerged from the back of the truck, moved around the rear of the buildings and crept behind the bakeshop.

A four-door sedan and a white bobtail truck were positioned near the back door of the shop. Two men dressed in thick coats and fur caps shuffled from the building, carrying wooden crates toward the rear of the truck. They glanced around suspiciously as they hauled the burden to the bobtail.

Shouting, one of the pair dropped his crate and reached inside his coat. Katz stepped forward, aware the man had already spotted them and that further attempts at concealment were futile. The Phoenix commander braced his Uzi machine pistol across his prosthesis and aimed the stubby barrel at the man.

"Nie!" Katz ordered, drawing on his limited vocabulary of Polish. "No! Don't try it!"

The man dived to the ground and yanked a pistol from his pocket. Katz followed him with the Uzi and fired before the opponent could use his handgun. A 3-round burst from the Uzi drilled into the man's chest. Thrashing and kicking, the gunman slid under the truck and came to rest against a rear tire. Blood splashed his overcoat and the pistol slipped from trembling fingers. The man stared up at the undercarriage of the truck without moving.

The second man jumped behind the truck and drew his weapon. Rafael Encizo tracked the man through the sights of his Uzi and triggered. Bullets tore into the fleeing figure's upper thigh and hip. The man cried out as projectiles ripped out chunks of flesh and muscle.

The powerful high-velocity punch hurled the man to the pavement. He landed hard, stunned by the terrible pain. However, he still held his pistol. Unwilling to risk the possibility that his opponent might use the weapon despite his injuries, Encizo rushed forward and nailed the fallen man with another trio of Parabellums.

McCarter and James darted to the bakery door. The Briton lobbed an SAS "flash-bang" grenade through the open threshold while the black badass covered him and watched the windows. A shape appeared at a second-story window. A man leaned over the sill, a double-barrel shotgun in his grasp. James raised his Uzi and fired.

The gunman's torso jerked and his shotgun clattered to the ground near James's feet. The body slumped lifeless across the window sill, arms dangling and dripping blood. James continued to watch the windows and roof until the grenade exploded.

The "flash-bang" grenade was designed to daze and disorient rather than destroy. The blast was loud but not deafening and accompanied by a brilliant flash of white light. McCarter dived through the doorway, his body low and Uzi held tightly to his chest. He hit the floor in a shoulder roll and slammed into the legs of a stunned opponent who was temporarily blinded by the grenade blast. The man gasped as he was thrown off balance.

McCarter felt the man tumble over his back and shoulders. The Briton landed in a kneeling position and stared up at two figures who were still dazed and blinded. One man covered his eyes with one hand and held a Walther P-38 pistol, pointed at the ceiling, with the other. The other man had a gun in his belt but raised both hands overhead and kept his eyes shut.

The British ace was reluctant to shoot, since neither man presented any immediate danger. He glanced around for other opponents. The room was a professional kitchen with large ovens, freezer, shelves with plates and utensils and a long preparation table. McCarter found no other opponents in the room.

Calvin James entered and swung his Uzi toward the two men who staggered around in a half-blind state. He didn't notice the third man who had tripped over McCarter's hurtling form until the fellow rose and slashed the barrel of a Swedish-made M-45 submachine gun at him. Steel struck steel, and the Uzi was jarred from James's fingers.

The Chicago badass reacted to the unexpected attack by thrusting his paratrooper boot at his opponent's ribs. The gunman groaned from the painful blow, and James pushed the muzzle of the Swedish subgun toward the ceiling as the man triggered a useless salvo into the plaster. The barrel was hot in James's fist, but he held on and swung his free hand at the gunsel's throat. The side of his hand missed the intended target and chopped the hoodlum in the mouth.

Blood oozed from the man's split lips, but he still struggled to wrench the M-45 from James's grasp.

Gary Manning stepped into the kitchen and discovered the deadly tug-of-war. The big Canadian quickly smashed the base of his Uzi between the shoulder blades of the man wrestling with James. The blow stunned the thug and allowed the black commando to yank the M-45 chopper from the guy's weakened grasp.

He rammed the butt of the weapon into his opponent's gut. The man doubled up with a half-choked gasp, and James whipped the steel barrel across the goon's skull. The man collapsed in an unconscious heap as the gunman with the Walther P-38 regained enough awareness and vision to attempt to use his weapon.

As the pistolman swung his German handgun at James and Manning, McCarter opened fire from his kneeling stance. A trio of Uzi rounds pierced the would-be attacker's chest, solar plexus, heart, sternum and lung. The impact hurled the poor fellow across the room. He was dead before his body slammed into the freezer door and slumped to the floor.

"S'il vous plaît, messieurs!" the only opponent still on his feet exclaimed, thrusting both hands overhead in surrender.

"Keep your hands up!" Manning ordered in rapid French as he approached the man. "Turn and face the wall. Put your hands flat on the surface, feet shoulder-width apart...."

Movement drew the Canadian's attention to an archway in which a figure appeared, a compact sub-machine gun in his fists. Manning glimpsed the gun-man's round bearded face as he snap-aimed the Uzi and squeezed the trigger. The face vanished in a spray of crimson-and-gray brain matter.

The French stooge who was ready to surrender charged when Manning opened fire on his comrade. He lunged for the Canadian's right arm and the Uzi. Manning hit the guy under the chin and sent him staggering backward into the table.

Manning followed the guy and cracked the steel Uzi against the hood's forehead. The man sprawled across the tabletop, stunned and bleeding at the hairline. Manning plucked the pistol from the dazed man's belt and hammered the butt into his opponent's chest. The guy jerked weakly, uttered a faint moan and passed out. The Canadian warrior struck the goon's confiscated pistol into his own belt.

James and McCarter rushed to the archway as Encizo and Katz entered the kitchen from the back door. The black tough guy from Chicago held the M-45 he had taken from a vanquished opponent. He peered through the archway into the service portion of the bakery, where cakes and pastries were displayed in glass cases. Several tables with chairs were located in the small dining section. Harsh glare from police spotlights flooded through the wide front windows of the shop. Warsaw cops had been posted in a wide circle around the bakery in case Perse and his people managed to elude Phoenix Force. They had been told to hold their fire to avoid hitting the Phoenix commandos inside. Captain Potocki was in contact with the police by radio and could inform them if they needed to change tactics.

Bullhorns bellowed commands from the street. Voices announced that the police had the bakery surrounded and ordered Perse and his followers to surrender. The orders were given in both Polish and French to be certain of being understood. The tactics were intended to confuse and disorient the enemy as much as to encourage them to surrender. Hopefully the distraction would assist Phoenix Force with the raid within the shop.

James and McCarter didn't find anyone in the front of the shop. They climbed a flight of stairs to the second story. Light streamed from the top of the stairs as James carefully poked his head around the panels flanking the steps to glance up the passage. At the top of the stairs he glimpsed a shape with a pistol in hand.

"Shit!" James exclaimed, jerking away from the stairs as three shots snarled from above.

The bullets pelted a wall. Plaster dust spit from the ragged holes. James watched McCarter take a "flash-bang" grenade from his belt. The Briton began to pull the pin, but James placed a hand over the grenade and shook his head.

McCarter nodded. He realized James's evaluation of the situation was correct. If they lobbed a grenade up the stairs, it might fail to reach the top and roll back. Even if it reached the top, the gunman might kick it down the stairs.

James took the grenade from McCarter, but didn't pull out the pin. He figured the opponents upstairs had heard the earlier explosion, unless they were deaf, and would assume the grenade would be live. Hoping the trick would work, James swung his arm around the edge of the panel and hurled the grenade upstairs.

Both James and McCarter hoped the gunman was distracted as they swung their weapons around the panel and opened fire up the stairwell. The opponent was watching the grenade tumble down the stairs as the wave of 9 mm slugs slammed into his body and spared him the necessity of deciding what action to take. He died instantly and tumbled down the stairs.

The Phoenix pair could see no one else at the top of the stairs. James watched while McCarter took another grenade from his belt. This time he chose a concussion blaster and pulled the pin. He heaved the grenade to the top of the stairs with ease since there was no longer a need to stay behind cover while throwing.

The grenade rolled into the narrow corridor upstairs. The Phoenix pair moved behind the panel shield at the base of the stairs and waited a couple of seconds for the grenade to explode. The blast shook the building. Plaster dust spilled from cracks in the walls and ceiling. The concussion explosion would have neutralized any opponent in the upper corridor and probably stunned anyone on the floor.

McCarter and James charged, weapons held ready. The corridor was a shambles with billows of dust and fallen bits of plaster scattered across the floor. McCarter didn't hesitate and dashed to the nearest door. He kicked it in and found an abandoned bedroom.

James was the first to see a ladder at the opposite end of the corridor. It extended to a trapdoor in the ceiling. The black warrior jogged to the ladder. He discarded the M-45 subgun. The barrel and frame would be too awkward to get through the small opening. James drew his Walther P-88 from shoulder leather with one hand and plucked a "flash-bang" grenade from his belt with the other.

The black badass pulled the pin and tossed the grenade up through the trapdoor. There was a loud bang and a bright flash. James sucked in a tense breath and scrambled up the ladder. McCarter shouted for him to wait, but James was already halfway through the open trapdoor.

He emerged on the roof where a short, pudgy man dressed in a gray jacket and white trousers stood less than three yards away. He pawed at his eyes with one hand and waved a pistol in the other. A black briefcase was positioned near his expensive Italian shoes.

"Je ne peux pas voir!" the man exclaimed as he nearly tripped over his own valise.

"I know you can't see!" James replied in curt French. "But I can, *monsieur!* Drop the gun and—"

The guy cursed and tried to aim his weapon in the direction of James's voice, his eyes still covered. Unfortunately his effort was too successful and James had to open fire. The Walther roared as James squeezed the double-action trigger twice. Orange flame jetted from the muzzle and seemed to streak across the rooftop to burn into the fat man's stomach and chest.

James watched his opponent collapse in a trembling lump. Blood stained the man's jacket and a ragged bullet hole at the heart revealed the Frenchman was dead. James sighed and shook his head as he approached the corpse. McCarter climbed through the trapdoor and saw his partner kneel beside the dead man.

"You okay, Cal?" the Briton asked.

"A little pissed off," James answered. He examined the dead man's pistol. It was a French-made MAB autoloader. "This dumb bastard made me kill him. He was blind from the glare and tried to shoot me. Goddamn it! I hate having to take out a guy under those conditions."

"Better you than him," McCarter declared. He noticed that the sounds of battle had ended. "I think this little rumble is over. All things considered, I don't reckon it went too badly."

"Could have been better," James replied grimly. "This chubby stiff fits Perse's description, and he would have been a lot more useful to us alive."

James gathered up the briefcase. It was locked. He was tempted to jimmy the latch with his Blackmoor but decided it would be better to take it to the others downstairs. Although unlikely, there was a possibility the case was booby-trapped or rigged with a destruction mechanism to obliterate whatever was inside if opened incorrectly. Manning and Encizo were familiar with such things. He'd let them figure out how to handle the case.

"I sure hope there's something else in this thing than Perse's deed to the bakery and some overdue mortgage bills," James commented as he headed for the trapdoor.

"Maybe the bloke packed his lunch," McCarter said with a shrug.

12

"The officers outside want to know what they're supposed to do now," Captain Potocki declared as he held a two-way radio transceiver in one hand and his unfired Wz-63 submachine gun in the other. The Warsaw cop was glad he didn't have to use the weapon during the raid.

"Tell them to keep civilians away from the area," Katz answered. The Israeli sat at a table in the kitchen of the bakery and took advantage of the opportunity to light up a cigarette after the battle. "We've got two live prisoners and about half a dozen dead. Have your men pull the ambulance in front and bring in two stretchers with restraining straps."

He turned to James and McCarter. "Johnson, you supervise any medical treatment those two hoods require," Katz instructed. "Masters, go with him and help guard the prisoners. No offense to the Warsaw police militia, but we don't want to take any chances with our captives. They may be our first real source of information about this cocaine business, and we can't have them escaping or getting themselves killed."

"We'll take care of 'em," James assured him, placing the briefcase on the table. "I took this from the guy on the roof. I think he was Jean Jacques Perse himself. Too bad I had to do the bastard. He might have had some answers for us."

"The first question I would have asked him would have been—who the hell tipped you we were coming?" McCarter said gruffly.

"Tipped?" Potocki asked, puzzled.

"Perse and his people were pulling out of here," Katz explained. "They were loading crates into the truck and they were armed and ready for trouble. It might be a coincidence, but there's a good chance someone alerted Perse and told him we were going to raid the bakery tonight."

"*Co to znaczy...*" Potocki began. He was startled by this claim and lapsed into his native language. The cop switched back to English. "What does this mean? Is there a spy within our group at the safehouse?"

"The enemy may have an informer in the police militia and found out about the raid that way," Katz answered. "They didn't appear to have much time to get their merchandise out of here and flee. That would mean they didn't receive the warning until it was too late."

"Speaking of merchandise," Manning began as he hauled one of the crates into the kitchen. "Let's see what they were so eager to load into that truck."

The Canadian had located a hammer and used the claw portion of the head to pry loose the wooden lid on the crate. He pulled some packing straw from the container and found several large china plates separated by folded newspapers. Potocki shook his head grimly.

"I pray to God we haven't made a terrible mistake," he said, staring accusingly at Katz.

"You might remember they started shooting at us, Captain," Rafael Encizo said dryly as he headed for the table and took out a small leather kit from a pocket.

Manning took all the plates from the box and pushed aside more straw at the bottom. Then he removed two clear plastic bags, each filled with roughly one kilo of white powder. Manning tossed one of them to Potocki.

"Have your lab run some tests on that stuff," he told the cop. "I bet it won't turn out to be flour. There are about six more bags just like it at the bottom of this box."

"We found eight crates," Encizo commented as he opened his leather kit and removed two lockpicks. "If they're all loaded with cocaine, it's quite a haul."

The Cuban turned his attention to the valise. He probed the lock with the slender steel tools, turned them slightly and heard a click as the latch opened. Encizo finished unlocking the case and opened the lid. Inside the container were stacks of paper money. Some of the cash was in twenty-zloty bills, but most were French and Swiss francs.

"I guess every baker needs some dough," James commented as he gazed down at the case. "How much you figure is in there?"

"With the combination of monetary units that's hard to say," Encizo answered. "A couple hundred thousand maybe. Depends on what sort of currency you want to count it in. Damn sure enough to get Perse out of the country if that's what he had in mind."

"Let's hope those two can answer some questions," Katz remarked, glancing at the two semiconscious goons lying on their bellies, hands and ankles bound. "What kind of shape are they in?"

"They got rapped on the noggin," James replied. "Might have concussion or even skull fractures. They may not be able to talk for a while. Anybody check the pulse rate on these clowns?"

"When we cuffed them," Manning confirmed. "Pulses are strong and heartbeats seemed steady. They seemed to be breathing okay. You're the expert, Johnson, but I don't think either of them is really hurt."

"Fine," Katz declared. "Let's get them out of here and search the place before letting the police forensic team do their work. Since we can't trust all of them, we'll need to do as much as possible before we let them in."

"I hope you're wrong about an informer," Potocki said. "What will we do if there is one?"

"Continue with our mission," Katz replied as he ground out his cigarette in a saucer. "Although that may not be easy to do."

ZBIGNEW ZABLOCKI STOOD by the Mermaid Monument as a layer of sleet blew across the Vistula River. He turned up the collar of his overcoat and lowered his head to try to shield his face from the stinging darts of half-frozen moisture in the angry wind. Zablocki stuffed his hands into his pockets and stamped his booted feet to try to stay warm in the miserable weather.

He wished Colonel Durnov had picked a more agreeable meeting place. Being so close to the river seemed to increase the night chill, and Zablocki resented being forced to get anywhere near the Mermaid Monument. He considered the statues to be the most ridiculous historic site in Warsaw. Why anyone would consider fantasy sculptures of mythological females with fishtails to be of any cultural value was beyond Zablocki's comprehension.

At last Durnov arrived. The Russian officer emerged from a black Volkswagen along Kosciuszkowskie. He wore a greatcoat and sable hat and didn't seem uncomfortable in the bitter cold. Zablocki suspected Russians had an abnormal fondness for the cold. He had never known a Russian who didn't seem to prefer winter to the warmer seasons. Durnov wasn't an exception. The Soviet colonel actually smiled as he approached Zablocki.

"Guten Abend," Durnov greeted. *"Wie geht es Ihnen?"*

"Sehr gut," Zablocki lied. He thought it a bit cheeky for Durnov to ask "How are you?" when the answer was obvious.

The men continued to converse in German to reduce the chance of a passerby understanding them.

"The Americans sent some kind of special team to investigate our operations here," Zablocki began, his teeth chattering. "Our source hasn't been able to learn much about them, but they seem to be very skilled and professional, whoever they are."

"I know," Durnov replied grimly. "Evidently some KGB agents working out of the Soviet embassy have already had an encounter with these mysterious strangers. I don't know the details, but this team may be the same unit the KGB has been trying to find for the past eight years. The files I've seen on this American superteam suggest they're exceptional commandos, espionage operatives and experts in unconventional warfare. More than one KGB operation was ruined by these men."

"Apparently one of your KGB comrades told them about one of Gautier's men here in Warsaw," Zablocki declared. "Those American bastards had already called in an Interpol agent from Austria, and they managed to put together enough information to postulate that this Frenchman could be dealing cocaine for the Corsican syndicate here. They launched the raid less than an hour ago. You may have heard gunshots on your way here."

Durnov's expression hardened. He gazed at the river, his face unprotected from the razorlike wind as he contemplated the unexpected events. "Mácka has put a great deal of time, money and effort into this mission," the colonel declared. "This is an unforeseen problem, but we can't allow it to stop us. The mission was going well until this happened. We continue as planned with one small adjustment to deal with these capitalist trash."

"You want me to have them killed?" Zablocki inquired.

"Give the job to Rzewuski," Durnov replied. "He's done this sort of work before. Recently he's had quite a bit of practice with terminating obstacles."

"It's one thing to kill an innocent, unsuspecting American businessman, and quite another to tackle a group of highly trained professionals whom you have already confirmed are extremely dangerous."

"Tell Rzewuski to use whatever methods are necessary," Durnov insisted. "I don't care how many men he needs for the job or what has to be done to accomplish it."

"Comrade Colonel," Zablocki began, "I'm not questioning orders, but I think we should consider the possibility this wouldn't solve our problem. If we terminate this group, the Americans will simply send another to take their place."

"They don't have another team like this one," Durnov snapped acrimoniously. "Just take care of it, Zbignew. I have business to attend to elsewhere. Mácka is putting together an operation in another East European country. The less you know about it the better."

"I understand," Zablocki assured him. He did understand. Durnov was concerned that the Mácka mission in Poland might fail and the Russian intended to protect further efforts of the covert organization in case that happened.

"You have a difficult task," Durnov said as he turned toward the VW. "I know you're dedicated to our cause and I have faith in the ability of you and those brave comrades who are carrying out orders in the trenches."

"Thank you, Colonel," Zablocki replied. "We'll try to deserve your confidence."

"I'm sure you will," Durnov stated. *"Do svidaniya."*

Having spoken the traditional Russian farewell in his native language, the Soviet officer headed for the car. Zablocki watched Durnov climb into the Volkswagen.

"Until we meet again," Zablocki muttered. "If indeed we do."

13

Sunlight streaked the Monument to the Heroes of the Ghetto and created a scintillating effect against ice formed at the peak. It seemed as if a layer of diamonds had been set in a crescent shape near the summit of the memorial. The glitter seemed inappropriate on this solemn structure, a commemorative to the courage and determination of the resistance fighters from the Jewish ghetto who fought the Nazis during the occupation of Warsaw in World War II.

Gary Manning gazed at the monument as the car passed while heading north on Marcelego Avenue. The Canadian recalled a comment Lech Walesa had once made, referring to the Holocaust: ''Poland is a country where two people once lived; now one is mostly dead.'' Many of those Jewish people had died as warriors fighting Hitler's minions. Not docile victims of the Nazi death camps, the ghetto guerrillas had battled against incredible odds with inferior weapons. Most were slaughtered in the one-sided conflict, yet they died as brave soldiers, defiant to the end.

"Something on your mind?" Encizo inquired when he noticed the pensive expression on the Canadian's face.

"I was just thinking that this country has gone through a hell of a lot in its history," Manning answered. "It would be nice if Poland got a break after all those hard times."

"We could all use a break once in a while," the Cuban said with a shrug.

The driver of the vehicle was a Warsaw police sergeant selected by Potocki to act as chauffeur and interpreter for the two Phoenix commandos. Sergeant Bohomolec drove the car onto Mariana Avenue and headed for the Gomulka Clinic.

Manning, Encizo and the Warsaw policeman entered the hospital. Other cops were already present as well as Inspector Schmidt. While Sergeant Bohomolec spoke with his fellow officers, the Phoenix pair asked Schmidt about news concerning the two enemy thugs who had been brought to the clinic.

"Your friend Mr. Johnson has been supervising the medical treatment of those two," the Interpol agent replied as they met in the hospital administration office. "He says one man has a concussion and is still in a coma. The other has a neck sprain, but Johnson seems more concerned about a heart murmur. He says neither man can be interrogated in the most efficient manner at this time."

"We know what he means," Encizo assured Schmidt.

The physical condition of the injured goons would prevent Calvin James from using scopolamine. The truth serum was a powerful drug and could be fatal if given to an individual with serious health problems. James regarded captive opponents as medical patients under his care. He wouldn't risk harming a subject under these circumstances by injecting the serum even if this prevented the possibility of getting vital information.

"However," Schmidt continued as he tapped the lid of a briefcase, "I've taken photographs and fingerprints of the hoodlums. I'll fax them to my headquarters and run an Interpol check on them. The Warsaw police are also going to look into the background on those two, but one of them had a French passport, so Interpol and the Sûreté have a better chance of finding his criminal history. He may even be using his real name on the passport. Perse was stupid enough to do so."

"Sometimes investigating a man's past can help uncover things about the present," Manning commented. "Is the other cretin a Polish national?"

"He wasn't carrying any identification," the Austrian agent answered, "but he's been muttering in Polish while in a coma. Johnson and Masters tell me the enemy at the bakery were both French and Polish. Apparently you've got one of each upstairs."

"Neither one of them is much use to us right now," Encizo remarked. "Well, Johnson and Masters have had a long night. We came to relieve them so they can get some sleep. After we make sure the security's tight enough, we may not stay long, either.''

"I thought you wanted to supervise the security personally as long as these men were in the hospital,'' Schmidt said, eyebrows raised slightly.

"If we can't interrogate them because they're in such poor physical condition,'' Encizo replied, "then they aren't in any shape to escape. One of them is in a coma. It's pretty obvious he doesn't present much of a threat, and he certainly won't be going anywhere for a while. If the Warsaw police and the Polish Security Service can effectively guard those two, we'll let them do it. No sense in having the members of our unit tied up baby-sitting.''

"We're trying to investigate some other leads,'' Manning added. "We can't afford to be undermanned. And time is something we can't waste. Too many lives are at stake.''

"I understand,'' Schmidt assured them. "But you did find a large shipment of cocaine at the bakery. Perhaps that was the entire supply.''

"More than half the crates were loaded with bags of hashish instead of coke,'' Encizo explained. "Still, we found about forty kilos of that white poison. It would be nice to think that was all the cocaine in Poland, but we can't count on that. Even if it is, we don't know who's responsible or how they're getting it into the country.''

"Or what their true motives are,'' Manning added. "If these sewer rats were just concerned with making a profit, why did they murder two American businessmen and try to frame them with enough cocaine to choke a hippopotamus? Gangsters might want to throw suspicion on someone else, but it's hard to imagine they'd also throw away that much dope just to make the charade more convincing."

"I agree," the Interpol agent said with a nod. "So much for any hope that this was finished and I could go home. My wife is less than happy about how much time I spend on assignments. Being unexpectedly rushed here to Poland without even being able to tell her any details isn't going to help my marital situation."

"Sorry, Schmidt," Encizo replied with genuine sympathy. The members of Phoenix Force knew better than anyone that covert operations required one to sacrifice anything that resembled a normal personal life. "If this wasn't so damn important, we wouldn't have brought you into it."

"I understand," the Austrian assured him with a weak smile. "It's part of my job. Shall I show you to the room where those two charming drug peddlers are staying?"

"The cops will take us up," Manning answered. "You should go back to the embassy and see what you can find out about the photos and fingerprints. We'll be in touch."

Manning and Encizo stepped into the corridor. The strong scent of hospital disinfectant assaulted their nostrils. The Cuban found this smell disgusting. It reminded him of a long recuperation at the U.S. Army Hospital in Nuremberg, Germany, in 1986 after a bullet creased his skull during a mission. He had had to spend months in the hospital before he fully recovered.

"Good," Sergeant Bohomolec announced as he approached the Phoenix warriors. "I found you before Superintendent Kniazin."

"Who the hell is he?" Manning asked.

"*I* am Police Superintendent Kniazin," a voice declared in curt English with barely a trace of accent.

He was a diminutive man with a narrow, pinched face and hard hazel eyes. Kniazin removed his cap and stuck it under his arm. His hair was clipped close to his skull, which contributed to his mean appearance. A pair of burly uniformed police officers stood behind Kniazin to reinforce the nasty little fellow as he glared at Manning and Encizo.

"Pleased to meet you, Superintendent," Encizo said with a thin smile. "Or is that a wrong assumption?"

"You Americans have made quite a few wrong assumptions since you decided to try to take over police business in Warsaw," Kniazin replied snidely. "It's time for you to be corrected in certain matters."

"Really?" Manning asked. "I suppose you're going to enlighten us, Superintendent."

"I happen to be Captain Potocki's superior," Kniazin declared. "He didn't get my authorization for that so-called raid last night."

"Did you happen to notice the 'so-called' drugs confiscated during that raid?" Manning inquired.

"I'm more concerned with the number of men killed by your rash actions during that assault on the bakery," Kniazin told him. "Warsaw isn't Washington, D.C., or New York City. Perhaps you're accustomed to gun battles in the cities of America, but we don't intend to tolerate that sort of thing in Poland."

"Certainly you don't want to tolerate narcotics in Warsaw," Encizo commented, trying to stay calm in the face of the superintendent's accusations. "I'll admit the raid could have gone better if we'd had more time to gather information about Perse and his operations. Still, not a single civilian or police officer was injured. We planned the operation to put them at as little risk as possible, and I'd say the results support our opinion that we acted accordingly under the circumstances."

"You people killed six men and the other two are hospitalized due to your excessive behavior," the superintendent insisted. "I would call that a disgraceful example of American brutality."

"What do you call all those young Poles who've died in drug-related incidents?" Encizo asked. "We're trying to help bring an end to that in Poland."

"You Americans would do well to terminate the drug problem in your own country before you try to tell us how to deal with our problems here," Kniazin told the Cuban. "The slaughter of six men in Warsaw isn't the sort of thing we intend to put up with. I'm certainly not going to allow you to torture the two wounded men in the hospital beds upstairs.''

"Torture?'' Manning scoffed. ''We don't use those sort of tactics. Sergeant Bohomolec was with the police at the bakery last night. Why don't you ask him if we used extreme violence beyond what was necessary to defend ourselves and capture the enemy?''

"Actually,'' the sergeant began sheepishly, ''I wasn't inside the building to witness the battle....''

"Okay,'' Manning told Kniazin quickly. ''Don't ask him. Ask the provincial governor if we don't have authority in this case. What do you call a province here? A *voidvodeship?*''

"I see you've done some research on Poland,'' Kniazin said dryly. ''There are actually forty-nine *voidvodeships* here and three cities with provincial status. Warsaw is one of them. The police militia is responsible for law enforcement here. That means my authority is what matters.''

"To hell with this,'' Encizo said with a sigh. ''Let's just relieve our partners, check security and let the superintendent do his job.''

"I want all of you out of here,'' Kniazin insisted. ''You foreigners are threats to the peace of Warsaw and law and order in the city.''

"Xenophobia strikes again,'' Manning muttered with disgust.

"Superintendent,'' Encizo began, frustrated with the conversation, ''let's go up to the room. Our partners will leave. You and your men can stay with us until we've finished checking the security of the prisoners. Unless there's a problem we'll happily leave, as well."

"That's a fair compromise, Superintendent," Sergeant Bohomolec declared.

"I don't think we need your help again," Manning told the Warsaw cop, still annoyed with Bohomolec's former comments.

"All right," Kniazin reluctantly agreed. "We'll follow your suggestions. However, I intend to report this to my superiors and advise them to have all of you deported from Poland."

"You do that," Manning invited. "Just don't prevent us from doing our job. Your government won't be happy if you jeopardize foreign aid from America. We have authority from the President of the United States himself. Want to bet we can't convince him to shave off a couple of million from the aid to Poland?"

"Blackmail?" Kniazin said with contempt. "Is that standard procedure with you Americans?"

"It's standard procedure with politics everywhere," Encizo said with a shrug. "That's because it works so well. Let's get this over with, Superintendent."

They headed for the elevator at the end of the hall. Manning almost refused to step into the car due to his paranoia about booby-trapped elevators, but he figured the risk was minimal and entered. The Canadian was uncomfortable and eager to get out of the little compartment as it traveled up the shaft. Manning was a bit claustrophobic, and being in the car with five other passengers didn't make the trip any better.

The doors opened on the fourth floor. Manning was relieved to be the first out of the elevator. Encizo patted him on the shoulder. The Cuban was aware of his partner's feelings about elevators. He didn't share the attitude, but he understood it.

A uniformed policeman met them in the hallway. Manning and Encizo were dressed in casual street attire, suitable for the winter weather. They had to show the police guard identification before he would let them pass. Kniazin and Bohomolec spoke briefly with the officer. The two big cops who accompanied the superintendent silently followed their commander.

Another cop was stationed outside the room. The men approached and the officer at the door immediately knocked to signal those inside. The door opened and a weary Calvin James appeared. He nodded at Encizo and Manning.

"I hope you guys have some good news," James remarked. "Even some bad news might be an improvement. Things have been sort of boring here."

James had donned a white hospital smock over his black fatigues. A stethoscope hung from his neck. James looked at Kniazin quizzically.

"Schmidt filled us in on the condition of your patients," Manning explained. "Any change?"

"Nope," James answered. "I think the one in the coma might soon regain consciousness, but we won't be able to use truth serum to interrogate him for a couple of days at least."

"You're not handling these patients any longer," Kniazin announced, thrusting a finger at James. "I certainly won't allow you to administer any drugs to them."

"What's your problem, pal?" James asked with a puzzled expression.

"He's a police superintendent and he's upset because we've been operating in his jurisdiction," Encizo answered.

"Uh-huh," James commented with a nod. "How many creeps mixed up with the drug traffic in Warsaw have you caught, Superintendent?"

"I haven't killed any," Kniazin replied in a hard voice.

"Bet you never got close enough to one for him to try to kill you, either," the black warrior remarked.

The superintendent opened his mouth to respond, but Manning interrupted. "We're going to relieve you and Masters," the Canadian explained. "You guys must be ready for sleep."

"Sure could use it," James admitted. He took a two-way radio transceiver from the pocket of his smock. "I'll tell Masters to get up here."

He spoke into the radio. Twenty seconds later David McCarter appeared from a stairwell. The British commando carried a coat draped over an arm to conceal the Uzi machine pistol in his fist. A nine-inch metal cylinder was attached to the stubby barrel.

McCarter, clad in black fatigues, didn't attempt to hide the Browning pistol holstered under his arm.

"You're not very subtle," Manning remarked with a sigh. "That's a little excessive for a civilian hospital."

"That's why I put a silencer on the Uzi," McCarter said with a grin. "Seriously, I figure this was the best way to discourage people from using the stairs. It's the greatest weakness to the security here."

"You're concerned two injured men could manage to get to the stairs?" Kniazin asked, shaking his head. "That seems quite absurd."

"I'm not worried about those two bastards," McCarter explained. "But some of their mates might try to rescue them or shut them up permanently. That's our main concern right now."

"You and Johnson can go now," Encizo announced. "Just hide the hardware while you're leaving. We'll see you later."

"Fine with me," McCarter replied. "This is bloody boring here."

McCarter and James packed their gear and headed for the elevator. Manning entered the room where the two enemy hoodlums lay in their beds, guarded by yet another Warsaw cop. The man in the coma was surrounded by an oxygen tent and connected to machines to register life functions. The other thug stared at Manning with unfettered hatred. He sported a neck brace and his head was bandaged. The Canadian recalled he had taken this guy down with a rap across the skull.

"Bonjour," Manning declared, remembering the man spoke French. *"Comment allez-vous?"*

The man spit at Manning. The glob of saliva fell short of its target and landed on his bed sheets. He moaned and reached for the neck brace. The act of expectoration had only served to aggravate his injury.

"I guess that means you're not doing so well," Manning said with a shrug. "Pity."

The hood was handcuffed to the metal rail by the bedside. There were iron bars in the window. Even if the police guards were sloppy, it would be difficult for the prisoner to escape.

Bohomolec and one of Kniazin's companions entered and addressed the cop on duty in rapid Polish. He nodded and left. Manning asked Bohomolec what was going on.

"The superintendent has ordered that only two officers are to guard the prisoners," the sergeant explained. "One outside the door and another by the elevator. He says it's a waste of manpower to use more than two since the hoodlums are obviously in such bad physical condition they couldn't possibly escape."

"Jesus," the Canadian muttered, and moved to the door.

The two guards who had been stationed in the hall and by the elevator were gone. Kniazin had assigned one of his men to the latter post and waited for the other officer to step from the room. Kniazin seemed pleased by the disgruntled expression on Manning's face as the Canadian emerged from the room, followed by Sergeant Bohomolec.

"What the hell do you think you're doing, Superintendent?" the Phoenix commando demanded.

"I'm assigning a sensible number of men to a job that may not even require a single officer," Kniazin replied. "The Warsaw police militia has other duties besides catering to the paranoia of foreigners."

Rafael Encizo approached from the end of the corridor. He had checked other rooms to ascertain that there was no easy access from fire escapes or ladders outside. The Cuban had heard enough of the conversation to realize Kniazin had reduced the guards on the prisoners.

"You're not taking this seriously enough, Superintendent," Manning insisted, looking for support from Encizo.

"I don't think we can convince him of that," the Cuban replied with a sigh.

Manning reluctantly agreed with his partner. The Phoenix pair recognized they would be more apt to get results by contacting Jowialski and urging him to influence the Warsaw police.

"Gentlemen," Kniazin declared, pleased that he had won, "come with me."

"Mind if we use the stairs?" Manning urged.

Kniazin shrugged. He decided he could afford to be magnanimous since things were going his way. The superintendent, Manning, Encizo and Bohomolec

entered the stairwell, their footsteps echoing as they
began to descend with Kniazin leading. He felt tri-
umphant and wanted to savor the control over the
others.

"I suppose you people are with the CIA," Kniazin
commented, taking a pack of cigarettes from his
pocket. "We had to tolerate the KGB for decades when
the Russians controlled Poland. You'll find we're an
independent people and don't appreciate meddling
superpowers of any sort."

"Somebody is meddling with Poland by bringing
cocaine into the country," Encizo reminded him.
"Too bad you're not more concerned about that."

"If it's our problem, we'll deal with it," the superintendent replied as he fired up a cigarette. "We don't
need to be told what to do by the CIA, and I certainly
don't need your help to do my job."

The explosion roared above them. The stairwell
seemed to vibrate from the blast. Kniazin grabbed the
handrail and gasped with astonishment. Manning and
Encizo immediately reached inside their coats and
drew their pistols.

"Like hell you don't need our help," Manning
sneered as he bolted up the stairs.

14

"Get downstairs and cover the damn elevator!" Encizo told Kniazin and Bohomolec. The Cuban galloped after Manning as he spoke. "Put men on each floor to cover all exits!"

"Rozumiem!" Bohomolec replied. He realized he had answered in Polish due to the stress. "I understand. Be careful!"

Kniazin said something in an excited voice, but Encizo didn't waste any time trying to guess what the superintendent was talking about. He charged up the stairs, taking two or three risers with each stride. Manning had already reached the landing to the third floor and prepared to mount the remaining steps to the fourth.

The door above burst open, and three men dressed in white hospital orderly uniforms started down the stairs. Seeing Manning, they came to an abrupt halt. The first man grabbed a pistol in the waistband of his white trousers.

Gary Manning snap-aimed his Walther P-88 and squeezed the trigger twice. Crimson spiders appeared

in the center of the man's chest. The gun slipped from
the man's fingers as he fell against the handrail and
slid down the stairs. One of his comrades dropped to
a kneeling position by the top post of the rail and
pointed a small black handgun at Manning.

The Canadian threw himself onto his belly as a shot
snarled from above. The enemy bullet ricocheted
against concrete and whined from wall to wall. Manning fired back and saw his round spark against the
metal post the gunman was using for cover. The third
opponent retreated into the hallway while his pistol-
wielding partner leaned around the post and tried to
get a better view of Manning.

Encizo reached the landing and thrust his arms forward, Walther held in a firm two-handed grip. The
gunman saw the Cuban too late and tried to reposi-
tion his weapon to deal with the new threat. Encizo
opened fire. A Parabellum hit the opponent in the
right rib cage and knocked him back. The gunman
triggered. The shot went high and shattered a glass
plate and light bulb in the ceiling.

Manning and Encizo fired in unison. The enemy
gunman's white shirt turned scarlet, and he slumped
lifelessly against the doorjamb. The Phoenix pair
cautiously mounted the stairs, P-88 blasters held
ready.

The corpse stirred slightly as the door eased open.
A dark sphere, smaller than a baseball, rolled along
the floor through the gap. The Phoenix pair immedi-

ately recognized the item as a Soviet-made F-1 hand grenade.

"*¡Madre de Dios!*" Encizo exclaimed as the grenade tumbled between the two men.

The Cuban kicked the grenade. It plunged through the bottom rung of the handrail and dropped two stories down the well before hitting a landing. Crouching, Encizo and Manning covered their heads and faces and opened their mouths to try to equalize the pressure in their ears.

The explosion rumbled below and the stairs quaked as if about to collapse. Their ears still ringing, Manning and Encizo rushed to the door. Dust rose up from the stairwell and a fire alarm sounded on the second floor. The two warriors could only hope no one was hurt.

Manning grabbed the dead man by the door and pulled the corpse upright. He pushed the corpse through the door into the hallway to the fourth-floor ward.

Two pistol shots exploded and Manning felt the dead man's body jerk from the impact of the slugs. He shoved the corpse aside, dropped to one knee and thrust his P-88 in the direction of the gunshots. Two figures in white shuffled backward to the elevator. One bogus orderly was already inside the compartment. The other, moving toward the open elevator, pointed a pistol at Manning.

The gunman had been taken off guard when he fired into his own dead comrade. Manning's tactic distracted him long enough to allow the Canadian to train his Walther on the opponent and fire.

The man howled and clutched his belly with one hand as he tried to fire back at Manning. Two more shots from the Canadian nailed the gunman in the chest and the side of the neck. Blood spewed as the man stumbled backward into a wall.

The man in the elevator hastily swung a pistol with a silencer at Manning. The Canadian ducked as the muffled weapon coughed twice. Bullets pelted the doorframe. Manning and Encizo thrust their pistols around the corner and triggered. Then Manning dived into the corridor and rolled across the floor while Encizo covered him from the door.

The elevator doors shut with the gunman inside. Encizo shouted to Manning to stay put in case the elevator stayed on the fourth floor. Manning glanced at the corpses in the hallway. The two cops Kniazin had assigned to guard the ward were dead. One lay near the elevator, not far from the body of the gunman Manning had taken out. The other officer was sprawled outside the room where the two prisoners had been.

Rubble and plaster dust littered the threshold of the room. A fire alarm blared inside and smoke rolled from the doorway. Manning didn't have to look inside to realize what had happened. The killers, disguised as orderlies, had killed the police sentries and lobbed a grenade into the room to assassinate the injured hoodlums inside. The blast must have ignited the oxygen tent and the fire had set off the alarm. The scent of charred flesh revealed that the sprinkler system had been inadequate to douse the flames before they had reached the patient who had been in a coma. He would never come out of it now.

Manning turned back to the elevator and saw that the direction light beside the doors had switched on, illuminating an arrow pointing up.

"He's headed upstairs!" the Canadian announced.

"Sneaky bastard," Encizo growled as he bolted up to the fifth-floor ward.

The Cuban pushed through the door to the hallway. A nurse helping a patient in a wheelchair gasped when she saw the pistol in Encizo's fist. He ignored her and looked toward the elevator down the corridor. The up light was still on. The elevator was headed higher.

"Prosze wezwac milicje!" a voice called somewhere in the ward. Encizo recognized the expression as a plea for someone to call the police.

His Polish was too limited for him to understand the words being exchanged among the rooms and in the hall. The voices sounded alarmed. Explosions and gunshots in a hospital were hardly routine. Encizo hoped none of the hospital staff had been hurt as he headed up the stairwell to the sixth floor.

The Cuban pushed the door open slowly. To prevent unwanted attention, he thrust his pistol into his coat pocket before he stepped into the hallway. A nurse and an orderly were helping an elderly patient with a walker step through the corridor. A beefy man dressed in a white smock with a clipboard under his arm waited by the elevator. The doors began to open.

Encizo approached, hoping he didn't look suspicious. Too late, he realized his coat was smeared with plaster dust and the knee of one pant leg had been torn. When the gunman disguised as an orderly emerged from the car, he instantly spotted Encizo as one of his enemies.

The guy's eyes widened and he lunged for the unsuspecting doctor. The medical man cried out as the gunman grabbed his smock and yanked him forward. The killer adroitly stepped behind the innocent bystander and jammed the muzzle of his gun into the doctor's ribs.

Encizo drew his pistol, but the enemy held the doctor as a shield. The man barked something in Polish. Encizo didn't understand a word. Nonetheless, it wasn't difficult to guess that the son of a bitch was trying to use the hostage to convince Encizo to either put down his weapon or allow the hoodlum to escape via the elevator.

"No way," Encizo replied, shaking his head. "You're not going anywhere."

The doctor trembled and his eyes pleaded with Encizo as he whispered something that could have been a prayer. Encizo sympathized but kept his attention focused on the gunman.

The hoodlum's lean, hard features expressed tension and fear. He didn't see any emotion in the face of the tough Cuban. Encizo held the Walther in a firm Weaver's combat grip and stared at his opponent through its sights. The gunman's eyes darted from side to side. He looked for some sort of way out or a sign that someone might try to convince the determined Hispanic to lower his gun.

The only exit was the elevator behind the man and his hostage. The down arrow had lit up and the elevator was already descending the shaft. Several people, witnessing the deadly drama, sheltered in doorways. Even the old fellow with the walker had been moved out of harm's way. The gunman was on his own and he didn't have too many options.

The hostage was useful only if the tactic held Encizo at bay. It was clear the Phoenix pro wasn't about to drop his gun, and killing the hostage would leave the gunman an open target with no cards left to play. He couldn't surrender and no one would be coming to his aid. That left one choice.

The gunman swung his gun at Encizo. He used the doctor for cover as he tried to aim and fire at Encizo. The shot burst like thunder in an echo chamber. Encizo had waited for the man to offer him a decent target. The extended arm wasn't much, but he shot before his opponent could do so.

The bullet ripped through muscle and bone above the gunman's elbow. His hand popped open and the pistol fell to the floor. The man staggered and clutched his shattered arm. Encizo kicked the pistol across the floor. The thug's glassy eyes and stunned expression revealed there was no fight left in him as he slumped into a corner.

The elevator doors opened. Superintendent Kniazin and two uniformed policemen emerged. Encizo patted the doctor on the shoulder and tried to assure the frightened man that it was over. The Cuban turned to Kniazin and suggested he talk to the guy.

"Are you sure this is the last of them?" the superintendent inquired as he glanced at the wounded man in the corner.

"I think so," Encizo replied. "Check the fourth-floor rooms and closets to be sure nobody's hiding. It's not very likely, but it never hurts to be sure. It's not very probable they'd send more than four men to handle a job like this."

"Did . . . did they succeed in killing the prisoners?" Kniazin asked, reluctant to learn the answer.

"Yes," Encizo confirmed, "and the two cops you put on duty. I'm sorry, Superintendent."

"How did they get past the guards?" Kniazin said with a frown.

"They were disguised as orderlies," Encizo answered. "Maybe we can ask this bastard."

The thug suddenly arched his back as pink foam bubbled from his lips. Encizo pushed the man to the floor. The goon's body continued to convulse. Encizo smelled a strong scent that resembled almond extract.

"What's the matter with him?" Kniazin asked, confused by the man's actions. "If he needs a doctor . . . this is a hospital . . ."

"A doctor can't help," Encizo said grimly. "It's cyanide. The son of a bitch bit on a suicide capsule."

"He's dead?" the superintendent asked with astonishment.

"As dead as they come," Encizo replied, shaking his head. "And our hope of getting any information about these people might be just as dead now."

15

Konrad Schmidt emerged from the taxi in front of the Austrian embassy. Philippe Vaché watched the Interpol inspector from a café across the street. The Corsican peered over the top of a newspaper. He had pretended to read the morning issue of the *Trybuna Ludu* while he sipped hot tea from a glass. A patient man, Vaché had waited for more than an hour for Schmidt. He wiped the glass with a napkin to remove fingerprints, tucked the newspaper under his arm and slipped on a pair of gloves before he left the café.

Schmidt paid the driver and turned to walk to the embassy. He didn't notice Vaché cross the street at a fast trot, head bowed, the brim of a fedora pulled low across his face. Stanislaw Rzewuski stepped from the back of a sedan parked by the curb and walked toward Schmidt, a bag of groceries cradled in his arms. The Polish agent pretended to slip on the icy sidewalk and dropped the bag. Melons, cartons and meat wrapped in butcher's paper spilled onto the pavement.

Rzewuski shook his head and bent to pick up the groceries. Schmidt blocked a rolling melon with a foot and stooped to pick it up. His back was turned to Vaché as he straightened and prepared to hand the melon to Rzewuski. The Pole smiled and took the fruit from Schmidt.

"Dziekuje bardzo," Rzewuski said, thanking Schmidt.

Vaché stepped behind Schmidt and thrust the point of an ice pick into the Austrian's right kidney. The Corsican killer drove the blade in deep with a quick shove and continued to walk past his victim with a rapid stride. Schmidt's body jackknifed from the pain in his punctured kidney. His mouth opened to scream, but Rzewuski's arm shot forward to jam the melon into the Interpol agent's face. The blow muffled Schmidt's cry and knocked the wounded man off balance.

The Austrian fell to all fours. Rzewuski quickly grabbed Schmidt's briefcase. Vaché opened a door to the sedan and climbed inside. He left the door open and Rzewuski hurried into the car and pulled it shut. Henryk Wankowicz, behind the wheel, had started the engine the moment Rzewuski and Vaché had gone into action. He quickly pulled away from the curb and stepped on the gas pedal.

The car bolted along the street. Since traffic in Warsaw was relatively light, the sedan had no difficulty racing from the scene. Konrad Schmidt lay sprawled on the pavement as snowflakes fell on his lifeless face.

KATZ RECOGNIZED the unmarked car driven by Captain Potocki as it pulled to the curb outside the Victoria Intercontinental Hotel. Potocki opened a door and Katz entered, greeting Gary Manning and Rafael Encizo, who were already inside. Then the vehicle headed west on Krolewska Street.

"Schmidt has been murdered," Potocki announced grimly. "Two men ambushed him in front of the Austrian embassy less than an hour ago. They killed him in broad daylight. The assassins were bundled up in cold-weather clothing and no one saw their faces. Schmidt was killed with an ice pick. The blade was smeared with garlic to cause blood poisoning even if the wound itself failed to be fatal."

"That's an old Mafia tactic," Katz remarked. "Probably used by the Corsican Union, as well. Sounds like the enemy has gone on the offensive against us."

"It gets worse," Manning declared. He told Katz what had happened at the hospital.

Encizo added to the story and explained how the wounded gunman had committed suicide with a cyanide capsule. "That's not standard behavior for gangsters," the Cuban stated. "More the sort of thing one would expect from a professional espionage agent."

"What are we dealing with?" Potocki wondered aloud. "The enemy seems to know too many details about us for just luck."

"We've definitely got an informer," Katz said, "not just a mole in the police militia. The police didn't know about Schmidt. Only a handful of people knew why he was in Warsaw."

"I'm in the police militia and I knew about Schmidt," Potocki declared. He glanced at Katz. "Does that mean you suspect I'm the informer?"

"Right now I have to suspect everyone who isn't a member of my team," Katz admitted. "That includes you. However, I don't think you're the most likely candidate, Captain. We wouldn't be discussing this with you otherwise."

"I'm relieved to hear that," the cop answered. "Any reason why you trust me more than Jowialski?"

"More than Staszic," Katz assured him. "The fact that he's in the CIA doesn't exclude him from being an enemy agent. You're a less likely choice because you actually participated in the raid on Perse's bakery. You had ample time to warn the enemy, and they were in the process of pulling out when we arrived. However, they probably would have been gone if you had alerted them as you were assembling police officers for the raid. During the raid, you could have either alerted the enemy or ambushed us from behind."

"Of course, you could just be clever enough to play along to get our confidence," Encizo remarked. "But

I think we've all got a strong suspicion who the mole is.''

"Really?" Potocki asked with surprise as he steered the car onto Prezedmiescie Street and drove toward the pharmacy safehouse. "Do you mind telling me who it is?"

"Yes," Katz answered. "I'm afraid we do mind. No offense, but we still have to be a bit suspicious of you."

"I just wish I knew who I should be most suspicious of under these circumstances," the Warsaw cop said with obvious frustration. "How are we going to deal with this problem?"

"The first thing we do when we reach the safehouse is call the hotel and tell Johnson and Masters to get out of there," Katz answered. "I didn't see any point in waking them when you contacted me, but I didn't know how serious this had become. If the bad guys killed Schmidt, it means the rest of us are certainly on their hit list, as well."

"What then?" Potocki inquired.

"I'm still trying to put a plan together," Katz confessed. "This is an unexpected turn of events and we're really not prepared for it."

"Well, we'd better come up with something quick," Manning commented as they approached the safehouse. "There may not be much time to—"

The pharmacy suddenly exploded. Windows shattered and glass and merchandise spewed from the gaps. Potocki stomped on the brakes and brought the car to a jarring halt. Dust and smoke billowed from the building. An alarm blared and people rushed into the street. Flames crackled within the pharmacy.

"Jesus," Manning rasped as he opened the door. He bolted from the vehicle, followed by Encizo.

They rushed to the building. Hundreds of pills were scattered among the shards of broken glass outside the pharmacy. Other items had also been hurled from the store portion of the safehouse. The fire inside was growing, but Manning approached the entrance. The door had been blown off its hinges. The Canadian felt the heat of the blaze as he peered inside.

The shelves and display cases lay in disarray on the floor. The Polish agent disguised as a pharmacist was slumped over the counter, his head bleeding from a shrapnel wound. The fire raged from the rear of the shop. The explosion had apparently occurred in the basement where the safehouse was located.

Manning slipped out of his coat and draped it over his head. He drew a sleeve across his nose and mouth and charged inside. Encizo prepared to follow the Canadian's example. A shop owner from another building brought a fire extinguisher. The Cuban approached the man and pointed at the fire extinguisher.

"I need that," he said, pointing at himself and hoping the gestures would convey the meaning.

Potocki appeared next to Encizo. He spoke to the shop owner and extended his hands as he said, *"Prosze mi to dać!"*

The man recognized the police uniform and gave Potocki the fire extinguisher. The cop turned to enter the pharmacy as Manning staggered from the threshold, the injured Polish agent draped over his neck and shoulders.

Fire danced along the hem of Manning's topcoat and the sleeve of the motionless Polish agent's sweater.

Potocki quickly aimed the extinguisher at the pair and sprayed them with foam. The blaze within had escalated to such a degree that they couldn't venture inside to search for others.

Encizo helped Manning lower the injured man to the snowy ground. Manning tossed off the smoking coat and coughed forcibly. He scooped up some snow and wiped it across his face and neck. The Canadian breathed deeply, trying to force the smoke from his lungs and throat.

"Are you all right?" Katz inquired as he approached.

"Yeah," Manning croaked, coughing once more. "There weren't any customers in the shop. No civilians got hurt at least. If Jowialski and Hugo were downstairs, they're finished. No way they could survive that."

"Staszic was supposed to be here, too," Potocki stated. "The explosion may have killed all three of them."

"Four," Encizo announced as he knelt beside the man who had been carried from the pharmacy. He took two fingers from the man's neck after searching for a pulse. "This man's dead."

"Shit," Manning rasped, shaking his head with anger.

"You did all you could," Katz assured the Canadian.

Cars came to a stop in the street. Sirens wailed in the distance. The Phoenix trio and Potocki were unnerved by the incident. It was another unexpected blow to the mission. They looked at the pharmacy as the fire began to consume the building from within.

"What happened?" a familiar voice demanded in a shocked tone.

They turned and saw Ignacy Jowialski approach from one of the cars in the street. The Polish intelligence agent glanced from the safehouse to the four men, his expression a mask of astonishment.

"You're alive," Manning remarked with surprise.

"That's obvious," Jowialski replied, staring at the Canadian. "I asked what happened."

"The safehouse is gone," Katz answered. "So is anyone who was down there. Why weren't you in there?"

"*Co...*" the outraged Jowialski started to reply in Polish, then caught himself in midsentence and switched to English. "What does that mean? Are you accusing me of something, Wallburg?"

"The goddamn building blew up," Encizo said harshly. "We were supposed to be here to meet with you and Staszic. Just a lucky break you weren't here when it exploded?"

"I was at the hospital," Jowialski replied, clearly offended. "Hugo became very ill. I took him to the hospital and he was diagnosed as suffering from food poisoning. Botulism. That's why we weren't here. Satisfied?"

"Not quite," Katz told him. "What about Staszic?"

"Toni was in the safehouse," Jowialski said with a sigh. "He must have been killed unless he was out of the building by some miracle."

"Miracles are rare," Encizo stated. "You and Hugo must have used up the supply for a while."

"I don't appreciate these accusations..." Jowialski began.

"We haven't made any yet," Katz said sharply. "Let's get out of here."

"Where are we going?" Potocki asked.

"Back to the hotel," Katz answered. "Jowialski, you'll follow the captain's car. I'm riding with you."

"Charming company," the Polish agent muttered as he headed for his vehicle.

HUGO TWARDOWSKI SAT UP in the hospital bed with surprise when the door opened and three visitors entered his room. Katz, James and Jowialski shuffled in and closed the door. James leaned against it and smiled at Hugo.

"A private room," the Chicago badass observed. "Not bad. How you feeling? Botulism is a bitch, ain't it?"

"Uh . . . yes," Hugo replied as he watched Katz and Jowialski approach the bed. "I'm still ill, but I feel better now."

"I'm not surprised," Katz remarked. "The doctor said it was a rather slight case of botulism. Not even close to being life-threatening."

"Mr. Jowialski knows how sick I was," Hugo said, looking at his boss. "What's wrong?"

"There was an explosion at the safehouse," Jowialski explained. "We were lucky we weren't there, Hugo."

"Apparently Mr. Wallburg and his friends weren't there, either," Hugo remarked. "I hope no one was hurt."

"Hurt?" Katz inquired, raising his eyebrows. He leaned over the bed as he added, "Oh, yes, someone was hurt."

His left arm swung to drive his fist into Hugo's stomach. The man gasped from the unexpected pain. His mouth fell open, and Katz quickly thrust the steel hooks of his prosthesis between Hugo's jaws. The Pole uttered a choking sound and tried to reach for the Israeli's wrist.

"Don't try it," Katz warned. "I might yank your tongue out by accident. I really don't want to do that. Now one of your teeth is false and contains a cyanide capsule. I'm going to move the hooks along your molars. When I touch the one that contains the suicide pill, you blink twice. If you don't, I'll yank out any tooth that seems to be in the most likely position. I might have to pull out five or six before I get the right one. That's up to you, Hugo.''

"I didn't pack any Novocain," James commented as he moved a chair to the door and jammed the backrest under the knob. "You might be in for a real nasty dental experience, pal."

Katz moved the hooks inside Hugo's mouth. The man in the bed suddenly blinked twice. The Phoenix commander asked him if he was sure. Hugo blinked twice again. With exceptional dexterity Katz clamped the false tooth between the tips of his hooks and worked it loose, then examined the white plastic molar.

"Thank you for confirming our suspicions," Katz told Hugo. "Until this moment I wasn't one hundred percent certain you were the informer."

"The botulism didn't convince you?" Hugo asked with a sigh.

"Not completely," James informed him. The black commando removed a small medical kit from his belt as he spoke. "It was still possible Jowialski gave you food poisoning so he could use it for an excuse to be out of the building when the pharmacy exploded. By taking you to the hospital it would make you look more suspicious than him. If you'd been smarter, you would have given him the botulism instead of yourself. Not too much. If your botulism had been more serious, you wouldn't have been such a likely suspect.''

"But that wasn't the only mistake you made," Katz added. "The night of the raid on Perse's bakery you tried to delay us for an hour or two by telling us that lame story about Perse having a mistress and she might have a child and they both might be at the bakery. You suggested we wait while you tried to learn more details with your computer."

"You managed to warn Perse," James commented, "but not soon enough. When Schmidt was murdered this morning, it proved one of four people had to be the informer. Staszic was out of the running because you killed him with that explosion. Potocki wouldn't have had a chance to plant the bomb at the safehouse. That left you and Jowialski here."

"What would you have done if Hugo didn't have a cyanide capsule in his mouth?" Jowialski inquired.

"We would have given you both a dose of scopolamine," James answered as he removed a syringe from his kit. "After we questioned you under the influence of truth serum, we'd know which one was guilty."

"I'm glad it didn't come to that," Jowialski said dryly. He glared at Hugo. "I still find it hard to believe you're a traitor."

"*I'm* a traitor?" Hugo sneered. "You and the others who turned against communism and sold yourselves to the capitalists of the West like whores are the traitors. You've betrayed the martyrs who sacrificed their lives fighting the Nazis. You betrayed the prin-

ciples and philosophies taught to us since childhood."

"That's such a sad story," James snorted as he approached the bed, syringe in hand. "Maybe you'll
have a chance to write about it if they send you to
prison for life instead of executing you for treason."

"Treason?" Hugo began.

"The government in power decides what treason
is," Katz reminded him. "Of course, murder is still
murder and you're responsible for quite a few, indirectly and directly."

"Now you're gonna answer some questions for us,"
James said, pointing the needle at Hugo. "Lucky me,
I got to see the information on the medical examina-
tion when you came in here. You're healthy enough to
handle a little scopolamine. Even got the right dose for
your size and weight, pal."

Hugo tried to leap up and strike the syringe from
James's hand. Katz slammed the heel of his palm into
Hugo's breastbone and knocked him back onto the
mattress. James grabbed one wrist and twisted Hugo's arm as he positioned the needle at the vein in the
crook of the elbow. Katz clamped the hooks of his
prosthesis around Hugo's other wrist and grabbed the
man's throat with his single hand. The Israeli stared
into Hugo's eyes.

"Go ahead and resist," Katz invited with an unpleasant smile. "Give us the excuse to beat you to a
pulp before Mr. Johnson administers the scopolamine. Every civilized man has a savage inside him.

You struggle and you'll see how uncivilized we can be."

Hugo looked away, genuinely frightened. He didn't struggle as James injected the truth serum. The black warrior wiped the Pole's arm with a cotton ball dabbed in alcohol. He nodded at Katz. They held Hugo until he drifted into a drug-induced stupor.

"Jowialski," Katz began, "it's best that a subject under scopolamine be interrogated in his native language. We'll tell you what questions to ask and you translate for us. All right?"

"Of course," Jowialski agreed. He looked at Hugo and shook his head. "I've known this man for years, but I never really knew him at all. This is my fault, too. I chose Hugo for this operation."

"So you misjudged the guy," James said with a shrug. "We all misjudge people from time to time. That's part of being a human being, Ignacy. Accept it and get on with the job. We still have to nail the bastards who are really responsible."

"Indeed," Jowialski replied. "Let's do it."

16

"The organization calls itself Mácka," Katz explained as he sat at the table in Captain Potocki's kitchen. "That's Russian for 'mask.' It apparently consists of hard-line Communists who aren't willing to accept the changes under *glasnost.*"

"There's nothing worse than a sore loser," McCarter commented, popping the cap from a bottle of Coca-Cola.

Potocki's small apartment was crowded with seven men. However, the captain proved to be a good host and prepared *kolduny,* boiled potatoes and soup for his guests. Potocki placed bowls of the latter dish on the table for Phoenix Force and Jowialski. Encizo inhaled the aroma of the rich cream soup.

"Lobster?" the Cuban inquired.

"Crayfish," Potocki replied.

"So who's behind this Mácka outfit?" Manning asked as he spooned some soup. "An offshoot of the KGB?"

"Some KGB are certainly involved," Jowialski answered. "The conspiracy includes Communist extremists throughout Eastern Europe—Poland, East Germany, Czechoslovakia and possibly Hungary and Romania, as well. There may even be Mácka agents in Yugoslavia and Albania. Hugo wasn't certain. He doesn't know much about Mácka outside of Poland."

"Well, let's start by taking care of the bastards in this country first," McCarter suggested as he sipped his Coke.

"The head bastard here seems to be named Zablocki," James declared. "You might recall his name came up in conversation a while back."

"Former member of the Sejm," Potocki confirmed. "In fact, we ran a check on him to learn what he's been up to since 1989."

"You mean Hugo did it?" Manning asked with a sigh. "I don't think we can have much faith in anything he told us."

"The Warsaw police also looked into Zablocki," Potocki answered as he stood by the stove and prepared to serve the *kolduny*. "Naturally he's still a member of the Communist party and a leader of one of the major trade unions. Ironically enough, for a man who supposedly hates capitalism and free enterprise, Zablocki is also the owner of a pier in Gdansk and has other property that he rents to individuals and businesses."

"Gdansk?" McCarter said thoughtfully. "Isn't that where Solidarity started back in 1980?"

"Yes," Potocki confirmed. "Another irony. Zablocki is doing business in the same port city where Walesa and opposition to communism began."

The captain placed plates of *kolduny* and potatoes on the table. The Polish dish resembled ravioli. Potocki assured Katz that the *kolduny* was stuffed with lamb, not pork. The Israeli nodded and thanked him for this consideration.

"Isn't Gdansk located to the north?" McCarter asked. "By the Baltic Sea?"

"That's right," Jowialski replied. "It's always been a major port and done a great deal of trade with the West even when the Communists were in power. Is that important?"

"Maybe," Manning commented. "The Baltic Sea separates Poland and the Scandinavian countries. That includes Sweden."

"The Swedish coast is the closest of the Scandinavian countries," Potocki said with a nod. "I see your point. The Interpol check that Schmidt ran on Perse claimed the Corsican gangster had formerly lived in Sweden before he moved to Warsaw."

"And some of the weapons used by the enemy at the bakery were Swedish firearms," James added. "Sounds like there might be a connection."

"So you think the Corsicans have been smuggling cocaine into Poland from Sweden?" Jowialski mused. "That would make sense, considering Zablocki's pier at Gdansk."

"And Mácka hired the Corsican Union members to provide the drugs in order to make the cocaine traffic appear to be a scourge brought to Poland by Americans and the corrupt system of democracy and free enterprise," Katz stated. "Proof that all the old Marxist claims about capitalism as the great evil of mankind are true."

"Insane," Potocki muttered, shaking his head.

"That's a simplified explanation," Katz said. "There's certainly more involved in the machinations of Mácka than this scheme. Efforts to undermine the economy, prevent goods and services under Solidarity, that sort of thing. These people are unscrupulous and clever. They know better than to try to pull down a nation with only one operation."

"But if we can stop them now," Jowialski declared, "we'll bring an end to Mácka's influence in Poland for good."

"You'll stop them for now," Encizo corrected. "Didn't you ever hear that 'the price of freedom is eternal vigilance'? You always have to stay alert to threats from groups such as Mácka. They're not always subversive clandestine organizations, either. Sometimes the threat comes from elected officials and appointed bureaucrats. Bankers, industrialists, union leaders, all sorts of people can be more concerned with gaining personal power and influence than preserving the freedom of their country."

"Taking out Mácka is our concern right now," McCarter insisted. "So let's get this Zablocki character and wring some information out of him."

"That's an appealing notion," Katz admitted, "but if we get Zablocki, the others will run for cover. It might take months or years to find them all. The cocaine traffic might be stopped for a while, but there's a very good chance it will continue unless we reach the source." The Phoenix commander turned to Potocki. "Can you find out what goods foreign ships have been delivering to Zablocki's pier?"

"Especially from Sweden and other Scandinavian countries?" the cop inquired. "Naturally there are records kept on such matters with the Gdansk shipping industry. It shouldn't be difficult to get that information."

"Good," Katz replied. "The enemy may or may not have agents within the police militia, but I'd say we can trust the officers we worked with during the raid on the bakery. Superintendent Kniazin may not win any personality prizes, but he's certainly not a Mácka agent. It may sound a bit indecorous, but I suspect he might also welcome a chance to redeem himself after his error in judgment at the hospital, and we can use that to enlist his aid."

"He felt pretty guilty since two of his men were killed as well as the prisoners," Manning confirmed. "I think he'll be more than willing to help us."

"Then we'll have him get the information about foreign trade to the pier," Katz declared. "Mácka may already know about Captain Potocki and he may be under surveillance. Hopefully the enemy is still trying to figure out exactly what happened. They certainly know the safehouse exploded, but Hugo hasn't contacted them. They'll know something went wrong. It may not take them long to locate us. However, it's unlikely they'd actually attack us at police headquarters."

"Well, we'd better finish dinner and be on our way," McCarter advised.

"In fact, I don't think we have time to finish eating," Katz replied. "The meal is excellent, Captain, but we've got a lot to do and we may not have much time to get it done."

"If we all survive, you can help me wash dishes," Potocki said with a slight smile.

SUPERINTENDENT KNIAZIN was eager to assist Phoenix Force and their allies. He offered them the use of his office and conference room and agreed to contact the authorities in Gdansk. Kniazin also sent four cars of police to fetch Hugo from the hospital. Potocki had assigned two of his most trusted officers to guard the informer until he could be placed under arrest and put in a jail cell.

Kniazin soon had results for Phoenix. He had discovered that a cargo ship called *Odin's Merchant* had made several trips from Oland Island, off the coast of Sweden, to Zablocki's pier at Gdansk. The captain of *Odin's Merchant* was a man named Ingvar Vatten.

Kniazin asked Interpol in Stockholm to run a background check on Vatten.

"Vatten has been involved with trade to Poland since 1980," Kniazin explained, consulting his notes. "Although he's only recently been making frequent trips. He doesn't have much of a criminal background, but he did stand trial for manslaughter in 1981. Vatten killed a man in a barroom brawl and put another fellow in the hospital with a broken arm, collarbone, a smashed jaw and several broken ribs. Charges were dismissed because the jury decided Vatten acted in self-defense. There were two opponents against Vatten in the fight, but he was clearly more than a match for both of them."

"A formidable man," Jowialski remarked.

"A very powerful man," Kniazin added. "Physically at least. He killed his opponent in the brawl by breaking the fellow's neck with his bare hands. Interpol doesn't have any proof Vatten is involved in smuggling, but his income has increased dramatically recently. Most interesting is the fact that most of his crew are French."

"The Corsican-Swedish-Polish connection," McCarter mused as he fired up a Player's cigarette. "I guess that's one form of international relations."

"Now the most important item," Kniazin announced. "According to the shipping manifests at both Oland Island and Gdansk, *Odin's Merchant* is due to arrive at Zablocki's little harbor tonight at 8:00 p.m."

"I'll be damned," James said with a sly grin. "Here I thought Christmas was a couple of months ago."

"We're getting a nice big present—Vatten, the cocaine he's bringing in and whoever will be there to receive the shipment," Manning said.

"Don't forget Zablocki," Encizo added. "We'll have more than enough evidence to nail him, as well."

"We have enough to bring him in for questioning right now," Potocki declared. "We can hold him here while the raid is in progress. Afterward we should have a strong enough case to put the Communist bastard behind bars for the rest of his life."

"Good idea," Katz agreed. "Superintendent, why don't you and Mr. Jowialski see to Zablocki? Take along some extra men. He might have bodyguards and may react violently when cornered."

"It will be my pleasure to deal with him," Kniazin assured Katz. "Your team and Captain Potocki will conduct the raid on the harbor?"

"We wouldn't miss it," McCarter answered with a grin.

"Unfortunately some of our gear was at the safehouse when it exploded," Manning explained. "My assault rifle and Uzi were there as well as some plastic explosives."

"Did that contribute to the explosion?" Jowialski inquired.

"Probably not," the Canadian demolitions expert replied. "C-4 doesn't detonate easily. It usually requires a special blasting cap or primacord. An explosion near it might detonate some C-4, but that's unlikely. Speaking of which—has Staszic's body been found?''

"There wasn't much left of the corpse," Kniazin said grimly. "Human parts were found among the rubble, but we haven't been able to identify them yet."

"Poor Toni," Jowialski said sadly. "He was supposed to return to the United States in the spring. He loved America, but he loved Poland, too."

"I know," Encizo said with a weary nod. "I also know my Uzi was at the safehouse when the bomb went off."

"I lost my M-16," James said with a shrug. "But I had my Uzi at the hotel, so the bomb didn't get it."

"My bloody crossbow was there when the safehouse went up," McCarter added. "I had my Uzi and handguns at the hotel, but we also had a lot of spare ammunition at the pharmacy hideout. That's all gone now."

"I know," Katz said as he tapped the hooks of his prosthesis on the lid of his briefcase. "I've got my Uzi in here and three spare magazines. Nine millimeter Parabellum ammo is pretty rare here in Poland. We'll just have to make do with what we've got. Can the police supply subguns to my men who lost their Uzis?"

"We can provide you with some Wz-63 submachine guns," Kniazin answered, describing the technical specs of the weapon.

"What's the cyclic rate of fire?" Manning inquired.

"Six hundred rounds per minute."

"Fifty rounds less than the Uzi," the Canadian commented. "That's okay because we're not familiar with the weapon and the slower cyclic rate will make it easier to control."

"We also have a few R-SVD sniper rifles," Kniazin added. "The R-SVD is similar to the Russian Dragunov rifle. We have some on hand for special police situations."

"You're our best rifle marksman," Katz told Manning. "Do you want to go with the R-SVD instead of a subgun?"

"I'm not familiar with the Dragunov-style rifle," the Canadian answered. "Since we'll probably have to go in to get the enemy, I'll use a close-quarters weapon."

"Yeah," James added. "That's my opinion, too."

"All right," Katz said, glancing at a wall clock, "it's almost seven o'clock. We've got a little more than an hour to get ready to meet *Odin's Merchant* when it arrives. That doesn't leave a lot of time to assemble the best, most trustworthy officers."

"I'll take care of that," Potocki assured him. "But I can only get six or seven officers who I can vouch for and who also fit the requirements for the job."

"That will have to do," the Israeli replied.

"But you don't know how many opponents you'll be faced with at the pier," Kniazin warned.

"We'll sure find out," Calvin James replied with a sigh.

17

The icy wind blew across the Gulf of Danzig and swept sheets of snow and hail over the Lenin Shipyard in Gdansk. The Three Crosses Monument stood defiantly in the storm. The commemorative had been erected in honor of Solidarity members who had died during protests against Communist control in the early 1980s.

Stanislaw Rzewuski stared at the monument from the Zablocki pier. Even in the blizzard the tall crosses were clearly visible. The sight sickened Rzewuski. The memorial to the slain dissidents had actually been put up in 1984 when the Communists were still in power. He considered this recognition of "enemies of the state" as legitimate martyrs to be the beginning of the transformation of Poland from communism to democracy. When the government allowed the Three Crosses to go up, it had encouraged an invasion of capitalists, in Rzewuski's opinion.

He stood on the pier as the chill bit through his topcoat and made his flesh crawl. Rzewuski folded his arms on his chest and turned to the lights that ap-

proached from the Baltic Sea. His scarf was pulled
across his mouth and nose for protection from the
cold, but Rzewuski's eyes weren't covered. Snowflakes fell on his lashes as he watched the ghostly lights
gradually draw closer.

Pierre Gautier and Philippe Vaché shivered and
stood near the door of the warehouse, eager to get out
of the cold. The Corsicans didn't see the necessity in
waiting outside on the pier to greet *Odin's Merchant*.
Rzewuski was apparently displaying his willingness to
face the hostile elements to prove he was as manly as
the sailors who ventured upon the Baltic in such miserable weather. He had invited the Corsicans to join
him outside so he could have an audience and subject
them to the same ordeal. The Polish bastard was willing to freeze his own ass off just to force them to do
the same.

The door opened and Henryk Wankowicz stepped
from the building. He wasn't property dressed for the
bitter cold. His body trembled as he called to Rzewuski in Polish. Gautier didn't understand most of
Wankowicz's words, but he did notice the urgency in
the man's voice.

Rzewuski suddenly returned to the warehouse; the
Corsicans quickly followed. A man named Podstoli
was seated at a transceiver radio unit in the storage bay
area. He didn't remove the headset from his ears as he
turned in his chair and looked up at Rzewuski.

"We have confirmation of the results of the explosion at the pharmacy in Warsaw," Podstoli ex-

plained. "The public news broadcasts haven't been reporting the entire story. The police and the Security Service have managed to keep the number of casualties from the news media. Only two were killed by the explosion."

"Damn it," Rzewuski cursed with anger.

"*S'il vous plaît*," Gautier urged. "*Je ne comprends pas—*"

"*Un instant*," Rzewuski snapped, annoyed by the Corsican. He didn't care that Gautier didn't understand the conversation in Polish, and the damn gangster could wait until he was ready to translate.

"None of the American specialists were among those killed," Podstoli continued. "In fact, two men fitting the descriptions of the one-armed man and the tall black one visited Hugo Twardowski at the hospital. When they left the room, two Warsaw police officers were assigned to guard the patient."

"Instead of giving him bacterial toxin for a mild case of botulism I should have put cyanide in the vial," Rzewuski muttered. "That idiot should have waited for the Americans to arrive at the safehouse before he set the timer on the bomb and left the building."

"Perhaps we should terminate him before they move him from the hospital," Mikolaj Kochanowski suggested.

"Too late," Podstoli stated. "The police have already moved him."

"They probably got enough information from him already," Rzewuski commented. "Twardowski's knowledge of this operation was limited. He didn't know me by name or any details about how we were getting the cocaine or the termination of the American businessmen. However, Zablocki recruited him. The enemy probably knows about Zablocki, and it won't be long before they guess we're using this harbor to import cocaine."

"Twardowski may have committed suicide," Wankowicz said. "He was equipped with a cyanide capsule."

"And the Americans had the police guard a corpse in the hospital?" Rzewuski said, shaking his head. "Then they moved him and somehow made Hugo appear to be alive? That's wishful thinking and too farfetched to rely on. One of the American experts—the black one, I believe—is adept in the use of scopolamine, according to previous reports from Twardowski. We must assume they have successfully interrogated Hugo and learned about Zablocki. They may even have put enough pieces of the puzzle together to suspect what we're doing here."

"What should we do, Comrade?" Wankowicz asked, a trace of fear in his tone.

"*Odin's Merchant* is coming into port," Rzewuski answered. "We have to get the shipment now. It's too late to send it back and we'll need the cocaine if we're to continue the mission. We have to strike this base as quickly as possible and go into hiding until we can evaluate what to do."

"We'll start preparing to leave," Wankowicz said with a nod.

Rzewuski finally turned to Gautier and Vaché. He explained the crisis in rapid French. Rzewuski opened his coat and reached inside to draw his P-64 Polish Makarov as he spoke. The renegade agent stuck the pistol in a coat pocket so the weapon would be easier to reach in an emergency.

"You intend to leave after the drugs are delivered?" Gautier demanded. "What are Philippe and I going to do?"

"Get on *Odin's Merchant* and have Captain Vatten take you to Sweden," Rzewuski suggested. "You can't stay in Poland. Anyone with a French passport will be under suspicion, and neither of you speak Polish well enough to pass as natives."

"If the authorities know about this pier, they may also know Vatten is bringing the drugs into the country," Gautier complained. "Interpol may be waiting for him when he returns to Sweden."

"So have Vatten take you to Copenhagen or Helsinki," the Polish agent replied. "They won't be covering Denmark or Finland. Not yet, anyway. Anywhere along the Baltic might be a good choice."

"Vatten will be very displeased," the Corsican warned.

"Why should he be any different from the rest of us?" Rzewuski said bitterly. "That seagoing gangster will have to cope with this the same as we must. He doesn't have much choice."

"He'll demand more money," Gautier declared. "Especially if he has to take Philippe and me to another port and perhaps go into hiding himself."

"Half his crew consists of Corsicans under your command," Rzewuski answered. "You can force Vatten to take you if necessary. Or even kill him and take over the ship. Vaché has another ice pick, doesn't he?"

"Oui, monsieur," Vaché assured him with a hard stare. "And my steel will work as well against Polish flesh as Swedish."

"You're not really stupid enough to threaten me?" Rzewuski inquired as he thrust a hand into the pocket with the pistol. "Even if you could kill me, my men will take care of you and Gautier before either of you can leave this warehouse."

"You still owe us a great deal of money," Gautier declared. "You goddamn Communists think you can cheat the Union de Corse?"

"I'm afraid you'll have to accept that loss as bad luck in a business venture," the Pole said with a sneer. "You're only concerned with money, and as ultracapitalists you must have encountered such setbacks in the past."

"Revenge is a word that may have been invented in Corsica," Vaché hissed.

"Calm yourself, Philippe," Gautier urged, placing a hand on his friend's shoulder. "We must accept the reality of the situation."

Gautier knew the odds were in favor of Rzewuski and the Polish agents. This wasn't the time to seek revenge. He knew enough about Mácka and its members in Poland to see to getting retribution in the future. Simple survival had to be their first concern for the moment.

"Post guards and tell them to stay alert," Rzewuski told Wankowicz and Kochanowski. "The rest of you start packing our merchandise in the truck. We'll burn the warehouse when we leave to destroy any evidence that might be overlooked. Arm yourselves. We may not complete this night without a fight."

THE VAN MADE its way through the cobblestone streets of Gdansk. Two trucks followed and carefully kept pace with the lead vehicle. The city still retained a medieval atmosphere, and the winding, narrow streets weren't made for modern traffic. The town hall and several churches were constructed in Gothic style. Many of the houses had balconies of carved stone.

However, Phoenix Force and the Warsaw police militia didn't have time to admire the architecture. The vehicles moved to the Langgarten section of the city. The difference between the old and new portions was stunning. Langgarten, the modern part of town to the north and west, featured universities and spacious gardens. The streets were wider and the lighting far better than in the old section.

"We're approaching the Lenin Shipyard," Captain Potocki announced as he drove the van. "Zablocki's pier is approximately two kilometers to the northeast."

"Radio the drivers of the trucks," Katz instructed. "Tell them to separate and move into the predetermined positions. We want to cover the enemy from all sides. A horseshoe formation at the pier should do it. The only other option they'll have will be to jump into the bay. Since the water must be freezing, that would be a very stupid move."

"They might run to *Odin's Merchant* if it's in dock," Potocki remarked as he peered through the windshield. The wipers slid to and fro in a constant effort to ward off the snow.

"That won't do them any good," Katz answered. "The ship is a target, too. If it has arrived, we'll take it down. If it hasn't arrived, we'll wait for it and give Captain Vatten and his crew quite a surprise."

"Perhaps we'll be lucky and the ship will still be docked at Oland Island," Potocki commented. "Considering the weather, Vatten may have decided not to set sail. Kniazin told Interpol in Stockholm about that Swedish misfit being involved in drug trafficking. The authorities may take care of Vatten and his group for us. If he set sail and discovered the weather was too harsh, he may have headed back to Oland. If so, he'll find Interpol waiting for him."

Katz nodded. "All one can do in a combat situation is try to prepare for whatever happens. The trouble is, you never know what the other side's going to do."

Potocki wished the Israeli hadn't made this observation. He was already nervous about the confrontation. The police captain and the other Warsaw cops lacked the experience of the Phoenix commandos and were unaccustomed to gun battles and life-and-death conflicts. The captain wondered how the five superprofessionals from the United States had managed to retain their sanity if they had to face this sort of challenge as a regular part of their job. He suspected the men of Phoenix Force might be a little crazy, yet he admired their madness because it consisted of the courage and determination that could save nations.

The police captain radioed the new instructions to the drivers of the trucks. Katz rolled his head slightly to loosen taut muscles due to tension. They were approaching a battlefield. He could sense it as surely as a bird could sense an approaching storm.

Katz was uncomfortable in the front seat. The heater worked all too well, and the Israeli and the others in the vehicle were bundled up for protection from the cold. He wore a field jacket with a liner, a wool cap and military field pants. His Uzi machine pistol was on his lap and he carried the Walther P-88 in a shoulder holster outside the jacket. A canvas case on his right hip contained a gas mask.

David McCarter and three Warsaw cops were in the rear of the van. The British ace was dressed and armed in a similar manner to Katz. The police carried Wz-63 choppers or R-SVD sniper rifles. They were equipped with tear gas canisters and two grenade launchers. McCarter glanced out the rear window and watched the trucks turn onto another street.

"We must be getting closer," the Briton remarked, cradling his Uzi in the crook of an elbow.

"The shipyard is straight ahead," Potocki replied, tightly clenching the steering wheel.

"We have to get off the road and continue on foot," Katz announced. "The enemy may have lookouts posted. The weather is actually an advantage. The heavy snowfall will reduce the visibility of any surveillance cameras they might have. More important for the safety of Gdansk and the people here, there won't be many workers on the docks tonight. The threat to innocent bystanders will be minimal."

"The streets are virtually deserted tonight," Potocki added as he looked for a place to park. "Gdansk isn't much for nightlife in the winter. Sopot is a major resort area between here and Gdynia, but it isn't very popular this time of year."

"I wonder why," McCarter said sarcastically. He glanced at the steadily falling snow and wondered how many degrees below zero the temperature had dropped.

He got a better opportunity to judge the weather as they left the vehicle. The fierce cold was a shock after being in the heated van for hours. Half-frozen snow crunched under their boots as they walked to the Lenin Shipyard. Katz took a two-way radio from his belt and contacted the other members of Phoenix Force.

Calvin James and Gary Manning were with a group of Warsaw police in a truck to the south of Zablocki's pier. Rafael Encizo and Sergeant Bohomolec were part of the third portion of the assault force. They had left their vehicle to approach the pier from the east.

"Everyone's in position," Katz announced as he returned the radio to his belt. "This is it, gentlemen. One way or the other we finish the mission tonight."

18

When *Odin's Merchant* arrived at Zablocki's pier, the cargo ship docked and men carried wooden crates from the vessel along a gangplank to the pier. A large, powerfully built figure marched to the warehouse, hands thrust into the pockets of his topcoat. The dark blue cap and his impressive physique identified him as Captain Vatten even from a distance.

Gary Manning observed the Swedish smuggler through a pair of binoculars. The Canadian commando slowly scanned the pier. Two guards were posted outside the warehouse. They didn't carry weapons, but Manning noticed each sentry stood near a PMK assault rifle. A Polish version of the Soviet AK-47, each PMK was within arm's reach of a sentry.

"They're concerned about appearances," Manning whispered to Calvin James. "They don't want the place to look like an armed fortress, but they're prepared for trouble nonetheless."

"Let's see if we can give them more than they're ready to handle," James replied.

Manning glanced at his partner's Uzi and wished he was also armed with a familiar weapon instead of a Wz-63 subgun. The Phoenix pair and two Warsaw policemen used another warehouse for cover as they approached the Zablocki building. There was little cover or potential camouflage between their position and the enemy base. Stacks of crates were located on the pier itself, but these offered more shelter for the enemy than for the assault force.

Encizo and other cops covered one flank. The unit led by Katz, McCarter and Captain Potocki formed the third portion of the horseshoe of fighters to hit the base. They were as close as they could get without being spotted. There was no subtle way to handle the situation under the circumstances.

James turned to a police sharpshooter named Goszczynski. He doubted he could pronounce the guy's name, so he merely addressed him as "officer" and whispered some brief instructions. The cop nodded and raised the buttstock of his R-SVD rifle to a shoulder. He aimed as a voice bellowed from a bullhorn to order the men inside to surrender to the police.

One of the sentries immediately reached for his rifle. Goszczynski squeezed the trigger of his sniper gun. The shot echoed in the crisp, cold air. Sparks erupted when the copper-jacketed slug struck the steel frame of the guard's PMK assault rifle. The sentry jumped away, startled and frightened.

He dropped to his knees behind a crate and began to unbutton his overcoat to reach inside for his pistol. James rushed him and stomped a boot on the guy's arm to knock it aside before he could grab the weapon.

The sentry, seeing the muzzle of James's Uzi pointed at his face, remained on his knees and slowly raised his hands to shoulder level. More shots sounded across the pier as the raid continued. James couldn't afford to spend time with the guard. He swung another kick and slammed the boot heel into the man's chin. The sentry's head snapped back and he slumped to the planks. James knelt beside the fallen figure and quickly bound the man's wrists together at the small of his back with a set of unbreakable plastic riot cuffs.

Manning jogged past James and the defeated guard. He noticed the black warrior was frisking the sentry after securing the fellow's wrists. James confiscated a P-64 pistol from the guard's shoulder holster. He stuck the gun in his belt and tossed the PMK rifle beyond the guard's reach. James left the sentry and headed for the warehouse.

The second guard at the base had also reached for his assault rifle when the bullhorn sounded. He stepped right in the path of a police sniper's bullet when he grabbed for his gun. Although the sentries were taken out, some of the men on the pier hid behind crates and readied their pistols. Others rushed around on the decks of *Odin's Merchant*. Two carried Swedish M-45 submachine guns.

Police fired cartridge-style grenades. The projectiles exploded on the pier and aboard the ship, dispersing clouds of tear gas. The enemy coughed and cursed as Phoenix Force and their Warsaw allies donned gas masks and rushed forward.

The men by the crates pawed at their eyes as tears fogged their vision. They spit and snorted to shake off the effects of the gas. Through misted eyes and the haze of falling snow they saw figures headed for the pier. The Phoenix commandos and cops resembled invaders from another planet. The rubber masks with bug-eyed lenses and plastic filters created a fearsome appearance.

Encizo opened fire with a Wz-63 as he charged. A spray of 9 mm projectiles raked the crates used as enemy cover. Already at a disadvantage due to the gas, the opponents were startled by the barrage of bullets. Most ducked for cover. One gunman attempted to return fire with a French MAB pistol. His shot was poorly aimed and the round shrieked past Encizo's head by almost a foot. The Cuban blasted into the opponent's face and chest.

The gunman collapsed beside two fearful comrades. Crouching behind the crates, they thrust pistol barrels over the wooden boxes to fire without exposing their heads. The desperate tactic was ineffective, and they relied on sheer luck to hit a target. Nonetheless, one of the Warsaw cops cried out and doubled up from a bullet in the abdomen.

Rafael Encizo dived to the plank walk and slid across the icy surface to the crates. Approaching from the opposite side of the pier, Katz and McCarter hurled more grenades at the enemy. Tear gas billowed as Encizo crawled around some crates and trained his Wz-63 on the enemy. Encizo held his fire because the gunmen, staggering blindly and nearly choking, appeared to be already out of the fight.

A volley of full-auto rounds suddenly slashed across the pier. Two enemy gunmen were thrown to the planks in bloodied heaps. Encizo was surprised by this and realized that the shots had come from the open doors to the bay area of the warehouse. Three opponents with subguns had cut down some of their own men as they ruthlessly hosed the pier with high-velocity fire.

Another Warsaw cop also went down as a trio of bullets slammed into his chest. Encizo stayed low and moved to a crate for cover. Bullets splintered wood from the corner of the box, and the Cuban ducked to avoid flying slivers. A boot stomped down on the frame of his Wz-63. He glanced up to see that an opponent had accidentally stepped on the gun. The guy was stumbling around with one hand over his eyes. He had no idea Encizo was there or that he had pinned the submachine gun.

The Cuban released the gun and grabbed the man's coat front with both hands. He yanked hard and pulled the dazed opponent face first against the crate. The man's forehead struck the wood hard, and he slumped unconscious next to Encizo. Another half-blind gunman saw his comrade fall and began to point a pistol at Encizo.

A shape suddenly appeared behind the triggerman. Katz swung his prosthesis and snared the opponent's arm above the wrist with the steel hooks. He yanked downward, and the man cried out and fired a useless round into the planks near his feet. Katz swept his Uzi machine pistol into the side of the gunman's head. The steel frame connected with the skull and the man wilted to the pier.

More shots erupted from *Odin's Merchant*. Encizo and Katz found themselves in a bad position. The gunmen at the bay doors and those at the ship were laying down a cross fire with the Phoenix pair in the center. They held their fire and stayed low, behind cover, while other members of their unit responded to the enemy threat.

Captain Potocki and two other cops had found cover by a pair of automobiles parked by the warehouse. Potocki ordered an officer armed with a grenade launcher to fire into the bay area. A cartridge grenade shell streaked through the open doors and exploded. A concussion blast shook the warehouse. The gunmen within were hurled to the concrete floor, stunned.

Although blood oozed from his ears and nostrils, Mikolaj Kochanowski held on to his Wz-63 and started to rise. Although the Polish agent's eardrums had been ruptured, he tried to aim his weapon at the

Phoenix warriors by the crates. Katz and Encizo aimed and fired first. Half a dozen 9 mm shredders tore into the Polish gunman and sent his corpse sliding across the concrete floor.

The police officer with the grenade launcher suddenly dropped the weapon and fell back, arms outstretched, a bloodied hole in his forehead. Potocki and the other cop with him ducked behind a sedan as more bullets from an enemy subgun punched the metal skins of a row of vehicles.

Potocki reached for the fallen grenade launcher and fed a fresh concussion grenade into the breach. The other cop braced his R-SVD sniper gun across the roof of the car and peered through the telescopic sights. The police sharpshooter zeroed in on the head and shoulders of a gunman near a handrail on *Odin's Merchant*. The guy carried a French FAMAS assault rifle. He had tied a cloth around his mouth and nose for protection from the tear gas and donned a diving mask for additional insurance. The improvised gear seemed to work well enough to allow him to use his weapon with some degree of accuracy.

The police sniper triggered his rifle and rocked slightly from the recoil. A 7.62 mm bullet shattered the faceplate on the gunman's diving mask. The man fell back onto the deck as bits of crimson-stained glass fragments flew from his bullet-smashed mask and ravaged face. Two more opponents rushed to the rail wearing diving masks and air tanks strapped to their backs. Each held a regulator mouthpiece in his teeth with an air hose attached to the valve of a tank. The diving gear protected them from the gas fumes just as it allowed one to breathe underwater.

The pair opened fire. One launched a stream of submachine gun rounds at the crates where Katz and Encizo were stationed. The other man gathered up the FAMAS and fired at Potocki and the police marksman. Neither gunman noticed David McCarter as the Briton surreptitiously made his way to the edge of the pier. McCarter raised his Uzi, squeezed the trigger and hosed the pair with a long burst of 9 mm devastation.

Hit point-blank in the chest, one man tumbled to the deck. His companion caught two bullets in the left shoulder and arm. The impact spun the guy around. More Uzi rounds slammed into the air tank attached to his back. The gases in the tank included concentrated hydrogen and oxygen. These ignited with a vengeance. The tank exploded and splattered its owner across the deck of *Odin's Merchant*. Flames burst across the port side.

"Bloody hell!" McCarter exclaimed as he dodged a chunk of fiery debris then leaped over the handrail.

He glanced down and saw the charred remnants of a human leg amputated at the knee. The Briton realized the air tank worn by the other gunman could blow if the fire reached it. He bolted from the pier as Captain Potocki aimed the grenade launcher and triggered another explosive shell. The projectile hit the cabin section and the concussion blast shattered portholes and tore a door from its hinges.

The explosion hurled a man across the stern of the ship. He tumbled over the handrail screaming until he plunged beneath the surface of the chilly Baltic. *Odin's Merchant* was still rocking from the blast when the second air tank exploded. Chunks of the deck and burning human flesh spewed from the blast as the fire aboard the ship intensified.

Gary Manning moved to a side door of the warehouse and inserted some gray puttylike substance in the lock and hinges. Calvin James stood by, guarding the demolitions expert as he prepared the CV-38 charge. Manning inserted a detonator into the plastic explosive and gestured for James to stand back.

As they stepped to the corner of the building, they heard the sounds of battle across the pier. *Odin's Merchant* was virtually destroyed and burning rapidly. Two unarmed figures staggered down the gangplank, arms raised high in surrender. Enemies still fought the assault force at the bay doors to the warehouse, but the Phoenix warriors and Warsaw police clearly had the upper hand.

The charge exploded. Manning glanced around the edge of the building and saw that the door had been thrown about eight feet. Automatic fire snarled from the doorway from one or more opponents inside.

Manning, his back to the wall, carefully approached. He yanked the pin from a tear gas canister and tossed it across the threshold without exposing himself to enemy fire. James moved forward and fired to discourage a counterattack. The Canadian unslung the Wz-63 subgun from his shoulder as the badass from Chicago kept the enemy busy.

Tear gas fumes floated from the doorway. The shooting inside the building ceased and the Phoenix pair heard violent coughing. Thankful for the protective masks, the pair swung around the door. Manning ducked low and James remained high to shoot over his partner's head. Inside, two stunned gunmen were poised with Polish subguns. Wankowicz and Podstoli tried to see through a veil of tears and control the hacking and coughing created by the tear gas.

"Give it up!" James shouted, his voice muffled by the rubber and plastic strapped to his face.

The Polish agents didn't understand English, but the meaning of the Phoenix pair's weapons was obvious. Wankowicz growled with anger and swung his Wz-63 chopper toward the door. Podstoli followed his comrade's action. It was a desperate and hopeless act of defiance. James and Manning opened fire before their half-blind, half-choked opponents could trigger.

"Jesus," James muttered as he stared at the bullet-riddled corpses. "Why didn't the dumb bastards give up?"

"If we had been in their position," Manning commented, "we probably wouldn't have surrendered either."

James scrutinized the storage area he and Manning had entered. More crates and cardboard boxes were stacked near the walls. Tools and machine parts were kept on shelves in one corner of the room. A number of kegs were labeled Sjotunga.

"I don't think that's Polish," Manning remarked. "Must be kegs from Sweden."

"What's that word mean?" James asked.

"How the hell do I know?" Manning replied gruffly.

The Canadian stepped closer and noticed that one of the lids was missing. He peered into the keg and saw that it was jammed with frozen fish. Manning was intrigued because the room wasn't refrigerated and seemed an unlikely storage area for the product. He reached into the keg and pulled out one of the fish.

"It means 'sole,'" the Canadian announced as he identified the species of fish.

He inspected the fish inside the keg and discovered a bag of clear plastic lodged between the layers of frozen sole. Manning extracted the bag and discovered it was filled with white powder. He handed it to James.

"Looks like we found part of the cocaine shipment," Manning remarked.

"Pretty fishy," James added as he tossed the bag into the keg.

Without warning a stack of crates and boxes was hurled down on the Phoenix pair. James managed to jump clear of the avalanche but Manning didn't. Heavy containers crashed into the Canadian and knocked him to the floor. Captain Vatten stood where the crates had been—the big Swede had pushed them over. A cloth was tied around his nose and mouth and he wore a pair of goggles, but he didn't carry a weapon.

James pointed his Uzi at Vatten. The captain raised his hands and spread the fingers to show he was unarmed. The black warrior held his fire, reluctant to shoot an opponent who didn't have a weapon or present an immediate threat. Manning groaned and began to stir beneath the pile of boxes and crates.

"Cochon noir!" Pierre Gautier snarled as he stepped from a doorway, MAB pistol in his fist.

"Your mama," James rasped, dropping to one knee as he swung the Uzi toward the new threat.

Gautier's autoloader barked. The tear gas had reached the Corsican's nostrils and eyes. His vision was impaired and his shot missed James by several inches. The American commando's Uzi blasted a trio of slugs into Gautier's barrel-like belly and chest. The gangster fell backward, blood streaming from his torso.

Vatten lunged for James, massive hands aimed at the black man's subgun. Fists hit the captain under the ribs. The unexpected and powerful blow sent Vatten staggering into a wall. He hissed from the pain, puzzled by the attack until he saw that Gary Manning had risen from the mound of fallen crates.

"I guess you're okay," James remarked, relieved to see his Canadian partner unharmed.

"Just bruised a little," Manning answered. His attention was still fixed on Vatten, fists balled and poised for combat.

The Swedish smuggler froze as James swung the Uzi toward him once more. Manning's Wz-63 was still buried beneath some cardboard boxes. The Canadian reached for the P-88 in shoulder leather under his arm.

"Shit!" James exclaimed as another figure rushed from the doorway.

Philippe Vaché screamed in raw fury and charged, ice pick clenched in his fist. The Corsican killer didn't seem to notice the tear gas fumes. His eyes remained wide open, ablaze with anger akin to madness. His mouth was twisted into a bestial snarl.

James tried to redirect his Uzi as Vaché closed in. The Phoenix fighter's attention was fixed on the ice pick in case he had to dodge the deadly blade. Vaché suddenly twisted in midstride and swung a roundhouse kick at James's subgun, propelling the Uzi from James's grasp.

Manning turned toward Vaché, yanking his Walther pistol from leather. Vatten's fist hammered the Canadian's wrist, and the P-88 popped from his hand. The Swede jabbed his elbow into Manning's chest and stunned the Phoenix fighter. Vatten didn't give his opponent a chance to recover. He grabbed at Manning's head and clutched the rubber snout of the gas mask. The smuggler turned sharply and pulled Manning off balance, hurling him into the wall.

Vaché lunged for James's belly with the ice pick. The black Phoenix pro barely managed to sidestep from the path of the blade. He slapped the forearm above the ice pick to redirect the weapon. With the side of his hand, James lashed Vaché across the shoulder blades. The blow staggered Vaché, but James was frustrated because he had intended to strike his opponent at the base of the skull or nape of the neck.

The Corsican unleashed another savage kick. Vaché's heel slammed into James's stomach. The commando doubled up with a gasp, but his left hand streaked to the handle of the Blackmoor Dirk sheathed under his right arm. Vaché turned and thrust the point of his ice pick at James's face, trying to plunge the steel through a lens of the gas mask to puncture an eye socket.

James dodged the attack and slashed the six-inch blade of his dirk into the ice pick. Steel clanged. The blow nearly struck the ice pick from Vaché's fist. The Corsican glared at the knife in James's left fist. He didn't see the black man's other fist until it smashed into the side of his jaw.

Vaché groaned and stumbled back. He slashed wildly with the ice pick to keep James at bay as blood trickled from his mouth. The Corsican hissed like a serpent and feinted with the ice pick, hoping the tactic would distract James. He swung a high round-house kick at his opponent's head.

The black fighting machine ducked as Vaché's foot whirled above his head. The Blackmoor Dirk rose and slashed deeply into the gangster's calf muscle. Vaché screamed and attempted an awkward thrust with the ice pick. James easily dodged the attack and punched the point of the knife into the Corsican's midsection. Three inches of double-edged steel sunk into Vaché's flesh. James jumped back to avoid a final desperate lunge by the wounded opponent.

James's boot tagged Vaché's wrist and knocked the ice pick from the dying man's fingers. Vaché dropped to his knees and clutched the handle of the knife still jammed into his solar plexus. His mouth fell open as blood gurgled into his throat.

"I bet Schmidt felt the same way when you killed him," James growled. "You son of a bitch."

He kicked Vaché in the face hard and broke the killer's jaw. The blow also knocked Vaché unconscious. This was an act of mercy that allowed Vaché to die without further pain. It was probably more than the assassin deserved.

Captain Vatten had continued his assault against Gary Manning while James and Vaché enacted their duel. The Swede pinned Manning to a wall, grabbed the gas mask in one hand and used it for a handle as he slammed the back of the Canadian's head into the wall.

Manning's skull throbbed as he swung a left hook at his opponent's face. His fist jarred Vatten's jawbone and allowed Manning to break the Swede's hold. He pumped a knee into Vatten's gut and quickly grabbed the big man's coat sleeve with one hand and a lapel with the other. The Canadian jammed a hip into the captain's belly, turned and judo-tossed Vatten to the floor. As he sailed through the air, Vatten swung a boot and kicked Manning just above the right kidney. The Canadian fell into the wall once more, his side aching. Through the lenses of his gas mask made foggy by his labored breath, Manning saw Vatten rise from the floor. The Swede clasped his hands together and swung them like an ax at the Phoenix crusader's neck.

Manning sidestepped the attack. As Vatten's fists hammered the wall hard enough to crack plaster, Manning hit him with a hard right cross. The captain swayed from the punch. The commando punched Vatten's chin and kicked him between the legs. Vatten uttered a choking gasp and doubled up in agony.

Gary Manning put his opponent in a frontal headlock with one hand and placed his other on Vatten's shoulder, gripping his own wrist to tighten his deadly, viselike grip. Vatten realized what was about to happen but had no time to act. Manning twisted fiercely and bone cracked in the Swede's neck. Vertebrae gave way and the spinal cord snapped. Captain Vatten's body went limp and lifeless in the Canadian's grasp. Manning allowed the corpse to fall to the floor.

"Oh, man," James said as he tried to catch his breath. He looked down at Vatten's body. "You know, we were lucky neither one of these dudes came at us with a gun."

"Yeah," Manning agreed as he wearily located his fallen Wz-63 subgun. "Everybody has some luck once in a while. I'm sure glad we had some this time."

Both men were aware that one day their luck would run out. They knew eventually there would be one last mission for each member of Phoenix Force. Each one would certainly come to a violent end.

Of course, that was something they had known from the beginning. James considered this as he retrieved his Uzi.

"At least we don't have to fret about how we'll handle retirement," he muttered.

"What's that?" Manning inquired.

"Nothing important," James assured him. "Let's see if the others need our help wrapping up this mess."

19

Stanislaw Rzewuski withdrew into the office as Rafael Encizo fired a burst of submachine rounds at the Polish agent. Bullets chewed off pieces of the doorway as Rzewuski pressed his back to the wall, P-64 pistol in his fist. The scent of tear gas drifted into the office from the bay area of the warehouse. Rzewuski realized he couldn't hold out much longer. The invaders were too well armed and skilled.

Apparently the others had already been taken out. Rzewuski was alone. He still had his pistol with three extra magazines and one F-1 hand grenade. It was more than enough weaponry to deal with most situations, but inadequate to handle his present crisis. Rzewuski knew the Mácka operation was already ruined. He couldn't hope to salvage the mission. He had two options: surrender or die.

Rzewuski had no trouble making a choice. He considered himself to be a true patriot: not to Poland, but to the creed of the Communist movement that had dominated his life. If he had to die for this cause, Rzewuski would die as a hero to the beliefs he had served with total loyalty and dedication. And he would take as many of the enemy with him as possible.

The office was indefensible. The invaders would soon box him in and use tear gas or concussion grenades to render Rzewuski helpless. He considered tossing the F-1 blaster at Encizo in the bay section, but decided this would probably be futile. There was ample cover available and the enemy could duck behind crates to protect themselves. The Soviet grenade was Rzewuski's most powerful single weapon. He didn't want to waste it.

The renegade agent glimpsed movement at the window by the desk. Seeing a uniformed figure outside the glass, Rzewuski opened fire with the P-64. Glass shattered and the Warsaw policeman fell from view.

He shoved the F-1 into a coat pocket, tugged at his cap to be certain it was firmly on his head and drew a forearm across his eyes. Rzewuski charged the window and leaped forward. He hit the glass pane with all his weight behind it. The framework gave way. Glass smashed apart. Broken shards stung his neck and jaw, but he was otherwise unharmed by the bold tactic.

Rzewuski landed awkwardly and tumbled to the ground. He glanced at the corpse of the man he had shot through the window. Rzewuski began to reach for the dead man's submachine gun as a figure appeared at the corner of the warehouse. The agent swung his pistol at the shape and triggered twice. The cop retreated from view and Rzewuski bolted from the pier.

Captain Potocki and the police sharpshooter were still stationed by the two automobiles when they saw the man in the tattered overcoat run toward them. The cop with the R-SVD rifle swung his weapon at the approaching figure but hesitated, unsure if the man in the coat was friend or foe.

Rzewuski didn't hesitate. He quickly aimed and fired a lethal slug into the sharpshooter's heart. Continuing toward the cars, Rzewuski pumped another round into the policeman's upper torso. The rifle fell from the officer's grasp as his bloodied body tumbled into the side of the sedan. His corpse slid to the ground as Potocki tossed the empty grenade launcher aside and drew his side arm.

Captain Potocki never had a chance. Rzewuski was less than six feet from the Warsaw cop and shot him twice in the face. The unfired handgun slipped from Potocki's fingers as the back of his skull exploded and brains and bone fragments splattered across the hood of the sedan.

"Goddamn bastard!" David McCarter exclaimed as he saw Rzewuski slaughter the policemen.

The British commando ran across the pier and fired at Rzewuski. The Polish agent ducked behind the sedan as bullets scraped the car's roof. He opened the door, slid behind the steering wheel, stuck the key in the ignition and turned on the engine. A Parabellum shattered the window on the passenger side. Rzewuski grabbed the gearshift and stepped on the accelerator.

The car shot forward and headed away from the pier. McCarter's Uzi spit at the retreating vehicle. Bullet holes lined the rear of the sedan as smoke rose from the spinning tires. Rzewuski crouched low behind the wheel, pressing his foot on the gas.

Seeing Rzewuski's attempted escape, McCarter raced to the other car. The driver's door was open but the keys weren't in the ignition. Too much to hope for, McCarter thought as he fished a Swiss Army knife from a pocket. He used the screwdriver blade to pry loose the keyhole section of the ignition and worked the blade inside.

"Come on," McCarter rasped, pumping the gas. "Work, you mechanical son of a bitch."

He knew sometimes this trick could start a car, sometimes not. The engine suddenly growled to life. McCarter hit the stick and the car lurched forward. He glimpsed Encizo running toward the vehicle, but there was no time to pick up the Cuban to "ride shotgun." Rzewuski already had a head start, and McCarter was afraid the car might stop running if he let up on the accelerator.

Encizo watched the car race after Rzewuski's vehicle. He cursed under his breath, perturbed with the actions of the Briton, which seemed rash and reckless from Encizo's point of view. Then he heard Katz calling from the bay doors of the warehouse. The Israeli emerged from the building and jogged toward Encizo. He stopped abruptly when he spotted Potocki and the other dead cop.

"Damn it," Katz said bitterly as he gazed at the bloodied remains of two allies. "I'd hoped we could pull this off without losing any of our people."

"Unfortunately these aren't the only ones who didn't survive the raid," Encizo informed the Phoenix commander. "A couple of Warsaw police were hit and I found another dead cop at the side of the building. The *cabrón* who killed Potocki and at least one of the other officers got away in a car. McCarter took the other car and chased after the bastard. Thick-skulled cockney should have taken me with him instead of charging off to play lone avenger."

"I'll get the keys to the van," Katz announced. He didn't want to go through the pockets of Captain Potocki to retrieve the keys, but he wouldn't give this unpleasant task to one of his men. "See if any of the English-speaking policemen survived the battle. If one of them is familiar with Gdansk, have him drive a truck or car and try to catch up with David and his quarry."

"That bastard will have to be pretty slick to outwit or dodge McCarter," the Cuban commented.

"He had to be clever, ruthless and very dangerous to make it out of here," Katz said grimly. "Cal and Gary met me in the building. They took out a number of opponents, including someone who appears to be Captain Vatten and at least one Corsican. They also found part of the cocaine stash. I'll leave one of them here to help the cops round up prisoners and make certain none of them are playing possum. The other will come with me in the van."

"Right," Encizo said with a nod. "I just wish we'd parked our vehicles closer to the pier."

"I wish we'd had enough men to form a tighter ring around the area so no one could have escaped," Katz said with a sigh. "When you find a Warsaw cop who understands English, ask if he can contact the Gdansk police by radio. Maybe the local law enforcement can cut off the enemy driver before he can get out of the city."

"They're probably already headed this way," the Cuban replied.

ENCIZO HAD GUESSED correctly. Sirens screeched as a caravan of police cars raced through the streets of the Langgarten section of Gdansk. Seeing the flashing lights of the cop vehicles headed for the Lenin Shipyard, Rzewuski swung off the main avenue onto a side street.

David McCarter followed Rzewuski's car around the corner, the tires of his vehicle skidding on the icy pavement. McCarter clenched his teeth and rolled with the skid, slowing down just enough to avoid going out of control. He didn't know what model car he was driving, but it handled similar to an old Ford gearshift. The Briton pulled out of the skid and continued after his opponent.

Rzewuski saw the car in his rearview mirror and realized he was being tailed by one of the invaders at the pier. The Polish agent's foot was fixed on the accelerator, but the pursuer was closing in fast. Rzewuski grudgingly admired the other man's driving skill. The car was following him at a rapid pace and he couldn't outrace or evade his opponent.

The vehicles streaked toward the Gdansk Polytechnical University. The massive brick-and-stone buildings were a blur in the snowstorm as the cars hurtled past. McCarter held his Uzi machine pistol in his left hand and thrust it out the open window. Trying to aim a weapon at a moving target while driving a vehicle at top speed on slick, hazardous roads was no small feat. McCarter was glad there was no other traffic on the street or pedestrians in sight as he opened fire.

Two slugs plowed into the trunk of Rzewuski's sedan. McCarter didn't know where the other rounds went. The Uzi clicked on empty. The Briton had exhausted the ammo in the magazine. He tossed the machine pistol onto the seat beside him and drew the Browning Hi-Power from shoulder leather.

Frustrated, Rzewuski fought to maintain control of his vehicle. The Communist couldn't return fire and effectively steer the sedan. Twisting around to shoot at an opponent at his rear while driving in the treacherous weather would be virtually impossible. He hoped to reach the old town section and outmaneuver his pursuer on the narrow, winding cobblestone streets.

The renegade agent's eyes widened when he saw two sets of flashing lights in his path. A pair of Gdansk police cars blocked the street. Parked lengthwise, ends meeting in the middle of the street, the cop cars formed a blockade. Officers stood by the vehicles, pistols drawn, gesturing for the speeding sedans to halt.

Rzewuski extended his arm through the car window, the P-64 autoloader in his fist. He fired three rounds at the police. One cop crumpled to the pavement, hands clutched to his belly. The others bolted for cover, unaccustomed to finding themselves in a gun battle. Rzewuski gripped the steering wheel and charged.

The sedan rammed the rear quarter sections of the police cars. Taillights shattered and metal crunched as the impact separated the vehicles and created a pathway for Rzewuski's auto. The trunk on one police car popped open as the sedan plunged through the blockade. McCarter continued to chase his opponent and tagged one of the cop cars with his front bumper in the pursuit.

The police opened fire on both vehicles. McCarter ducked low and cursed as a bullet smashed a rear window. He kept going, determined not to lose his quarry. Rzewuski's sedan had lost a headlight, and part of the front fender hung loose and scraped the pavement as the Pole reached the old town district.

The twisting, curving streets were like an icy roller coaster. The cars rocketed across the frosty surface.

McCarter struggled to keep his vehicle on the road as he raced after Rzewuski. He cut a turn too quickly and banged into a bus stop bench, denting a side panel. The Briton held on to the wheel and stubbornly followed the Pole.

He triggered the Browning. He was more accurate with the familiar pistol he had used all of his adult life. The Hi-Power felt as natural in his hand as a pen or a fork.

His first shot shattered the rear windshield of Rzewuski's sedan. The car weaved wildly as the Pole responded to the 9 mm messenger that sizzled inside the vehicle. McCarter targeted the outline of Rzewuski's head and fired again. The projectile missed because the cars were moving too fast, too unpredictably. It punched a hole in the front windshield near Rzewuski and cracked the heavy glass.

"I'm not through with you yet, you bastard," McCarter growled, and fired two more rounds.

The left rear tire of Rzewuski's sedan exploded and the hubcap popped off. Rzewuski's car swung into a skid and whirled across the street like a giant top. It crashed into a stone wall outside the church of Saint Mary. The passenger side of the sedan crunched against the barrier. The hood burst open and steam hissed from the radiator.

McCarter steered his car to the curb and eased on the brake with steady pressure to prevent going out of control. When the automobile came to a halt, he stepped from the car, the Browning in his fist. He watched Rzewuski's vehicle, unsure of the fate of the driver. The crippled sedan appeared to be lodged in the wall. McCarter didn't see the Pole as he crouched by his car for cover.

Snow showered down on the Phoenix commando and the wail of police sirens echoed in the distance. The great Gothic church towered above him as McCarter gripped the Browning in a Weaver's combat hold and used the car door for a shield.

"You've had it!" he called out to the smashed car. "Get your arse out of there and give up!"

He didn't know if the driver understood English. McCarter wasn't even sure if the man was alive or conscious. The wreck was bad enough to be fatal, but he had seen men walk away from worse. McCarter himself had survived crashes that were at least as severe as that the sedan had experienced. Although curious, the Briton remained by his cover and waited. This was one occasion when time was in his favor.

A metal sphere sailed from a window of the sedan. It hit the cobblestones in front of McCarter's car and rolled beneath the front fender. McCarter knew what the object was and bolted. The grenade exploded before he could reach cover.

The car blew apart. Metal and flaming petrol scattered across the street. The explosion filled the night with angry light, and a concussion wave hit McCarter like a backhand swipe from an invisible god. He was thrown off his feet and tossed eight feet before he crashed to the hard, frozen pavement. Blackness descended across the Briton's vision and bright orange comets and supernovas popped inside his head.

McCarter fought the seduction of unconsciousness. He felt his battered and bruised body stir. Pain traveled up from his limbs and spine as he crawled across the cobblestones. The Phoenix pro placed his palms on the ground and tried to get to his knees. His body wouldn't respond. He shook his head. Dark cobwebs drifted across his vision. He grunted from the effort as he rocked back on his knees and blinked.

The veil lifted and he stared at a tall, lean figure that seemed to float toward him. McCarter saw the stern expression on the face of Stanislaw Rzewuski. The man cradled a broken arm to his chest, but held the P-64 pistol in the other fist. A ribbon of blood trickled from a scalp wound above the Pole's marble-hard eyes.

"You . . . you did well, CIA man," Rzewuski began in English, his voice weary and breath ragged. "But I did just a little bit better."

He pointed his pistol at McCarter. The Briton had lost his Browning. He looked up at Rzewuski and managed a thin smile as he braced one hand on the ground and placed the other at the small of his back. "I don't suppose you'll let me have one last cigarette?" McCarter inquired, staring at Rzewuski's face.

"Sorry," the Polish agent replied sincerely. "There isn't time for such social niceties. This has to be a very informal, one-man firing squad."

"I reckon you're right about that," McCarter admitted.

He suddenly threw himself to one side as his hand swung from the small of his back, the snub-nosed Smith & Wesson revolver in his fist. The little backup piece spit flame the instant McCarter produced it. A .38-caliber bullet slammed into Rzewuski's chest before the Polish agent realized what had happened.

Rzewuski staggered backward. He felt a lung burst and pain filled his body like hot lava. The Pole triggered his P-64, and a 9 mm slug sparked against the cobblestones near McCarter's supine form and whined as it ricocheted past the Briton's ear. The Phoenix warrior's nerves screamed inside his brain and he returned fire with the S&W.

Two more .38 slugs smashed through Rzewuski's chest. His heart was reduced to mashed pulp and the impact pitched him backward to fall to the pavement. Rzewuski's arm rose, pistol still in his trembling fist. He fired one last shot into the cold night sky. Then his arm dropped as he surrendered to death.

McCarter slowly lowered the .38 revolver. He exhaled a tense breath and inhaled deeply. The cold air tasted sweet and filled his lungs. The Briton was still alive and it felt good to breathe and have blood running inside his veins.

The euphoria of surviving the deadly encounter subsided, and McCarter felt the pain of dozens of bruises. His head began to spin and his side ached as if needles were jammed in his rib cage. He started to get up, but his legs wouldn't support him. He tumbled to the ground as the world became a warm black blanket of unconsciousness. The sirens grew closer, and McCarter smiled, aware the cops would find him before he could freeze to death.

"Take your time," he muttered as his senses drifted away. "Nobody's going anywhere now...."

20

Ignacy Jowialski and Superintendent Kniazin met Katz at the hospital's emergency room. Kniazin had the unenviable task of trying to explain why the Warsaw police had conducted a raid on the Lenin Shipyards without consulting the police in Gdansk. As the superintendent spoke with the local police brass, Jowialski and Katz moved to a solarium to talk privately.

"I understand Captain Potocki and several other officers were killed," Jowialski said sadly. "The captain was a good man."

"Yes," Katz agreed. "Some other police were injured, including one Gdansk officer who's being operated on right now."

"What about your people, Wallburg?" the Polish intel man asked.

"Masters was battered and bruised by an explosion," Katz answered. "He has a couple of cracked ribs and lots of black and blue marks, but no broken bones or serious internal injuries. Considering the fact that a grenade exploded before he could reach cover, he was very lucky. Masters will spend the night in the hospital, but he should be able to leave in the morning. A number of the enemy are here, as well. Corsican gangsters as well as Mácka agents. I'm afraid they're all low-level characters. The leaders at the pier all seem to have died during the battle."

"Too bad," Jowialski said with a sigh.

"They didn't leave us much choice," Katz assured him. "What about Zablocki? Did you and Kniazin arrest him? There's certainly enough evidence to hold him now."

Jowialski looked down at the floor and shook his head. "Zablocki was already gone," he explained. "Apparently he packed his bags and fled before we could arrest him. He must have suspected the Mácka operation was falling apart. Zablocki has probably left the country by now, but we've got agents and police watching for him at roadblocks, airports and train stations all over Poland."

"He's a big fish," Katz said. "I hope you catch him, but the conspiracy Mácka was conducting here is finished. Even if you don't find Zablocki, he's no longer a threat to your country."

"I know," Jowialski said with a smile. "You'll be glad to hear that the president of Poland has already contacted the President of the United States to explain what's happened and to assure him that Polish and American relations will return to normal. A press conference will be held tomorrow morning. The Communist conspiracy will be exposed and the accusations of American involvement in drug trafficking here will be put to rest.''

''And the reputations of two innocent businessmen who were framed as drug dealers and murdered by Mácka will be restored,'' Katz said with satisfaction. ''Their families will still have to deal with grief, but they won't have to contend with the shame and doubts associated with accusations that their husbands or fathers were smuggling cocaine.''

''That's true,'' Jowialski agreed. ''So you've completed your mission, Mr. Wallburg. Congratulations. I doubt we could have done this without your help.''

''It's our job,'' Katz replied with a shrug. ''We'll be going back to the U.S. tomorrow. Our control officer may already have another mission for us.''

''I admire you more than I can say,'' Jowialski told Katz. ''But I certainly don't envy you. Do you think the failure of the drug trafficking mission by Mácka will be enough to make the organization disband?''

''No,'' Katz said with a sigh. ''I wouldn't count on that. I have a feeling we haven't seen the last of Mácka.''

ZBIGNEW ZABLOCKI DROVE the Volkswagen through the snowstorm that swept across Dresden. The city was best known as a target site for British and American bombers during World War II. Dresden had been reconstructed and restored after the war, but it remained a grim and forbidding place, in Zablocki's opinion.

He had driven all night to cross the border into what had once been East Germany. All his instincts had warned him to run from Poland. Colonel Durnov had left because he had suspected the mission could fail. The effort to kill the Americans at the safehouse in Warsaw had failed and Hugo Twardowski had been interrogated at the hospital. These events had convinced Zablocki it was time to leave before the sky crashed down on him.

Zablocki listened to the radio as he drove. He had heard unconfirmed news reports of explosions at a pier at the Lenin Shipyard. There was no doubt in Zablocki's mind what this meant. His survival instincts had been correct. He had left Poland just in time.

The VW struggled through the snow to the train station. It was quiet in Dresden and the station seemed deserted. The winter was bad this year, Zablocki observed. It was bitter and cold throughout Eastern Europe. The weather suited his attitude at the moment. Zablocki parked near the railroad tracks and took out a pack of cigarettes. He didn't know how long he would have to wait.

A few minutes passed and a familiar figure approached the car. Zablocki was relieved to see Klaus Schoffer. The former SSD agent approached the VW and climbed into the front seat beside Zablocki. Schoffer brushed snow from his overcoat and looked at the Pole with an expression that seemed to contain a trace of pity.

"I'm glad you got my message, Klaus," Zablocki said. "Everything has gone very badly in Poland."

"I know," the East German replied with a nod. "The details are obscure, but we already know Mácka operations in your country have failed."

The sound of an approaching train rode along the rails. The lights of the locomotive drew closer and the noise increased as Schoffer leaned back and unbuttoned his coat. The German folded gloved hands on his chest as he watched the train come nearer.

"The last time we met was at the Berlin Wall in 1989," Schoffer remarked. "That was a very bad day. A great disappointment for all of us still committed to the goals and convictions of communism."

"This is a bad day, too," Zablocki mused. "I had no choice. I couldn't remain in Poland."

"I understand," Schoffer replied. "You need protection from the authorities of your country."

"Not only my personal safety is at stake," Zablocki insisted. "If I am arrested, they may use truth serum to learn more about Mácka. Our entire organization is in jeopardy if they capture me."

"I know," Schoffer said with a nod as the train rolled into the station.

He suddenly drew a small pistol. Zablocki opened his mouth and stared at the gun. Schoffer didn't hesitate and shot Zablocki above the right eye. Blood splashed the inside of the windshield as Zablocki slumped behind the steering wheel. The noise of the train concealed the sound of the small-caliber weapon.

"You were right, Zbignew," Schoffer remarked as he tossed the pistol into Zablocki's lap. "We couldn't risk allowing you to be captured."

Schoffer stepped from the Volkswagen and buttoned his coat. He thrust his hands into the pockets as he walked away. It was indeed a cold winter, Schoffer thought as he headed for his own vehicle parked several blocks away.

A cold and very bitter winter...

These heroes can't be beat!

Continue to celebrate the American hero with this collection of never-before-published installments of America's finest action teams—ABLE TEAM, PHOENIX FORCE and VIETNAM: GROUND ZERO—only in Gold Eagle's

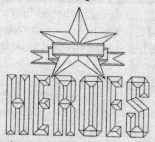

Two additional action-packed volumes are available:

HEROES: Book I $5.99 592 pages

ABLE TEAM: Razorback by Dick Stivers
PHOENIX FORCE: Survival Run by Gar Wilson
VIETNAM: GROUND ZERO: Zebra Cube by Robert Baxter

HEROES: Book II $5.99 592 pages

PHOENIX FORCE: Hell Quest by Gar Wilson
ABLE TEAM: Death Lash by Dick Stivers
PHOENIX FORCE: Dirty Mission by Gar Wilson

In the Deathlands, the only
thing that gets easier is dying.

JAMES AXLER

DEATH LANDS®
Moon Fate

Out of the ruins of nuclear-torn America emerges a band of warrior-
survivalists, led by a one-eyed man called Ryan Cawdor. In their quest
to find a better life, they embark on a perilous odyssey across the ravaged wasteland known as Deathlands.

An ambush by a roving group of mutant Stickies puts Ryan in the clutches
of a tyrant who plans a human sacrifice as a symbol of his power. With
the rise of the new moon, Ryan Cawdor must meet his fate or chance
an escape through a deadly maze of uncharted canyons.